For Kaye,
With very many thanks.
Josie

Let me ... ... I'd like
to read the ... ... member!

THE WEAK AGAINST THE STRONG

JOSIE MOUNSEY

FriesenPress

Suite 300 - 990 Fort St
Victoria, BC, V8V 3K2
Canada

www.friesenpress.com

First Edition — 2020

ISBN
978-1-5255-6445-1 (Hardcover)
978-1-5255-6446-8 (Paperback)
978-1-5255-6447-5 (eBook)

1. FICTION, THRILLERS, HISTORICAL

Distributed to the trade by The Ingram Book Company

He lies like an eyewitness.
Old Russian Proverb

Something unpleasant is coming when men
are anxious to tell the truth.
Benjamin Disraeli

ACKNOWLEDGEMENTS

During the years I spent writing this novel, many people helped by reading and commenting on parts of the manuscript. Special thanks go to Prim Pemberton and the individuals who participated in her Wednesday afternoon workshops, Creative Writing in Cabbagetown, for offering critiques and suggestions: Ann Bjorseth, Ilene Cummings, Sylvia Daigneault, Philip Jessup, Gobnait McAnoy, Barb Nahwegahbow, Steve Thompson, and Andy Webster.

Alan Cumyn, my mentor in the Creative Writing program at the Humber School for Writers, provided invaluable advice, interest, and encouragement, particularly in the early stages of this novel.

Thanks also to Kim Echlin, my first Creative Writing teacher at the University of Toronto. Kim's encouragement and gentle criticism were exactly what new writers need. The genesis of this novel was an assignment in Kim's class to write about an overheard conversation. Who knew where that simple exercise would lead?

I especially want to thank my husband, Joe, who is my greatest love, friend, and supporter, and who allows me the time to pursue my writing projects and keeps things going on the home front, so that we at least get to eat one decent meal each day.

DEDICATION

To the millions of victims of sex trafficking,
both adults and minors, throughout the world,
and to the brave souls who put their lives on the line
to help them and to try to bring traffickers to justice

To the memories of my parents,
Albert and Helen Hance, who taught
me good values in life and the importance
of kindness

To my late best friend, Wiebke Smythe, who
encouraged me to continue writing this story

To my husband, Joe, who is always there for me

PROLOGUE
PETROGRAD, RUSSIA–1917

Dima and Ira Galichin's son, Sergei Dmitrievich, had no first-hand memory of the momentous week that heralded the start of the Bolshevik Revolution. He was twenty days old at the time.

In the darkening days of October 1917, the nation was in ferment and disintegration as Vladimir Ilyich Lenin and the Bolsheviks manoeuvred for power, demanding peace negotiations in the light of the country's military failures. Many aristocratic families who had fled to their country estates were now seeking exile in foreign lands, as peasants and soldiers, carried along on the rising tide of violence sweeping across Russia, rose up against landowners.

In Petrograd, fog rolled in from the Neva. Huddled in his coat, hurrying to meet a client in the gloom on Liteynyy prospekt late on Thursday afternoon, Dima Galichin's step was heavy. He worried about the safety of his parents, who had left Petrograd six months ago, fearing what would happen in the wake of the abdication of the Tsar and the rise of Bolshevism. None of his parents' friends had heard from them. *If only there was a letter ... anything.* During the 1905 Revolution, Dima's father, Alexander Ilyavitch Galichin, like many others of noble birth, had supported the aims of the newly-formed Constitutional Democratic Party, known as Kadets, and was vociferous in defence of workers' and minority rights, including Jewish emancipation. Later, he had taken a less prominent stance in the Party, preferring to work quietly in the background, arguing for the rights of citizens and influencing legislation. But over the years he had become increasingly disillusioned with the way the Party lurched from one crisis to another. Last year, he had further distanced himself as the Kadets' opposition to the government's conduct of the war became more vociferous, all but accusing government ministers of treason.

If only I knew they were safe, Dima sighed as he walked on. It was as if they had disappeared into the ever-darkening cloud enshrouding Russia. He thought back to the last time he saw his parents. "You must leave. Take Ira, before the baby is born. Come with us. Do this one thing we ask," his father had pleaded. Dima had tried to reason with him, lift him out of his morose mood, but his father had waved an arm around the array of law books lining the bookcases in his study, gripped Dima by his shoulders, stared into his eyes, and hissed: "It will be a massacre! What good will the rule of law do us then? Tell me that." The fight had seemed to go out of him and he slumped onto a chair.

As Dima left that day, his mother had hung on to him, pleading that he should go with them to Finland. "What sort of world will your child, our grandchild, be born into here?"

Why didn't I listen to them? Tension was now at fever pitch in the city. There were constant reports that soldiers were walking away from the vermin-ridden trenches at the front. They were short of weapons, ammunition, and food and blamed the workers in the rear for the shortages that cost so many comrades their lives. Today, he had heard that crowds of soldiers invaded munitions factories, forcing workers at gunpoint to increase production. *Where will it end?*

Not since the terrible plague years of the seventeenth century had Russia's cities known such dire shortages. Petrograd was hardest hit. The surrounding areas produced little grain, and nearly all food products had to be transported over inadequate rail networks clogged with military supplies. Rumours circulated that Jews were hoarding food, and while women shivered in line for meagre portions of black bread, members of the Soviet gorged on white bread, butter, and cake. Thousands of workers demonstrated in the squares and streets calling for the overthrow of the government, for the confiscation of food and money from the bourgeoisie, and for the seizure of Russia's mills and mines.

Dima clasped his leather satchel closer to his body. *What will become of us?* He swallowed hard as he thought of his wife, Irina, and of their son, Sergei, so small, his life still ahead of him. But what life? *Papa was right. There is nothing here for us. Whatever Ira says, we must think of ourselves and our child,* he resolved. It would be difficult. In the past few months, Ira had displayed a new resolve, a stubbornness, ignoring his pleas not to venture out on her own, not to become involved. She and her friends had cleaned up an old bakery by the Nikolaevskii Station and were providing soup and anything else they could lay their hands on for the women who were forced to work long hours in factories to support their families while the men were at the front. *If only she would be more careful. There's the child to think of now.*

He quickened his pace. *I won't listen to her. We must leave. Her parents? They will be a problem. She won't go without them.* But how could he persuade Ira's father who, like many writers, now hoped for a new and better life here? Dima had tried to appeal to him, saying that nothing peaceful could come out of this widespread violence. "Once peaceful people have turned into assassins," Dima had railed. "It's too dangerous for you here. Why not join your friends, the other writers and poets who have already gone to the Crimea?" His pleas were in vain.

But Ira and the child. We must. We have to … Dima stopped in his tracks, suddenly aware of the roar of voices. Out of the swirling fog, a soldier ran toward him, weaving wildly around, his great coat open. As the man drew level, his breath came in noisy gasps. He grabbed Dima's coat sleeve and gripped the cloth. Dima stared into the man's ashen face, the brown peaked cap pushed back off his forehead.

"Pazhalusta! Pazhalusta!" the soldier shrieked. "Pamagite! Pamagite!"

Within seconds an angry mob was upon them. The young Cossack's eyes were wide with terror. His hat was knocked off and the hands of his pursuers tore at his hair. Dima tried to wrench himself free, but the soldier's fingers hung on to his sleeve. They were both swept along with the crowd, Dima's cries of "Khvatit! Khvatit!" drowned by demented shouts of "Kill him! Kill the thief!"

Dima was dragged to the ground. His gloved hand pulled frantically at the soldier's fingers, bending them backwards until his arm was free. As he struggled to get to his feet, a blow to the left side of his face knocked him sideways. His cries mingled with the piercing screams of the Cossack and the thud of countless boots trampling and kicking with manic purpose. Bent double, Dima lurched through a gap in the barrage of legs. The air was cold on the edge of the crowd. His body was drenched in sweat. Blood pulsed noisily through his temples. Each breath brought a stab of pain in his chest as he stumbled toward a shop doorway. Faces peered out through the windows. He dropped to his knees in the corner and covered his head with his arms.

It was quiet now. Not even the rumble of wheels. He looked around. The now silent mob was drifting away. Two remained, rifling through the soldier's pockets, forcing his legs upwards and tugging at his boots until they came free. The legs fell to the ground. The men slapped each other on the shoulders and strode away, swinging boots and a belt, above their heads.

Everything seemed to be happening in slow motion. Dima got to his feet and took a few faltering steps toward the twitching body. He stared. The face was a mangled pulp. Pieces of ripped coat were scattered around. The Cossack's uniform jacket and shirt had been wrenched open, and where his chest had been there was now a cavity oozing dark rivulets of blood. The lower part of one leg lay at a disjointed angle; the bare foot rested in a puddle of water, footcloth by its side. Dima's trembling fingers hovered above the body, not daring to touch.

He felt his way almost blindly back into the shop doorway. People started to come out of the shop. His whole being shook and bile rose into his mouth as he leaned against a doorpost. When he turned toward the street, streams of people seemed to come at him, dim in the gloom. The wheels of wagons began to grind again.

He could no longer see the body. A small crowd had gathered around. A woman clutched a young child's hand as they hurried past. Her eyes met his briefly. She quickened her pace, dragging the child behind.

The jangle of horses' harnesses was loud. The noise reached a crescendo. Dima's feet were unwieldy weights as he staggered into an alleyway. In his mind he saw again the mutilated body. *What could I have done? There were so many of them. Like a pack of wolves pursuing its prey across the steppe.* He stumbled farther and leaned against a wall. Fog swirled around, illuminated by flickering candles in windows. He sat down on a stone doorstep and winced as he pressed his fingers to his cheekbone. A muffled methodical boom pounded in his head. He looked down. Where was his satchel?

We have to get out of here. What if Ira is attacked? The baby. He fought back to his feet and looked around, unsure which way to go. Buildings towered above him. At one end of the alleyway he could see shapes tinged yellow by the fog. They were getting bigger. He began to run in the opposite direction. His breath came in laboured gasps. The faster he ran, the closer the footsteps seemed to get. He banged his fists on a door … again and again … then staggered on around a corner. He was now bent over holding his chest, the noise of footsteps reverberating like thunder all around him. He raised his head. A dark, elongated shape blocked out part of the light. As he covered his head with his arms, it came down on him.

PART ONE

CHAPTER ONE

MONTRÉAL, CANADA–JUNE 1967

"Maman! Where are you going?" four-year-old Mitch cried from the front seat. The car door slammed. His voice became louder: "I want to go with you." He knelt up on the seat, face pressed against the window, trying to see where his mother was. She had gone.

"Maman! Maman!" he wailed, struggling with the handle on the car door. It opened and he slid to the ground. Leaving the door open, he ran after her, following the click of her heels up a driveway. *Why didn't she take me with her?* She'd never left him alone in the car since the day he locked himself in. "Mama!" he yelled.

She turned and held up a hand to him. "Stay right there, Mitch." Her voice was the one she used when he spilled things.

"Don't leave me, Maman," he pleaded, close to tears, and ran after her.

"Silly, I'm not leaving you." She came toward him. "But there's something I have to do. You have to wait here … just for a little while."

Tears ran down his face and plopped on to the driveway.

She stooped down, placed the parcel she was carrying on the ground and hugged him. "You have to be brave, like Charlot," she cajoled.

He wanted to be brave like Charlot. Every night as Maman read *Les Aventures de Perrine et Charlot* to him, Mitch imagined he was the orphaned Charlot stowing away with his sister, Perrine, on a big wooden boat to escape a horrid old aunt. They went to New France, which Maman told him was what part of Canada was called a long time ago. Mitch could scarcely breathe with the excitement of the stories, and for one whole week, unless there was a tempting treat to be had, refused to respond to any name but Charlot.

"If you're good, we'll go to the *Pâtisserie,*" Sophia whispered now.

"Can I have *pain au chocolat?*"

"First, you have to wait here." She kissed the top of her son's head. "Promise?" Mitch nodded and she picked up the parcel and walked toward the house.

He wiped his tears away with the back of a hand. His bottom lip trembled. *What's in the parcel? We always choose presents together.* He took two steps toward her.

At the top of the stone steps, Sophia turned and looked back at him. Then she raised her right hand and knocked on the door. Mitch crept toward her. Some moments later, the door opened and a man appeared. He had a long grey beard and was big. Mitch took a step back. At first, he couldn't hear what they were saying, then the man raised his voice. "I told you never to come here again." He waved his arms at her. "We don't want to see you. Go away!"

Mitch wondered what the funny words meant. They didn't sound like any words he had heard before. He twisted a lock of hair around and around in the fingers of his right hand, as he watched his mother.

"Who is it?" A woman's voice this time.

"It's me, *Muter*. Sophia."

Mitch edged closer. He was now at the bottom of the steps.

"Sophia. You shouldn't come here. Please ... you must go."

"Go inside. I will deal with this."

"*Muter*. We are going away. To Russia."

"I won't tell you again, we don't want you here," the man bellowed. "You've made your choice."

"*Muter. Muter.* Please," Mitch's mother cried.

"Get out! Get out!" The man started to push roughly at her.

She was now teetering on the edge of the steps, holding out the present. "*Muter*. I've brought you something." Her voice was shrill.

"We don't want you here." The man grabbed the top of her arms and started to shake her. "Do you hear? Go away!"

His words were mixed with Sophia's cries of, "*Muter. Seit azoi gut.* Some pictures of your grandson ... Mitch."

At the sound of his name, Mitch clambered up the steps. "Don't hurt her! Don't hurt Maman!" he shouted and reached for her skirt. He tripped and fell down hard on the stone. The door closed with a bang. He started to wail.

Sophia hauled him upright, knelt on one knee, and held him close. "It's all right. It's all right. There's nothing wrong." She breathed into the top of his head.

Mitch sniffed loudly.

"Are you okay?"

His knee hurt and he held a hand over it as she rocked him gently; he could feel her body trembling.

"You're bleeding!" she said, looking at the trickle of blood seeping between his fingers. She opened her purse, pulled out an embroidered handkerchief, folded it quickly into a makeshift bandage, and tied it around the scrape on his knee.

"I d ... didn't like that m ... man." Mitch sobbed and burrowed his head into her neck. The fingers of his right hand gripped one edge of her jacket.

"It's all right, darling. He's just upset." Sophia's voice was barely audible. Tears coursed down her face as she clutched her son. "Okay now?" she whispered after a few moments.

Mitch's sobs subsided and he watched as she reached out for the parcel and stood up.

"Didn't they want the present you got for them?"

"I'll leave it here; they can have it later."

"Can I have it?"

"No, it's for them." She bent down and tucked the parcel into a corner beneath a profusion of white flowers trailing from a planter. "We must go." She wiped her eyes quickly with the tips of her fingers.

"Can we go to the *Pâtisserie* now?" Mitch asked.

"Later," she said and took his hand.

"You promised!"

She looked down at him; a weak smile lifted the corners of her mouth. At the end of the driveway, she turned and looked back at the house. Then she squeezed his hand and they stepped onto the sidewalk.

In the car, she sat for a few moments with her hands on the steering wheel, staring ahead.

"I didn't like it when you left me," Mitch whined.

"I'm sorry," she said and undid the handkerchief from around his knee. "It's stopped bleeding now, my brave soldier." She ran her fingers through his mop of unruly brown curls. "Now, why don't we drive down to the river and buy an ice cream?"

"But you promised. You promised we could go to the *Pâtisserie*."

"We'll do that too. Later." She dropped the handkerchief into her purse, which she tucked behind her seat, then started the car.

"Who was that nasty man, Maman?" Mitch asked as they pulled slowly past the driveway.

"I'll tell you later."

At the ice cream kiosk, Sophia lifted Mitch up to see the shiny pictures on the poster at the side of the counter. He pointed first to the cone filled with pink ice cream and then slid his finger slowly toward the neapolitan. *Yumm. That one has chocolate too.*

"Perhaps a little scoop of both?" the man in the white coat behind the counter tempted. Mitch nodded enthusiastically.

Alongside the towpath by the river, he ran behind bushes and trees, peeping out, pretending he was Charlot checking that the horrid aunt hadn't followed them across the ocean. A blob of ice cream spilled out of the cone onto the grass.

"Mitch. Come and sit here for a while," his mother called. He ran back to the path and saw she was sitting on a bench. "Sit here just while you finish your ice cream." She patted the seat next to her.

With another lick of the ice cream, he asked, "Do they have ice cream in Russia?"

"I'm sure they do."

"But why do we have to go? I like it here." A trickle of chocolate ice cream dripped onto his shirt.

Sophia sighed, took the ice cream from him, unwound the paper napkin from the cone, and dabbed at his shirt. "I don't know how you get in such a mess." She licked around the edge of the cone and used her tongue to push the remaining ice cream further down before giving it back to him. Then she tilted his head backwards and ran the napkin around his lips.

A duck squawked and, with wild flapping of wings, rose into the air as a rowing boat drifted toward the bank on their side of the river. *"Fais attention, Papa!"* a young boy shouted from the boat. *"Assis-toi, Antoine!"* the boy's father cautioned, struggling with the oars.

"Is he going to fall in, Maman?" Mitch asked excitedly, jumping to his feet.

"Antoine! Assis-toi!" the man commanded again as the boat rocked from side to side. It hit the bank. The child wobbled for a second or two then sat down clumsily in the bow.

Mitch laughed loudly. Sophia put a finger to her lips and shook her head at him. They watched in silence as the father used one of the oars to push the boat away from the bank.

Mitch flopped onto the bench and took a bite out of the cone. "Why do we have to go?" he started to wail again. Before Sophia could reply, he shouted, "I don't want to! I won't!"

"Shush, now. Calm down. This is silly." Sophia patted his leg. "You want to see Papa, don't you?"

"I ..." he hunched his shoulders and turned away from her. He didn't know if he liked the man in the photograph Maman had in the frame on her night table. "I want to stay here," he said.

"Darling, I can't go through all that again. If I could change it, I would." She pulled him toward her. He began to cry. She stroked the side of his head.

"What about my friends?" he gulped between sobs.

"You'll soon make friends. New friends. They're just little boys and girls the same as you."

"I don't like girls." He edged along the seat away from her.

"Papa and I will make everything all right, you'll see."

Mitch poked a stick between the gaps in the wooden slats of the bench. He didn't like Russians. The ones he'd seen at Expo were scary. There had been a big statue of a man who looked like a horrid monster. Mitch had clung to Maman's hand and looked around for spies—Patrice, his friend, had told him the Russians are our enemies and they send people here to spy on us. "Look at the Sputniks," Maman had urged, pointing up to the roof of the exhibit. Mitch had wriggled free from her hand and run outside, darting around people's legs. When he'd looked around, he couldn't see her. "Maman! Maman!" he'd wailed. A lady bent down and tried to comfort him. Then his mother had grabbed his arm and held on to him hard, telling him what a naughty boy he was. Her voice had frightened him, making him cry louder. Later, she'd dragged him to see a giant hammer and what looked like a yellow moon. He couldn't remember what it was. The hammer had been so big, Mitch was sure it belonged to a giant.

"When we get home, why don't we learn some more Russian words?" Sophia broke Mitch's reverie. "We'll surprise Papa when we see him."

"Patrice said they have real guns there. Like cowboys have. And they put people in prison."

"Don't be silly, darling. Of course they don't. Papa's Russian and he doesn't have a gun, does he?" As she spoke, Sophia's words reinforced in her mind how little she knew of Mitch's father's life. "And he's not in prison."

"They'll put me in prison. That's what Patrice said."

"Now you are being silly."

"Why do we have to go? I don't want to. I want to stay here," he sobbed loudly.

Sophia sighed. "Mitch, I've told you. Papa's not allowed to come here."

"Why not?"

"It's just that he's Russian and he's not allowed to live here, so we have to go to Leningrad to live with him." She looked at Mitch. "It'll be fun ... and I'm sure they'll have ice cream."

Mitch stuffed the remains of the cone into his mouth and sat with swollen cheeks, arms folded across his chest. He stared intently at the scrape on his leg, and an idea came into his head. *I'll tell Patrice that I hurt my knee in a scuffle when Charlot's big wooden boat sailed up the river and I helped him fight the baddies— the ones in the rowing boat.* He giggled softly to himself.

"Mitch." His mother's voice jolted him from his imaginary life. "Those people, this afternoon ..."

"Who were they? Why did that man shout at you?"

"That was my father ... my parents."

He looked up at her.

"Your grandparents."

"But you told me ... you told me they are in heaven; that's what you said."

"I know. I was going to explain when you are older. When you could understand."

"That was a lie, Maman. You told a lie."

Sophia bit her lip.

"You said if I told a lie, bad things would happen to me." He looked down at his sandals.

"I'm sorry, darling. I was just trying to protect you." She took a deep breath. "Those people, your grandparents, we quarrelled because they don't like Papa."

"Why?"

"It's just that Papa belongs to ... well, he doesn't really belong to any church. And my parents are Jewish. Hasidic Jews." A frown creased Mitch's forehead and she explained. "Like the men in the long black coats and black hats that we sometimes see on the streets."

"The ones with the funny long curls?"

Sophia nodded.

"Will my hair be like that when I get big?"

"If you like."

"Then I wouldn't have to go to the barber, would I?"

"That's true," she laughed, thinking of how, in observance of her faith, she hadn't allowed Mitch's hair to be cut until his third birthday. She had always hoped ... *Best not to think about that,* she told herself now. "It's all a bit complicated. You see, when I was a little girl, my parents arranged with the parents of a little boy that when we were both grown up, we would get married."

"Did you like him, Maman? The little boy?"

"I don't remember him when he was young, but when we were older, we met a few times. He was nice, but I didn't love him. And then I met Papa, and I really loved him." A strange look—half smile, half frown—crossed her face. "But my parents wouldn't allow me to see him, so ..." She paused for a moment then spoke quickly. "So I left home and they were very angry."

Mitch wondered what it would be like to have a grandmother and a grandfather, even one who shouts. He had Grandmother Irina Arky-something in Leningrad. She was to live with them, and he was to call her *Babushka*. It was a funny name, and he thought she must be very old, like Jean-Pierre's grandparents. Maman had told him Papa's father died in a kind of a war. An October-something. Mitch thought that was right. It couldn't be anything nasty—October was when he had his birthday. *Maybe when I'm five I won't have to go to Russia. Perhaps I can go to see these grandparents here in the big house. They could take me to the zoo or on picnics.* Jean-Pierre's grandparents took him to the zoo and the circus. Sometimes to their cabin too. It was by a lake and they had a boat. Mitch wondered if his grandparents had a boat. He could pretend he was Charlot.

"Maman? Could we wait and go to Russia another time?"

"No, darling. We have to go soon. Papa's waiting for us."

"But we could take Papa to see those people. They will like him. They won't shout at him."

"Perhaps some other time." She paused. "Now, what about that *pain au chocolat*?"

"Do they have those, too … in Russia?"

CHAPTER TWO

EN ROUTE TO LENINGRAD—JULY 1967

Sophia sank down into the middle of the three seats on the left side of the aircraft. She leaned back and closed her eyes, trying to ignore the chaos all around. A fresh wave of loud voices filled the air, and she opened her eyes and saw the backs of two women. They were standing in the aisle, jostling each other, arms outstretched as they each tried to squeeze large bags into the overflowing open-fronted racks above the opposite row of seats. Both had jet-black hair swept into a tall bouffant style that rose some inches above their heads. One wore a dark blue suit, the other a shapeless, grey print dress, which, when she turned around, had large moisture stains under the arms. Their towering topknots wagged as their voices rose to a crescendo.

"Maman?" A small voice came from the window seat and she felt Mitch's fingers grip her arm. "Are they going to fight?"

"No, darling. I don't think so," she murmured. She watched as a stewardess jammed both bags into the rack above the seats two rows ahead. The woman in the suit eased her skirt down over bulging thighs, patted the sides of her hair into place, and flopped into a seat on the other side of the aisle from Mitch and Sophia.

"Let's do up your seat belt," Sophia urged, fumbling with the buckle. The belt fastened, she leaned across Mitch and stared out of the window. All she could see was the concrete apron. She swallowed hard in an effort to overcome the emotions that were threatening to overwhelm her. *Pull yourself together. There's nothing to keep you here,* she told herself sternly, trying to dispel the images of long-ago happy times with her parents that were flashing through her mind. Then a different image stuck: her father's face, contorted with anger. She felt again his hands pushing at her on the front doorstep a few weeks ago, dispelling any lingering hope of reconciliation. *Foter? Why does it have to be like this?*

"What's wrong, Maman?" Mitch's words jolted her out of her reverie.

"Nothing, darling ... just happy that we'll soon be seeing Papa. That's all."

"Will he know who we are?"

She nodded reassuringly, determined not to let her mind run down the familiar track where she imagined Sergei's blank stare as he searched for some resemblance to the woman he had last seen, for those brief few weeks, over five years ago. *Of course he'll know me,* she admonished herself.

She had lost weight, but during the past few months her friend, Simone, had done her best to fatten her up. "At least I know you've had one good meal this week," Simone said each Sunday lunchtime, to the amusement of Mitch and her own large brood of children as knives and forks scraped on plates. Simone was her only real friend from the old days—but Simone wasn't Jewish. Everyone else cut her dead in the street or crossed to the other side of the road to avoid the embarrassment of coming face to face with her. Even her brother had turned on his heel and disappeared down a side street when she walked toward him, pushing Mitch in his stroller. *But there, in the Soviet Union, with all the anti-semitic propaganda, who will want to be friends with a Jew? A Zhid! Especially after the Six-Day War last month.* So why was she taking her Jewish son to live in a country where his heritage was despised? She had tried to convince herself that he didn't look Jewish and that he bore more than a passing resemblance to Sergei. Tears sprang up in her eyes. In other circumstances, she would have been proud of his dark hair, eyes, his nose.

"Who is that man?" Mitch interrupted her tortured thoughts, pointing to the passenger sitting the other side of Sophia. "Can't he talk?"

"I'm sure he can, but he's busy," she whispered. She glanced at the stiff figure by her side. The man, dressed in a brown suit, had stepped into the aisle to let them into their seats, the stern expression on his face unchanged as Sophia mumbled her apologies. He was now reading a typewritten document and, as she watched, jotted something in the margin. Her eyes scanned the page. Judging by the letters, it was written in Russian. *It's all a jumble to me,* she thought miserably.

Simone's husband, Luc, had tried to teach her the most commonly used words, enough to get by. "I don't understand your problem," he said, a look of exasperation on his face. "You, of all people, should find it easy. Some of the characters are similar to Hebrew." Although Hasidim generally use Yiddish among themselves, and Hebrew is considered a holy tongue reserved for prayer and study, Sophia didn't know why she found the language confusing either.

The aircraft jolted and moved slowly backwards. A female voice crackled over the loudspeaker; Sophia had no idea what was said. As they taxied to the runway, the uneasy feeling in her stomach intensified. She looked straight ahead, fighting back tears, unwilling to take a last look at the country she had always called home. Soon their home would be in that far-off land behind the Iron Curtain. She shuddered and reached for Mitch's hand.

Two hours or so later, Sophia passed their untouched dinner trays to the stewardess, relieved that she would no longer have to stare at the unidentifiable mass of food that had solidified before her gaze. The man sitting next to her had been smart, refusing food and opting for several shots of vodka. He lit a cigarette now and she breathed in the aroma of the strong Bulgarian cigarettes Sergei smoked ... or had all that time ago. She thought of the way he used to let the cigarettes burn through almost until they scorched his fingertips.

"Maman?" Mitch knelt up on his seat. "Can the wind break the glass in the window?"

"Of course not."

"Are you sure?"

"Yes, I'm sure. The windows are that thick." She held a thumb and forefinger, some way apart, in front of his face. "Not even a huge giant with a big hammer could smash them."

"But that big hammer ... the one at Expo ... a giant could get that."

"That's silly. Now why don't we read your book?" She reached into her bag under the seat in front. "It's your favourite." She held the well-thumbed *Les Aventures de Perrine et Charlot* and pulled Mitch's feet out from under him with her free hand.

"I don't want to read the stupid book. I want to go home," he shouted and kicked the back of the seat in front. An eye appeared through the gap between the two seats.

"Pardon," Sophia mouthed her apology and tucked the book into the seat pocket. The eye disappeared. "We have to sleep first," she spoke softly to her son.

"I want to sleep in my bed." He clutched both armrests as the aircraft started to bump around. "I want to go home. I don't like it here. It's horrid!"

"Shush, darling. You're just tired." Sophia pulled the straps of the seat belt around him and fastened the buckle. "Let's make you nice and cozy." She reached for a blanket that had fallen onto the floor and covered his legs with it. "Now, why don't we have some of the nice sandwiches we brought from ..." The word "home" froze on her lips. She quickly pulled out Mitch's old brown bear from the seat pocket. “We’ll have to get him a new eye when we get to Russia, won’t we? I’m sure Papa will know the best place to get one,” she said.

“The giant, Maman. While I’m asleep, he won’t hit the window with his big hammer, will he?”

“Of course not. There aren’t any giants in the sky. They live on the ground, don’t they?”

“Do they live on the ground in Russia?” he whispered.

“No. They can’t get across the sea. Now let’s try to get some sleep.”

Mitch clutched the bear to his chest and began to chew one of its ears. Sophia turned her head into the side of the seat and watched Mitch’s chest rise and fall. His arms and legs twitched a few times then his breathing became even; soon the bear’s head flopped to one side.

The cabin lights were dim. Now and again the murmur of voices or a cough punctured the drone of the engines. Sophia leaned back and tried to bring a vision of Sergei into her mind, but over the years his image had faded. She reached for her purse and pulled out a photograph. With a fingertip, she traced the outline of his square jaw, his lips. He was standing by the frozen river, his dark clothes and serious expression at odds with the pristine whiteness of the scene. What did she know of this man … the father of her son and the man with whom she was going to share her life?

Sergei had travelled to Canada from Leningrad as a legal adviser assisting a group from the Soviet Union looking for ways to link up with a children’s charity in which Luc was involved. Sophia was press-ganged into joining the welcoming party at the airport. He stood head and shoulders above the others as the party emerged into the Arrivals hall. But it wasn’t just his unusual height that made him stand out for Sophia. There was an aura about him, an immediate connection, a quickening in her stomach that made her feel weak every time she looked at him, heard his voice from across a room. Even after all these years, she still imagined she could hear it.

On the way from the airport that day, he had sat next to her as she drove him and two other members of the party to the home of one of the charity volunteers in the city. His English was good, but conversation stilted. The following day, Sophia helped serve supper for the group at Simone’s home. Her hand shook as she handed Sergei a bowl of soup. A splodge spilled onto the sleeve of his jacket. She gulped, dumbstruck, unsure what to do. He dabbed ineffectively at the stain with a paper serviette, and then Simone guided him to the kitchen, where he removed his jacket and she applied water to the stain. Sophia followed, mumbling apologies.

"It does not matter," he'd told her, a comforting hand on her shoulder. Her eyes fixed on the wave in his iron-grey hair, the way his almost coal-black eyes sparkled in amusement at her embarrassment.

Simone had held up the jacket, which by then had a large water stain. "I'll dry it with my hair dryer. It won't take a minute," she said, and disappeared into the hallway.

Sergei's voice was low when he spoke again: "I would like to meet you somewhere ... a cup of coffee?" Sophia nodded. "We have to be careful." He explained quickly that the man sitting at the end of the table nearest the window was from the KGB—the Soviet security police. "He's here to make sure we don't get too friendly with local people!" Sergei grinned at her.

During the three weeks that followed, evading the KGB minder had become a game, at least to Sophia. The tension added to the drama and excitement. Beneath it all, a growing love. She skipped classes at the university—something she had never contemplated before—persuading a friend to let them use her room in one of the residences. It was there that their son was conceived.

She looked at the photograph again now. It was taken a few hours before the group's visit came to an end. She could still remember the feeling of dread that consumed her as she thought of life without Sergei. How could she continue? There had to be a way to be together. He had explained that corresponding would be difficult. Friendships with foreigners were frowned upon and letters from overseas opened by the authorities. "I will try to get a message to you. There are ways, but it will take time. It's a circuitous route. The letter will tell you how to reply."

For weeks, Sophia had drifted from day to day, unable to pick up the threads of life as she waited for a message or a letter. She couldn't concentrate on her studies and wandered the city revisiting the places they had been together. When the weather was bad, she feigned illness and stayed in her room at home, going over in her mind every inch of his body, how they had made love until they were both exhausted. When the letter arrived, passed to her by Luc, she no longer had to feign sickness. She knew she was pregnant with Sergei's baby. She lay for hours on her bed, gently massaging her stomach, hoping that the baby within felt some semblance of the love she felt for his father and for him. Their child was a boy—of that she was sure. But as morning sickness weakened her, she began to have desperate thoughts, to worry about the future for her baby. What had she done? Would she ever see Sergei again?

Alone in her room, she had agonized over the words she would use to tell her parents. With their rigid religious views, how would they accept that, rather than marry the good Jewish boy they had chosen for her, she was pregnant by someone from the Soviet Union? And there was the age difference. Hasidic thought expects that a bride and groom should be about the same age as each other. Sergei was twenty eight years her senior. She would have to make her parents understand, tell them of the love she and Sergei felt for each other.

One evening, while the three of them ate dinner, she had gathered her courage and begun to tell them of her feelings for Sergei. "It is out of the question. Put him out of your mind!" Her father's knife and fork clattered onto his plate. "You are promised to Avraham. He is a good man. He will make a good husband." She had tried to reason with him, telling him that she didn't love Avraham. It was Sergei she loved. "Forget him! It is Avraham you will marry!" Her father banged his fist on the table to punctuate his words. Sophia had shifted in her seat, appealing silently with her eyes to her mother. For a moment, a flicker of compassion washed across her mother's face, then she turned away.

"Avraham will not want me," Sophia gulped. "I am carrying Sergei's baby."

Her father's face had screwed up with anger and disbelief. "You are telling us you are pregnant? By ..." he spluttered, unable to find strong enough words. "You would choose a man like that over your religion, your family, your country?" He pushed his chair back noisily and got to his feet. "You disgrace our family name. You're no better than a whore!" He threw his napkin onto the table. Sophia slid down in her seat, shoulders hunched. "They are our enemies. Communists, the lot of them! Don't you know what they did to our people?"

Her mother had pleaded with her. "You hardly know him. We will make arrangements for the child. No one will know. Things will be as before." *Arrangements?* Sophia stared at her mother, unable to accept what the word implied. "You'll forget that man in time, but you'll never get over the loss of your family."

Sophia had left the house that evening, clutching a suitcase. "You're not wanted here," were her father's last words.

For weeks, Sophia had moved aimlessly from one borrowed room to another, her savings dwindling. She went back to classes for a few weeks, but knew she had to find work if she was to provide for her child. Luc arranged for her to work for a few hours each week helping one of his elderly female clients sort out the affairs of her recently-deceased husband. Sophia loved the peaceful atmosphere in Celeste's home, the way a photograph could send her into fond reminiscences of happy times she and her husband shared. It gave Sophia hope for her own future, one she desperately hoped she would share with Sergei and their child.

On a warm summer day, she had sat on a bench in Simone's garden and read again a letter that had arrived that morning from Sergei. It had been written some weeks before, just after he learned he was to become a father. Although the news must have been a shock, the strength of his love for her and their baby spilled from the page. He wrote of the time when they would be reunited. 'It won't be easy, lyubov' maya,' he warned, 'but we will make it work somehow'. As the sun warmed her body, she imagined she could feel his hands caressing her swollen breasts, moving down to her stomach, feeling the flutterings of the child within.

She looked now at her son ... their son ... sleeping in the aircraft seat at her side. She ran a hand through his hair, agonizing again over whether she was doing the right thing bringing him to an unknown land, to a father he had never met. A man she hardly knew. A man with whom she would share a bed. How many times, alone in her bed in Montréal, had she longed to feel his body next to her, have him make love to her? *But now?*

She touched their son's cheek gently, remembering how when the nurse handed the tiny baby to her in the delivery room, an odd mixture of love and panic flowed through her exhausted body. She had cried huge sobs, which the medical staff mistook for tears of happiness. In reality, she was terrified that this scrap of humanity was now dependent on her. In that moment, she had grown up, gulped back tears, and told herself she could do it. She had so much love for this child, they would get by.

Secretly, she had harboured the hope that her parents would accept what she had done and love their grandson. Simone tried to talk her out of visiting her old home. But Sophia wrapped her two-week-old son in a blanket and watched from the other side of the street as her parents walked down their driveway on their way to the synagogue, the synagogue where on Mitch's eighth day the *mohel* would have performed the *brit milah,* the sacred ritual circumcision, and where Mitch would have received his Hebrew name. *Ari* is the name Sophia had chosen—*Ari* with its meaning of lion, strength, and fearlessness, all qualities her son would need in the difficulties ahead. On that day, as Sophia looked across the street, Mitch had started to cry. Her mother stopped and looked around. Sophia stepped back into the shadows and clutched her baby to her breast, unwilling to subject him to rejection. Later, Simone confessed she had taken it upon herself to go to see Sophia's parents. She shook her head, a comforting arm around her friend's shoulders. "Maybe if I go there when my father is out, my mother might ..." The rest of Sophia's words were left unsaid as she looked into Simone's troubled face.

In the years since then, Sergei's commitment to Sophia never faltered. How could she not love this man who wrote of his love for her and their son, believing that one day they would be together? She never shared the doubts that haunted the night hours, the fear of having grown apart from the man she had known for those few short weeks. What did she know of him or his life in a country where every movement was controlled, where their son would be subjected to a life of limited opportunity?

Just after Mitch's second birthday, Luc mentioned the possibility she might join the delegation from the charity in their upcoming visit to the Soviet Union. A new excitement and purpose filled her waking hours. Mitch would stay with Simone, and she arranged a temporary leave of absence from the school where she was working as a teaching assistant. She shopped for clothes and gifts for Sergei, guessing at his size and tastes. It wasn't to be. The Soviet authorities refused to sanction the group's visit. The night she learned of the decision, she cradled Mitch in her arms and cried until she fell into exhausted sleep.

She hoped a miracle would happen and Sergei would be allowed to return to Canada. But permission had finally come through—Sophia and Mitch were to join him in Leningrad. After the initial euphoria, a cold chill gripped her stomach. For days, she stared into space, her mind tormented with thoughts of life in the Soviet Union ... or a future without Sergei and a father for her son. Love won through. Her mother was wrong. She had never got over her love for him.

She remembered now how excited he was when he wrote with news that he and his mother had moved from the *kommunalka* and been assigned a larger apartment. "It's the perfect place for all of us." When Sergei first mentioned that his mother would live with them, Sophia had searched for words that would not wound. He was insistent, telling her that in the Soviet Union, families live together. 'It's a necessity, and the older people help look after the grandchildren,' he wrote. But Irina Arkadyevna sounded like a formidable woman. Her husband was killed at the time of the October Revolution, and Sergei told tales of his mother's fortitude as she struggled to bring him up on her own. Was this what Sophia wanted for her son? A life without a father? No. They would be a family. The four of them.

As the engine noise droned on, a vision of her own mother's face, illuminated by the glow from the candles of the menorah, washed unbidden before Sophia's eyes. Then it faded and was gone.

It was mid-morning when she watched the runway race beneath the plane and felt the wheels bump down on the tarmac at Sheremetyevo Airport.

"Are we there, Maman?" Mitch asked. "Will Papa be here?"

"We're in Moscow, darling. You remember?" She looked quizzically at him. "We have to get another flight to Leningrad, where Papa will be waiting."

"But I don't want to get another flight. I want Papa to be here." When Sophia didn't reply, Mitch raised his voice. "I want him here ... I don't want to go on another stupid plane. They're horrid!"

"Calm down." Her voice was low, her mind already racing through the possible scenarios that awaited them in the terminal building.

The aircraft lurched to a stop. Mitch turned from the window, his eyes wide. "Maman! There are soldiers. They have guns!" he breathed.

"The soldiers won't hurt us," she began, silently cursing herself for not preparing him for this. Luc had joked that although the official explanation was that the soldiers ensured no one came into the country who shouldn't be there, it was more likely that the military were guarding the aircraft in case anyone tried to escape the byzantine restrictions of the so-called utopian society. A scowl from Simone had warned him not to continue.

"Will they shoot us?" Mitch's voice was a mere whisper. "Patrice said ..."

"Forget what Patrice said," she snapped. "He doesn't know. Now get your things together."

The stench of aviation fuel rose up to meet them as they stepped out of the aircraft. Sophia blinked against the bright light, gripped Mitch's hand firmly, and started to descend the steps.

Inside the terminal building, she tried to decipher the signs, but fatigue had washed-out her brain. She followed the other passengers and joined the end of one of the lineups in front of the officials in the boxed-in areas.

"I'm hot," Mitch declared and jabbed the toe of one shoe onto the floor.

"I know," she commiserated. Sweat trickled down her back, and she fanned her son with the passports and forms she held in one hand. "Better now?"

"Isn't the lady hot?"

Sophia turned around. An old woman stood behind them. Her black cardigan was buttoned up and the scarf around her head tied in a knot under her ample chin. "I expect she is," she said wearily.

"Ty govorish' po russki?" the woman asked in a low voice.

Sophia stared, uncomprehending.

"Rebёnok?" The woman gestured toward Mitch with a hand.

"Mitch ... my son." As Sophia spoke, Mitch sidled up to her.

The old woman put out a tentative hand and ran it along the fabric of Sophia's skirt.

Sophia smiled, turned, and pushed their bag forward with her right foot. She looked along the lines of people. They waited patiently, talking quietly among themselves. *Not like at home,* she thought. Then she remembered that this was now their home. She looked around the stark room. There was a staleness in the air, as if the very breath of life had been sucked out.

She glanced at the paper in her hand. It was filled with Luc's neat handwriting—a phonetic list of the likely things the officials (guards, he called them) might ask and how she should reply. They had rehearsed the words over and over. Now, to her stricken gaze, the paper contained a jumble of indecipherable symbols.

They shuffled forward; the uneasiness in the pit of her stomach intensified with each step. She watched as documents were checked, and she heard official stamps thump down. Her eyes followed the receding backs of people as they disappeared into the gloom behind the guards' booths. What lay beyond, she could only imagine. Mitch pulled his bear out of the bag and clasped it to his chest with both arms. His shirt hung out of the back of his pants; she bent down and tucked it in. Then she hugged him and whispered, "It's going to be all right. It's going to be all right".

"I'm hungry, Maman, and thirsty," he moaned, resting his head on her shoulder.

"I know," she murmured. They had hardly eaten anything since they left Montréal, and the water in the galley on the plane had run out hours before they landed. "We'll get you something after we've checked in for our next flight. A nice cold drink and maybe some ..."

"I don't want to go on another plane." His shoulders drooped. The bear dangled at his side.

Finally, they reached the front of the line. She hooked her bag over an arm and took Mitch's hand. They both jumped involuntarily as the guard barked out an order and beckoned them forward. "Come, Mitch," she said, approached the booth and slid their documents through the slot in the glass. The world fell silent. She looked at the guard's pockmarked face; he picked up one of the passports, opened it at the page with the picture, raised his head, and stared at her. Colour rose in her cheeks, and her hand went to her neck, her fingers pulling the lapels of her blouse together. Then he put down her passport, opened Mitch's, and leaned forward to look at him. Mitch wriggled free from her grasp and buried his face in her skirt.

"Kak dolgo vy budete zdes'?" the guard growled.

Her hand trembled as she looked at her notes, desperately trying to make sense of what he had said. The words on the page blurred and the room seemed to tilt at a crazy angle. She gripped the small wooden ledge in front of her and opened her mouth to speak but quickly bit back the Yiddish words that came into her mind as she heard again Luc's words: *You must be careful. Asserting Jewishness conflicts with being a loyal citizen.* At that moment, she felt as though she stood between two worlds, belonging to neither.

"Kak dolgo vy budete zdes'?" the guard's voice boomed out again. He thumped his fist on the counter, his face puce.

"My zdes' ... " Her lips were unable to form the rest of the words. Sweat pricked her skin and she felt the fabric of her blouse sticking to her back.

"W... What's he s ... s ... saying?" Mitch sobbed.

Sophia felt too many shreds of dignity to join him ... yet.

"Can I help?" A tall, grey-haired man in a dark suit had stepped out of the adjacent line. "He is asking how long you will stay here," he explained in English as he put his briefcase down on the floor beside her.

"Thank you," she gulped. "Could you tell him that we are here to join my ... my son's father in Leningrad. He is a Soviet citizen. We are going to live here.

We have permission. The papers." She gestured to the documents the guard was holding.

The conversation went back and forth for some minutes; then the guard slid the documents toward Sophia and pointed a finger to a closed door at the far side of the room.

"It seems that, as you are here as a permanent resident, you have to be seen by someone else," the man in the suit explained. "In the office there."

Sophia picked up the documents, a look of helplessness on her face.

The man checked his watch. "If you like, I can wait with you and make sure they have someone who can speak English, someone who understands."

"I don't want to delay you," she began.

"Sleduyushchiy!" the guard barked, motioning to the old woman behind them to come forward.

"I think we'd better get out of the way," the other man suggested, "before this fellow here loses his temper completely."

"But you'll lose your place," she said, taking Mitch's hand and moving to one side.

"Don't worry, my dear. I have some time before my next flight. As you probably know, we foreigners are only allowed to travel on a limited number of flights, just to maximize the inconvenience." He grinned and began to pick his way between the people and their assortment of bags and boxes. "One of the first things you learn in this God-forsaken country is that in public people are mostly wary of speaking to foreigners. They never know who will inform on them."

"Do you live here?" Sophia asked. They were now in front of the closed door.

"Me? No! I'm here on business. I wouldn't last long in this sort of place. They'd banish me to Siberia!" he laughed. The sweat felt cold on Sophia's back. "Now, let's get this sorted out," he said and rapped on the door loudly.

CHAPTER THREE
LENINGRAD–JULY 1967

Four hours later, Sophia and Mitch approached the exit in the baggage hall in Leningrad. Three guards sat behind a table—beyond them, an open doorway where shadowy figures drifted past. A mixture of excitement and panic rippled through Sophia. Sergei was so close. The other side of the doorway. Waiting. She stopped and closed her eyes for a moment. *What if he isn't there? What if he doesn't recognize me? Will I know him?* Her feet felt glued to the ground as she tried to stop the scene that seemed to take over her mind in her sleeping and waking hours. It was there now, running through her head. The darkness beyond the door, her frantic search for the man who had fathered her son. The crowds. They washed to one side, revealing a figure crouching in a corner. It rose up and came toward her. It had her father's face, but an emaciated body. It reached out, trying to pull Mitch toward it. She held on fast to her son's hand.

"Maman! You're hurting me!"

Her son's voice penetrated the darkness, and she loosened her grip on his hand and began to walk forward. The guards at the exit were chatting amongst themselves as Sophia and Mitch drew level. The one closest to them waved them on. Sophia took a big breath and walked through the doorway. Mitch trailed behind. A sea of faces stared at her—a fixed tableau, unmoving. She couldn't see anyone who looked like Sergei, or the Sergei she remembered. The noise added to her confusion as she looked for a way through the press of bodies. "Stay close," she urged, clasping her son's hand more firmly.

Then hands gripped her shoulders and she looked into almost coal-black eyes. The suitcase handle slipped from her grasp. "It's you. It's really you," Sergei breathed, looking from her to Mitch and back again. He cupped her face in his hands. For a second or two her body was rigid. Then he kissed her gently and gathered her into his arms. She buried her face in his shirt, tentatively at first. His body was warm, and she began to breathe in the smell of cologne mixed with the odour of Bulgarian cigarettes.

"I've missed you so much." She sobbed into his shirt.

"Lyubov' maya, lyubov' maya," he murmured, hugging her closer.

"There were soldiers. With guns!" Mitch's insistent voice came to them as they drew apart.

A softness spread across Sergei's face as he looked at his son. It was a moment before he stooped down and murmured, "The soldiers won't hurt you."

Mitch backed away, hunching his shoulders, his arms wrapped around his chest.

"It's Papa," Sophia encouraged. Her right hand on Mitch's back, she pushed him gently forward. She felt his body stiffen. "Go on. Give Papa a hug."

Sergei held his hands out to him. "Papa is here now. No one will hurt you ... *moy syn*." Mitch came toward him, head down, staring at the floor. "He's such a fine boy ... a fine boy." Sergei reached out and gathered his son into his arms. After a moment, he picked Mitch up and drew Sophia into their embrace, his breath warm on the side of her face. "I can't believe you're really here. After all this time." His body shook as he sobbed.

When they drew apart, Sophia noticed that Sergei's face was thinner; the front tooth he had chipped just before leaving Canada now bore a gold filling. The overhead lights picked out streaks of white in his hair. "Let's get you out of here," he urged as a large woman tried to push past. "Now, Mitch," he said, lowering Mitch to the ground and wiping his own eyes with the back of his hand, "you must hold on. Keep right behind me, both of you." He took the bag from Sophia, picked up the suitcase, and held it in front of him as he forced his way through the mob.

Sophia gripped the back of Sergei's blue shirt and bent into him, pushing Mitch into the space between them. The heat of people was all around. The cloying smell of sweat mingled with stale tobacco smoke. Faces stared at her, mouths open as they shouted to each other. Sergei's voice rose above the rest: "Let us pass! Let us pass!" Daylight seeped through as they reached the edge of the crowd, and she let go of Sergei's shirt.

"Leonid should be out there somewhere." Sergei said, putting the suitcase down and motioning toward the doors.

"Leonid?"

"Leonid and his wife. They share an apartment with my friend, Vera Kishinevskaya. You remember, I told you about her?"

Sophia's brain felt like mush.

"I'm tired. Carry me," Mitch whined, sidling up to his mother.

"My poor wounded soldier needs to be carried, does he?" Sergei laughed loudly and knelt down. "Papa will carry you." Mitch looked at Sophia; she nodded, and he climbed on to his father's back, looping his arms around his neck as he had seen other boys do with their fathers. "Hang on," Sergei called to Mitch. He picked up the suitcase, his elbows gripping Mitch's legs. "It's pandemonium out there," he added to Sophia as he struggled upright. "Hold on to my arm."

Outside, a cloud of diesel fumes hovered above the people thronging the sidewalk. "Take no notice of them. They're just trying to earn money," Sergei commented as yet another man with a battered face attempted to steer them off in the direction of a car. *"Nyet! Nyet!"* he barked when hands reached out to pull at the suitcase. Mitch hid his face in the back of his father's neck. "There's Leonid." They stepped into the roadway and dodged between the slowly moving traffic toward a black car parked on the other side of the road. A well-built, grey-haired man, dressed in black pants and a collarless white shirt, hurried toward them and took the suitcase from Sergei. "Let's get you into the car," Sergei said, lowering Mitch to the floor.

Leonid swung the suitcase into the trunk of the car, slammed the lid down, and turned to Sophia. He bowed his head slightly. *"Zdravstvuyte."* His grin revealed perfect teeth.

Sophia hesitated for a moment and then offered her hand. His grip was firm.

Inside the car, she leaned back into the seat as they pulled away. Her eyelids felt heavy. A cacophony of horns blasted as cars tried to turn across the traffic and pedestrians ran across the road. After a few minutes, they were clear of the airport and turned onto a wide road, bordered by scrubby grassland. Cars vied for position with open-backed trucks piled high with wooden boxes and crates.

Mitch was now kneeling on the other back passenger seat, talking non-stop to his father, who was sitting in the seat in front of Sophia. "Is this our car?"

"*Nyet*. This is Vera Kishinevskaya's car. She's Papa's friend."

"Will she be my friend too ... Papa?"

Sergei grinned. "Of course she will. I've told her all about you. She's looking forward to meeting you ... both of you."

"Where's our car?"

"We don't have one yet."

"Why not?"

"Well, it's different here. You have to put your name down on a list, and then when your turn comes, you get your car."

"But when will we get it?"

"Soon. We're luckier than most people. I'm on a special list where I work."

"What colour will it be? I like blue. Bright blue!"

"We don't have a choice."

Sergei's voice sounded flat to Sophia's ears. She remembered how when she drove him in her father's car in Montréal, he enthused over the leather upholstery. She hadn't understood his excitement. "It's only a car," she had teased. It made sense now.

"I still can't believe you are here." Sergei grinned at her. "And as beautiful as I remembered."

Sophia looked down at her cream-coloured skirt, which was spattered with unidentifiable stains. Her blouse hadn't fared much better. *I dread to think what my face and hair look like,* she thought, carefully avoiding a glimpse of herself in the rearview mirror.

"And Mitch, Babushka Irina has made you some of her special *vatrushka*," Sergei said.

"Is that my babushka?" Mitch asked.

"Yes, she's your babushka."

"Will she have presents for me?"

Sergei laughed loudly. "I'm sure she'll have something for you."

Sophia watched the street scene slip by. Women emerged from shops, carrying string bags bulged into odd shapes with what looked like vegetables and bread. Despite her exhaustion, she couldn't help exclaiming as they passed an ornate pastel-painted building.

"It isn't all drabness here," Sergei quipped.

Maybe it will be all right, she told herself. She leaned back in her seat and closed her eyes, concentrating on the sound of Sergei's voice as he answered Mitch's questions or spoke to Leonid. His voice was as deep as she remembered ... the voice that had spoken words of love to her in the narrow bed in which they had clung together in Montréal, sleepy from making love. Now his words spun around and around in her head like the drone of aircraft engines, until she felt as though she was tilting backwards, unable to fight the cloying sense of tiredness any longer.

Some minutes later, the clang of a tram jolted her awake. She looked around, at first unable to focus her eyes on anything. "You are tired, *lyubov' maya*," Sergei murmured. She took the hand he offered over the back of his seat. It was warm and soft like the rest of his skin. The skin she had longed to feel during the lonely years. At first, she had awoken in the night, imagining his fingers gently caressing her body. But the memory of their lovemaking faded. Now, as their eyes met, a flush came to her cheeks. *What will it be like lying next to this man ... this man I hardly know?* It had seemed so easy, so natural, before. "Where are we?" she asked.

"Moskovskiy prospekt. We'll be home soon."

The traffic slowed and Leonid shifted through the gears noisily. The car ground to a halt level with a group of women. Each was armed with a long-handled brush and pan, and Sophia watched as they swept litter from the sidewalk. The young woman closest to the car was dressed in a brown and yellow skirt, or perhaps it was a dress, topped with a long turquoise top buttoned down the front. Around her head she wore a red scarf. Wisps of blonde hair had escaped from the front and dangled over her face as she worked. Sophia met the woman's steady gaze. Her eyes were vivid-blue; despite their bright colour, they had a dullness about them.

"Those women back there," Sophia began as the car pulled away. "Is that the only job they can get, sweeping the streets?"

"It's work. They earn money," Sergei replied and turned to look at her. "Some of the older women do it to augment their pensions."

"But it doesn't seem right. The young ones. Surely they deserve better? A chance in life."

"My darling, the Soviet Union is like everywhere else. Some people will always be less fortunate than others. That's just the way."

They were now travelling parallel to a dirty, yellow tram, which swayed and clanged along tracks on a strip of land in the centre of the road. It ground to a halt alongside a line of people. Leonid jammed on the brakes of the car as a man and woman ran across the road. He put his head through the open window, and by the tone of his voice and angry gesture, she guessed the words he shouted were less than polite.

A few minutes later they crossed a bridge over a narrow strip of water. "That's the Obvodny Canal," Sergei said. "This was all swampland before Peter the Great worked his miracle and built the city. Such a magnificent city."

"Do they have boats on there?" Mitch asked, pointing a finger out of the window. "Can we go?"

Sergei turned and grinned at Mitch. "We'll go on Sunday on the Fontanka ... and afterwards we'll have a picnic."

"Yes! Yes!" Mitch shouted, bobbing up and down on the seat. *I can be Charlot.*

"We're almost there," Sergei said as Leonid did a U-turn across the oncoming traffic and then turned into a side street. Sophia looked out of the open window. Tall buildings towered above, blotting out the daylight. At least, she thought it was daylight. Her wristwatch told her it was six o'clock, but her body felt as though it was the middle of the night. The car slowed and Leonid inched it through a narrow archway into a courtyard.

Sergei's face lit up with excitement as he helped Sophia out of the car. Mitch scrambled after her. "Where do I play?" he asked.

"Why, just over there." Sergei pointed to a low-rise building, in front of which was a slide and a sandbox behind a wire fence.

"But who will I play with?"

"I'm sure there are lots of other children around," Sophia added with a certainty she was far from feeling. The only people she could see were three men sitting at a small table on the far side of the courtyard. It looked as if they were playing some sort of board game.

"The other children from the child care centre." Sergei bent down level with his son. "See, that's where you will be going with all the other little children." Mitch's bottom lip trembled. "And it's not far from our apartment. Maman and Babushka will be able to look out of the window and wave to you."

"Will they speak French? The children?"

"You will soon be speaking Russian, my son."

"What floor is it? Our apartment?" Sophia asked, looking up at the lines of laundry strung around the outside of the windows.

"The fourth. We're on the fourth floor."

She looked to where Sergei pointed, trying hard not to let dismay show on her face as she took in the grime-spattered building. She felt as though a tight band was wrapped around her chest, forcing air out of her lungs. The buildings around the courtyard hovered over her, tilting downwards, and she shifted her gaze toward the ground, taking shallow breaths until the feeling of panic subsided and she began to breathe more easily.

"It's nicer than the *kommunalka* Babushka had before," Sergei murmured. "We have our own kitchen. It's only the bathroom we have to share." He kissed the side of her face. "It'll be okay. You'll see." He picked up the suitcase. "Now let's get you both inside."

With a slight bow of his head, Leonid got back into the car, started the engine, and pulled away. Sophia gripped Mitch's hand and followed Sergei across the cobbled courtyard, trying not to think of their apartment in Montréal, sunlight streaming in the windows, the little garden where Mitch had learned to ride his bicycle. As they reached the big wooden entrance door, Sophia noticed two old women sitting on chairs along the outside wall. They both stopped knitting and looked Sophia and Mitch up and down. Sophia was too exhausted to hide the stains on her clothes. The door creaked and Sergei ushered them into a dimly lit hallway. "The women," he said as he inclined his head toward the door, "we jokingly call them *dezhurnyye.* Busybodies really. Most buildings have them. They like to think they're important, watching who comes and goes. Soon everyone will know you've arrived."

"It smells horrible." Mitch's voice echoed around the hallway.

Sophia had been trying to ignore the stench—not a smell she could identify. Bile rose in her throat as she followed Sergei toward a narrow, green-painted door, at the side of which concrete steps spiralled upwards. Sergei put the suitcase on the floor and pressed a button at the side of the door. Clangs came from the elevator shaft. "The elevator's a bit small, but it usually works, unlike in some buildings." After a moment or two, he pulled the door open, slid back the metal grille, and stood to one side to allow them to get in. It was dark inside. "The light bulb," he pointed to the empty socket in the ceiling, "people steal them. Trade them for vodka." A pulse throbbed in Sophia's temple and the beat of her heart seemed to fill the space as the elevator jerked and rattled upwards.

"It's scary in here. I don't like it," Mitch whispered and hid his face in Sophia's skirt.

"Mama will be so pleased to see both of you," Sergei's voice came from the darkness. "She didn't sleep last night. Or the night before." The elevator shuddered to a stop and he pushed the metal grille and door aside. Sophia took a deep breath and stepped out, pushing Mitch in front of her.

They were in a narrow passageway, lit by a single bulb. The brown paint on the walls was chipped and the stone floor worn into a groove down the middle. "It's along here," Sergei said. Sophia shivered.

"Some of these are just one-room units. There's nowhere to store things," Sergei explained as they inched sideways around a bicycle, an old bedframe, and cardboard boxes piled haphazardly against the wall. At the end of the corridor, they turned a corner. "Here we are," he said and stood to one side.

At that moment, the door in front of them opened and a slightly-built woman stepped out. Sophia swallowed hard and tried to find her voice.

CHAPTER FOUR
LENINGRAD—DECEMBER 1967

From her place at the window, Sophia watched a piece of paper whipped up into a spiral of snowflakes in the courtyard. She checked her watch. *The children will be out to play in two minutes.*

"Why are you still doing this?" Irina Arkadyevna cautioned. "He has to learn you can't always be there watching over him." Although Sergei insisted they only speak Russian, when he wasn't home the two women often conversed in English. Ira had learnt the language from her maternal grandmother, who had come to Russia as a governess.

Sophia knew her mother-in-law was right, but what harm was there in giving Mitch a reassuring wave when he came out to play with the other children?

"You'll have to stop it some time, otherwise you'll still be doing it when he's ten!" Ira shook her head. "Let the boy settle on his own, make friends. He'll survive."

Sophia wasn't sure her son would survive in this austere society where individuality is scorned. She had witnessed it herself in the child care centre where the younger children were herded into the bathroom to sit on tin potties—all in the name of marching in step with the collective!

She stared out of the window, hungry for a glimpse of Mitch. The door opened and a knot of children spilled out into the playground. She scanned wrapped figures. Searched for the red woollen hat. She waved. He didn't look up but instead ran to the wooden slide and began to climb the icy steps. Sophia held her breath. When he reached the top, she waved again. He hurtled down the slide to where a little blue-bundled figure waited, and then the two of them ran to the sandbox and began to throw snow at each other. As Sophia moved away from the window, an odd mixture of relief and sadness washed through her.

"I know it's been hard for you coming here." Irina Arkadyevna slumped down onto a chair and smoothed the oilcloth covering the table. "If only I'd been as brave."

"Brave? You're one of the bravest people I know." Sophia poured coffee into two cups and placed one on the table in front of Irina. "You brought Seryozha up on your own. Not many people could have done that," she said, reaching for her own cup.

"I did what I had to. But none of it would have happened ... if only ..." Ira sighed loudly as Sophia sat down opposite her. "If only we'd left when Dima wanted to. He would still be alive. None of it would have happened."

"I'm sure you did what you thought was right."

"*Nyet!* I was stubborn. I wouldn't listen. He pleaded with me. 'We'll go to Finland.' I can hear his voice now. 'There's still time, Ira. Please. We must leave for the sake of the child.' But I thought if I stayed, I could help those poor women whose husbands were at the front. We made soup for them." She rubbed her right eyebrow with a fingertip. "Soup! Can you believe I thought more of making soup than for the safety of my husband and child?"

"Don't be hard on yourself," Sophia murmured.

"It was my fault. The whole thing. My parents too. My father, he was a writer. Lived in another world where he thought that after the Revolution he would be allowed to write freely." She gazed off into the distance before taking a deep breath and continuing. "They were both taken. I was never able to find them."

She gulped back tears. "It was only my Dima and his parents who saw how things would be. That we all should leave before it was too late. His parents, they went to Finland. No one knows what happened to them." She shook her head. "They were good people. Always helping anyone in need. My poor Dima. He was like them." She took a gulp of coffee. "His friends and I, we scoured the streets for two days looking for him. We found him. In an alleyway. There was no overcoat, shoes, money. People must have walked past him." She clasped her hands together. "I always hoped he died quickly. If he had lain there wondering why I hadn't come ..." Her voice trailed off and she stared, unblinking, straight ahead.

Sophia got to her feet and put an arm around Ira's shoulders. Sergei had never told her the circumstances of his father's death, only that he died during the October Revolution. She assumed he was a soldier, but there were no pictures in the apartment of a stiffly-erect uniformed figure looking into an unknown future. She shivered now as she thought of the young Ira running through the streets searching for her husband, and of Sergei just a few weeks old. A baby who would never know his father. *At least that won't happen to Mitch,* Sophia comforted herself, and took a quick peek out of the window. The red hat was bobbing around the playground.

Irina Arkadyevna's head was now bent forward, her long grey hair entwined into a loose plait, wound around her head and held in place by the tortoiseshell clip Sophia had bought in Montréal. The store was filled with fripperies, the kind that brighten otherwise dull lives. Mitch chose a big glittery slide, but she persuaded him that Babushka Irina would prefer something less flamboyant. Now she wasn't so sure. The young woman who must still lurk somewhere inside the worn-out body deserved some glitter, a chance to recapture the youthful years taken from her by violence and hardship.

Sophia thought of her own life, the decisions she had made, the feeling of fear that had gripped her at the thought of coming to the Soviet Union. How scared she was of meeting her future mother-in-law. *In some ways, I'm like her. I thought only of myself. Nothing of my family, how they nurtured and loved me.* She remembered again the evening nearly six years ago. "Don't do this, Sophia," her mother had pleaded. Sophia had turned from the dressing table and looked at her mother's red-rimmed eyes, the hands twisting a handkerchief around and around. "*Muter.* Why can't you understand? I love him so much ..." The lump in her throat had threatened to choke her, and she quickly threw a few more things into the suitcase and snapped it shut.

And now, because of the love she and Sergei shared, she had brought her son—their son—to this harsh place where he hardly laughed, couldn't converse properly with his friends, and was deprived of any chance to learn about his Jewish heritage or go to Hebrew school. When he turned thirteen, he would miss his *bar mitzvah*, where he would have taken on all the rights and obligations of a Jewish adult. If Irina Arkadyevna branded herself as selfish for thinking of others when she should have taken her son to safety in another land, then she, Sophia, was guilty of a far worse crime.

Sophia's mind went back to the letter she had received yesterday from her friend, Simone, in Montréal. It was written in October and had taken weeks to get here via the unofficial route Luc had set up.

> *Did you hear, my dear Sophia? On Sunday in Ottawa, on the fiftieth anniversary of the Russian Revolution, hundreds of people hurled eggs at the Soviet Embassy and chanted, "We'd rather be dead than Red!" Can you believe that? I'm so worried about you and dear little Mitch. Please write and tell me you are okay. Yesterday, on CBC Radio (on "Cross Country Check-Up," you*

remember the program?), a woman who once lived there for ten years rang in and said that in the Soviet Union, you aren't even allowed to smile. Luc says that's ridiculous, but please tell me it isn't that bad there. I can't bear to think of you living like that.

Sergei's brow had creased into a frown when he read the letter. "Sophia, for all our sakes, you must tell her not to write such things. Anyone might get hold of it. Tell her life is good here." Later, he told her to destroy the letter. "It will be better for us all if you don't have letters from people over there." She memorized every word Simone had written before tearing the letter into tiny pieces.

"It's over fifty years now since he died." Irina Arkadyevna's voice cut into her thoughts.

"We could go to his grave. Take flowers if we can find some. Is it close?"

Ira nodded her head.

"Perhaps on Sunday?"

"He would like that."

* * *

Later the same day, Sophia stirred the pot of soup on the stove. She stood for a few moments looking at Sergei slumped in an armchair. His eyes were closed, the dark rings around them like holes in his gaunt face. She knew her being here was difficult for him. They were still waiting for permission to marry—she was a foreigner and a Jew. After Mitch was born, she had changed her surname to Galichin; it was all she could do to bind the three of them together as a family. But marriage was different. Sergei was urging her to denounce her religion. It would make it easier, ensure they were all safe. In her darker moments, Sophia thought she should leave. Disappear. Without the stigma she brought them, Sergei and Mitch would be accepted. But how could she leave the two people she loved most? One night, she confessed her thoughts to Sergei.

"How could you even think of it?" he cried. "Losing you would be worse than losing my legs, my hands, my mind. Everything!" He made her promise never to have such thoughts again. She prayed every night that, despite her presence, Sergei and Mitch would be allowed to lead normal lives and be happy.

She went back to the stove and gave the soup another stir, comforting herself with the thought that things were changing slowly. Mitch seemed to be making friends, and Sergei's job was going well. Earlier this week, he had accompanied his boss to Moscow for two days. She had missed the reassurance of his body in their narrow bed in the corner of the living room when she awoke, drenched in sweat, from the dream that plagued her. Her breath came in noisy gasps as she tried to dismiss the figure she saw so vividly. It had risen from a deep pit. At first it had the face of her mother; the brown eyes looked at Sophia kindly, the voice soothing, welcoming, drawing her toward it. Soft hands reached out and touched Sophia's hair. Then sharp fingernails dug into her scalp and she twisted and turned, her hands pulling at the fingers which were locked in a vice-like grip. The flesh was deathly cold—a cold such as she had never known. Wizened old crones appeared from nowhere, their loose flesh hanging in folds as they poked bony fingers at her. She felt herself falling down into the pit. Faces peered at her, their sharp noses like beaks, their mouths dark holes as they chanted words she could not understand. *Stop it! Stop it!* Sophia told herself now, taking the spoon out of the pot and dropping it onto the side of the stove.

She turned toward the window. In the courtyard, the headlights of a car cut through the darkness. In a dimly-lit apartment opposite, she made out the shapes of people gathered around a table. It was Friday evening, the time when Sophia should be reciting the blessing and lighting the Menorah. She had packed it carefully in tissue paper and nestled it amongst the clothes in the wooden chest— the chest that still hadn't arrived from Canada. "It will be here soon," Sergei had consoled. Sophia thought otherwise. *It's a sign of my unworthiness; the only remaining symbol of my faith has been taken from me.* She had asked Sergei if there was a synagogue she could visit when no one else was there. "There is only one left in the city. You mustn't go anywhere near it," he cautioned. "People from there have been arrested, imprisoned. The *militsiya* watch. There are informers. You would be followed back here. We would all be labelled as enemies."

During the past few days, Sophia had begun to think her faith was subsumed in her need to be accepted. Waiting in line outside a store that was rumoured to be getting a supply of toilet paper, she listened to the gossip of the other women, silently praising herself that she understood most of what they said. Then, despite the chilling bite in the air, she started to sweat as one woman repeated jokes about the *Zhidi,* told to her by her husband. "Yeah, those dirty Jews," the other women muttered as the narrator began another story. "An old Jew shuffling up Bol'shaya morskaya is clonked on the head by dislodged pieces of a building. Goddamit, there's no place for a good brick to fall down in this country!" To her astonishment, Sophia found herself joining in the laughter that followed. She was unable to stop.

Now she rocked gently back and forth, trying to recall the sound of her father's voice as he recited Kiddush, and the soft laughter as one or other of her mother's sisters told stories of their early life in Hungary. As a child, Sophia had perched on a chair in the kitchen, listening to the women arguing over some long ago incident in the *Unterland. Tante* Hani would pause as she chopped potatoes, waving a knife at her sister to emphasize her words: "*Umsin!, Jozefa.* That wasn't how it was." Sophia could almost taste the *shlishkes,* their stuffing of *lekvar'.*

She felt Sergei's arms around her, smelled the odour of cigarettes. "Is Mama asleep?"

She turned and rested her head on his chest. "I think so. Her legs were aching again. It's too much for her, all this walking, lining up."

"I know, but she has always done it. Come and sit down for a while." He led her to the armchair and tucked a cushion behind her back as she sat down. "We have to be patient. We should have our car soon. Things are definitely getting better. Did I not tell you they would?" Sophia nodded. "And don't forget that Vera Alexandrovna said Leonid would drive you in her car, as long as they have enough fuel."

Vera Alexandrovna had done so much for them already. Only last week, when there was still no sign of the wooden chest arriving from Canada, she insisted on giving Sophia some of her clothes. "They will look so much nicer on you." Sophia swallowed her pride and accepted. "Who else do I have to give them to? Treat them as an early wedding present. Even if you did steal the one man in the world I ever wanted to marry!" Vera laughed. Fear must have been written on Sophia's face, and the older woman added quickly, "Don't worry, my dear. Sergei and I have never been more than good friends."

Sophia assumed that Vera had had a relatively easy life. If not, how could she have kept her enthusiasm and zest for life? How wrong she was. Sergei told her that Vera was born into the aristocracy, and when she was a small child, the Red commissars ransacked her family home in Petrograd. Her parents and a few loyal servants gathered the children together and fled to their country estate outside Vyborg on the Gulf of Finland. Like many of their peers, the Kishinevskis had no interest in politics. They were good employers, caring for the families who depended on them for their livelihoods and homes. But this did not shield them from the hatred that welled up in the local peasants. Even in the cultural mix of the lands along the Finnish border, previously loyal servants became assassins, carried along with the rising tide of violence sweeping across Russia. Vera and her older sister, Olga, hid in the stables the night the horde of men from the village rampaged through the house, the flames of their anger fanned by vodka. The two children clung together under their coverlet of straw until the tumult could no longer be heard. Too frightened to venture into their home, the girls ran to the house of the local doctor. The next day, he broke the news to them that their parents had been killed.

The two girls lived in poverty in the new classless society. That was until a prominent member of the Party became obsessed with Olga's beauty and her soaring operatic voice. Her patron brought Olga to live, as his mistress, in Leningrad, and she soon persuaded him that having her sister with her would complete her happiness. They lived secretive lives in comparative comfort until the patron died. Then, with the help of influential friends, the two women managed to melt into obscurity. Vera nursed Olga through a painful illness until she died ten years ago.

What must Vera think of me, whining about my pathetic little problems? Sophia thought now, getting to her feet and going to the stove. *At least I have memories of a happy childhood spent with my parents. And a husband and child.* She looked across to Sergei. He met her gaze, and the familiar feeling of excitement ran through her body. She remembered now that first night in Leningrad, how nervous she had been undressing and lying next to him. She was tired, but their pent-up longing had swept aside any inhibitions as they explored again each other's bodies, reaching a climax that came quickly. As she had drifted into an exhausted sleep that night, Sergei had covered her body with kisses, just as he had in that borrowed room in Montréal, the room where their son had been conceived.

Now their son was sitting cross-legged on the floor, looking at the book Sergei brought back from Moscow. At first, Mitch had tossed it to one side, unable to hide the look of disappointment on his face. Sophia knew he hoped for a toy car. "You'll like it, Mitch. Timur, the boy in the title," Sergei explained as he picked up the book and held it so that his son could see the cover, "he and his friends form a secret club to do chores and favours for people whose men are away serving in the Soviet Army. You remember the soldiers we saw in the parade?"

Mitch nodded enthusiastically, and Sophia wondered what had happened to the child who was terrified of the soldiers at the airport. *He seems to be slipping away from me,* she thought. *But perhaps I am slipping away from them.* She closed her eyes and tried to calm the feeling of panic that washed through her.

"Is it the rug, *lyubov' maya*? I thought you liked it."

She opened her eyes and met Sergei's enquiring gaze. "It's lovely," she murmured. He had put his name down on a list over two years ago, and today his grin stretched from ear to ear as he unrolled the rug to reveal reds, blues, and splashes of green. It was now hanging in pride of place on the wall. "We're luckier than most. Some people never have such luxuries," he told her. *Since when has a rug been a luxury?* Sophia kept that thought to herself, consigning it to the part of her mind where only she was allowed to go.

"Papa?" Mitch put the book down. "Why do you read the paper backwards? Is that how you're supposed to read here?"

Sergei laughed softly. "Come and sit on my knee and I'll tell you a little secret," he said, straightening the newspaper. Mitch scrambled onto his lap at the kitchen table. "Now, this is how it's done," he began. "You have to look for clues on the back pages. That's where you find the real news."

"But why?"

"Well, it's clever really. See here. On the list of people who have died, there are lots of people who died on the same day, some from the same families. Now when we look at the front page," he said as he turned the paper over and pointed, "it tells us that there was an air crash in the United States. You know where that is, next to Canada?"

Mitch nodded.

"But the air crash was really here in the Soviet Union, and all those people who died must have been in it."

"But ... isn't that a lie?"

"Not really. It's a game. A game of national pride. You see, the United States is our enemy."

"The soup's ready." Sophia dropped the spoon onto the counter. "I'll wake Mama."

Twenty minutes later, they sat around the small square table, knees almost touching. "Papa, who is little Volodya?" Mitch asked.

"Little Volodya? Why, that's Lenin," Sergei replied, wiping a crust of bread around his bowl.

"You remember, Mitch—the picture in the children's centre." Sophia didn't mention the statue that had frightened Mitch at Expo.

"We sang a song about him today." Mitch sat upright in his chair and began to sing loudly. "The Tsar was like the English King, but Lenin's team was stronger ..."

"Prekrati eto!" The words escaped Sophia's lips before she could stop them.

They were all silent for a moment, then Irina Arkadyevna leaned toward Sophia and patted her hand. "It is because they have no religion. They worship Lenin," she whispered. She then turned to Sergei. "On Sunday, Sophia and I thought it would be nice to visit your father's grave. It's over fifty years ..."

CHAPTER FIVE

LENINGRAD–LATE JUNE 1968

Sophia cradled the envelope in her hands. Her breath came in shallow gasps as she stared at her mother's neatly-formed handwriting. For years she had tried not to hope that her parents would find it in their hearts to forgive her, welcome Mitch into their family. But now? *You have to know,* she told herself. With trembling hands, she tore the envelope open and smoothed the flimsy paper. For a moment, her stunned mind was incapable of stringing the written words together. Then her mother's message came into focus:

> *My Dear Sophia,*
> *Although your dear foter forbade me contacting you, you were never far from my thoughts. Now he has gone. The end came suddenly. So suddenly that not even I had the chance to say goodbye.*

"Oy gevalt!" Sophia cried. *Tate? Dead? No! He can't be.* She gripped the edge of the table. Tears spilled down her cheeks—tears that had been locked inside for years. Tears she never allowed herself to shed for fear of losing her grip on life. "He's gone," she gulped. "*Tate's* gone." An image of her father came into her head. For a few seconds, he seemed to be with her, in the room. He smiled. The smile she remembered from her childhood. *"Tate ... "*

A minute or two later, she mopped her eyes with her apron and began to read again.

> *He was in the garden. It was a bright, sunny day, and he was tying back the tulips.*

Over the years, Sophia had hardly dared to imagine the garden draped in sunlight, Mitch running across the lawn toward his grandparents while she watched through an open window.

> *Your friend, Simone, she said she would arrange for my letter to get to you. She is worried, as she hasn't heard from you for a long while. I pray you are okay. Too much time has been lost already.*

Sophia read on and then caught her breath.

> *He is my only grandchild, and too many years have been wasted. Please say you'll come, Sophia.*

Sophia's mind raced ahead, picturing herself and Mitch walking up the front steps of the house in Montréal. Her mother would open the door and reach out to touch Mitch's face. She could hear her mother's voice: "*Yoy ... yoy ... yoy.* Such a wonderful boy."

Minutes passed. Feelings of sadness, joy, regret, washed through her. She would never again hear her father's voice, the gruff tones that had always softened when as a child she climbed onto his knee and looked into his face. He would hug her close and murmur that she was forgiven for whatever naughtiness she had committed. *Why couldn't he forgive me when I found the man I love? It would have been so different.* She would still have come to Russia to be with Sergei, but there would have been memories of Mitch's early years, of celebrations wrapped in the warmth and love of a family. There would have been letters, pictures of picnics by the canals, Mitch's first day at the child care centre. Those opportunities were lost. And now, her father had been dead for almost a month and she hadn't known.

She imagined her brother and the other men gathered together in dark overcoats and hats. The Rebbe intoning the blessing, mourners shovelling earth into the grave. She shivered, got to her feet, filled the kettle, and put it on the stove. Even if things had been different, she could never have got back to Canada in time to support her mother in her initial shock, to share the sense of bereavement, to comfort her. To be a daughter again.

That afternoon she sat at the kitchen table, pen in hand. Time passed. *What's wrong with you?* she asked herself. Over the years, she had composed so many letters in her head—the words she would say to her parents if she had the courage to write to them. But now, the words wouldn't come. How could she express the emotion she felt? How could she atone for all those lost years? She let her thoughts drift, imagining her mother in the quietness of what had once been a family home, sitting at the table in the kitchen, a solitary meal in front of her. Could this be the woman who had cooked for so many Passovers, Friday night dinners? She had to reach out, comfort her. The words started to flow: reminiscences of times with her father when they were a happy, united family, when it seemed the joy would last forever. She told her how she and Mitch couldn't wait to see her.

She paused, wondering how she would explain to Mitch the death of his grandfather. She doubted it would have much effect on him, as he never really knew him. But lately it had become difficult to gauge how Mitch would react to anything. Some days she felt she didn't know her son—young as he was, he no longer seemed a child, with his wan face and serious expression. He had lost his sense of mischief, of childish fun. *A visit to Canada will do us both good,* she resolved. *I'll find the money somehow.*

She took up her pen, telling her mother she would write again as soon as she had obtained the necessary permit to travel. Her mother hadn't mentioned Sergei, and had addressed the envelope to "Sophia Weitz," her name from her other life. Sophia didn't tell her they were now married. For a moment, her thoughts went back to that dismal ceremony—so different from the joyous occasion her father had promised her from the time when she was just a little girl. *"It will be a time of rejoicing. The beat of drums, the music rising. My hands on your covered head, my whispered blessing, a call from the heart: My child, be happy. Be healthy. Be loved."* The young Sophia had danced around, secure in her father's love. Sophia shook the thoughts from her head now. Before signing the letter, she added the hope that one day they could all be together. *One step at a time,* she told herself and sealed the envelope.

* * *

Day after day she waited in line at the Office of Visas and Registration. The queues were long and her heart heavy as she listened to the gossip, the tales of Jews turned away. In the Arab-Israeli conflict in June of last year, the USSR had switched sides and now actively supported various Arab regimes against Israel. An increasing number of Soviet Jews had applied to emigrate to Israel—almost all were refused permission to leave. But still they came, pursuing a faint hope, a dream. Those waiting in line told stories of friends or relatives whose applications were turned down on the pretext that at some point in their careers, they had been given access to information vital to Soviet national security. Sophia bolstered her flagging spirits, telling herself her case was different. She wasn't applying to go to Israel, and she couldn't possibly have had access to sensitive information. Her absence would only be temporary. So how could they refuse?

One evening, after almost two weeks had passed, she arrived home to find Mitch sitting on Babushka's lap. His eyes were red, his cheeks flushed. "What's the matter?" she asked, placing a hand on his forehead. He squirmed and turned his face away from her.

"The other children said he is a traitor. Good Soviet citizens don't want to leave," Babushka said softly.

"No one will talk to me. It's all your fault!"

"They will soon forget," Babushka comforted, directing a scowl in Sophia's direction. "How about one of your favourite candies?" she tempted, shifting Mitch to one side and delving in her apron pocket for the chocolate candy wrapped in blue paper decorated with a picture of a brown squirrel holding a huge nut. Mitch's hand closed around it.

Sophia slumped onto a chair at the table. Sergei and Babushka had warned her this could happen. Somebody must have seen her in the lineup and spread the story that she was trying to leave the country. Nothing was secret here, with the thin walls and the two old gossips who sat in the entrance swapping stories with anyone who passed by. Sergei had pleaded with her. "Please don't do this, Sophia. The boy is settling down. It will make things difficult for all of us."

She pointed out that he had left the country with the charity group—after all, that was how they had met—so why was it okay for some and not for others? He didn't have an answer. "What sort of country requires you to have a visa to leave?" she threw at him. He looked at her with eyes filled with sadness.

Each night she lay in bed too frightened to sleep, imagining the sharp fingernails of her nightmare as she was dragged into a pit. Each morning as she set out again to take her place in the long lines, she told herself she owed it to her mother to see her one last time.

Now she looked across at her son. He was sucking the sweet as Babushka sang softly to him. The words went around and around in Sophia's head. "I spell you into sleep ..."

"I will go on my own," Sophia murmured. Babushka nodded as she sang.

Early the next morning, Sophia walked briskly past the two old women who were already at their posts outside the entrance door, knitting needles clacking. From the knowing looks they gave her, she knew word had already spread of the argument she and Sergei had last night. Although they usually spoke in English whenever they disagreed, their raised voices aroused curiosity. She was unable to rid her mind of Sergei's angry words, how he accused her of being selfish, of putting their child's happiness in jeopardy. She had tried to explain, but he hadn't understood, railing at her for undermining everything he had worked to achieve. "When I come back ..." she had begun to say. From the agonized look on his face, she finally understood. "Of course I will come back," she said. "I would never leave you and Mitch. I promised." Later, standing at the kitchen window, she had watched the early morning light creep across the courtyard, her arms wrapped around her upper body, imagining how it would feel to be once again in her mother's embrace. She couldn't give up this chance of seeing her again. She needed to feel her soft fingers, not the claws that haunted her dreams. *Just one last try,* she resolved. *The damage is already done, wasn't that what Sergei said last night?*

She was earlier than usual, and the lines were shorter. Blood pulsed noisily through her temples when in late morning she slid her papers across the desk to the official. He scrutinized every word, glancing up at her from time to time. His face gave nothing away. Then he put the documentation to one side and stared at her. His eyes were cold. "We can grant you an exit visa." He paused, picked something out from between his teeth, and wiped his fingers on the edge of the desk. "But you will not be allowed to re-enter the Soviet Union."

"What? But why?" Her questions went unanswered. "You can't do that. My husband, my child. They are here." She leaned closer to the man, and words rushed out of her mouth. "It's inhumane. All I want to do is visit my mother. She is old. I may not get the chance to see her again." There was no response. "Please. My father has died. My mother, she needs me. We haven't ..." Her voice petered out as the official picked up her application and tore it in half.

"Sleduyushchiy!" he barked and motioned to her to step aside.

For a second or two she was transfixed, unable to move. She felt a hand on her arm, pulling her to one side. It was the hand of a young woman who had been a couple of places behind her in the line. "You must do as they say. Don't make trouble for your family."

Sophia looked dumbly at her for a moment and then nodded her head, stumbled back to the desk, gathered up the rest of her documentation, and walked unsteadily toward the door. *Don't make trouble for your family.*

PART TWO

CHAPTER SIX
LENINGRAD—OCTOBER 1976

Mitch looked at the crumbling facades of the buildings, broken windows, rubble piled on the footpath. *This can't be the right place,* he thought, checking the address on the scrap of paper. He shifted his school bag to his other hand and began to make his way farther along the street. He hadn't gone far when a large black dog ambled out of an alleyway; its ribs protruded sharply. It growled and Mitch stepped into the road. As he did so, a young girl appeared at the dog's side. Her shoes flapped where they had split across the toes. She wore a shapeless brown coat. Her skin was sallow. She spat at Mitch. The dog barked. The girl laughed. Mitch started to run, not stopping until he was sure the girl and dog weren't following. In the gathering dusk, it was difficult to see the numbers on the doors of the buildings. He soon realized he had gone past the place where Vanya lived and hurriedly retraced his steps.

He hadn't told anyone where he was going. He felt a thrill of excitement staying out late after school. Lots of boys at school did so, but Mitch had never been asked to join them. He listened enviously to their tales of playing banned pop music in smoky basements, drinking illicit liquor, and of the girls who joined them, never knowing whether to believe their tales. Several times he had suggested to his only real friend, Vanya, that they look for some excitement themselves, but Vanya always said he had things to do. At first, Mitch wondered if he had a secret girlfriend, but when girls sidled up to him, directing smiles his way, Vanya didn't seem to notice. For a fourteen-year-old, Vanya was unusually serious, often engrossed in this or that mathematical problem he was intent on solving, or pacing around the schoolyard, his mumbled words never missing a beat; Mitch would walk in silence at his friend's side, matching his steps.

Now Mitch was worried. Vanya hadn't been at school for several days. "Forget about him. You know what his type are like," the other boys jeered. What was Vanya's type? Maybe they were jealous of the ease with which he sailed through school work, always attaining the highest *pyatorka* grade. Admittedly, he didn't look like most people—his skin was dark. *But what difference does that make?*

Mitch asked himself as he pushed open the battered entrance door. He would gladly swap his own pale, pimpled face, for Vanya's exotic complexion.

Inside the building, his shoes beat a constant rhythm on the concrete stairs as he wound his way upward. The smell of urine brought back memories of the first building he and his family had lived in. On the second floor he squinted in the gloom, checking for numbers among the myriad signs that peppered each door. At last he found the right one and banged loudly several times. He heard footsteps. A voice came from within: *"Kto tam?"*

"Zdravstvuyte!" Mitch ventured. "I ... I'm looking for Vanya. I'm his friend from school."

Bolts slid back and the door opened slightly. Part of a face appeared; the one visible eye looked Mitch up and down. Then the door opened wider and he stepped inside. He waited while the old woman eased the bolts back in place. "Along there. Last door." Mitch walked slowly in the direction she indicated. A young girl with tousled red hair peered around the edge of a door. She held a baby. Snot dangled from its nose. From behind a closed door came the sound of raised voices. Mitch quickened his pace. At the end of the corridor, he looked back. The old woman nodded her head and he knocked on the door.

It was opened by a dark-skinned woman, who Mitch assumed to be Vanya's mother. After he explained who he was, she ushered him into a small, dimly-lit kitchen. A young girl, scarcely more than five years old, stood back against the wall. A pot bubbled on the stove, and Vanya's mother gave it a stir before pulling back a curtain into what appeared to be the only other space. "Vanya?" Mitch cried and hurried toward a narrow bed along one wall. A blanket covered the lower half of Vanya's body; above that, his ribs were bound with rags, his right arm in a sling. *"What ... ?"*

"It's nothing," Vanya grinned, revealing broken front teeth and swollen lips.

"But you're hurt." Mitch dropped his bag onto the floor. "What happened?"

"He was looking for mushrooms on the edge of the city, to sell to make a bit of money for us," Vanya's mother began as she pulled the blanket further up her son's body. "His father. He was sent to a detention camp six months ago." She let out a long sigh and sat on the edge of the bed. Her daughter sidled up to her.

"Papa is coming home. You said he was," the child whined.

"Of course he is, Klasha. Papa will be home soon," she comforted, one hand cradling the child's head.

“What happened to your husband?” Mitch’s voice was almost a whisper.

“He did nothing. Someone he worked with ... she said she heard him telling people communism was dead, the Americans would triumph. She made it up to save herself,” she sneered. “And now my Vanya.”

“But who did this?” Mitch ventured.

“The *militsiya*. They were rounding them up, people like us.” She pointed to the dark skin on her arm to illustrate her point.

“Why would they do that?”

“He’s a good boy, but they don’t care who they take.”

“But why?” Mitch’s words hung in the air. He looked from Vanya to his mother, and then back to his friend. “What did you do?”

“*Nichego!* Nothing at all!” Her words were bitter.

“Forget it, Mitch. It could have been worse.” Vanya winced as he tried to shift himself up in the bed. Mitch reached out to help, but Vanya waved him away and slumped onto the pillows.

“They don’t want us here now,” Vanya’s mother lifted Klasha onto her lap and ran her fingers through the child’s hair.

Mitch sat down on a chair at the side of the bed and leaned forward.

“It was good when we came here. There was nothing for us in the United States.” She stared into the distance before speaking again. “The University in Moscow. Patrice Lumumba University it was later called. My husband, he did well there. It was 1960, and the Communist Party, they subsidized everything. He was one of the first students to graduate. An Engineer, that’s what he was.” There was a note of pride in her voice.

No one spoke for a moment or two. Then the silence was punctuated by the sound of raised voices in the corridor. Vanya’s mother shifted the child off her lap and got to her feet. “Another argument about the bathroom.” She shrugged and gave the pot a stir before continuing. “They used us. Trying to show the world how tolerant they were of those of other races, those with black skin. There were lots of African Americans. They used us to discredit racism, capitalism. The only way forward was communism. That’s what they said. And now, they don’t want us here.”

Mitch noticed how her faded clothes hung on her. He saw now the patched, mustard-coloured wallpaper, the cracked, brown linoleum. A candle on the *krasnyy ugol* cast an ethereal shadow on an icon. It was different to the icon of the

Byzantine saint that Babushka kept in her room, which had mournful eyes set in an unnaturally small, elongated face. From what he could see, this one depicted the Virgin Mary—both she and Jesus were black, as black as coal.

"Why did they do this to you? I don't understand ..." Mitch began.

"We changed our names. Gave our children Slavic names," Vanya's mother interjected. "Thought it would make us fit in."

"But you're Russian. I don't understand why they would do this to you."

"Let it go, Mitch. Now, tell me what I've missed at school."

Over the next few minutes, Mitch did his best to relate the events at school, which now seemed silly and irrelevant. "I'll try to come back to see you on Sunday," he concluded. Getting to his feet, he buttoned his coat and picked up his schoolbag. Klasha watched his every move from where she was now standing by the window. Mitch grinned at her and she pursed her lips, suppressing a giggle.

In the corridor, Vanya's mother slid back the bolts on the main door. "When will he be back at school?" Mitch asked.

"They ripped his clothes to shreds."

"His clothes?"

"He can't go back to school until he has something to wear," she whispered.

Mitch silently berated himself for not realizing his friend only had one set of clothes. "I ... I'll sort out some of mine. Drop them off," he promised.

"Be careful," she cautioned as she opened the door and peered up and down the corridor.

Outside the building, his heart thumped loudly. Mist hung around the few working street lamps as he clattered along the sidewalk. The dog was still in its position. Mitch ran to the other side of the street. As he drew level, the dog lurched alongside, barking and snapping at his heels. He rounded the corner into the main street. The dog dropped back.

Cold air stung Mitch's throat as he tried to regain his breath. A tram clanged to a halt a few yards away. He ignored it. He needed to walk. To think. His father had always told him that the Soviet government looks after its citizens, ensuring they all have a decent place to live and food on the table. "Every member is equal, unlike in the United States, where everyone is out to outdo everyone else." *Then why are Vanya and his family living like that? Why should it matter what colour their skin is?* Mitch asked himself. *It doesn't make sense. They aren't bad people or lazy.*

They haven't been drinking. And all the other people in those buildings? If we're all supposed to be the same, why don't they have everything we have?

An old man walked toward him, and Mitch stepped to one side to allow him to pass. He wore an old army overcoat, his hollow cheeks illuminated by a street lamp. Their eyes met. A strange feeling ran through Mitch, causing an involuntary shiver as he recalled an incident a few days ago. A man dressed in the same sort of coat. It was evening, and they had been eating their meal when a knock came at the apartment door. His father had hurried into the hallway and, ignoring Maman and Babushka's orders to finish his meal, Mitch had leapt to his feet and peered into the hallway before Babushka could pull him away. She had grabbed his arm, closed the door, and pushed him back to his place at the table, but not before he had seen the man and heard Papa's whispered admonishment: "I told you not to come here. It isn't safe." Papa had put on his jacket and coat and kissed Maman on the cheek, saying he would be back later. Then they were both gone. Now Mitch watched the old man as he walked slowly along the side of the road. *There are many men that look like him in the city,* he told himself, his thoughts returning to Vanya.

He walked for an hour or so, not noticing the pastel-coloured palaces with their ornate stone carvings of huge birds, around which he had once woven childish stories. As he walked, the truth came to him. *It's all a fantasy, a fairy story.* Was there supposed to be a moral there, like a Krylov fable? *Why didn't I see the things right under my nose?* He had thought everyone was treated the same, lived like his own family, where his father went to work and brought money home to provide food for them all. They now lived in a larger apartment. He hadn't realized that things were different for Vanya's family—his father had been arrested, his friend had to work to earn money, when everyone knew it was illegal to work until you were much older. *I believed everyone was taken care of. Isn't that what I was taught? What Papa said?* He kicked a stone with the toe of his shoe and watched it ricochet off the side of a shuttered building. "It's a joke! A fucking, sick joke!" he yelled.

On the edge of the canal close to home, he sat on a bench. Fog hung above the water and he shivered. For a second or two, everything was still. In this supposedly perfect place, even the water was scared to move.

CHAPTER SEVEN

LENINGRAD–JANUARY 1977

"Our whole lives have been a lie," Mitch yelled. "It's all a farce. Why did you make me believe it?"

"Keep your voice down," his father hissed. "Do you want us to end up in Comrades' Court?"

Mitch dropped his voice an octave. "Us? That's not likely to happen to us. Do we have black skin?" he scoffed, pushing up the left sleeve of his shirt and looking at his forearm.

"Your mother is Jewish," Sergei whispered. A look of fear flickered in his eyes and he put an arm around Sophia. "It's got to stop. You can't go around jeering at everything in public. The *dezhurnaya,* she heard you. She told Babushka." He sighed loudly. "We have to hope she doesn't report you."

"Give her a fistful of roubles and a bottle of vodka. She won't remember." Mitch shrugged. "I suppose you want me to end up being a good Party member like you. Defend the system. Ignore what's going on. Is that it?"

"Mitch, please. We've been through this before. It's for your own good. It's the only way you'll get into university," Sophia pleaded. "It's bad enough anyway, without ..."

"So you admit it's bad!" Mitch sneered.

"Don't speak to your mother like that," Sergei snapped. "We've done our best to make sure you've had a happy life, not gone without. I don't think you realize how difficult it's been. It's stuck in my gut to be subservient to people ... people like that damned ..."

"Why do you, then?" Mitch cut in.

"I'll tell you why." Sergei took his arm from around Sophia and gripped Mitch by the shoulder. "So that you and your mother don't suffer anymore than you have to."

"Suffer? You think we don't suffer?" Mitch knocked his father's hand away. "We've suffered every day since we came here," he spat. "Maman and I were happy in Montréal."

"Prekrati eto!" Sophia glared at Mitch before turning to Sergei. "He doesn't mean it. He doesn't know what he's saying."

"Don't I?" Mitch turned his back on them and stared out of the window. "We only came here because of him."

"You think I don't know that?" Sergei spun him around, his face close to his, and hissed, "You think I haven't suffered too? Seeing your mother shunned by scum who belong in the gutter. Having to swallow my pride and work for people I dislike. Defend people who are as guilty as hell. You think I like that?"

Mitch took a step back.

"I do it every day for you and your mother. It's the only way I have of keeping you safe."

"Please, both of you, this isn't getting us anywhere." Sophia's voice broke the tension. Sergei turned and sank onto a chair. The tick of the clock took over the space around them.

Mitch breathed heavily as a fresh wave of anger took hold of him. Anger at the injustice of it all. Anger at the lie that was the Soviet state, where innocent individuals like Vanya's father are packed away to prison, and where criminals, both in and out of uniform, get away with beating people up and giving false statements. Why had he been stupid enough to believe the propaganda? He hadn't seen what was right under his nose. The people who don't have warm clothes or a decent place to live, the arrests of those who don't conform to the system. As a child, he was swept along toward the bright, shining future that would be his if he followed the path of communism, embracing Lenin's dream of a society where everyone was equal, and rosy-cheeked children waved flags and sang songs. He had gazed in awe at posters of heroic tractor drivers and factory workers devotedly building the paradise that was the Soviet Union. But where were these supposedly happy people? He had been stupid, participating with gusto in the *Oktyabryata,* marching in parades, reciting ditties about Grandpa Lenin. As a ten-year-old he had relished the rituals of the Young Pioneers, staunchly proud of his starched white shirt, crisply ironed black shorts, and fiery-red tie. He had practised for hours to master the precise forty-five degree salute, the goose-step march. At the sound of bugles and drums, he was consumed by a passion that for years he thought was nationalistic pride. He now realized it was fear that made people step in time to the beat of the official dogma, where dissidence resulted in loss of privileges, jobs, and the right to the basic necessities of human life. He felt betrayed, adrift in a sea of misery and uncertainty.

"Mitch?" His mother's voice jolted him from his reverie. "We know you care, that you were upset about Vanya. But what we are saying is for your own good. You have to keep your thoughts to yourself."

"That's why Vanya was beaten up! Because people like him," Mitch growled and glared at his father, "don't even have the guts to protest."

Babushka, who had been a silent observer, struggled out of her chair and hobbled over to Mitch. "You don't know anything about your father," she said, jabbing a finger into his chest. "How he .... "

"Prekrati eto!" Sergei jumped up and grabbed his mother's arm.

"He's not fit to be your son!" She shook off Sergei's hand. "He needs to know the way you risk your ..."

"*Nyet!* Mama. Leave it!" Sergei commanded. "Not now."

Babushka glared at Mitch for a moment or two before continuing. "You think you're smart, but I'll tell you something ..."

"Mama!" Sergei interjected. *"Nyet!"*

"It's okay. Let me talk to the boy. Try to get some sense into his thick head."

"That's not fair!" Mitch protested.

"Life's not fair, wherever you live. But the really smart ones play them at their own game, manipulate the system." She began to wheeze. "Do you think your father, or anyone, believes all that rhetoric, the empty phrases? *Nyet!* It's what they do to survive. What we all do. They lie to us. We know they're lying. They know we know they're lying." She paused to regain her breath. "But they keep lying anyway, and we keep pretending to believe them."

"Where's the sense in that?" Mitch snapped.

A glint of daring lit up Babushka's rheumy eyes. "What you have to remember is that they can't get into your mind. Can't know what you're thinking."

"But ..." Mitch began.

"But nothing! You'll do as you're told and go to the komsomol meeting and apologize as though you mean it." Babushka gasped the last few words, her body taken over by the wracking cough that was always with her now, summer or winter.

"Mama, you need to rest," Sophia said, putting an arm around her. "Let me take you to your room." She paused at the doorway, looked over her shoulder, and shook her head at Mitch.

CHAPTER EIGHT
LENINGRAD–JANUARY 1978

Mitch reeled back against the wall. His head hit the stonework, and for a few seconds the ground tilted one way then the other. He sank down, pulled his knees into his body, and covered his head with his arms, bracing for the next blow, uncertain from which direction it would come. *You have to get away … run … run … you have to get away … run.* Around and around the mantra went in his head, building momentum, propelling him onto his knees, hands splayed out on the ground in front of him. "Shit!" he screamed as a boot clamped down on the fingers of his right hand. He looked up into the face of his assailant. The militiaman leaned forward, increasing the pressure on Mitch's hand. Mitch took a sharp intake of breath and tensed himself for the agony that would come when his fingers were crunched into the ground. Time ticked on. Then the man laughed loudly and moved his foot away.

Mitch scrambled to his feet and pulled his injured hand into his chest, sliding his other hand along the wall as he edged away. The militiaman followed, matching his pace, slapping his nightstick into the palm of his hand … once, twice, three times. Then the point of the stick jabbed into Mitch's left shoulder, pinning him to the wall. "You come back here and I'll break your ass! Mother fucker!" he spat. His breath was rancid, and Mitch turned his head away. *"Zhopa!"* the man sneered and, with a final jab of the stick into Mitch's shoulder, turned on his heel. Mitch was rooted to the spot as he watched him run to join the rest of the thugs. Nightsticks rose and fell. Mitch turned away, trying not to imagine the blows raining down on the defenceless group of men huddled at the side of the kiosk. Their agonized cries followed him as he wove a haphazard path across the station concourse. At the door, he stopped and looked back. The militiamen were now dragging their victims in his direction. *It's hopeless; you can't help them,* he told himself and pushed the door open.

Outside, an icy wind whipped across the forecourt. Mitch moved quickly into the shadow of a doorway at the far end of the building. He watched writhing bodies dragged across the roadway and thrown into two *militsiya* trucks. There was no sign of Vanya. *Maybe he's hiding somewhere.* A loud sob rose in his throat as the vehicles roared away.

It was quiet now except for the howling of the wind. He waited a while before venturing into the station again. It was almost deserted. *We shouldn't have come here,* he berated himself as he careened around, checking the places Vanya might be hiding. They had been handing out cigarettes to some of the hapless people who sheltered in stations and other public places. Tonight, the group included an amputee whose leg stumps were so infected that the stench had turned Mitch's stomach. *I should have tried to help them, done something.* He leaned against the wall in the washroom and fumbled in his coat pocket for his cigarettes and matches. *What harm were they doing?* he asked himself and shook a cigarette from the packet. He knew they would be driven out of the city and abandoned in forest areas, where most of them would perish. And Vanya? He swallowed hard and lit the cigarette with trembling hands. *Maybe he got away, went home or to the kafe. If not, with a bit of luck, he'll only be beaten up and left on the city streets.*

Luck! How sick is that? In the crazy world of the Soviet Union, Vanya's black skin made him a target for random searches and detention by the police and security forces, on the pretext of fighting crime and enforcing residential registration requirements.

Mitch flexed the fingers of his right hand; they throbbed, but it didn't feel as though any were broken. He prodded the lump on the back of his head, winced and then slid a finger into his mouth. One tooth was loose, but that was nothing compared to what might have happened to Vanya. Tears dribbled down his cheeks and he ground the cigarette into the floor. He thumped the wall with his left hand and yelled "Bastards! Bastards!" over and over. His voice echoed back. Then there was silence.

Later, in the darkness of the corridor of the *kommunalka* where Vanya lived, Mitch paused for a few seconds to regain his breath—the freezing night air had sliced through his lungs like a knife. He banged loudly on the door with his left fist. "Vanya! Vanya!" He rapped again and again.

"They're not here," a woman's voice came from within.

"I must see them," he yelled. "I have to find Vanya." There was silence. Mitch leaned against the door and pleaded, his fingers tracing the gouges in the wood, the peeling paint.

"We don't want any trouble." A man's voice this time. "You must go."

Mitch thumped on the door again. When there was no response, he scurried along the corridor, feeling along the wall until he came to the stairs. Then he clattered down them as fast as he could. Outside, he moved quickly through the narrow alleyway to the rear of the building and shouted up to the second floor: "Vanya! Come on. Open up. It's me, Mitch." Curtains twitched, and then a window opened on a higher floor, and a bottle crashed to the ground next to where Mitch was standing. He scurried back down the alleyway and huddled in the entrance to the building, in case Vanya or his mother or sister came home. After smoking two cigarettes, he gave up.

Vanya wasn't at the *kafe* either. There was only one other customer—an old woman. Mitch's teeth chattered as he asked the man behind the counter whether he had seen Vanya. "Not today. Hardly any customers this evening," he replied, shrugging his shoulders. *"Kofe?"* he asked, already slopping some into a cup. Mitch slid a few coins across the counter, picked up the cup, and took it to a table in the corner.

He kept an eye on the door, hoping it would open and Vanya would burst in, his familiar lopsided grin on his face. Then everything would be all right. He took a gulp of coffee; it burnt his mouth and sprayed over the table as he spat it out. His shoulders sagged as he leaned back in the seat. For years nothing had seemed right. He was still living a lie, still marching to the official beat. A year ago, he had done as Babushka said: pleaded his case at the komsomol kangaroo court, apologized for his lapses, and pledged allegiance to the Party and its superior aims. His inner voice had rebutted every word. He took part in komsomol activities, sang in the choir, attended drama class—all things a good communist does. Babushka had been right. There was something strangely satisfying in playing them at their own game, making them believe he subscribed to their lies.

Inwardly, he scoffed at the Party posters and sagging anti-American slogans declaring the United States a country of unemployment, starvation, racial injustice, warmongers, and imperialist designs. Whenever he had the chance of not being overheard, he listened to *The Voice of America* and the BBC on a Grundig radio; its frequencies reached beyond jamming range. He developed a fascination for dissidents who spoke out against repressiveness, and avidly devoured underground *samizdat* material, which he stuffed under his mattress to join the dog-eared copies of banned Western novels. Novels that transported him to a land where people didn't fear a knock on the door in the silence of night, and where young people like him listened to pop music in public and wore denim jeans. The only people who wore proper blue jeans here—not the ones made of hard fabric that chafed your legs—were the *Sovetskiye Detki,* the children of so-called influential families. The same kids who were protected from expulsion from schools by family connections.

Now the old woman struggled to her feet. Her lips were blue. *She's probably living in a damp basement with rats for company.* The thought made Mitch shiver. A blast of cold air rushed in as the woman opened the door and disappeared into the night. *At least Babushka hadn't had to live like that,* he thought.

Some months after Mitch suffered the humiliation of admitting his failures to the komsomol session, Babushka took to her bed. On Sundays and after school each day, he spent time with her, reading aloud or listening to her reminiscences. One day she told him to take out the big box from the bottom of her cupboard. He placed it on the side of her bed, and she lifted out volume after volume of his grandfather's law books, cradled each one in her hands and smelled them, as if searching for a trace of her long-dead husband. "He was a good man." There was pride in her voice. "Many of the lawyers only accepted criminal trials where they could earn high salaries. Not my Dima. He took on the cases no one else wanted ... the people who couldn't afford to pay. The victims." She stared at the book in her hand before continuing. "During the Siege, I almost burned them in the *burzhuika.* Your father and I, we were desperate. We had no firewood, no food. But it would have been like destroying the holy scriptures." She had begun to wheeze. Mitch picked up one of the books and leafed through it until her breathing eased. "I hid them away. It was all I had left of him, his son and his books." The fading afternoon sunlight picked out the dust on the books, the grey palor of her skin. "In the war, I made sure your father didn't go." She gripped Mitch's hand and whispered: "I knew a doctor, an old friend of your Dedushka. He gave me a certificate to say that my Sergei had a chronic lung disorder."

"Shouldn't he have fought like the other men?"

She leaned toward him. "The violence in this country took my husband. Was I to let them take my son too?"

Mitch had run a finger carefully over the name written in cursive script inside the front cover of the book he held: *Dmitriy Alexandrovich Galichin.* The idea that had been running through his mind for several weeks congealed into a decision. "Babushka," he began. "I've decided. I'm going to be like Dedushka and Papa. I'll work hard and become a lawyer."

"I knew you would, *moi galubchik.* But first you have to do well at school, have a recommendation from the komsomol. Remember, that's part of the game." She slumped back on her pillows.

Two weeks later he had stood between his parents and watched Babushka's coffin lowered into the ground. Her voice seemed to rise out of the grave, the strong voice that was hers before the congestion in her lungs rendered it a mere rasp: "Take care of the books. Use them wisely."

Now Mitch drained the dregs of his coffee, pulled his coat collar up around his neck, and got to his feet. *I must find Vanya.*

CHAPTER NINE

LENINGRAD—MONDAY, MARCH 24, 1980

Mitch sat the other side of the table from Vanya's mother, Tatiyana Ruslanovna Cherkasova, their tea untouched. The mournful eyes of the Virgin Mary stared out from its place in the holy corner. As they had done many times in the two years that had passed since the January night when Vanya disappeared from the station, Mitch and Tatiyana Ruslanovna talked about what might have happened. They could only speculate and share their grief. His body had not been found until the ice thawed.

"There's no end to the misery in this country." Tatiyana's voice was low. "You heard the announcement this morning about the explosion last year in Sverdlovsk?"

"The government denied it, didn't they?"

"They're still denying there was an explosion. They want us to believe it was a natural outbreak of anthrax in the area." Tatiyana snorted. "A thousand people died from eating tainted meat! Can you believe that?"

Mitch shook his head in disgust; everyone knew the anthrax leak could only have come from a secret military installation.

"There's many will choose to believe them." She sighed. "But how many mothers have died or lost their sons, their daughters, their husbands? I ask myself." When Mitch didn't answer, she went on. "My Vanya. He had such a bright future. Such a clever boy. A mathematician. That was what he wanted. My son, a mathematician. Maybe in Leningrad, or even Moscow. He would have ..."

As Mitch listened to Tatyana Ruslanovna constructing a life for her dead son, he stared at the photograph of Vanya propped against a dish on the wooden chest of drawers. His lopsided smile was there as it always had been. Mitch tried to sear this affable vision of his friend into his mind to blot out the image that haunted his sleep. The Vanya who came to him at night had empty sockets where his eyes should be. His cheeks bore the marks of cigarette burns, his mouth wide open as if to speak. A viper's head emerged from the mouth. Its forked tongue darted in and out. Then would come the pounding of hooves, and Vanya's voice reciting the words of Pushkin's poem[1]:

"How terrible he was in the surrounding gloom! …
What strength was in him!"

The horse came closer and reared on its hind legs, foam spewing from its mouth as it hovered over Mitch. Vanya's voice rose to crescendo:

"And in that steed, what fire!"

In the silence that always followed those words, Mitch looked up. It wasn't a full-blooded stallion he saw, but the inert statue of The Bronze Horseman in Senate Square. He felt again the terror he felt as a small child, when his father had pointed up to the statue, telling him of the legend that enemy forces would never take Leningrad while the horseman kept guard. He had gripped his father's hand, scared to look up, sure the towering figure would spring to life and come clattering down on them.

1 'The Bronze Horseman,' narrative poem (1833) by Alexander Sergeyevich Pushkin (1799-1837), written about the equestrian statue of Peter the Great in St. Petersburg, and the great flood of 1824.

CHAPTER TEN
LENINGRAD–MARCH 1982

A fug of cigarette smoke hung in the air of the dingy, one-room apartment on the edge of the city. Mitch's gaze strayed nervously from one to another of the four fellow students perched on chairs around the room. *I hope they don't think it was me,* he worried. The group met occasionally, sometimes drinking too much, always talking in hushed tones about the work of dissidents such as Andrei Sakharov, who two years ago was exiled to Gorky for speaking out against Soviet troops being sent to Afghanistan. They shared whatever *samizdat* material they could lay their hands on. It was mostly just talk, but Mitch enjoyed these impromptu sessions, the feeling of comradeship, a shared hatred of the ruling regime. They were always careful, never meeting on campus, sometimes on an otherwise deserted canal bank in a semi-derelict part of the city, usually with little advance warning of time and place.

Not careful enough, Mitch told himself now. They should have known something like this would happen. It was how this dysfunctional society worked. Children informed on parents, neighbour informed on neighbour, worker informed on worker. Within the university there were those who informed on the activities and ideological inclinations of other students. A law degree was often a way into the political, foreign, and counter-intelligence services. The next generation of spies—people who toed the Party line and would turn in their own babushkas for the glory of the cause.

Now two of the group were missing, rumoured to have been booted out of law school. They were good students, so the only feasible explanation was that someone had informed the authorities of their membership in the clandestine group. *What if they come for the rest of us?* Mitch shifted uncomfortably in his chair. Seeds of doubt ran through his mind as he looked at the four other people in the room. He thought he knew them. He may not like one or two of them, but he had trusted them, and now one of them must have betrayed them. So who was it?

Irina Grigorievna Kislova chewed the fingernails of one hand; the other hand gripped the back of her neck, as though propping up her head. Her short black hair was unevenly cut and stuck out at curious angles. She wore too much makeup for Mitch's liking—her cheeks glowed red in a clown-like way. She was known to have a few intimate male acquaintances, one of whom was an American student who allegedly provided the makeup and Levi's jeans she habitually wore. She didn't seem to have any political ambitions, and her course grades were good enough that she wouldn't have to inform on anyone in order to be rewarded with a pass mark. *Maybe she let something drop to one of her lovers.*

It can't be Yura. Yuri Ivanovich Trubetskoy was Mitch's closest friend—his only real friend now. They had met during their first week in university, and a comfortable rapport quickly developed between them. After Yura's father was killed in an industrial accident ten years or so ago, his mother had taken Yura and his two sisters to live in Kaliningrad, where she looked after an elderly aunt in return for board and lodging for her young family. He had confessed to Mitch that as a teenager at school he accepted bribes of money for cigarettes and drink by writing essays for some of his idle or dumb classmates, always making sure their grades were never quite as good as his own. *It can't be him,* Mitch told himself again. *He wouldn't betray us.*

His attention shifted to Zviad Andreiovich Zubov. He had never understood how Yuri could bear to share a dormitory with this crass specimen of humanity. At almost thirty years of age, Zviad Andreiovich was the epitome of *Homo Sovieticus.* He came from a proletarian background, had worked on a collective farm, served three years in the Army, and was a staunch Party member. Desirable qualities that could guarantee a place at university. He rarely attended classes and seemed to idle away his time dreaming of weekends when he could return to his family *dacha* outside the city and dig potatoes. *Surely it can't be him?* Two weeks ago, he obtained a really sensitive *samizdat* publication and helped distribute it, which would have incriminated him in the eyes of the authorities. *Unless that was a setup.* Zviad Andreiovich looked up now, a ponderous expression on his face. His eyes met Mitch's, and the two men stared at each other for some moments.

That left Arseny Efimovich Jakobic, the only real Jew amongst them. Although Mitch had never been close to Arseny Efimovich, he felt a certain sympathy for the man whose obvious Jewishness—the nose, the black curly hair—was hard to hide. And then there was his surname. His mother was Russian, so why hadn't his parents done as others often do and given their son her surname? Arseny had been the most enthusiastic member of their group, regularly disseminating information on discrimination on the grounds of religion. *Maybe the authorities put pressure on him. It was him or us.* Vanya's mother's words came back to Mitch: *"She made it up to save herself."*

* * *

Two weeks later, Mitch pulled his jacket collar up to shield his neck from the wind sneaking through the warped frame of the dormitory window. Despite the draught, rancid cooking fumes hung in the air. Zviad Andreiovich forked the last piece of fried potato into his mouth and sat back in his chair at the small table. A trickle of fat ran out of the corner of his mouth; he wiped it away with the back of his hand and belched loudly.

Mitch turned away and began to poke the screwed-up rags back into place in the window frame. He could barely bring himself to speak to Zviad now. Within hours of the evening when they had gathered in that dingy room, Zviad had revealed himself as the informer. He had approached each member of the now-defunct group, demanding certain favours or money in return for keeping silent. Mitch and Yuri had done a joint deal, pooling their resources to scrape together enough money to provide a regular supply of women willing to have sex with Zviad. At first it was simple; there was never any shortage of women willing to ply sexual favours for much-needed money or scarce goods. But the price had gone up when word of Zviad's deviant sexual desires spread. Yuri and Mitch had added the inducement of a bright future for the lucky woman who may one day become Zviad's wife. "Any day now, he will be rewarded with a lucrative career for his services to the Party." Mitch hated these half-truths, but it was better than the fate of the original two members of the group who had disappeared and were now known to be in Afghanistan with the other unfortunate bastards, wielding a kalashnikov as part of the Soviet attempt to impose socialist practices on Afghan society. Even now, Mitch dreaded the military training that would start in his fourth year at university. What would he do if forced to aim a gun at a human being?

"Cigarettes. Do you have any?" Zviad Andreiovich's question interrupted Mitch's thoughts, and he turned from the window. Zviad was now peering myopically into the pockmarked mirror, arranging strands of greasy hair across his scalp. He stank of perspiration, his pants were stained, and his sweater had holes in both elbows.

Mitch tossed a packet of cigarettes onto the table before checking his watch. If he left now, he would avoid the embarrassment of coming face to face with whichever female Yuri had managed to entice. "Tell Yuri I had to leave. I'll see him in class tomorrow," he threw over his shoulder as he left the room.

* * *

The next afternoon, Mitch ran across S'vézdovskaya líniya dodging between a boxy little Zhiguli and a truck belching fumes into the air. He was late for Professor Bakunin's lecture again and knew that as he tried to creep in unnoticed, the professor would pause and stare at him, the thick lenses of his glasses giving his eyes a strange piercing quality, as if he alone could crack the intricate code of Mitch's mind.

Mitch's mind. A mystery to Mitch himself. He had paced the streets late last night, and countless other nights, questioning his feelings, his doubts. What was he to do with his life? Every path he took led down a blind alley to more disillusionment. The thrill of nervous excitement on his first day at law school six months ago had dissipated into despondency. He had been naive to think he could work within a system where justice could be bought, where guilty people walked free, and the innocent were convicted on the basis of false statements given by so-called witnesses. And where people like Zviad Andreiovich Zubov prospered. Thankfully, it looked as if the blackmail would soon be over. This morning, Yuri had told Mitch that in less than two months, Zviad would move to Alexandrov to take up a job—his reward from the authorities. The two had done an impromptu dance, slapping each other on the back.

Mitch knew he should accept how things worked in this fucked up country. He was luckier than most. He had free tuition and a modest stipend, and it was better than doing compulsory military service. The work wasn't difficult—he had quickly discovered that all legal theory is reduced to easily memorizable formulas applicable to any case. He could get his law degree, build a successful career, bribe judges, fix verdicts for high paying clients such as the black-market bourgeoisie, and get rich like the other *prestupniki*. Occasionally, he would do a volunteer stint for the sake of his record as a good citizen, or inform on some unsuspecting person to earn credit with the Party, all the while piling up a heap of money that he would use to buy his way out of the country. But who would pay? The people who couldn't defend themselves against the might of the Soviet state, that's who. So what difference could Mitch Galichin make? He couldn't take on the Soviet monolith. But was he going to give up and watch innocent people beaten to a pulp for the crime of the colour of their skin, or their religious beliefs, while the state-sponsored thugs responsible went unpunished? Where was the justice in that?

Now at the entrance to the university, he fumbled in his overcoat pocket for his cardboard pass, emblazoned with the official stamp and a photograph that bore a passing resemblance. The elderly woman guarding the door fixed him with a sour look. Mitch found it difficult to distinguish one of these women from another. Whatever the weather, their stout bodies were wrapped in coats of an indeterminable hue, their heads swathed in scarves, and their chunky legs planted in boots. Some students cultivated a friendly banter with these guarders of the doors, easing their passage through the system with a well-timed gift of an orange or a blemished apple. But Mitch didn't see why he should do this. On days when he forgot his pass, he did what Russians habitually do—he circumvented the system and squeezed through a gap in the barrier when the old women looked the other way.

Inside the courtyard, he took a drag on his cigarette and looked up at the windows of the second-floor lecture room. Professor Bakunin would already be in full flow, his monotone voice reciting a diatribe on the history of the Communist Party of the Soviet Union, one of the five political education courses students were obliged to attend. Mitch had heard it all before, seen for himself the results of the struggle for the supposed higher form of human society. Professors recited the bold print, paying tribute to the superiority of the socialist system and the glorification of Soviet workers; students made notes. Mitch found it difficult to pay attention. Last week, he was jolted out of a daydream by a thump on his desk. "If you wish to continue your studies at this university," the professor said, his voice cutting through the silence in the room, "you will concentrate on the subject in hand. Is that clear?" Mitch muttered his apologies, his eyes focused on a pulse that throbbed in the professor's temple.

Mitch wasn't sure he wanted to continue his studies, but today in the class he made copious notes and tried to make it look as though he was interested—it was part of the game. As the lecture finished, he gathered his belongings together and walked quickly out of the room, ignoring the scowl Professor Bakunin directed his way.

* * *

The following day, Mitch discovered a note pinned to an inside page of his paper on the principles of scientific atheism, which Professor Nekrassov had marked. He read the note and turned the paper over on the desk. Why did the professor want to see him? The mark for the paper was good, so it couldn't be that. *Why me? And why does he want to meet away from the campus?* The professor had asked that Mitch meet him the following evening at an address on the edge of the city. He grimaced, wondering if it was something to do with the *samizdat* stuff. *I'll kill that fucking Zviad!* he cursed, stuffed the paper into his briefcase and joined the other students as they filed out of the room. He hesitated in front of the professor's desk. The professor looked away.

At eight o'clock the next evening, Mitch turned his father's car into a side street near the building where the meeting was to take place, pulled into the edge of the road, and switched off the engine. He opened the car door, removed the windshield wipers, and tossed them into the footwell before locking the door. Like most things, spare parts for cars were in short supply, and it had become a habit to remove anything that could be pilfered. The uneasy feeling in his stomach intensified as he turned the corner and walked toward the building. *What if it's a setup? That rat Zubov's reported me to the Party? I should have told someone where I was going.*

The entrance door creaked as he pulled it open. Inside, he blinked into the gloom, searching for the stairs to the basement. Then he grasped the iron handrail and walked slowly downward. At the bottom of the stairs, a single light bulb hung from the ceiling. The smell of damp clogged his throat and nostrils. *It's not too late.* He turned and looked back at the staircase. *They'll find you wherever you are,* he thought gloomily and began to grope his way along the corridor. He tapped on the door. It opened, and a giant of a man filled the doorway. The "Come in" was uttered in such a soft, almost effeminate, tone that it took Mitch a second or two to connect man and voice. The face that looked down at him was masculine, the pale skin mostly hidden by a heavy, grey moustache and beard and a thick mop of frizzy, black hair. His large hand on Mitch's shoulder propelled him along a corridor. They entered a room filled not with the gloom of subterranean living Mitch had expected; canvases streaked with bright colours adorned the walls and were propped against every available surface.

A chair scraped across the floor. Professor Nekrassov came toward him, extending a hand; Mitch hesitated and then gripped it. The professor looked different. It wasn't his hair—there isn't much you can do with a shaved head—and he was still wearing the red scarf that was always wound around his neck. Gone was the serge suit, and in its place were dark casual pants, a brown-check shirt, and a sleeveless beige sweater. As Mitch slipped his coat off, Yuri Ivanovich stepped out of the shadow behind the door. Mitch raised his eyebrows; Yuri shrugged.

"You must both be wondering why I asked you here," the professor began. "Let me first introduce my good friend, Borya. Boris Konstantinovich Yastremski." The professor paused while Boris Konstantinovich gave an exaggerated bow and shook Mitch and Yuri's hands. "A lawyer—a somewhat disgraced lawyer, I should say." Borya grinned and bowed again. "But now, as you can see, an artist."

Mitch looked at the vivid pictures covering the far wall—not the works depicting the heroic past or harmonious future favoured by the intelligentsia. Rich splashes of colour filled the canvases and warmed Mitch's soul. Although the feeling of uneasiness hadn't left him, he felt a strange affinity with this man whose avant garde style had most likely condemned him to life in a basement, where people who didn't conform were forced to exist.

Professor Nekrassov pulled out a chair at the table and sat down. Mitch and Yuri followed suit. Both sat stiffly upright. Boris Konstantinovich paced around the room, moving pictures and grunting, a puzzled look on his face. Then, apparently satisfied, he sank down onto the remaining chair; it gave an ominous creak. They talked of generalities. *Be careful,* Mitch cautioned himself. *This could still be a setup.*

Borya reached across and pulled four shot glasses toward him, closely followed by a bottle. The liquid in the neck of the bottle gurgled as he slopped it into each glass and slid them across the table. Then he got up and, raising his overflowing glass, proposed a toast: *"Za vstrechu!"* Now on their feet, the other three echoed his words and downed the liquid in one gulp. Borya ran the back of a hand across his lips and refilled the glasses. One shot quickly followed another. "Have some food," Borya commanded, indicating the plates of *blini,* slices of cheese, and cake studded with raisins and sprinkled with sugar. Mitch ate gratefully, anxious not to drink on an empty stomach—earlier, he had done no more than play with the meal his mother set before him.

"Don't look so worried," the professor smiled, "I have observed you both carefully, and Arseny Efimovich Jakobic has vouched for you. So ... I think I can trust you." He looked enquiringly from one to the other; neither moved. "I need help with some work. Something I think you would both be interested in."

With the vodka, a warm feeling of comradeship began to wash through Mitch. He looked across the table at the professor, seeing him in a different light from the stiff, unapproachable man who rapped out texts, brooking no dissent. Boris Konstantinovich looked at the now empty bottle, put it on the floor, leaned sideways in his chair, pulled another bottle out of a cupboard, and refilled the glasses. They drank in unison. *Govno!* Mitch cursed to himself as he fought to control the burning in his throat. *Christ, this stuff's lethal.* When desperate people couldn't afford vodka, they took to *Samogon,* illicitly distilled vodka sometimes containing cleaning fluid, medical disinfectant, and the like. Mitch tugged at his shirt collar and pushed his glass away. His nose started to drip, so he pulled a handkerchief from the pocket of his pants. His head felt as though it was going to burst, and one look at Yura's puce face confirmed he was in the same state.

"Wh ... what are you going to do with the paintings?" Mitch croaked in an effort to divert attention away from their plight.

"What can I do? Give them away?" Borya's tone was mournful. "A friend, he was going home to Poland. He wanted to take some with him, to sell them and send the money to me. But the bastards wouldn't give permission. Said they were too abstract. Not Soviet enough. I ask you," he said, looking around the table, "if that was the case, surely they'd want to get them out of the country. Wouldn't want dangerous paintings contaminating the great Soviet experiment." He poured himself another drink.

An hour or so later, Mitch's thoughts ran around and around in his head. He could hardly pin one down. Out of the cotton wool clogging his brain, he vaguely recalled Professor Nekrassov asking for their help with some work he was doing. Something to do with victims of the Stalin era. *You have to be careful*—the thought floated off with Borya's high-pitched voice as he started to sing. The words sounded vaguely familiar. Borya's voice faded and he stood up, filled his glass, slopped what was left into the professor's glass, and shook the empty bottle first over Yuri's glass then Mitch's. "Vlad Vysotsky. Songwriter, poet, dissident. Departed friend," he declared. He drained the glass in one gulp and rambled on, reminiscing about the feeling of solidarity in the crowd as the *militsiya* had tried to keep the masses from taking over a public square in Moscow on the day of the funeral of Vysotsky, the demigod of the Soviet underground. "We sang his songs, chanted his words, the greatest words ever written about this ugly system."

Some time later, Mitch and Yuri emerged into the night and wove their way along the street, an arm around each other's shoulders. It had been a strange evening, but for the first time in a long while, Mitch felt happy. Deliriously happy. They had escaped the wrath of the Party, and soon Zviad Andreiovich would be gone. Their pace was slow, and at a street corner they paused in front of a billboard and stared at the plethora of advertisements offering an array of services, dubious and otherwise. The words jumped around in front of their faces, and Mitch laughed as he reached out and tried to catch a word that seemed to be floating in the air. White flakes drifted down on him, and for a moment he thought it was snowing. Then he turned and watched as Yuri tore up another handful of paper tabs, which he had pulled off the advertisements. They cascaded into the air, and Mitch twirled around, his arms outstretched in the paper snowstorm. He slipped on the icy surface, and Yuri grabbed him. *"Ya p'yan,"* Mitch slurred, hanging on to Yuri's coat with both hands as he tried to regain his balance.

"Those two. The professor and Boris Konstantinovich. What do you think of them? Do you think they ... you know?" Yuri asked.

Mitch stared into Yuri's face and grinned. "Do you think the professor keeps his scarf on when they ... ?

Their laughter rang out like a peal of bells in the night.

CHAPTER ELEVEN

LENINGRAD–SEPTEMBER 1982

The sidewalks were bathed in the iridescent bluish lights of street lamps as Mitch jumped off the tram. It wasn't his usual stop, but he needed exercise, time to think. There was a spring in his step, and his briefcase swung at his side. It was the end of the first week of the semester, and he was feeling more positive than he had felt for years. Six months ago, it seemed as though the system was suffocating him, but the cloud of darkness that trapped him for so long had lifted that night in Boris Konstantinovich Yastremski's apartment. Mitch would never forget that evening or the following morning when, on waking with a loud thumping in his head, he remembered the car. He managed to fend off his father's angry words by promising to have the car back by the time Sergei returned from work. By a quirk of luck, it was still where he had parked it, with all its wheels intact.

He hadn't seen Boris Konstantinovich again, but just thinking of the solidarity of the defiant masses at Vladimir Vysotsky's funeral gave Mitch a sense of comradeship, empowerment. He wasn't alone; bubbling beneath the seemingly compliant surface of society, a whole army of people hated the system as much as he did.

During the summer recess, Mitch and Yuri had worked secretly on the research they had, in their inebriated state, promised to do for Professor Nekrassov, who was running a *pro bono* clandestine legal advice service for the victims of Stalin's vicious rule. Court cases had been going on since the dictator's death in 1953, but it was risky business—even though over two decades ago Khruschev publicly denounced Stalin, those who exposed crimes and repressions under Stalin risk prosecution for alleged slander.

The professor was the one taking most of the risk; hopefully, no one would be able to trace the research back to Mitch and Yuri. But they were still careful. Even without Zviad Andreiovich's presence, it was too dangerous to work in Yuri's room at the university. On the pretext of preparing papers for the next semester, they worked in Mitch's bedroom, being careful to lock incriminating papers away. You never knew who might be snooping around. Recently, the *dezhurnaya* had taken to knocking on the apartment door, usually on the pretext of checking that the water system was functioning properly, or some such made-up excuse. Her visits usually coincided with when his father was out, but Maman had become skilled at blocking the doorway to stop the nosy old woman from venturing into the hallway. Whenever Mitch and Yuri heard someone at the door, they frantically secreted their papers behind stacked boxes in Mitch's armoire.

As they worked, legal tomes and documents (depositions, hospital reports, employment records, personal statements) littered the surface of the makeshift desk as they tried to make sense of medical terminology and written evidence from witnesses supporting the claims of victims. Today, the professor had slipped Mitch a new case, that of a Polish Jew who had spent the early years of the Stalinist era in a labour camp. The man's allegations were all too familiar. The sulphurous fumes of the copper smelter at Karabash in the Urals, where he and his wife had been forced to work, caused her premature death and his chronic lung disease.

Although Mitch hated lying to his parents about what he and Yuri were doing, the work gave him a sense of satisfaction. He was beating the system. His legal training wasn't in vain. He would graduate and take whatever job the authorities assigned him and, in his spare time, continue to help victims of State repression and injustice. He wasn't sure how, but he owed it to Vanya and others like him to find a way.

With this more optimistic approach to life, the horrific visions of Vanya that had plagued his dreams vanished. He still thought of his friend, but his memories were happy ones, and each night he drifted into untroubled sleep.

This evening, Mitch was newly inspired. He and Yuri had sat in on a clandestine gathering where the professor, other scholars, and human rights advocates spoke of the need to keep the spotlight of public attention on the plight of Andrei Sakharov in exile in Gorky. Mitch and Yuri had taken a circuitous route to the meeting venue, jumping off trams between stops, checking over their shoulders every few minutes in case they were followed, reminiscent of the spy novels Mitch loved to read when he could get his hands on them.

"Doctor Sakharov is a symbol of human freedom. He is also a human being who deserves to live with his family in freedom and dignity. It is up to us all to use our contacts in the outside world to show what is going on here. Or are we going to live up to Alexander Solzhenitsyn's damning indictment of the Russian intelligentsia as nothing more than people with diplomas and good jobs?" The speaker paused here and looked around. "*Nyet!* We must keep Sakharov and others like him ... Yuri Orlov, Sergei Kovalev ... I don't need to spell out their names, we are all familiar with them ... in the forefront of people's minds. We need to keep up the pressure throughout the world to demand their release." Mitch and Yuri knew the names quoted. In 1974, Kovalev, the biophysicist and founder of the first Soviet human rights association, was charged with "anti-Soviet agitation and propaganda," and after seven years in labour camps in the Perm region and Chistopol prison, was now in internal exile in Kolyma. Like Sakharov, Orlov was once a prominent nuclear physicist but was fired for his human rights activism and was now incarcerated.

Mitch listened to the inspiring words, his feelings a mixture of respect and fear for the brave people who were willing to put aside their personal safety for the greater good of others. He wondered whether he would have the courage to be like them. "We have to work toward a world where we are able to speak without fear of repression, where we have freedom from religious persecution and to travel abroad and return home freely. One day this repressive regime will change, and when it does, we will be ready," the last speaker concluded. *And I'll be ready too,* Mitch had vowed to himself as he and Yuri got up to leave.

On the journey home, he thought of his mother and the way fear forced her to outwardly abandon her religion. How he, her only child, who had been born into the faith of Hasidic Judaism, must never let that fact be known, and how his mother had been denied the chance to visit her own mother, his grandmother. Like Sakharov and other imprisoned dissidents, they were stripped of the basic freedoms millions of people throughout the world take for granted.

Mitch paused now in front of a ground-floor apartment window and lit a cigarette. Paint flaked off the grime-encrusted wooden frame, and a light from within illuminated a crimson banner bearing testament to the inhabitants' devotion to the Party. A crude poster pinned to the banner depicted joyous peasants in colourful traditional dress. Above them floated white doves of peace. Mitch snorted loudly and walked on.

CHAPTER TWELVE

LENINGRAD–SEPTEMBER 1982

In the lecture hall the following week, Yuri whistled softly under his breath. "Where's she been hiding?"

Mitch looked up from the notes he was reading and followed Yuri's gaze. A young woman stood in the aisle. Her hips were clad in a figure-hugging black skirt, and her tight cream blouse, cinched-in at the waist, emphasized the fullness of her breasts. The outline of her nipples dimpled the fabric. Someone stood up to let her into a spare seat near the end of the row in front of where Mitch and Yuri were sitting; they gaped, open-mouthed, as she wiggled her body from side to side, adjusting her skirt with a free hand before sitting down.

"Things are definitely looking up here," Yuri murmured.

Throughout the lecture, Mitch tried to ignore the woman. By the look of her clothes, she came from a wealthy family, and he had long ago vowed he wanted nothing to do with people like that—people who get rich while others starve. But his eyes constantly strayed, noticing the way her dark brown, shoulder-length hair curled outward at the edges and how every now and then she tossed a lock of hair back off her face. As they left, he looked around for her, but she had vanished into the crowd.

During the weeks that followed, he couldn't get her out of his mind. So who was she? It hadn't taken Yuri long to find out. Her name was Nataliya Alekseevna Lipovskaya. "Nataliya, Natasha, Natashinka," Mitch said the names softly to himself when he was on his own, relishing the sounds they made. But what was he, Mitch Galichin, doing thinking about a woman like that? It was said that Nataliya Alekseevna's father was an art dealer who dealt in the so-called masterpieces depicting the Soviet Union's glorious past, currently favoured by those who could afford inflated prices. *Probably stolen from the Hermitage or somewhere,* Mitch thought crossly. *Don't even think about her,* he told himself as a vision of Boris Yastremski's vibrant paintings flashed into his mind.

But he found himself following Nataliya Lipovskaya, transfixed by the way her skirts moulded around her thighs, how the muscles in her buttocks tightened as she took each step. Alone in bed at night, he imagined she was lying beside him, his hands running over her breasts, downward over the slight bulge of her stomach.

Yuri egged him on to ask her for a date. "Go on, Mitch. What have you got to lose? You know you fancy her."

"She's not my type. I've never even spoken to her."

Once or twice as she walked toward him, he cleared his throat—there was no harm in saying *"Zdravstvuyte."* It never happened. "She wouldn't look twice at me. She's always with that Maxim Shevchenko," he told Yuri. Yesterday, between classes, he'd watched the two of them leaning on Shevchenko's car. She'd wound her arms around his neck as he pressed his body against hers. "Shit!" Mitch had cursed. *Who can compete with a shiny black Moskvitch?* According to Yuri, Shevchenko's father was a fat cat bureaucrat. Rumour had it that the elder Shevchenko had grown rich on a scam in the Ukraine.

"Forget her. You don't stand a chance," Mitch mumbled to himself as he walked away.

CHAPTER THIRTEEN

LENINGRAD—MAY 1983

The day before the oral Criminology exam, Mitch spent the afternoon reviewing his course work in the law school library. *If you want to pass, you have to convince the examiners you believe the dogma,* he told himself as he committed statutes, phrases, and facts to memory.

Around six o'clock his brain could take no more. He yawned, stashed his notes in his bag, and got to his feet. After tomorrow he would be a free man … for a few months at least. Apart from Professor Nekrassov's research, he had no other commitments. The summer stretched ahead. He hummed softly to himself as he returned his pile of books to the counter. Outside, he lit a cigarette and then hurried around the side of the building. He was grateful his father had lent him his car. *Tomorrow, on the way home from the exam, I'll buy a bottle of something for him and flowers for Maman … maybe narcissus …* he resolved. He turned the key in the car door and threw his bag onto the back seat. Leaning against the open door, he took a few quick drags on the cigarette, then dropped the butt onto the ground.

"Mitch! Mitch! *Wait!*"

He turned around. Yuri Ivanovich was running toward him.

"I'm glad I caught you. Boy, do I have something to tell you!"

"What's all the fuss?"

"Give me a ride and I'll tell you," he grinned.

"Get in. This had better be worth it. I'm late all ready." Mitch got into the car, closed the door, and started the engine.

The passenger door slammed shut. As they pulled onto Universitetskaya Embankment, Yuri turned and looked at him. "Saturday night we're going to a party." Mitch was silent. "Don't you want to know where?"

"Not particularly, because I'm not going."

"*Khorosho*! I'll go to the Lipovskys' on my own."

Mitch eased his foot off the gas pedal. "You mean Nataliya Alekseevna Lipovskaya's?"

"The same." Yuri leaned back in the seat. "Still not coming?" He laughed loudly.

Mitch pulled the car into the side of the road and turned to face Yuri. "How are we invited to the Lipovskys? We don't know them."

"I do. I know her brother, Pyotr Alekseevich."

Mitch drummed his fingers on the steering wheel.

"Well, Tolik knows him," Yuri confessed. "He's taking his finals, and on Saturday he's celebrating."

Mitch stared ahead.

"And the lovely Nataliya will be there." Yuri shoved Mitch's arm. "Come on, Mitch. You know you like her. It's your big chance."

"I can't." Mitch checked the car mirrors and pulled away.

"What do you mean, you can't? Where are you going?"

"Yuri, I can't watch her with that … that Shevchenko." He spat the words out.

"But Mitch, that's the point. He's gone. Dropped out the week before exams started."

"He's probably sick or something. He'll be there on Saturday." *Running his fingers down her back, lingering over her buttocks,* he added to himself. He shook his head. He had spent the last seven months trying to forget her.

"Shevchenko's gone. Really gone." Yuri emphasized the last two words. "His father's been sent back to the Ukraine. Some scandal, or so Pyotr Alekseevich told Tolik."

"Why the hell didn't you tell me before?" Mitch yelled, wrestling with the steering wheel to bring the car back on a straight course.

* * *

On Saturday evening, Mitch looked at himself in the mirror in his bedroom. He leaned closer, examining a blemish on his right cheek. Then with both hands he tried to smooth down his mop of hair. When he took his hands away, curls sprang out at crazy angles from his head. *I don't know why you're bothering; she won't even give you a second glance.*

But what if she does? He hadn't had any experience with women. In truth, until he began to fantasize about Nataliya Lipovskaya, Mitch had never felt strongly enough about any woman. Since his early teenage years when other boys talked about nothing but girls and sex (or more likely sex and girls), Mitch had wondered if there was something wrong with him. Was he a homosexual, like the men who lurk in the shadows of restaurants, in alleyways, or in the seclusion of more private places, who had to be content with a fleeting linking of hands, perhaps a gentle touch on the face? More often than not, the *militsiya* turned a blind eye, but there was always the risk of prosecution, for homosexuality was still on the statute book. Now whenever he allowed himself to think of Natasha, he knew he would not spend parts of his life in dark alleyways. At least not with men.

"Mitch! How long are you going to be?" his mother called. "If you want us to drop you off, we'll have to leave soon."

"Five minutes," he yelled.

At the gatehouse outside the Lipovskys' building, his confidence took another dive. He let out a low whistle. *These people must be seriously rich ... or have a lot of influence.* The guard on the gate looked him over, scrutinized his identity documents, checked his name off a list attached to a clipboard, and disappeared inside the gatehouse. A moment later, the iron gate whooshed open and Mitch stepped into the compound. *This is way out of my league,* he thought to himself as he walked slowly across the courtyard toward the imposing building. Several cars were parked along the edge, mostly Volgas, the status symbol of the *nomenklatura*. There were also three other black cars. He paused. Is one of them Shevchenko's? At the base of the front steps he stopped, lit a cigarette, and stared at the stone carvings above the door posts.

"Aren't you going in?" Yuri's voice came from behind. Tolik was with him.

"I'm not sure ..." Mitch shook his head.

"Khuynya!" Tolik slapped him on the shoulder. "Come on. We're wasting drinking time!" He bounded up the steps and pushed open the front door.

Mitch and Yuri followed him into a large hallway lit with a huge chandelier, which dangled on a long chain. "Up here," Tolik called from halfway up the wide marble staircase. "Follow the noise!" The apartment door was open and they made their way to a room at the end of the corridor. The air was thick with cigarette smoke, and Mitch paused in the doorway. He couldn't see Natasha, but that wasn't surprising, as there was a crush of people.

"Let's find the drink," Yuri urged, putting an arm around the shoulders of both Mitch and Tolik.

"Tolik! Over here," a dark-haired man on the edge of the crowd beckoned.

"That's Petya. I'll introduce you."

Mitch hesitated.

"Relax, Mitch! Enjoy yourself," Yuri shouted in his ear as they followed Tolik around the edge of the room. "Have you seen her yet?"

"Zatknis'!" Mitch hissed.

Tolik made the introductions. "My parents are away for the weekend," Petya shouted above the noise of the music. "Vodka and beer. Over there." He pointed to a corner of the room. "When that runs out, there's plenty more."

At the makeshift bar, Yuri lifted a bottle of vodka out of a container of ice. He looked at the label then poured three shots. "Beats old Borya's *Samogon*!" he whispered to Mitch and downed his drink in one gulp.

Mitch thought of Boris Konstantinovich Yastremski's brightly daubed canvases. In contrast, from what he could see, the paintings on the walls here were dismal, the heavy gold frames the only hint of brightness. He swallowed his drink and held the glass out to Yuri for a refill.

"Want a beer too?" Yuri reached for a bottle and pushed the cap off.

"You're too generous!" quipped Tolik.

"Think I'd better stick to beer after this," Mitch replied, raising the vodka to his lips. As it slid down, it warmed his throat and relaxed the muscles in his jaw.

"There's Fedor and Maxim over there," Tolik yelled, gesturing toward a group standing in an alcove.

Mitch tightened his grip on the beer bottle Yuri proffered.

"It's not Shevchenko, you idiot. He's not the only Maxim in the world!" Yuri chuckled at the grief-stricken expression on Mitch's face. "I told you, he's in Kiev. Now where's the lovely Natasha?" he said, glancing around. "Come on, we'll circulate."

They moved slowly from group to group. Mitch envied Yuri his easy-going attitude; he seemed to be friends with everyone. After a while, Mitch went back to the bar and put his empty beer bottle in a crate on the floor. He scanned the faces of a group of people who had just arrived and then poured himself a shot of vodka.

He drifted around the edge of the crowd. People were dancing, gyrating to the beat of techno-pop music. Mitch couldn't identify the songs or the bands; they all sounded the same to him. "Come on, Mitch," Yuri yelled, swinging his hips and hoisting his beer bottle into the air. Mitch shook his head.

An hour or so later, a sweat-drenched Yuri caught up with Mitch in a room at the front of the apartment. Mitch was slumped in an armchair, an empty beer bottle on the floor at his side. "There you are," Yuri said, narrowly avoiding colliding with a huge plant. He swiped the leaves out of his way with one hand, groped for the arm of a chair, and collapsed sideways into it. He leaned toward Mitch, a grin on his face. "She's here, the lovely what's her name?" He paused for a moment then slapped the side of his head. "Natasha, that's it!"

Mitch thought Yuri's speech sounded slurred, or perhaps it was his own befuddled brain that had difficulty sorting one word from another.

Yuri leaned closer. "She's here."

"I heard you," Mitch drawled. *I'll only make a fool of myself if I talk to her.* "I can't think straight with this fucking music!"

"You need another drink, that's what you need." Yuri waved an arm and got unsteadily to his feet. "That'll put you right." He wove a haphazard path across the room and disappeared through the doorway.

Mitch looked down at the damp blotches that had spread across his shirt. *How can I see her in this state?* he asked himself. *It's no good anyway. She's never even noticed me, so why am I kidding myself?* He leaned back in the chair and closed his eyes. The thudding beat of the music pulsed through his brain. If his head would only stop thumping for a while, he would go home.

"You've found yourself a quiet place to sleep."

Mitch opened his eyes. The door to the room was now closed, and in front of it stood Nataliya Alekseevna. She came toward him, seeming to float across the room. He blinked.

"Are you okay?" she said and leaned over him. Her breath smelled sweet.

"I ... errr." He gulped and shifted in the chair.

A smile touched the corners of her mouth, dimpling her cheeks.

"It's the m ... music. A b ... bit too loud," he blurted out.

"Petya's parties are always rowdy," she laughed.

Mitch stared hard at her. She was wearing a white dress, which looked luminous in the glow from the table lamps. She straightened up and he saw the outline of her legs through the flimsy fabric.

"Haven't I seen you somewhere before?" She kicked off her shoes, sat down in the chair opposite, drew her knees up, and hugged them close to her body.

Mitch sat up. "The Faculty ... the Faculty of Law."

"I thought so. You're usually with the blond guy. The one with a gap in his front teeth."

"Yuri. Yuri Trubetskoy," Mitch mumbled. *Damn fucking Yuri! I knew she wouldn't be interested in me.* He looked down at his sweat-soaked shirt and started to lever himself out of the chair. "I was just leaving," he croaked.

"*Nyet.* Don't go." She got to her feet and perched on the arm of his chair, a restraining hand on his arm. "Stay and talk for a while."

He sank back. His arm tingled beneath her touch. "What do you want to talk about?" he asked.

"You, of course." Her right arm went around the back of the chair, and her hair fanned out across one side of her face as she looked at him. "You were going to tell me about yourself."

"Was I?" He searched for something to say. "What do you want to know?"

"Well, your name would do for a start," she laughed.

"Mitchell. Mitchell Galichin," he gulped.

"Mitchell ... that's an odd name. How did you come by that?"

"My great-grandfather. He was from England."

"Don't you have any other names?"

"Mitch. Everyone calls me Mitch."

"Then that's what I shall call you." She ran a hand through his hair. "You haven't asked my name."

"I already know it." He reached out tentatively and touched the ends of her hair.

Ten minutes or so later, the door burst open. "Well, what do we have here?" It was Yuri who spoke.

Mitch glared at him.

"Okay! I'm going!" Yuri grinned. "Be careful of him," he said to Natasha.

"I think he's sweet," she replied, standing up and smoothing the fabric of her dress. She leaned forward and kissed Mitch's lips. "See you next Saturday." She picked up her shoes and walked to the door. "The Panteleimonovsky Bridge, one o'clock." Her hand fluttered briefly, and then she disappeared through the doorway.

CHAPTER FOURTEEN

LENINGRAD—MAY 1983

The following week passed in a daze of nervous anticipation. On Thursday morning, Mitch toyed with his breakfast, his mind full of being with Natasha on Saturday. *What will she expect of me? What should I do? You'll have to take it slowly,* he told himself. *But how slowly is slowly?*

"Mitch! Did you hear what I said?" His father sounded irritated.

"Prastite?"

"What's wrong with you this week?"

"Nothing." He shrugged his shoulders. "Just the aftermath of exams."

"Your mother and I have been talking about what you're going to do this summer. You can't spend it lying in bed and moping around."

"I suppose not." His thoughts were still far away.

"Look, we're a man short in the bureau, and it would be good if you could come in and help. It will be useful experience. I've cleared it with our manager."

Mitch met his father's gaze.

"Tomorrow then."

"Tomorrow?" Mitch jerked upright in his seat.

Sergei pushed his chair back. "Make sure you're up in time. I'm not hanging about for you." He stooped and kissed Sophia on the cheek and then picked up his briefcase from its place by the doorway. *"Paka, lyubov' maya,"* he called to her as he walked into the hallway. A moment later, the front door closed.

* * *

On Friday, time dragged. Mitch sat for hours at a desk in the big room where the lawyers worked. He twiddled with the pen in his hand, now and again scribbling notes on points of law that might be used in the defence of his father's client, who had been caught stealing large amounts of food from the company for which he worked and selling them on the black market. The man was clearly guilty, but then so were many people. It was difficult; a vigorous defence could be seen as anti-Soviet.

"How's it going?" His father's voice came from behind.

"Okay." He thought guiltily of the heap of scrunched-up paper on which he had written "Nataliya ... Natasha" over and over again, and which now clogged one of the desk drawers.

"I'll be ready to leave in five minutes."

Mitch breathed a sigh of relief. *I'll make up for it on Monday,* he resolved.

In the car on the way home, Sergei drove for some minutes in silence. "Anything the matter, Mitch?" he ventured.

"*Nyet.* Everything's fine. In fact, life's great."

* * *

The next day, Mitch walked to the centre of the Panteleimonovsky Bridge, looked up and down the footpath bordering both sides of the road, and then turned and walked back to where he had started. He had lost count of the times he had done this. *Where the hell is she?* He pushed up the left cuff of his new dark blue shirt and checked his watch—it was almost two o'clock. *I'll give her another ten minutes,* he decided, stepping to the edge of the path and scanning the bridge again.

He loosened his shirt collar, lit a cigarette, and leaned over the iron balustrade. This was usually his favourite time of the year—the time of the "summer snow," when the soft white flowers of the *cheryomukha* coat the canals. He took a drag on the cigarette and watched the sun's rays sparkling on parts of the water not covered by blossom. The thud of traffic crossing the bridge reverberated through the balustrade.

He turned and scanned the bridge again. People passed like shadows drifting across his mind. He closed his eyes and tried to conjure up a vivid picture of Natasha in the hope that some mental force would make her materialize in front of him. He could see a lock of dark hair falling over one side of her face, her creamy skin, the dimples in her cheeks, and her brown eyes flecked with green. He held on to the image in his head for a few more moments and then opened his eyes. The eyes staring at him were not hers. These eyes were bright blue fringed with long eyelashes. The young boy was probably no more than two years old. He twisted this way and that, shoulders hunched, arms wrapped around his body as he tried to resist his parents' efforts to pull him away.

"Come, Tima," the child's father said and swept him into the air.

"Nyet! Nyet!" Tima cried and wriggled in his father's arms.

"*Morozhenae.* We're going to get ice cream."

Mitch watched the young family walk away. The child was quiet now, one arm around his father's neck, his whispy, blond hair floating up and down with each step his father took.

Perhaps she's gone straight to the restaurant, Mitch wondered. *Nyet. She wouldn't do that; we said we'd meet here.* Earlier in the week, he had worked himself into a froth of uncertainty, wondering if Natasha would remember the arrangements they had made, or whether she would even remember him. On Wednesday he garnered the courage to telephone her and was relieved to hear instant recognition in her voice. After he put the receiver down, he stood for a while, savouring the way she had said his name in her slightly husky voice.

Another few minutes, he vowed again and lit another cigarette. As he waited, all his earlier uncertainties came flooding back. *Why are you kidding yourself? You know she won't come. She's probably ...* His thoughts were interrupted by the blast of car horns and angry voices. A car had stalled in front of where he was standing. Mitch wondered whether he should ask the driver if he needed help, but the engine roared into action, a cloud of black smoke burst from the exhaust, and the traffic started to move again.

He leaned back against the balustrade, hands thrust in his new blue jeans. Early this morning, he had joined the end of a line near the farmers' market, resisting the temptation to pay someone further forward in the line for their place. He could barely afford the one hundred rouble cost of the imported jeans.

He looked desultorily across at the orange facade of the Mikhailovsky Castle. Legend had it that Tsar Paul I had the castle painted to match the colour of his mistress's glove. *Now that was some love affair.* He sighed, scanned the bridge one more time, and ground the cigarette butt with the toe of his shoe.

He walked slowly along the side of the Fontanka river, hands in the pockets of his jeans. He had imagined walking here with Natasha, her hand in his, the filmy fabric of the white dress—the one she had worn the night of the party—brushing against his hand. He stopped across the street from *Beau Monde,* putting off the moment when he would cancel the reservation and with it any hope of a relationship with Natasha. His eyes followed a clump of *cheryomukha* as it broke away from the side of the river bank. The breeze carried it into mid-stream, where it lodged against a floating carpet of blossom. He took a deep breath, walked across the road, and down the basement steps.

Inside the restaurant he glanced toward the table in the alcove. It was the table he and his parents always had when they could spare enough money to come here. Today, it was to have been his and Natasha's. From the back of the room, Alphonse, the elderly waiter, raised a hand in greeting as Mitch climbed onto a stool at the counter. Mitch heard him explaining the menu to someone. "*Foie de veau,* Madam? It is calf's liver."

Mitch stared at the posters on the wall behind the bar, following the span of the struts of the Eiffel Tower, the red boots, the black garter on the leg of the dancer from the Moulin Rouge. He looked at the labels on the bottles lining the shelves, not reading the words.

"Mitch! Why you sitting here?" Alphonse gripped Mitch's shoulder. "That is your table," he said with a flourish of an arm. "You know it is."

"I came in to cancel it," he mumbled almost to himself.

"She is on her way, Mitch. The lady. She called. She asked me to tell you to wait."

Mitch almost fell off the stool in his haste. "She did?" A grin spread across his face as he headed to the table in the alcove. "Bring over a bottle of that wine my parents always drink," he called to Alphonse. He saw now that the restaurant was quite full. An assortment of faces looked at him as he sank down onto the familiar green leather banquette.

His parents first brought him here nearly fifteen years ago, a few days after his mother's abortive attempts to secure exit visas. Mitch had still been sulking over being branded a traitor by his school friends. His mother had argued that they couldn't afford to eat out, but her protests had faded as she chatted in French with Alphonse, discussing each item on the menu. "Not that we can get the same ingredients here as in Paris," he confided. "But we do our best. There is always a way." He had winked at her and gone on to tell her that his parents fled to Paris after the Revolution. They died in France, and Alphonse came to Leningrad to seek out relatives. His mission was not successful, but he stayed. That first evening, Sophia leaned toward Sergei and said, "Oh, Seryozha, this is like being at home in Montréal." Over the years since then, his parents eked out their money to allow for the occasional meal at *Beau Monde* to celebrate birthdays or anniversaries. It was a continuing source of wonder that the restaurant survived, with its style and décor linked to the decadent West. The paint was peeling off the saffron-coloured walls, the leather seat of the banquette was cracked, the crockery mismatched. All restaurants were owned by the State, and it could only be assumed that someone in the hierarchy had a special fondness for *Beau Monde.* If not, how could it survive?

The minute hand of his watch moved steadily round. Through the basement windows he watched feet pass by. Every time the door opened, he looked up, hoping to see Natasha sweeping in, the white dress clinging to her slender legs. The more he drank, the more his spirits fell. *You have to face it; she's not coming. But why did she ring to ask me to wait for her?* He didn't have an answer. He swallowed hard and shifted in his seat. *That zhopa Shevchenko. He must be back, damn him!*

He plucked at the tablecloth with his fingers, brushing together crumbs from the bread that Alphonse had brought over to soak up the wine. He held the wine bottle up to the light; it was almost empty. The restaurant had emptied out too, and a waiter was gathering up tablecloths and napkins. Mitch drained the bottle into his glass and swirled the liquid around before gulping it down. It tasted bitter.

He reached into his back pocket and pulled out his wallet. Despite the money paid for the jeans, it was unusually full. He had dug into his meagre savings, and his father had given him an advance on what he'd earned yesterday, or what he would have earned if his mind had been on the job. He was cross with himself for letting his father down, as he suspected the money was coming out of his father's own pocket. *I'll make up for it. I'll go into the office every day this summer. Weekends too. Work for nothing.* He tried to ignore the empty feeling in the pit of his stomach. He grimaced, thinking of having to face Yuri. *Govno! He's bound to have told Tolik. And Tolik will have told ... Don't think about it,* he told himself and counted some notes from his wallet. He turned to look for Alphonse. It was then that he saw her.

"Mitch. *Prastite!*" She wove her way across the room between tables and chairs, words of apology tumbling out of her mouth. Mitch stood up. She ran one hand through her hair; her other arm clutched several brown paper parcels close to her body. The handles of her purse dangled from where they were trapped in the crook of her elbow.

He reached out and took her by the shoulders, his touch gentle. The fabric of her pink-flowered dress felt soft, and he could smell a light fragrance. As he held her, the packages shifted downwards and the scooped neckline of her dress revealed the curve of her breasts.

"Are you cross?" she ventured, a tentative smile deepening the dimples in her cheeks. "My mother was in a generous mood. I just …" She looked up at him. "I just got swept along."

He watched her pink lips moving as she spoke. Then his lips were on hers, tasting her gently. A door slammed somewhere behind them and he drew back quickly, one hand going to his lips. *"Prastite,"* he mumbled.

"Oh, Mitch, don't be silly." She laughed softly, reached out a hand, and stroked the side of his face. "It was nice." At that moment, one of the packages she was holding slid to the ground. "Can I put these down somewhere?" Their hands touched as they grasped a parcel. Then she leaned forward and brushed his cheek with her lips. "Any chance of getting something to eat?"

"I'll see what I can do," he said and piled the packages on the far side of the banquette.

Alphonse was straightening bottles at the back of the bar and raised his eyebrows as Mitch approached. "Okay, my boy?"

Mitch grinned. "Any chance of some food? I know it's late."

Alphonse paused, head on one side, and pursed his lips. "For you and the young lady, I think we can manage something. We have some fish left."

"Spasiba." Mitch turned and looked over to the alcove where Natasha was unwrapping one of the parcels. "I'll find out what she'd like to drink."

They ate salmon in a herb sauce, thinly sliced potatoes, and green beans. Although this was Mitch's favourite meal at *Beau Monde,* today he hardly tasted the food. His fork went methodically in and out of his mouth; his eyes never strayed from Natasha. *She's so beautiful. Perfect.* He returned her smile.

"Mamochka insisted I have these," she said, revealing a pair of strappy, high-heeled red shoes from their brown paper wrapping. "She has a friend who works in one of the stores," she whispered, "and she always lets us know when they are having a consignment in." She paused and speared beans onto her fork. "My father will go mad when he sees all the stuff we bought. She was off to meet him at The Astoria. After a few drinks he'll calm down," she giggled. "He always does." She put down her fork, picked up the shoes, and swung them by their straps. "They'll be perfect for our trip."

Mitch's glass slipped from his hand. "What trip? Where are you going?" He dabbed at the pool of water on the tablecloth with his napkin.

"Spain! Isn't it exciting?" Her eyes were wide. "My father's giving a talk in Madrid, and he decided it would be nice if Mamochka and I went with him." She tossed the shoes onto the banquette, picked up her fork, and dipped a piece of salmon into the sauce. "It's all fixed. Exit visas, the lot. My father can always fix things."

Mitch looked down at his plate, recalling his mother's red-rimmed eyes the day she returned empty-handed from the visa office.

"We can shop and do all the touristy things while he's working," Natasha continued. "Mamochka knows a dear little dress shop there."

Mitch glanced at the assortment of new clothing littering the banquette. "When are you going?"

"Saturday." She reached across the table and laid her hand over his. "Don't look so sad. There's nearly a week before then. We can spend the whole time together." She squeezed his hand. "Really get to know each other."

Mitch's heart thumped loudly in his chest. "But I have to work. My father. He's relying on me."

"He'll understand. Tell him you'll work all the hours he wants while I'm in Spain. We'll be gone for two weeks, so that gives you loads of time."

Shit! he cursed to himself. *What am I going to say to Papa? He'll be furious.* He looked up and met Natasha's gaze. *I've got to see her. I can't let this chance go.*

"Now, what shall we do today?" she asked.

At the end of the evening, he closed the door of his parents' apartment and leaned back against it. The chequerboard black and white linoleum, which had always seemed to give the hallway a cold, uninviting look, tonight was bathed in a soft light. He walked over to the door to the sitting room and opened it. The darkened room was empty, and he checked his watch. It was past two o'clock.

In his room he lay on the bed, clothes and shoes still on, staring at the ceiling. His heart raced as he recalled the tremor that rippled through his body as his fingers felt the area under her arm and then the soft tissue of her breast. She had turned toward him, brushed her lips against his, and breathed in his ear: "Let's dance." He was hypnotized by the flashing lights and the movement of her body in time to the rhythmic beat of the disco. His own body had gyrated; his mind stripped away the flimsy fabric of her dress.

Now he could almost feel her breath on his neck, her body pressed into his when the dance tempo slowed. He closed his eyes and imagined unzipping the pink-flowered dress, his hands on her creamy skin, running over her breasts. As the long twilight of the Leningrad night brightened into dawn, he slept.

* * *

The next day, the boom of the noon-day cannon from the Peter and Paul fortress cracked across the room. Mitch sat bolt upright in bed, jolted out of sleep. The windows reverberated, then silence. "Damn cannon!" he cursed and slumped back onto the pillows, the pounding of his heart taking over the quiet space around him.

He propped himself up on his elbows and looked down. He was still wearing his shoes, jeans (undone), and shirt. The shirt was twisted around his body, and he pulled at the cloth with one hand.

What day is it? he wondered and then let out a low whistle, recalling the feel of Natasha's body. He could never have imagined …

A tapping sound interrupted his thoughts.

"Your mother said I was to wake you if you weren't up by now." The tapping on the door became louder. "Are you here?"

Mitch swung his legs over the side of the bed. *"Khorosho!"* he called, fastening his jeans as he walked to the door. He knew Verochka Murmanevna wouldn't go away until she was sure he wasn't still idling in bed. "I'm up," he laughed and opened the door.

"Not before time." She wagged a finger at him. "They've gone for a drive to Pushkin. You could have gone with them if you hadn't been lazing in your bed." She fixed him with a steely gaze. "And why do you still have yesterday's clothes on?"

"You don't want to know!" He looked away to avoid the scowl he knew would follow his words. "Any chance of some of your *Kresty'yanskiy Zavtrak?*"

She clucked her tongue at him. "Mitchell Sergeivich! Don't you think I have better things to do at this time on Sunday than cook breakfast?"

He grabbed hold of her shoulders and gave her a noisy kiss, first on one wrinkled cheek then the other, then the first again.

"Tsh, tsh," she admonished, pretending to brush away the kisses. "And don't you be long," she called over her shoulder as she shuffled along the corridor.

Mitch watched her. Her footsteps were muffled, her feet clad in felt *tapochki*. She had a strange gait, as though at any moment her pear-shaped figure would topple over. But there was something comforting about her grey hair, honey-brown eyes, and the sweet smell of baking that always hung around her. Whatever the food shortages, Verochka Murmanevna always conjured up a meal. They no longer asked how she came by most of the ingredients. "Better not to know!" was all she said. She came to live with them a few weeks after Babushka died and had quickly taken over in the kitchen. At first, Mitch resented the intrusion and brushed off her attempts to ease his grief with kind words and tempting food. One day she cornered him, much as Babushka had, and told him what a selfish young man he was. Didn't he know how fortunate he was? Her own husband and son died in the Stalin terror. Her eyes clouded over as she spoke, and Mitch turned away.

Now he closed the door, rubbed sleep out of his eyes, and pulled back the curtains. Bright light flooded in, and he opened the window and put his head out. In the distance he could see the green copper dome of the Kazan Cathedral streaked amber in sunlight. On the opposite side of the street to the apartment, the carved saints above a doorway were half in shadow, half in light. A pigeon stood on one leg on the head of a stone figure; the deep turquoise of its neck feathers glinted.

When they first moved here, Mitch had spent hours at this window watching the *monakhi* of the Russian Orthodox monastic order entering or leaving the house opposite, their long-sleeved robes swaying as they walked. His father told him that the monks risked persecution or death, as their beliefs went against those of the State. Mitch had tried to sort one black-clad figure from another, so he would know if anyone was missing. Each afternoon when the light was starting to fade and shadows reached halfway up the walls, there came a procession of women. They all wore headscarves and brought covered bowls to the doorway. Mitch was sure they contained food. Babushka sometimes took her place in the group. One afternoon he waited in the dim light of the kitchen. He heard her letting herself in the front door, and as she hobbled into the kitchen, he jumped out at her from the shadows. She shouted at him for scaring her half to death and shooed him away, swatting him with her headscarf. He had heard that the monks had given up the pleasures of the earthly life. Now he smiled to himself. The air smelled especially sweet today.

He turned from the window, flopped down on the wooden chair in the corner, and eased his feet out of his shoes and socks. His body looked the same, but inside he felt ... different. The rhythmic beat of his heart seemed loud. *Has it always sounded like that?* The room looked strangely unfamiliar too; the objects that had inhabited his world were from another life. How long had the hollow eyes in that carved mask looked down at him from the top of the bookcase? He remembered now—his father gave it to him about ten years ago. The young Mitch found it scary, and one day when his parents were out, he carried the wooden kitchen stepladder into his room. The ladder wobbled as he stood on the top rung, but he managed to stretch his arms enough to push the mask into the shadows. He had hoped fervently that the power of the saints guarding the monks' house opposite would spread this far and protect him from the menacing, sightless eyes.

Now from the depths of a warm bathtub he lay back and imagined Natasha's naked body. He held on to the vision in his head, not wanting it to change, not wanting to miss an inch of her gently curved hips, the plumpness of her breasts. He wondered about the colour of the hair around the soft place between her legs and rubbed his penis with the fingers of one hand.

Wrapped in a towel, clutching his discarded clothes, he padded along the corridor to his bedroom. He could smell bacon and onions cooking and smiled to himself. Verochka Murmanevna could never resist a request for *Krestiy'yanskiy Zavtrak,* the peasant dish her mother taught her to make.

He dressed quickly in old grey pants and a black T-shirt; he would change later for his date with Natasha. He picked up his jeans from where he had dropped them on the floor and took out his wallet from the back pocket. It didn't take him long to count the notes. He frowned and counted them again. The drinks were expensive at the nightclub, but Natasha said it was the place to go, the hub of the underground rock music scene in the city. *Chort! I hope Papa's back before I have to leave,* he thought, pondering how he could explain his request for more money.

In the kitchen, Verochka Murmanevna ladled his breakfast onto a plate. "Don't touch the plate; it's hot," she cautioned as she clattered it onto the table in front of him.

Mitch dug his fork into the fluffy eggs and piled pieces of bacon and bratwurst onto the end. *"Vkusno! Vkusno!"*

"You and your compliments." Her voice was harsh, but the look on her face betrayed her pride.

As he ate, he thought about where he would take Natasha that evening. *Somewhere cheap,* he grimaced. *It's a nice day. We can walk and find somewhere quiet, secluded, and maybe ...*

"Aren't you going to see who's at the door?" Verochka's voice cut through his thoughts. "I can't do everything here!"

The pounding on the door started again as he walked along the corridor. He pulled the door open and Yuri burst in.

"Mitch, how did it go?" he yelled, slapping Mitch on the shoulder.

"Sshh. I'll tell you later." Mitch closed the door and headed back to the kitchen. Yuri followed, and pulled out a chair at the kitchen table. "Something smells good."

"Any of the *Khachapuri* left that you were making yesterday, Verochka? I'm sure Yuri could eat a piece."

"You young men. I can't keep up with you." She opened a cupboard door and brought out the remains of the bread. "I'll tell you ..." She paused, rifled in a drawer, and retrieved a knife. "You're lucky you've never known what it is to be hungry ... really hungry."

"Me, I'm always hungry," Yuri quipped.

"You joke about it!" She wagged the knife at Yuri, and he shifted back in his seat. "Starving! That's what I mean by really hungry. In the Blokada, some people even ate their dead relatives." She snorted and jabbed the knife into the bread. Mitch and Yuri exchanged grimaces as she put a slice onto a plate and pushed it across the table to Yuri. "You'll have to eat it like that!"

They ate in silence while she babbled to herself and washed dishes in the sink. Mitch put down his knife and fork and pushed his empty plate away. "That looks good," he said, leaning toward Yuri's plate.

"It is," Yuri spluttered, his mouth full.

"You can't still be hungry." Verochka turned from the sink and picked up Mitch's plate.

"He's in love," Yuri laughed.

Mitch threw him a threatening look.

"Lyubov'!" Verochka shook her head at Mitch, wiped her hands on a corner of her wrap-around apron, picked up the *Khachapuri,* and slammed it down on the table in front of him.

"You get going," Mitch suggested to her. "We'll see to the rest."

"Mind you do. I don't want to see the dirty dishes here when I get back," she chided, unwrapping the folds of the apron from around her ample waist. At this time every Sunday, Verochka Murmanevna headed off to meet the rest of her extended family at one or other of their homes in the city. Mitch had long suspected she imbibed too much vodka; when she returned, her steps were unsteady, and bright red patches lit up both cheeks.

When at last the front door slammed, Mitch said, "Yuri, I don't suppose you have any money you can lend me, just for a while?"

Yuri leaned forward. "Never mind that. What happened with the lovely Natasha?"

CHAPTER FIFTEEN
LENINGRAD—MAY 1983

As the day of Natasha's departure approached, Mitch counted the hours he had left with her. Saturday loomed like a cloud of poisonous dust. He wondered how he had ever existed without her, without the indescribable feeling that ran through his body when he looked at her. When they were together, he was a different person, swept up in her sense of fun, consumed by an overwhelming urge to throw his inherent cautiousness to the wind and have her. Anywhere. But what then? If he ever got that far, she would guess he had no experience with women.

In the Tauride Gardens on Thursday afternoon, sunlight danced through the trees, highlighting the burnished red tints in Natasha's hair. Mitch slid an arm around her waist as they strolled along the pathways. His heart raced, his feelings a mixture of tenderness and longing to be with her, not only in the sexual sense, but to be part of her life. *What if she meets someone else in Spain, a good looking, wealthy, sexually experienced ... ? Don't think about it.*

She broke away from him, and her screams of mock fear rang out as he chased her. At the bottom of a path at the side of a bridge, she stopped. Her laughter came in gasps as she tried to regain her breath. He careened down the path, reached out, and grabbed her. For a moment, they both teetered on the edge of the water. Then he regained his balance, pulled her into his arms, and smothered her laughter with his mouth. She took his hand, led him into the shadows under the bridge, and leaned back against a stone parapet. He kissed her roughly and pressed his body against her. His right hand caressed her breast and then ran down her thigh. He fumbled trying to get his hand under the hem of her full-skirted dress. "*Nyet!* Mitch, *nyet*!" He moved his fingers under the elastic of her panties. It was warm and moist between her legs. She twisted her body and pushed him away. "*Nyet!* Not like this." Without looking at him, she straightened her dress and ran out into the sunshine.

"Fuck!" he cursed and braced one hand against the curve in the wall. *How could you have been so stupid?* But she had led him on. He lit a cigarette and inhaled deeply in an effort to regain his composure. A few minutes later, he walked back up the riverbank.

He was relieved to see she was still there, leaning on the balustrade on the opposite side of the bridge. An elderly couple passed by, their pace painfully slow as he searched his mind for the right words to say. He drew level with her. "Natasha, I'm ..."

"I didn't want it to be like that." She turned toward him, wiping away streaks of mascara with her fingertips. "Not with you. You're not like the others."

"It's okay. It was my fault. I shouldn't have done it."

"I want it to be special with you."

"I don't understand."

"I didn't want to do it down there." She inclined her head toward the river. For a moment they both stared into the water. "I don't know what it is about you. You're different, not like the others. I've never felt like this about anyone else before."

He hardly dared breathe.

"I love you, Mitchell Galichin," she murmured.

It was a second or two before he took in what she had said. Then he clasped her tightly and buried his face in her hair. "I love you too." He tilted her face upward, and then his lips were on hers, and they were oblivious to the world around them. As they drew apart, she looked at her watch. "I have to go. I promised my mother I would help her decide what clothes to take. She's so indecisive."

Mitch's hands rested on her hip bones and he gave them a slight squeeze. "We'll have all day tomorrow. Won't we?"

She nodded. "Tomorrow morning, I'm going to take you somewhere, show you something."

Half an hour or so later, he kissed her goodbye outside the gate to her apartment compound and watched until she was out of sight. He walked home, hardly noticing anything along the way, her words running through his mind. *I love you, Mitchell Galichin. You're different. Not like the others. She said that.* He knew there had been others. Yuri told him that Shevchenko boasted about how many times he had been with her. "And he wasn't the first." Mitch hadn't wanted to listen, hadn't wanted to think of anyone else touching her. But now it was different. He couldn't turn back the clock. *"I want it to be special with you," that's what she said.* He sat down on a bench and lit a cigarette. *What if it isn't special? What if she's disappointed? What if I can't satisfy her?* He took a drag on the cigarette and watched the stream of smoke as it drifted out of his nostrils. *Maybe I should get some experience with someone else. Get them to teach me the tricks.* Yuri had told him about an older woman who for a few roubles would show young men special ways to excite a woman. But Mitch wanted his first sexual experience to be with Natasha, not with some old crone.

* * *

The next morning, he persuaded Verochka Murmanevna to pack some food for a picnic, cajoling her into using the can of salmon he found in the cupboard. "Who is this young lady?" she questioned. "Whoever she is, she must be special if you want me to let you have this." She held the unopened can toward him. "You know your father likes it."

"She's very special, Verochka. And Papa won't mind," he assured her, glad his mother or father weren't around to refute his words. He was already in their bad books for letting his father down.

"Does she have a name?" She worked the opener around the top of the can.

"Natasha. Nataliya Alekseevna Lipovskaya." He took two bottles of beer out of the fridge and put them into a bag.

"Well, when are you going to bring this Natasha to meet us?"

"Soon," he assured her as she mashed a thin layer of salmon on two slices of bread.

On Liteynyy prospekt, Mitch heard the tram clanking behind him as he ran toward the stop. Natasha, already waiting there, gestured to him to hurry. He willed his legs to go faster. The tram slid past and ground to a halt in front of her. The door opened, and she put one foot on the step. His breath came in loud gasps as he reached her. "You're all flushed," she laughed.

"Are you two getting on or not?" the driver asked impatiently. Mitch adjusted the straps of the bag and followed her up the steps. There weren't any spare seats, and as the tram swayed around, they clutched at handholds, their legs touching briefly. Mitch lowered the bag onto the floor between his feet and put his free hand around Natasha's waist, steadying her. She looked even more beautiful today in a pale-green, fitted dress with a white cardigan draped over her shoulders. He stared at her, still not quite believing her words of yesterday. "So where are we going?" he asked.

"You'll see." A smile deepened the dimples in her cheeks. "I'm going to show you I'm not just a good-time girl."

"I never thought you were," he lied. He leaned closer to her as the wheels of the tram screeched to a halt and an overly-large woman pushed past.

"So what's in the bag?"

"Sandwiches. Nothing very exciting," he said, thinking of the scant filling of salmon. "I thought we could have a picnic. It's supposed to be warm later."

"I see you've come prepared," she giggled, glancing at the blanket draped between the handles of the bag.

"Verochka Murmanevna ... she lives with us," he explained, "she said the grass can get damp at this time of year." He laughed, raising his eyebrows. Natasha looked down at her feet.

Fifteen minutes later, they stood outside what looked like a derelict building. "Down here," she said as she started to walk down the basement steps. "Be careful, some of the steps are crumbling."

Mitch followed her, hoping this was somewhere they could be alone, have sex. She propped open a door that hung at a crazy angle. Shrill voices came from within. "What's going on?" he asked.

She stood to one side and let him enter. He took a few paces and squinted into the gloom. There were children everywhere. A dozen or so darted around in the middle of the room, grabbing each other by a coat sleeve or shirt tail. The thud of their shoes on the concrete floor and the noise of their voices was deafening. "What ... ?"

"This is my other family," she said.

Mitch looked around. There were mattresses on the floor around the edge of the walls. A few were occupied by children, some sleeping, some staring into space. At a table in a corner, a young woman had her hands in a bowl. "*Privet,* Natashinka!" she called, drying her hands on her dress as she walked toward them. "You must be Mitch. I've heard all about you." Her wavy hair was so blonde, it was almost white, and it fell softly over her shoulders. "I'm Marina. Marina Stepanovna." She gripped Mitch's arm. "Natasha's friend."

"More like my sister." Natasha hugged Marina and kissed her cheeks. "Well, what's been happening?"

"The *militsiya*, they were here last night." Marina bit her lip. "They found drugs and took away two of the older boys. There was nothing I could do. I had to let them go."

"Which boys?" Natasha asked.

"The two I caught sniffing glue. But it's Mashen'ka I'm worried about." She gestured toward a mattress in a corner. "She screamed all the time the *militsiya* were here. I couldn't calm her." A frown creased her forehead. "She wouldn't eat her breakfast this morning, and she has a high temperature."

"I'll see what I can do," Natasha said, already approaching the small figure lying under a blanket.

Mitch stayed where he was. Two young boys, their faces streaked with dirt, the sleeves of their shirts dangling over the ends of their hands, chased each other around him. "What goes on here?" he asked Marina in a loud voice over the din.

"Quiet! Quiet!" Marina shouted and grabbed the boys by their arms. A hush went around the room for a moment. "Come over here, and I'll explain." She let go of the boys and steered Mitch to the table where she had been washing dishes. "She's so good with her."

Mitch looked over to the mattress in the corner where Natasha sat, cradling a child in her arms. A wave of tenderness washed through him as she smoothed the child's hair back from her face and kissed the top of her head. "What is this place?" he asked.

"It's a shelter. An unofficial shelter for street kids," Marina explained. "We set it up about six months ago. Natasha persuaded one of her father's friends to let us use it. Her father provides money for food and other necessities." Marina put two bowls to drain. "Many of the children are orphans or have run away from home to escape parents whose tempers, usually fuelled by alcohol or the inability to cope, lead them to do the most awful things."

"And Mashen'ka ... is that what you called her?" He inclined his head toward the young child.

"She was abandoned. One of our friends found her in an alleyway behind a food store, picking through garbage. She was filthy, covered in bruises. Her hair was matted in knots, but I cleaned her up." Marina paused and looked across at the child. "She's mentally retarded. We don't know her name or age, but Natasha named her Mashen'ka. It suits her, don't you think?"

Mitch nodded. *Jesus Christ! Who would abandon a young child? Particularly one like that?*

Marina turned to a stove on which a saucepan of *kasha* simmered, ladled some into a bowl, put a spoon in it, and handed it to Mitch. "Here. See if she'll eat this now," she urged.

He walked over to Natasha, squatted in front of her, and handed her the bowl. He touched the child's cheek with one finger; she smiled a crooked smile and stared at him with piercing blue eyes. A lump rose in his throat as he looked at the golden halo of curls that framed her face. *What hope is there for her … or any of them?* he asked himself as he sat down on the mattress and put an arm around Natasha.

A small group of children sat in a semicircle close by, playing cards; a shaft of light from a small window hovered over them. Despite the sunshine outside, the atmosphere inside was cold. The mattress on which they were sitting, and on which this child slept, was damp. He clenched his fists. *No one should have to live like this.* He thought of Vanya's mother and sister in two dingy rooms with hardly enough to eat. And Vanya in a cold grave. He shivered and leaned closer to Natasha. "I had no idea you were doing this." He breathed into her ear and hugged her with one arm.

"You thought I was an empty-headed woman whose only thoughts were of what I was going to wear or where the next party was going to be." Mitch didn't reply. "Admit it."

"I did."

Natasha spooned *kasha* into Mashen'ka's mouth. "You weren't far wrong. I sometimes wonder what I'm doing here. It all started as a bit of a game. I suppose I was rebelling against all the things my parents value. The way they live. Then the whole thing gained momentum, and the kids just kept coming." She sat Mashen'ka between them. The child's head lolled to one side.

Mitch ran a hand through Mashen'ka's hair; it was whispy soft. She looked up at him. The front of her faded blue top was stained, and a trickle of dribble ran down the side of her chin. Mitch reached into his pocket, pulled out a handkerchief, and wiped it away, swallowing back tears that threatened to engulf him. *What future does she have? How long can she survive in a place like this?* He tried to avert his gaze, but the blue eyes held him.

"Shall we get going?" Natasha's voice broke the spell.

"I don't mind staying. We should help ..."

"Marina can handle things." Natasha took the handkerchief from him and dabbed at a spot of *kasha* on the front of her dress. Then she laid Mashen'ka gently on the mattress, covered her with a blanket, and kissed the side of her face. *"Zasypai, moya prelest',"* she whispered.

"I'd like to stay ..." Mitch started to insist, but Natasha was already walking toward the door. He scrambled to his feet, picked up his bag from where he had left it by the door, and waved goodbye to Marina. She shrugged as she dunked some more dishes into the bowl of water.

Outside, the light was bright and, despite the warm breeze, Mitch shivered. "What will happen to her ... Mashen'ka?" he asked, hoisting the handles of the bag onto his shoulder.

"Who knows?"

"Don't you think she might be better in a hospital or State orphanage, where she has medical care?"

Natasha stopped walking and turned to him. "Do you know what those places are like?" she snapped. "She'd be classed as an *imbetsil*. No one would bother to feed her. She'd die!" She glared at him for a moment and then turned on her heel and walked quickly away.

"I'm sorry. That was stupid of me," he called as he hurried to catch up with her, silently berating himself for his insensitivity. Mashen'ka would be better in an orphanage, but he shouldn't have said so.

Half an hour later, they alighted from a tram at the corner of Millionaya ulitsa, walked along the Neva embankment and through the open wrought iron gates to Letnyi Sad, the majestic Summer Garden planned by Peter the Great. Sunlight filtered through tall leafy oaks and elms as they strolled along the wide paths which criss-cross the gardens. Mitch reached for Natasha's hand. "Am I forgiven?" he asked. She gave his hand a squeeze.

There were a few people about, mostly elderly couples walking arm-in-arm. Here and there, they came across mothers with babies in prams. They stepped to one side as a young woman ran after a tiny girl who was lurching toward the pink and white blossoms in the flower beds; the mother was a second too late and the child's squeal of delight rang in the morning air as she clutched a handful of flowers in her small fist.

Farther along the path, he paused and ran a hand over the surface of one of the statues. Although most of the first Tsar's grandiose fountains and pavilions were swept away in a flood in the eighteenth century, eighty or so marble statues remained, depicting the mythological gods and heroes so much a part of Russian folklore.

"I'll race you to the Summer Palace," Natasha said, letting go of his hand and setting off at a sprint. Her cardigan, which she gripped in one hand, streamed behind. When Mitch caught up with her, she was bending down in front of the entrance to the modest palace, adjusting one of her sandals. She had her back to him, and he put the bag down and crept up behind her, sliding his hands around her waist and lifting her to her feet. She leaned back into him.

"How did you know it was me?" he whispered into her ear. His fingers splayed out until they met across the slight bulge of her stomach and pushed her back, moulding her into his body.

"Not here, Mitch. Someone will see."

"Where then?" he asked.

"What about that pink-draped four poster bed in there?" She gestured toward the palace. "I always rather fancied that." She turned to face him.

He laughed.

"Let's sit on the seat over there and eat some of that food you've been promising me." She pulled him in the direction of a bench under the trees. "What do we have?" She peered into the bag now balanced on Mitch's lap.

He apologized for the salmon. She picked at a sandwich and drank most of a bottle of beer. He drained the last of his beer and looked at his watch. "It's two o'clock. What do you want to do now?" he asked.

"Well ..." She paused. "My parents will be out this evening. I was going to pack my case then, to be ready for tomorrow, but ..." She leaned toward him, the gap in the square neckline of her dress revealing her cleavage. "If I do that this afternoon, you might come to our apartment later. About eight?" She raised her eyebrows questioningly at him.

"I ... I'd love to," he gaped.

"Petya may be there, but he won't tell."

He gathered up the remains of their lunch and dropped it into a nearby bin. He was quiet as they walked back through the gardens. *Her apartment. Her parents will be out.* The most he had hoped for was finding a secluded spot here in the shade of the trees. *I'll be alone with her, except for Petya. The two of us ...*

"Mitch? Did you hear what I said?"

"Sorry. I was thinking of something ... something nice."

"I asked if you were going to miss me."

"Miss you? I'll miss you every minute."

"That's good." She put her arm through his. "Let's look at the Krylov statue. Papa used to take me there on Sunday mornings, just the two of us." She steered Mitch down a side path to the Tea House, where they mingled with a group of people around the bronze effigy of the great writer. Mitch smiled to himself as she rushed forward, pointing out excitedly the animals from Ivan Krylov's fables depicted in bas-relief around the statue. Written in the early nineteenth century, Krylov's innocent-sounding miniature dramas satirized contemporary social types in the guise of beasts. Like most Russian children, from an early age Mitch could recite lines from 'Hermit and Bear,' 'Multi-Colored Sheep,' and many more. As he grew up, he began to think more deeply about the messages behind Krylov's stories.

"Natasha, have you ever wondered why the State eulogizes tales that encourage laughing at public figures?" His voice was low.

She paused, her hand on top of the head of the figure of the lamb "It's not really that," she laughed. "Take 'Multi-Colored Sheep'. Now, the lion is smart. As a ruler, he can't destroy the sheep himself, so he comes up with a plan. He hires a wolf as shepherd. When the sheep disappear, the wolf is seen as a bad robber, and the mighty lion as good and merciful."

"And you think that's all right?"

"It's a fact. Some animals, or people, will always be stronger than others. There'll always be differences, and it's the smart ones—like the lion—who work the system and survive."

Mitch thought of Krylov's lines: *"The weak against the strong; Is always in the wrong."*[2]

He swallowed hard as an image of Mashen'ka flashed into his mind.

"You need the leaders to do what's best for the people. That's the way it works." She took his arm again.

---

2 From the satire, 'Multi-Colored Sheep' by Ivan Andreyevich Krylov (1769-1844), published in the 1860s.

"For some," he mumbled under his breath. The tales seemed more like a warning. A warning of how powerful the State—or the lion—is. "Why are we talking about this, anyway?"

"You started it."

As they headed to the tram stop, he had more important things than Krylov on his mind.

* * *

At two minutes to eight that evening, outside the Lipovskys' apartment, Mitch straightened his jacket, wishing he hadn't been so liberal with his father's cologne. He rang the doorbell and paced back and forth, hoping her parents hadn't changed their plans.

Petya opened the door. "Mitch! Come in. She's not ready, of course." In the sitting room Petya poured drinks, while Mitch looked around. He hadn't seen much of the apartment on the night of the party. Or perhaps he had and it hadn't penetrated his intoxicated brain. He remembered the large paintings on the walls and went closer now to get a better look. "It's Papa's passion—art," Petya said, handing Mitch a glass of brandy. "Does nothing for me," he shrugged. "My mother always jokes that one day he'll swap one of us for a Steen or a Mazzola," he laughed loudly.

The humour was lost on Mitch. He had never heard either of the names that slipped easily off Petya's tongue. His own laugh sounded stilted. He sipped his brandy.

Petya gestured to him to sit in an armchair. "Mitch, I know it's none of my business but…" He twirled an unlit cigarette between his fingers as he paced around. "There's something you should know about Natasha."

Mitch held his breath, willing Petya not to utter the words that would shatter his dreams … *Natasha has someone else.*

"It's my father. He spoils her, gives her everything she wants. She tires of things quickly."

Mitch breathed again and sat down.

Petya lit his cigarette. "Look, what I'm trying to say is … I don't think you can afford her."

"Isn't that for me to decide?"

"She has very expensive tastes."

"I know. But there's ..." Mitch stopped. How could he explain that sometimes feelings were more important? That being together was enough?

"Khorosho!" Petya snapped, waving his arm in a dismissive gesture as he sat on the sofa.

They sat in silence for several minutes until Natasha burst into the room. "What's wrong with you two?" She looked from one to the other.

"Nothing," Mitch said. She was wearing blue jeans and a plain red T-shirt, her hair pulled back into a ponytail. *She looks so young, as if she's just got out of school.* The thought excited him.

She perched on the arm of the sofa and ran a hand through Petya's mop of long hair. He shifted away from her. "What's the matter, big brother?" she teased. "You're going to miss me. Is that what's wrong? How sweet."

"I'm going out." Petya ground his cigarette into the ashtray, got to his feet, tucked an edge of shirt back into his jeans, and left the room without a backward glance.

"What's wrong with him?" Natasha looked quizzically at Mitch. "Did something upset him?"

Mitch shrugged, stood up, took off his jacket, and draped it over the back of an armchair. The front door slammed.

Natasha flopped down onto the sofa and patted the seat next to her. She lifted her arms, revealing several inches of bare midriff, and unwound the band securing her ponytail. Mitch could scarcely breathe as he sat down.

His arm crept around her back. He could see the outline of her nipples through the tight cotton top. His penis throbbed and hardened as he moved his other hand up under her T-shirt. She wasn't wearing a bra, and he felt her nipples stiffen. "You don't waste time." Her voice was low and husky as she pulled the T-shirt up further and cupped a hand under one breast. Her other hand pushed his head onto the upturned nipple. He pulled it into his mouth, and she moaned softly as he sucked first one breast, then the other, then the first again. His penis felt as though it was bursting out of his pants. She pushed him away gently, tugged her T-shirt over her head, pulled herself along the sofa, stretched out her legs, and offered him a breast again. He sucked hard on it, one hand following hers as she unfastened her jeans and eased them down. She had nothing on underneath. He let go of her breast and pulled her jeans off. Her pubic hair was the deepest brown. His gaze never shifted from it as he got to his feet, kicked off his shoes, undid his pants, and stepped out of them. His underpants followed quickly; his cock stuck out in front of him, pulsating. Her fingers touched the end of it. "That looks good." She pulled him down, guiding his penis between her legs. He slid inside, the sound of his breathing filled his head as he thrust farther in. "Harder! Harder!" she urged, arching her back and digging her fingernails into his shoulders. The pain felt good. He concentrated on the power of his cock thrusting inside her, blanking out everything else from his mind. "Don't stop! Don't stop!" she yelled. Then the sound of his own cries filled his head as his whole body exploded and sperm pumped out of him. It kept coming as she shouted for more. Her body convulsed beneath him.

He collapsed onto her, breathing heavily. After a while he shifted his head and pulled one of her nipples toward his mouth and kissed it gently, enjoying the feel of his penis still inside her. As it slid out, his fingers explored where it had been. It was warm and wet. Mitch Galichin, who had been a virgin at twenty, had fucked the most beautiful girl in the world. Fucked her good and hard. He raised his head and looked at her. She smiled. There was a softness about her features now.

He eased himself off her, twisting his body around to get a foothold on the floor. He knelt at her side and pulled her into his arms. "Natashinka," he breathed into her neck.

She kissed the side of his face. "Do you have a handkerchief? I'm in a bit of a mess."

He got up, took his jacket from the back of the chair, and pulled a handkerchief out of a pocket. She took it from him and he watched as she wiped between her legs, stepped into her jeans, and pulled them up over her hips. He couldn't believe how good it had been. At that moment, a thought came to his mind. He hadn't used a condom. *Chort! What if I've made her pregnant?*

She scrubbed at a wet mark on the sofa with the handkerchief and then turned the cushion over. "They'll never know," she giggled.

There were hairs peeking out of the front opening of her jeans. He reached out and touched them and then gathered his clothes together and followed her along the corridor to her bedroom. *What the hell. If I've made her pregnant, the damage is already done.* "What time will your parents be home?" he asked.

"Around eleven."

Some time later, he lay back on the pillow and listened to her regular breathing. She was sleeping. His gaze drifted around the room, making out the contours of the furniture. Everything seemed large compared to what he was used to, what most Soviet citizens were used to. He turned on his side, moulded his body around her, an arm across her waist, and drifted off to sleep.

He awoke with a start, shot up in bed and looked at his watch. Christ! It was 10:30. "Natasha, wake up!" He gave her bottom a pat. "I have to go, *lyubov' maya*." She turned toward him and opened her eyes a fraction. "Your parents will be back," he gasped, moving to the edge of the bed.

He dressed quickly and then sat on her side of the bed, stooping forward to put on his shoes. She leaned her head on his back, her fingers massaging between his legs. He turned and held her away from him. It was tempting. *If you don't go now, her parents will be back,* he told himself firmly. "My darling," he murmured and kissed her lips gently. *"Ya lyublyu tebya."* He eased her back on to the pillows, his gaze lingering for a moment on her breasts.

At the doorway, he listened—it didn't sound as though anyone was home yet. He turned for one last look at her, then closed the door quietly. At the front door, he remembered his jacket and grabbed it from the back of the chair in the sitting room and scooped up his handkerchief from where she had dropped it on the floor. He stuffed it in his pant pocket and pulled open the front door. He let out a startled gasp. A woman stood in front of him holding out a key, ready to put it into the lock. *It can't be Natasha's mother. Too young for her,* he thought thankfully. Then he remembered the housekeeper. Natasha had said it was her evening off. "Natasha's in ..." he strangled the word "bed" in his throat. He gaped at the woman; her hair was dripping water. "Is it raining?" he blurted. Without waiting for an answer, he walked quickly toward the staircase, thrusting his arms in his jacket as he went.

Outside, rain bounced on the sidewalk slabs, and Mitch gave the guard in the gatehouse a broad grin as the gate swung open. At the end of the street he turned the corner, sheltered in a doorway, lit a cigarette, and inhaled slowly, trying to recapture the indescribable feelings that had gone through his body when he and Natasha had made love. He wanted to hold them in his mind forever. Before tonight, he had always felt that the first time he fucked a woman he would shout the news to the world. But not now. He ground the cigarette out, pulled up his jacket collar, and went out into the rain.

* * *

The next morning, rain beat incessantly on the windows of his bedroom. He still couldn't believe last night really happened. He thought of how he had moved on her naturally, his lust, his need to possess her, guiding him. Or that was how it seemed last night. Now he was consumed with doubt. She had guided his fumbling. *She must have known it was my first time.*

Umbrella tops moved quickly along the street below as he stared out of the window, trying to recall every inch of her body. He remembered the darkness of her nipples, how they had hardened between his finger and thumb, the colour and feel of her pubic hair, the soft, warm place beneath. He picked up the handkerchief from the top of the bedside cabinet. The fabric was stiff now but still smelled of her. He inhaled the smell again before tucking the handkerchief into a drawer.

He looked at his watch. *She'll be at the airport now. Soon with each movement of the second hand she will be going farther and farther away.* The next two weeks stretched like a long, dark tunnel before him.

At that moment, the telephone in the hallway rang shrilly. He dashed across the room, pulled open the door, ran along the corridor, and grabbed the receiver. "Nata ...?" A man's voice, one he didn't recognize. "Papa! It's for you," Mitch shouted and rested the receiver on the table.

Toward noon he watched clouds scudding across the sky. The rain had stopped, and a watery sun shed fingers of light through gaps in the grey.

CHAPTER SIXTEEN

LENINGRAD—MARCH 1984

Mitch pulled together the lapels of his overcoat with one gloved hand and gripped them under his chin. "Why do we have to come out on a night like this?" he shouted. Natasha's answer was lost in the howling of the wind. They turned a corner and swayed momentarily, bracing themselves against another icy blast. At the bottom of the basement steps, he wedged the door open with one shoulder, wrapped an arm around her and guided her inside the bar. The door slammed shut behind them and they stood for a moment in the silence. Only two other people had braved the freezing night, and they were huddled together at a corner table. "Sit down. I'll get something to warm us up," Mitch said, handing her his *shapka* and gloves. He had just about enough money for a couple of drinks.

A few minutes later he carried a small tot of brandy and a glass of red wine to where she was sitting, body bent, long fur coat draped over her shoulders. The whole of her body shook as he handed her the wine. "Drink this, it'll warm you." She stared at the glass. "You okay?" he asked.

She shrugged, took a sip of wine, set it down, and ran the tip of a finger around the rim.

A pulse throbbed in Mitch's right temple. *She's going to tell me it's over. I know she is.* They had been together now for ten months, but for the past couple of weeks, she had acted strangely. She had missed most of her classes and made excuses when he suggested they meet. At first, he thought she was still upset over the closure of the children's shelter. The *militsiya* arrived one night in early December and took the kids away, including Mashen'ka. Natasha, Marina, and Mitch searched orphanages and mental institutions in the city, or at least those to which they managed to gain access; there was no trace of the child. But after the initial rage and flurry of activity, Natasha seemed to accept what had happened and threw herself into a round of parties and other social events. Mitch tried to convince himself that it was her way of coping with loss, but there was still the nagging doubt that maybe she hadn't cared that much. *"She tires of things quickly,"* Petya's words came back to him. *You're being unfair to her,* he told himself now, recalling the way she smoothed Mashen'ka's curls, kissed the top of her head. Maybe he didn't understand women.

Maybe she was tired of him. Two nights ago, he took her to the Mariinsky; Vera Kishinevskaya had given him the tickets. On previous visits, her excitement was infectious as she scanned the audience and waved to friends. That night, she sat silently, program unopened in her lap. After his efforts at conversation met with monosyllabic replies, he looked around at the ornate blue and gold auditorium with its painted ceiling of dancing girls and cupids. As the overture began, he held her hand. Tension coursed through her fingers with each movement of the conductor's baton.

Now, he picked up his drink and swallowed it in one gulp. *Whatever it is, I have to know. I can't go on like this.* A chill ran through his body as he stared ahead unseeing. She turned to him and opened her mouth as if to speak. "Natasha, I know what you're going to say." His words hung in the air between them.

"Do you?" she said, eyes downcast. "I don't think so."

"What is it?"

"I'm pregnant," she whispered.

His jaw dropped. "Did you ... Did you say you're pregnant?" Disbelief sounded in every syllable. She nodded her head slowly. He gaped at her.

Her body convulsed in sobs and she looked away.

"It's okay." He cradled her head to his chest and rocked her back and forth."

"Prastite, prastite," she cried into his jacket.

"It's not your fault." If anyone was to blame, it was him. She had said they should be more careful, but he felt invulnerable, swept along on a cloud of lust, not thinking, all the time wanting more of her. For the past few weeks common sense had prevailed and he'd used a condom. *Too late!* he thought now. "You're sure?"

She nodded and slid her glass toward him.

"When's it due ... the baby?"

She shrugged her shoulders. "October."

"Why didn't you tell me before?" He gulped down some of her wine.

"I was hoping I was wrong." Tears brimmed over again and ran down her cheeks. "I didn't know how you would feel." Mitch pulled his handkerchief out of his pocket and passed it to her. "We don't have to have it," she sniffed loudly, twisting the handkerchief around and around in her hands.

It would be easy to say get rid of it. Wouldn't it? He looked at her. Part of him was growing inside her. A son or a daughter. He fumbled in his jacket pocket for his cigarettes. "It'll be okay. I'll make everything all right, you'll see," he murmured, almost to himself.

* * *

"What were you thinking, Mitch? What's going to happen to you now? Your career, your whole life." Sergei's arms, which had been flinging out in all directions, now fell to his sides. "We had such plans for you."

I had such plans for myself. Mitch sighed and slumped forward in the armchair. The clandestine work he was doing for Professor Nekrassov had kindled in him a resolve—some might say a suicide wish—to use his legal training to defend those unjustly accused. In his more rational moments, usually when rumours circulated that the body of someone who had spoken out about corruption in high places was found floating in a river or nailed to a tree, his nerve failed him for a day or two. Then he consigned macabre thoughts to the back of his mind to join the other things it was better not to think about. But now he would have responsibilities. A wife. A child. His eyes followed a line in the pattern of the rug on the wall as it meandered into swirls: reds and blues, splashes of green.

"Come, Seryozha," Sophia urged. "Sit down. We must talk about this calmly."

"Calmly! He's twenty-one years old. They're both still at school, for God's sake. And you expect us to talk about this calmly?"

In the silence that followed, Mitch met his mother's gaze. He looked away, unable to bear the disillusionment in her eyes. His father paced around the room. Twice he stopped in front of Mitch's chair, his face puce, his jaw set. Mitch waited for him to speak, to shout. Anything but this.

"Papa. Please." Mitch stood up and walked over to where his father was now leaning with his hands on the windowsill, his back to the room. "I can't tell you how sorry I am. I wish this had never happened." He laid a hand on his father's arm. His father shook it off.

"How could you be so irresponsible?" Sergei turned around, his face contorted with rage.

"I know. But ..."

"I don't want to hear your excuses. Get out! Get out of my sight!" Sergei spat.

Mitch glanced at his mother; she looked away.

The silence in his bedroom was almost worse than the tension in the sitting room. He lay on the bed and stared at the ceiling. From time to time he heard raised voices. Even as he had tossed and turned in bed night after night, wondering how he was going to break the news, he never imagined the effect it would have. Loads of young couples had children while at university, so why was it different for him and Natasha? *We still have to tell Natasha's parents,* he grimaced, biting one of his fingernails down to the quick. She said her father would be angry at first. "But everything will be okay. He'll come around. Mamochka and I know how to handle him." Now Mitch wasn't sure anything would ever be okay again. He had thought that once it was in the open they would be able to make plans for a wedding, somewhere to live. But now? He closed his eyes.

Some time later his mother called from the doorway: "Mitch?" He didn't answer, and she approached the bed. "Papa's calmer now. We'll talk ... we'll work something out."

In the sitting room, she handed Mitch a cup of tea. Settling herself next to Sergei on the sofa, she reached out and gave her husband's hand a pat where it rested on his knee.

Sergei leaned toward the armchair where Mitch was sitting. "What do her parents have to say about all this?"

"We haven't told them yet. I'm going there later this afternoon."

"You must have made some plans, the two of you, about the baby."

"We've talked about what we're going to ..."

"You're both too young to be burdened with a baby," his father interjected. "You don't have to have it."

"For Christ's sake!" Mitch yelled. His cup rattled on its saucer as he banged it down on the side table. "An abortion?" His voice wavered as he said the last word. "Is that what you're suggesting?"

"Lots of people do. It makes sense."

"How can you even suggest that?" Mitch shook his head. "Hell! It's my child ... your own grandchild!"

"What else are you going to do? Tell me that." Sergei threw out his hands in despair. "You can't support a child and a wife. You're both still at university. It'll be years before either of you earn any money."

"We'll manage."

"Mitch, be sensible." His mother's voice had lost its warmth.

"What do you think I'm trying to be?" He leapt out of the chair. "I'm trying to take responsibility for my own actions. Isn't that what you've always told me? Isn't it?"

"What are you going to do? Give up your career?" His father was now on his feet.

"If I have to." Mitch hadn't yet got his head around how he could continue his studies and earn enough money to provide for a family.

"You know we don't want it to come to that," his mother said firmly, shifting to the edge of her seat. "But Natasha ... she's used to having everything she wants. You don't have that sort of money. And neither do we."

"You know nothing about her. You haven't even tried to get to know her."

"We know you've got yourself in debt already, trying to please her," Sophia countered.

"You're being unfair to her. You've no ..."

"You can't go on like that," Sergei cut in. "She'll ruin your life."

"You're a fine one to talk! Or have you forgotten? Maman's parents weren't over-enamoured with you."

"That was diff ..."

"No, it wasn't! Your marriage worked out, despite their objections. And ours will too!"

* * *

Late that afternoon, Mitch sat at the end of the sofa in the sitting room at Natasha's home—the sofa on which he had first made love to her. Unlike that magical evening when nothing else mattered, now his stomach felt as though it didn't belong to him.

Natasha and her father hadn't yet put in an appearance. Lena, Natasha's mother, was plumping cushions. She wore a moss-green, scoop-necked dress cinched in at the waist with a wide, gold-coloured belt. Her black hair—which, even to Mitch's untutored eye, looked too perfectly black to be natural—was tucked into a pleat at the back of her head and held in place by a long, amber-encrusted clip. Mitch thought she must have been attractive in her youth, but now her hips had run to plumpness, the plumpness of over-indulgence. He searched his brain for something to say to her. They had been through all the pleasantries, not that pleasantries came easily to Yelena Nicholaievna. From the start, both she and Aleksei Aleksandrovich, Natasha's father, were openly hostile to Mitch, making it clear they didn't think he was good enough for their only daughter. *I dread to think how they're going to take this,* he thought, trying to blot from his mind the cloud of silence that had descended on his own home. He pulled a packet of cigarettes from his jacket pocket, fanned them out, and offered them to Lena. She shook her head. His hands were unsteady as he lit one for himself and puffed nervously on it.

"I'll go and see where Natasha and Lyosha are," she said. Her high-heeled shoes clicked along the marble-floored hallway.

Mitch rested the cigarette on the side of the ashtray, got up, and walked to the window. The gloomy March sunlight of earlier had gone. He hated this time of the year when the day had hardly awoken before an impenetrable darkness descended again on the city. These past weeks, the blackness outside mirrored his mood. Natasha had wanted to tell their parents straight away, but he needed time to come to terms with the fact that he was going to be a father before the rest of the world burst in. Before the scene today, he had begun to enjoy the feeling that she was carrying his child. When he looked at her swollen breasts, he was overcome with satisfaction that he did this to her. He hadn't lost her, as he feared. Whatever the hardships, they had a future together. They made love as often as they could find somewhere to be alone.

One afternoon, they had crept into the now-abandoned premises where the street kids' shelter had been. They sank into the pile of mattresses thrown into a corner and, huddled beneath their coats, were oblivious to the rest of the world as they found new ways to excite each other. As they straightened their clothes, they heard a noise at the back of the room, and Mitch discovered an old man curled in the shadows, an empty bottle at his side. "It'll be tomorrow before he wakes up," he told Natasha. She was sitting on the edge of the mattresses, her fur coat buttoned up to her neck. Her teeth chattered; her eyes brimmed with tears. "Is it Mashen'ka?" Mitch asked. "If this one's a girl, we'll call her Mashen'ka," he said softly, sitting down next to her and patting her stomach. Natasha shook her head, telling him it was bad luck to name a baby before it was born.

Now, loud voices broke in on his thoughts. The door opened and Natasha ran over to him and grabbed his arm. "I've told them," she hissed.

"You've what?"

"You! You!" Her father barged through the doorway. He was a powerfully-built man, several inches taller than Mitch. His face was puce, his cheeks puffed out in rage. "*Zhopa! Zhopa!* How dare you," he howled, wrenching Natasha's arm away and grabbing the lapels of Mitch's jacket.

"Wait a minute," Mitch began, trying to shake him off.

"Ublyudok! Ublyudok!" Aleksei Aleksandrovich took a swing at him. Mitch ducked. The next swing landed on Mitch's chin and he stumbled backwards, knocking over a small table. He hit the floor. A leg of the table jammed in his side. He gasped for breath as Aleksei's fingers pressed into his neck.

"Lyosha! Lyosha!" Lena shouted, pulling frantically at her husband.

"*Nyet!* Papa! *Nyet!*" Natasha screamed.

Mitch clawed at the other man's wrists, trying to roll over and push the bulky form off his body, but he was pinned down.

"Nyet! Nyet!" Natasha's voice seemed far away.

It was a moment before Mitch felt the pressure on his neck ease, and he took several noisy gulps in an attempt to get air into his lungs. Aleksei was kneeling over him, breathing noisily, fingers bent as though still locked around Mitch's throat.

"Lyosha, please. Your blood pressure," Lena beseeched. She grabbed her husband by the arms and helped him to his feet. "Come. Sit down." She led him to the sofa, where he sank down, pulled a handkerchief from his pocket, and mopped his face.

Mitch coughed, sat up, and loosened his collar. His breath came in short gasps. "Are you okay?" Natasha asked and knelt down next to him.

"Get him out of here," Lyosha growled as he started to rise to his feet again.

"We have to talk about this," Lena placated, holding on to his arm, "discuss what's best for everyone."

"It would be best if he got out of her life. If she had never met him," he spluttered, wiping sweat from his forehead. "He'll never amount to anything!" He spat the words out.

Mitch opened his mouth to defend himself. Natasha shook her head and stood up. Mitch got unsteadily to his feet and stumbled to an armchair as far away from Lyosha as possible. He rubbed his jaw and then gently prodded his ribs where the table leg had been.

Natasha stood the table upright and replaced haphazardly the things that had been on it. Then she took a couple of steps toward her father. "Papochka, please listen." She rested her hands on his knees. "Mitch and I love one another. We want to be together."

"*Lyubov'? Lyubov'?* What do you know of love?" he sneered. "Love is a luxury, not a prerequisite for marriage or happiness. *Lyubov'!*"

Natasha turned from him and perched on the arm of Mitch's chair, her arm resting loosely across his shoulders.

"Look at him. *Zhopa!*" Aleksei Aleksandrovich cursed. "How does he think he's going to look after her and a baby? I tell you, he'll never amount to anything. He can't even look after himself, let alone support a wife and child."

"We'll manage. I'll get ..."

"Keep quiet! I don't give a shit what you think." He looked threateningly in Mitch's direction. "In my house you'll listen to what I say."

"Lyosha," Lena tried to interject.

"I should have put a stop to it at the start."

"Papochka, please." Natasha got up from the arm of Mitch's chair and squeezed between her parents on the sofa. "I know this is a terrible shock for both of you." She looked from one to the other. "But Mitch and I, we want to be together."

"You don't know what ..." Aleksei Aleksandrovich began.

"Give her a chance, Lyosha," Lena interrupted. "Let her speak."

For the next quarter of an hour or so, Mitch watched the two women manoeuvre the situation with quiet words, a gentle rub of Lyosha's back, a suggestion ventured here or there.

At the end of it all, Lyosha sat back on the sofa. "I won't pretend I like it, *lyubov' maya,*" he said as he put an arm around Natasha, "but Papochka will make everything fine. You'll see. Haven't I always sorted out my darling girl's problems?" A satisfied smile spread across his face.

Mitch seethed. *This is my problem! Our problem!* he wanted to shout. *We can sort it out, given time.* "Natasha, we can manage ..." he started to say. She wasn't listening. He stood up, thrust his hands in the pockets of his pants, walked over to the window, and stared at the ghost-like images of people moving around in an apartment on the other side of the compound. Their shadows were edged with an amber glow from lights within. Once, and it now seemed long ago, his life had been bathed in a golden glow—the protective world of a happy, secure family.

"Mitch," Natasha called. "Papa says he knows of an apartment we can have. He'll speak to someone first thing tomorrow morning. Isn't it exciting?"

Mitch turned from the window. She held her hands out to him. "We'll be able to afford it with my allowance and what you can earn in your spare time. Papa will help too." Her eyes sparkled with excitement.

It was all moving too fast. An ice-cold feeling gripped his stomach, his thoughts a strange mixture of relief that they would be able to get married and not be forced to live with the Lipovskys, and the sinking sensation that his whole life was spinning out of his grasp. If they would only give him time, he would figure out somewhere for them to live, a way to earn money. "We'll see," was all he said.

He refused the drink Lena offered him, mumbling that his parents were expecting him. As he put on his coat to leave, Natasha's brother arrived home. "Mitch, good to see you," Petya beamed. "You okay?"

"Don't ask, Petya. Don't ask." Mitch pulled the collar up on his coat.

"What's going on?" Petya looked from one to the other.

Natasha put an arm around Mitch's shoulders. "We're getting married," she beamed at her brother.

A grimace flickered across Petya's face.

"You must take care of her, my boy." Lyosha gripped Mitch's hand.

Mitch resisted remarking that that was precisely what he wanted to do if they would only give him a chance. The grip on his hand was too tight for comfort.

"And Mitch," Lyosha called after him as he pulled open the front door. "Don't worry about finding a priest. If it's what my precious girl wants, that won't be a problem. I know one who will marry you. I'll make it right with the Party."

CHAPTER SEVENTEEN

LENINGRAD—MAY 1984

A light drizzle washed the city streets. Mitch and Yuri sat in the back of the big black Volga, watching familiar sights slip past. "I could get used to travelling like this, couldn't you?" Yuri said, running his hand over the leather seats.

"Some chance." Mitch laughed nervously.

"Ask Natasha's father. He'll buy you a whole fleet of cars!"

Mitch scowled at Yuri. He had warned him not to say anything about the Lipovsky family. Mitch was unsure whether the driver worked for Natasha's father or maybe was a functionary for some other organization. You couldn't be too careful.

Bile rose in his throat and he took a couple of puffs of his cigarette. For the past couple of days, he had been unable to keep any food down. Natasha joked that she was the one who was supposed to feel sick, not him. Despite his mother's protests, for the last twenty-four hours or so he existed on a diet of black coffee, brandy, and cigarettes. Surely he shouldn't be feeling like this on his wedding day, but maybe all bridegrooms feel the same.

In the early hours of that morning, he had awoken drenched in sweat. The sound of laughter rang in his ears. His breath came in short gasps as he relived the dream. It was so real. Her hand was warm in his as he led her to a bed in a dimly lit room. They were both naked, and he watched as she lay back on the bed, holding out her arms. Her legs were spread wide and, as he moved toward her, a figure emerged from the shadows. It was shrouded in black, cheeks hollow, eyes sunken sockets. The skin hung in folds from its face, and wisps of black hair stood upright on the top of its head. Mitch tried to reach out, to stop it going near her, but a strange force held him back. The figure began to change. The cheeks puffed out, the skin darkened and shrank back into place, and the hair grew longer, thicker. "Vanya?" Mitch tried to put out a tentative hand. His arms felt locked to his sides. Then the laughter started; it came from nowhere and bounced around the room. Natasha's fingers clawed the air, a look of terror on her face. *"Nyet! Nyet!"* Mitch screamed as the figure climbed on top of her. Her limbs thrashed out and Mitch shouted, "Vanya! *Nyet! Nyet!* Leave her! Leave her alone!" Then she was still. The figure turned onto its back and crossed its arms across its chest. Vanya's face faded and all that remained were black garments hanging loosely over the bed. The laughter was still there.

Mitch had got out of bed, lit a cigarette, stumbled into the sitting room, and poured himself a drink. As it slid down his throat, he told himself it was just a nightmare brought on by pre-wedding nerves, worry over money. In the past few weeks, his whole life had been a nightmare. Instead of the feeling of relief he expected after they broke the news of Natasha's pregnancy, a black despondency settled on him. He hadn't been able to concentrate and was sure he had failed his exams. "It's not the end of the world, you can always retake them next year," Yuri said. But Mitch needed to earn money, and lots of it—his debts had reached frightening levels as he tried to keep up with Natasha's demands. His parents helped out but would be horrified if they knew the extent of his problems. Petya was right, Mitch couldn't afford her. But what could he do? He loved her more than he had ever thought it possible to love anyone. And there was the child … their child. He couldn't lose them both.

Now all he wanted was for the wedding festivities to be over. Today was the *Brakosochetaniye* ceremony at the *Zapis Aktov Grazhdanskogo Sostroyariya* (ZAGS) office, the obligatory civil registration. In three days, there would be a church service. Mitch couldn't understand why Natasha insisted on this. Religious beliefs were against those of the State, but her father had smoothed things over with Party officials (and undoubtedly bribed the powers that be) to give in to yet another of her demands. It seemed to Mitch that she was always looking for ways to challenge her father. He could understand if she was deeply religious or anti-Soviet—there was a growing movement among young people to rail against Soviet restrictions—but she wasn't. Natasha was carrying it too far … an excuse to spend more money, no doubt.

"Yura?" He turned now to his friend. "You haven't arranged any stunts, have you? My nerves won't take it."

Yuri grinned. "Relax. Weddings are supposed to be fun."

"I'll remind you of that on your wedding day."

"Married? Me? Why would I cut myself off from all those women out there? It wouldn't be fair to them!" He laughed loudly and brushed cigarette ash off the red sash that he wore, denoting his status as Mitch's best friend and witness.

The car slowed as it approached the security gates at Natasha's home. The guard nodded to the driver, and the gates swung open. Mitch looked up at the apartment building and groaned—a huge poster hung above the front entrance. "I'll kill Natasha's friends!" Despite the crudeness of the painting and the fact that some of the outlines had blurred with the rain, it was clearly meant to depict Mitch and Natasha sitting up in bed. Hovering over them was Lyosha, a picture frame in his hands that he was just about to bring down over Mitch's head. Mitch could only imagine the lewd joke that was written underneath—thankfully, the wording had run in the rain.

Averting his eyes from the poster, he got out of the car and ran up the front steps. Wedding etiquette demands that the groom collect the bride from her home, but before he can claim her, her friends put every obstacle in his way, asking devious questions, blocking staircases, and extracting cash if he fails to make the grade. "Aren't you glad she doesn't live in a high-rise block? It would take you all day to reach her!" Yuri quipped.

Natasha's friend, Marina, stood in the hallway, a red sash draped around the top half of her body. She held out six pictures of babies. Mitch had no difficulty identifying the young Natasha. The baby smiled up at him and he smiled back, a fractured smile. He slipped the picture into his jacket pocket, wondering whether their baby would look like her. By most standards, Mitch's rite of passage was easy. He danced, solved complicated enigmas, and sang a stupid song. As his voice rang out in the stairwell, he feared Natasha's father would appear and bark inanities at him; halfway through the song, his voice failed. He pressed some roubles into the hand of one of Natasha's friends, sprinted up the rest of the stairs and through the open doorway into the apartment. At the end of the corridor, he threw open Natasha's bedroom door, closed it behind him, and turned the key. She was standing in front of a window and turned to face him. The low neckline of her pink dress accentuated the fullness of her breasts. *"Krasivya ... Ya lyublyu tebya,"* he said and took her in his arms. The tension of the past weeks ebbed away.

Seconds later, what sounded like a hundred fists pounded on the door. Natasha took his arm and, amidst loud cheers from their friends, they walked into the corridor.

Outside, Mitch gave her a quick kiss before she got into the car that would take her to the ZAGS office. He glanced around, checking that his parents' car was in its place in the procession. Like the rest of the vehicles, it was decorated with balloons and ribbons. As they drove through the city, the rain stopped and the sun glinted on the stylized golden rings on top of the bride's car.

In the turquoise-painted room in the old palace, a well-worn recording of Tchaikovsky's *First Piano Concerto* crackled out of loudspeakers. On the ceiling high above, plump cherubs smiled down. As Mitch and Natasha walked to the front of the room, he averted his eyes from the bulky presence of Aleksei Aleksandrovich in the front row and looked instead at the grey-haired, black-suited official who stood before them. His red sash bore the emblem of the Russian Republic and the legend, "Proletarians of the World Unite." Mitch smiled nervously at Natasha as the official asked solemnly if they wanted to marry each other. Their voices affirmed in unison. Mitch took the gold wedding band the man handed him and placed it on Natasha's finger. Then he held out his right hand and she slipped his ring on. He stared at the glass of red carnations on the desk and listened to the impersonal voice of the official reciting the obligatory words: "The Executive Committee of the Soviet of Working People's Deputies of the city of Leningrad has empowered me to register the marriage of ..." Although it was their names that were read out, Mitch felt strangely detached; the whole tableau floated before him as though it was two other people who stood there.

Once the marriage papers were signed, the official spoke about the obligations of marriage and the need for mutual love and respect. "Do everything together, in happiness and in grief, in hope and in doubt, in defeat and in victory, in all family affairs." *Family affairs. We're a family now; no one can change that.*

The strains of Mendelssohn filled the room, and they shook the official's hand and took their internal passports in which their marriage had been registered.

The corridor was crowded with people waiting for the next ceremony as Mitch and Natasha's party made their way to the vestibule, where a celebratory glass of champagne awaited. Mitch watched from the sidelines as Natasha's friends presented her with flowers. When his mother's turn came, she gave her new daughter-in-law a spray of deep pink roses and kissed her on both cheeks. A surge of pride welled up in him; whatever their feelings, his parents always acted impeccably in public. It occurred to Mitch now that his father was a good-looking man—his almost-white hair added a softness to his wide cheekbones and high forehead. Sophia, elegant in a pale-grey dress and jacket, still had the slimness of youth. Mitch stepped toward them. "Mitch, darling," she said as she slipped an arm around his waist, "Papa and I ..." Her face contorted as she struggled to fight back the emotions that threatened to overwhelm.

"Maman, be happy for us," he said softly.

"We are. If this is what you want, then we are happy for you." Sergei put a hand on Mitch's shoulder and added, "For both of you."

Mitch held them in a silent embrace for a moment. "Now, where's the champagne?"

A short time later, Aleksei Aleksandrovich's voice boomed out. "Doesn't my Natashinka look beautiful?" He held Natasha's hand close to his chest and fondled her arm.

"She's especially beautiful today," Mitch replied.

"Now, my boy, you have to look after her."

"I will. Trust me." Mitch shifted from one foot to the other, wishing to God the wretched man would let go of Natasha's hand.

"If it was ..." Lyosha began.

"Lyosha. They have to get going." Lena's glass clattered onto the table.

Tradition demands that the bride and groom and a few chosen friends have pictures taken and lay flowers at memorials around the city. Although most couples pay homage at the statue of The Bronze Horseman in Senate Square, Mitch had made excuses to Natasha. "Everyone goes there. It'll be chaotic. Let's go somewhere quieter." She did not know the fear that rippled through his body whenever he approached Falconet's imposing memorial depicting Peter the Great seated on a rearing horse. Or the terrifying nightmares he had after Vanya's death—the pounding of hooves, the horse rearing on its hind legs, hovering over him. One day, not long after the nightmares stopped, Mitch picked up a book of Pushkin's poems. His heart raced as he read the words of the epic "The Bronze Horseman," in which the statue springs to life and pursues the lovelorn Evgenii through mist-shrouded streets. Just to think of it brought him out in a sweat.

On this their wedding day, they went first across the Palace Bridge to Vasilyevsky Island. Hand in hand, they stood before the Rostral Columns and gazed up at the ancient ships' prows studding the deep umber structures. At the Field of Mars, the air was heavy with the scent of lilacs as they knelt to lay a sheaf of white roses in front of the eternal flame. Mitch bowed his head. His thoughts were not only of the martyrs of the 1917 Revolution and the Civil War who were buried here. As the flame danced high, he prayed for the soul of Dmitriy Alexandrovich Galichin. Although Mitch had never known his grandfather, he had built up an image of him from Babushka's stories of his life—the life that was cut short in an alleyway during the dark days leading up to the Revolution. Now he added a silent plea, asking his grandfather to bless their marriage and their child.

CHAPTER EIGHTEEN

LENINGRAD - MAY 1984

Sophia stood just inside the entrance to the restaurant where Mitch and Natasha's wedding reception was starting to get underway. Judging by the bursts of loud voices coming from the room on the other side of the gilt-trimmed doors, many of the guests were already well into the alcohol. She looked at the pale-green walls and ornate white and pink porcelain architectural decoration of twisted columns, cherubs, and cameo medallions; she had always loved these great palaces, which were a reminder of the extravagance of Russia's Tsarist history and a welcome antidote to the greyness of Soviet life. Like the Russian peoples, many such buildings miraculously survived armed uprisings, blockades, and the Communist social experiment, rising from the ashes of disaster to what was always heralded a greater and more glorious age just around the corner. When the Bolsheviks nationalized the properties of the nobles and aristocrats, the room in which she stood would have been home to four families or more, with crude wooden screens and improvised curtains marking the amount of space allotted by official decree.

She and Sergei could never have imagined that one day their son's wedding celebration would be held in such a grand place. They had dreamed their dreams for Mitch's future—modest dreams in which he would marry a sensible young woman with old-fashioned values who loved him for his kind heart and innate sense of fairness. There would be grandchildren, family holidays, picnics, visits to the circus. She let out a gentle sigh and sat down on a chair, bracing herself for another barrage of words from Yelena Nicholaievna. She had already heard enough about Natasha's achievements to last a lifetime.

"And Sophia, you should have seen her when she walked onto the stage to receive the Sociology prize. That was one of our proudest moments. Lyosha said to me ..."

Sophia steadied the plate of traditional Bread and Salt of Happiness Cake where it rested on her knees. She hoped with all her heart that she and Sergei were wrong about their predictions for Mitch's future with Natasha. Their misgivings had taken hold when they had first dropped Mitch off outside the building where Natasha lived, and they had watched from the sidelines as their son was taken over by the Lipovsky family. Night after night, Sergei and Sophia lay awake discussing ways they might help. They suggested to Mitch that he and Natasha move in to part of their apartment; it was large enough for them all. Natasha would be able to continue studying and, more importantly, would be away from the influence of her parents. Mitch shook his head and told them that, although their idea made sense, Natasha's father had already paid the rent on an apartment, and Natasha and her mother had spent a lot of money securing furniture and other things.

Thank God she's found someone else to talk to, Sophia thought, glancing at Lena who was now in animated conversation with a grey-haired man in a dark suit. The cockade of royal blue feathers adorning her wide-brimmed hat bobbed up and down as she talked. Sophia supposed she would have to learn to tolerate the woman who was now Mitch's *tëshcha*. Not quite the mother-in-law she would have chosen for him.

In a strange way, Sophia admired Mitch's loyalty. Not a word of criticism passed his lips. But, oh, how she wished she could have her son back—the happy young man he was before he met Natasha. After his rebellious teenage years, he became content with life in small ways, studying and quietly planning his future. Now, each evening when they heard his key in the door lock, they braced themselves to pretend they were happy for him. It troubled them that their feelings were not genuine. In the past week, they reluctantly began to accept there was nothing they could do to change the situation. He was marrying Natasha, and soon there would be a baby, their grandchild.

Last weekend, both families had gone to the new apartment. Sophia and Sergei admired it all: the sofa, the dining room furniture, everything. They spoke optimistically, saying how much they looked forward to the arrival of their grandchild. On the way home in the car, Sergei told Mitch that they had put aside a sum of money in case he needed it. They hadn't revealed that it came from the proceeds of selling jewellery that Vera Alexandrovna had given Sophia as gifts over the years.

Now her eyes pricked with tears as she recalled her son's careworn face as he thanked them. She thought back to the boy he once was—always concerned about everyone else. She thought also of her own parents and of how, because of their opposition to her marriage outside their strict faith, they had missed out on the joys of a grandchild.

She gripped the plate tighter, remembering the day the letter from her mother had arrived, telling her of her father's death. Her sadness was tinged with joy that her mother wanted to see her again and to meet her only grandchild … joy that turned to anger and despondency as days passed trying to obtain exit visas. It would have been too late, anyway; she learned later that her dear *Muter* passed away before Sophia had received her letter.

"Oni zdes'! Oni zdes'!" Lena's voice cut through Sophia's reverie. She got to her feet and glanced over her shoulder to where Sergei stood. His face creased into an encouraging smile, and she felt the familiar flutter in her stomach as their eyes met. As Mitch and Natasha stepped through the doorway, Lena held out an icon and gave the traditional blessing to the young couple. Sophia swallowed hard and offered the cake. She was not going to miss a minute of her grandchild's life. There would still be family picnics and holidays. They would laugh at the antics of the clowns at the circus with Mitch and Natasha's child.

CHAPTER NINETEEN
LENINGRAD—MAY 1984

Three days after the *Brakosochetaniye* ceremony, a hush descended on the congregation in the church as Mitch and Natasha stood before the altar. The flame of the candle held by the priest cast an ethereal light on the veil over Natasha's face. Mitch looked at the band of flowers entwined with ribbon holding her hair in place, and then his gaze drifted to the folds of white lace draped over the bulge of her stomach. Their fingers touched as they wound around the base of the candle.

The priest's voice, intoning the blessings, ran like a mantra through Mitch's head. He thought back to the time years ago when his father brought him to a Russian Orthodox church. Sergei warned him that he mustn't tell anyone; it was their secret. "Religion isn't allowed," he explained.

"Like being a *zhid?*" Mitch asked.

His father ignored the question, telling him that people watch the churches and report to the Party. Mitch's eyes widened. *Spies,* he thought. "We'll risk it, just this once," his father had whispered as they crept through a side entrance and stood in the shadows. Mitch held his father's hand as bearded priests waved censers in the dusk of candlelight. He craned his neck to look up to the blue painted dome and the window where light streamed through. His father told him that the eight-sided dome was a symbol of the Russian star and represented the skies and heaven. "If you pray hard, your prayers will rise with the incense all the way to the very top of the dome and then to heaven." Mitch prayed as hard as he could, his head craned upwards. He saw the incense and hoped his prayers were there too. The young Mitch was untouched by the uneasy relationship between Church and State. For him, the church was a place of wonder and excitement as he watched ghost-like figures moving around, muttering, prostrating, and crossing themselves before the icons. He wanted to join them, to look at the little candles flickering in glasses, to peer into corners searching for spies. But his father gripped his hand firmly. Mitch moved his feet up and down, stretching his legs out stiffly in front of him, imagining he was a soldier marching in the parade.

Today, as Mitch and Natasha exchanged rings again, all the doubts and misgivings that had clouded his mind for the past few weeks faded. In this place, far removed from the restrictions of Soviet life, a new confidence came to him. He would sort out the financial mess. And what did it matter if her parents arranged everything? He and Natasha would be happy together with their baby.

He took Natasha's hand in his and bowed his head as they recited the prayer: "My bountiful God, I beseech Thee ... Foster between us the spirit of understanding and of peace, that no strife, quarrel, or misunderstanding may arise between us ..."

The voices of the choir began to float through the air, softly at first, as they sang the Nicene Creed. Then the powerful tones of the soloist seemed to lift the words upwards. "Begotten, not made, of one being with the Father ... Through him all things are made ..." Mitch thought of the new life growing within Natasha and vowed no harm would ever come to his son or daughter.

The liturgy ended and there was silence. Then the crowns were held above their heads by Marina and Yuri. As they sipped the symbolic cup of wine, Mitch and Natasha smiled at each other. From now on they would share their lives—the triumphs, the tribulations. They would meet them together.

The priest led them in procession around the sacramental table. Once, twice, three times. The final blessing passed as if in a dream, and then the voices of their families and friends filled the church as they wished Mitch and Natasha many years of blessings.

* * *

Some hours later, Mitch leaned over in the aircraft seat and looked at Natasha. She was pale and there were dark circles under her eyes. He still couldn't believe she was his wife. When he first saw her in the lecture hall, he had not even dared to hope for a date, let alone to spend the rest of his life with her. Looking back, it seemed he was a mere boy at the time. So much happened so fast. He had missed out on a stage in life—late-night drinking sessions, light-hearted dalliances, mad escapades. But that wasn't for him. He enjoyed having someone special for whom to care.

The noise of the aircraft engines droned in his ears as he recalled the look on his mother's face when he and Natasha arrived at the wedding reception three days ago. She seemed hesitant at first, but after they tasted the ceremonial Bread and Salt of Happiness Cake, she wished them happiness, good health, and prosperity in their new life together. Then she clasped him to her and whispered, "We'll always be there for you, Mitch."

Now he and Natasha were headed for England. Lately he had been obsessed by thoughts that this could be their chance to escape from the Soviet Union. They would bring their child up in a land where every movement wasn't controlled, and where he or she would be free to do or say whatever it wished. But that was fantasy. How could he leave his parents behind? "Be sure to come back," was his mother's tearful goodbye. The thought of never seeing them again was many times worse than living in that dismal society. He was embarrassed by the ease with which their exit permits were issued. *Why couldn't it have been as simple for Maman when she wanted to visit her own mother?* He knew the answer to that—Lyosha's contacts' palms had been greased.

The sound of the engine noise changed seconds before a voice came over the intercom advising passengers to return their seats to the upright position, replace tray tables, and fasten their seat belts to prepare for landing at London's Heathrow Airport. He stroked Natasha's cheek. "*Lyubov' maya.* Time to wake up."

Daylight had all but faded as the black cab whisked them away from the terminal building. Even in the dim light, everything looked bright. As they neared the centre of the city, lights shone in shop windows displaying a colourful array of clothes and other goods. Outside their hotel, Mitch counted out the unfamiliar money for the cab driver from the wad of currency Natasha had given him. It could only have come from her father. The check-in clerk was cheerful and polite as she handed them the key to their room and wished them a happy stay in London.

Mitch had never stayed in an hotel before, let alone one as luxurious as this. At first he walked around their room scared to touch anything. That night in their canopied bed, he dismissed the thought that Lyosha, or his cronies in London, were picking up the bill. *We're here now, and I might as well make the most of it,* he thought as he took Natasha in his arms. Their lovemaking was gentle. Afterwards, they lay together, skins touching, no need for words. He shifted his arm from underneath her neck and let her head fall back gently on the pillow. She was already asleep but stirred as he touched her breasts and then her softly rounded stomach; her figure had blossomed with the growing life inside her. In less than five months they would be parents.

Sleep eluded him, and in the early hours of the morning he turned on the bedside light. His eyes strayed to the panelled walls, following the intricate, painted design. He counted the decorative plates hanging on a wall—from one to seven—several times before shifting his attention to the small paintings arranged in a group of four. His feet sank into the carpet as he went closer to get a better view of the scenes depicted by the artist. They were all of country houses, if the surrounding greenery was anything to go by. In the bathroom, he leaned his hands on the marble countertop and looked in the etched mirror. He breathed in deeply. *You can never give her all this,* he told his reflection as he breathed out.

At breakfast the next morning, Mitch looked around at the men in dark suits, the women dressed in smart outfits. He studied the menu, uncertain what to order—there was so much choice.

Natasha was in good form. The morning sickness of earlier weeks had disappeared, leaving her with an enormous appetite. "These croissants are good, Mitch," she enthused, reaching for another from the napkin-covered basket.

Mitch put a chunk of croissant in his mouth. As he chewed, he recalled the taste of the *pain au chocolat* at the *Pâtisserie* in Montréal—the rich chocolate, the flakes of pastry on his fingers, how his mother laughingly scolded him for making a mess. For the past few years, those thoughts had been exiled to the place in his mind where he was afraid to go.

"What are we going to do today? We must go to Harrods. You won't believe that place, Mitch."

"I thought a walk in the park would be more your sort of thing," he joked.

"Later. We'll do that later."

They didn't have their walk in the park. By the time they got back to the hotel, they were exhausted. From where he was slumped in an armchair, Mitch looked out at the leafy canopy of trees lining the wide street. The traffic was at a standstill: shiny, sleek cars, huge trucks, their sides advertising a variety of unfamiliar products and services. In the stores, Mitch had been unable to take in the array of goods, the ease with which transactions were conducted without endless lineups. The bed was now littered with an assortment of bags containing shoes, makeup, sweaters. He had given thanks to God that Natasha was pregnant and most of the clothes she looked at wouldn't fit.

During the next few days, the unbounded energy of youth and love propelled them like a whirlwind around the sights of London. They fed the pigeons in Trafalgar Square, watched the changing of the guard at Horse Guards Parade, and peered hopefully through the railings of Buckingham Palace for a glimpse of the Queen—she was there, the flag hoisted aloft told them so. Early one evening, they walked hand in hand through St. James's Park; the gold-tinged light turned the lake to a rainbow of colours. They saw the ravens and the Beefeaters at the Tower of London. Natasha's eyes lit up at the sight of the Crown Jewels; Mitch steered her quickly out into the sunlight. He chased her along the Embankment, making loud ghoulish noises as she wove in and out of the iron posts, her screams of mock terror shrill in the warm, early summer afternoon. Passersby stopped to stare, but Mitch and Natasha inhabited their own world, the world of lovers.

On their last afternoon in London, they wandered through the John Lewis store, picking up garments, some so tiny it was unbelievable they would fit even the smallest baby. They bought a jacket in the softest white wool and a primrose and white cot blanket sprinkled with animal shapes. The blanket was a gift from Mitch's parents.

They left the hurly-burly of the city behind for the coastal villages and hauntingly beautiful Suffolk countryside. The tranquil setting of the Tudor-era hotel outside Woodbridge, which Sergei's friend had recommended, was a breath of fresh air for Mitch. Not so for Natasha. "What do people find to do in this place? It's so quiet. My father would hate it here. And my mother? She would go crazy!" Mitch felt strangely content.

On their last day, from the garden of a riverside pub, they watched boats bobbing at their moorings. Mitch had developed a taste for the local Adnams ale, but only allowed himself one pint—he needed all his concentration to drive around the sharp bends and narrow lanes. After lunch, as they headed toward Bawdsey Point, sunlight flickered, dappling the front of the car with the distorted patterns of leaves. Through the trees, Mitch caught a glimpse of dark shapes pointing out over the North Sea. He pulled the car into the side of the road. They were missiles, like the ones paraded in Red Square on May Day each year. These were aimed at the Soviet Union, at his family. For a moment, the sunshine disappeared.

Later, he sat on the sea wall and watched Natasha picking her way over the pebbles along the edge of the water. Waves broke in foaming cascades around her bare feet. He looked at a ship on the horizon. Beyond that was the land they called home.

CHAPTER TWENTY

LENINGRAD—OCTOBER 1984

Mitch swallowed the last mouthful of his lunchtime sandwich, retrieved a metal token from the loose change in his pocket, reached for the pay phone on the wall in the corridor, and dialled. The ringing tone purred in his ear, and he took a couple of paces, stretching the telephone cord to its limit. There were still a few stragglers hurrying toward the lecture hall. If she answered now, he might make it before Professor Petrov began. "Come on, Natasha. For Christ's sake, answer," he urged through gritted teeth. *I should have stayed home,* he told himself. The baby was due any day.

"These lectures are important, Mitch, if you're ever going to qualify," she'd insisted. She was right. He had failed all but one of his exams last year and was lucky he hadn't been thrown out. He was now retaking most of the previous year's syllabus and, to make extra money, working evenings in a *ryumochnaya* serving alcohol to people who had already drunk too much. Studying late into the night, he found it difficult to concentrate, but he didn't have much choice if he was ever going to graduate.

"Chort!" he cursed now, banged the receiver cradle up and down a couple of times, and dialled his parents' number. "Maman ..."

"Mitch! Thank God you called," his mother blurted out. "We've been trying to get you, but we didn't know which lecture you were in. Papa rang ..."

"What's wrong?"

"It's Natasha. The baby. It's on the way. It started just after you left this morning. Her mother drove her to the hospital. We waited here in case you called."

"I'm on my way." He slammed down the phone, grabbed his bag, and scooped his coat off the hook as he ran to the exit.

Twenty minutes later, he shifted noisily through the gears of the car—to be more accurate, his father's car—and slowed to a halt. He could see the hospital building in the distance over the tops of the sea of vehicles spread out before him. *Must be an accident,* he thought. *It's never like this.* "Come on! Come on!" he urged, drumming the steering wheel. *What if something's gone wrong and Natasha's ... Don't think about it,* he told himself. The traffic crept forward and he yanked the steering wheel sharply to the right, forced his way between two cars in the nearside lane, mounted the curb, and accelerated into a side street. He parked the car in the first available space, grabbed his coat from the back seat, and dashed across the road.

Pedestrians halted their steps to let him pass as he ran. His shouts of "*Propusti menya!* My wife's having a baby. I have to get there," produced an unfamiliar air of gaiety on the street. Passersby sped him on his way with cries of "Good luck!" or "God bless the child."

A toothless old babushka grabbed his arm. "Look after them, young man," she cautioned, a smile crinkling her wizened face.

"I will. I will." He waved a hand and continued his haphazard path along the main thoroughfare. Despite the chill in the air, he was sweating. He skidded to a halt in front of a flower seller, grabbed two bunches of pink and white flowers, and paced up and down while the woman sorted out the change from the deep pocket of the green apron she wore over her coat. Inside the hospital entrance, he yelled to the woman behind the desk, "Where's the maternity ward?"

"First floor. Take the stairs to the right," she called after him. "But they won't let you in. Fathers aren't allowed."

The nurse who met him at the entrance to the ward hardly looked old enough to have left school. "My wife, Natasha," he blurted out. "Nataliya Alekseevna Galichina. Where is she?" His heart was racing and he bent down to try to get his breath back.

"Your wife and your daughter are fine."

Mitch jerked upright and stared at her, his mouth wide open. "My daughter?"

"Yes, a baby girl. Born ..." She checked her watch. "Just over an hour and a half ago. It all happened quickly."

Mitch swallowed hard. *A baby girl? A daughter.* "Are they ... are they all right?

"They're both fine."

"Can I see them?"

"If it was up to me, I'd let you in. But it's the rules."

Mitch thrust the flowers toward her. "Can you give these to her ... my wife?"

She took the flowers, turned on her heel, and headed into the ward.

He lingered for a few minutes, staring at the door. *A girl, my little girl, she's just through there.* He took a few steps and peered through the glass in the top half of the door. The nurse was checking a chart at the bottom of a bed. Then she swished the curtains around the bed and disappeared behind them. He opened the door and listened. There didn't seem to be any other staff around, so he tiptoed down the middle of the aisle, his head swivelling from side to side until he found Natasha's bed. She was asleep, arms stretched out on top of the bedclothes, strands of hair fanned across the pillow. He edged toward the cradle at the side of the bed. His daughter's face peeped out of the swaddling blanket. Her eyes were closed, and he reached out and stroked the side of her forehead. Dark eyelashes lay like strands of silk on her cheeks. As he pulled the blanket away with one finger, a fleeting grimace creased her face. At that moment, a patient called for a nurse. "My precious girl," he whispered to the baby, blew a hurried kiss to the sleeping Natasha, and scurried out of the ward.

Later, sitting in an armchair at his parents' home, he tried to describe the perfection of his daughter's features. "You should see her. She has the sweetest face, the darkest hair."

"Oh, darling, I'm so excited. I can't wait to see her," his mother enthused. "I have lots of baby clothes packed away. I didn't dare give them to you before. I was so afraid something would happen and ..."

"She's spent weeks scouring the shops for fabric, yarn. Sewing, knitting," Sergei cut in. "Now what about some wine?" He rose from his chair.

"Oh, what a happy day this is!" Sophia grinned.

Mitch hadn't seen his mother so relaxed since before he broke the news of Natasha's pregnancy to them.

"Why don't you stay here tonight, Mitch?" she suggested. "You can eat with us. I don't like to think of you on your own."

"Thanks. I'll come back here after work. I should call the hospital to give them the telephone number."

"Not yet." His father poured wine into three glasses. "We have to toast our granddaughter. And your daughter, of course."

"To Anja Sophia ..." Mitch began.

"Didn't you talk about naming her after the little girl Natasha looked after?" his mother interjected. "Mashen'ka?"

"Natasha thought it might bring the child bad luck." Mitch didn't tell them that, in truth, Natasha hadn't mentioned the girl for months. He often wondered where she ended up. Probably lying in a cot in some institution, forgotten.

"But the baby ... she should use her patronymic."

Mitch shrugged his shoulders at his father's suggestion. "What's the point in calling her Mitchellevna, or whatever? Mitch isn't a Russian name." *I got along without a patronymic,* he added to himself. "Anja Sophia will be nice. More modern." He clinked glasses with his parents and said, "Anja Sophia."

PART THREE

CHAPTER TWENTY-ONE

LENINGRAD—JANUARY 1986

Mitch paced up and down the corridor outside Vanya's mother's rooms and then banged on the door again. *There must be something wrong. I should have come here before, checked on them,* he berated himself. He had only visited once since Anja was born fifteen months ago. There never seemed to be time.

After eventually graduating from law school, he had accepted the position in the Legal Bureau to which he was assigned, closed his mind to corruption within the court system, and swallowed angry words when criticized by the Party that his legal defence was not within the boundaries of appropriate Communist behaviour. *What do these blockheads know of 'appropriate Communist behaviour'?* he ranted to himself.

The door creaked open and he was relieved to see Tatiyana Ruslanovna. She was wearing an overcoat, fingerless gloves, and a shawl wrapped around her shoulders. As Mitch entered the tiny space that was her kitchen, he exclaimed, "It's freezing in here!" Ice coated the inside of the window.

"The heating, no one can fix it," she said, gripping the shawl together with the fingers of one hand.

"Surely someone can do something. You can't live like this."

"No one cares about the likes of us!" Tatiyana spat. She filled the kettle, put it on one of the already lit burners on the stove, and sank down onto a wooden chair at the table. "What does it matter?" She shrugged.

"But it ..."

"It's my Klavdiya. My Klasha. She has gone." Over the next few minutes she told him that Klavdiya, who was now fifteen, had disappeared. She had gone to work for a family in Greece. "It was just for a few months, to earn money for us. She's been gone six months." Her voice began to tremble. "I haven't heard from her."

"How ... how did she get permission to leave?" As soon as he uttered the words, he knew how stupid it sounded. Someone had fixed it.

"A woman, Klasha said, she was outside the school. She said she could get her a good job, lots of money, looking after children. She would arrange everything."

"This woman ... did you meet her?"

"She came here one day. She knew some of the local people. People I know. She has an office, an employment agency."

A feeling of dread washed through Mitch. He had heard similar stories over the past months.

"Not even a letter." Tatiyana Ruslanovna shook her head and explained that last week she had gone to the woman's office but was told that Klavdiya disappeared during the journey. "Gone off with a boy she met, that's what she said." She paused and wiped her eyes with the back of a glove. "Not my Klasha; she is a good girl."

Half an hour later, Mitch entered the office, the address of which Tatiyana Ruslanovna had given him. "She ran off. Met a young man," the tight-lipped woman told him. "When the ship docked, she disappeared."

"She wouldn't do such a thing. I know her. She would never run off without telling her mother."

"You don't know these girls. They take the first chance that comes along," the woman smirked.

A door opened and a thick-set man appeared. His head looked almost square and seemed to mould into his neck. He wore a black tracksuit, and Mitch's mouth went dry as he saw the tattoos on the back of both hands. *Vory!* The *vory v zakone* originated in Stalinist prison camps, and acceptance into the group was often marked by extensive tattooing, chronicling the member's criminal career. "What she has told you is right." The *vor's* words were slow, deliberate. "We are the victims here." He thumped his chest with his right fist. "We are the ones who should be complaining. We have lost money." He glared at Mitch.

Mitch's body gave an involuntary shudder as he looked into piercing dark eyes. He opened his mouth to speak, but the man cut him off with a hefty push to his shoulders.

"Tell the girl's mother (another push) that if she doesn't stop making trouble, we will pay her a visit."

The next shove sent Mitch reeling backwards. His arms flailed wildly as he struggled to regain his balance. Then a hand gripped his left arm so tightly that he yelled out. The man pulled open the door and flung him into the corridor. Mitch bounced off the far wall, juddering every bone in his body. The man lunged toward him again. As Mitch ran, jeers of "Mother fucker!" followed him down the corridor and out of the building.

CHAPTER TWENTY-TWO

LENINGRAD—JANUARY 1986

Two weeks later, Mitch faced Yuri across a table in the *stalovaya*; Mitch was now in the habit of eating at these canteens, which serve cheap, basic food. "Come on," Yuri cajoled. "It'll be good experience, and there are thousands of people out there who have no one else to turn to. Are you going to ignore them?"

Mitch stared at the murky liquid, which passed for coffee, in his cup.

"All I'm asking you to do is sit in an office for a couple of hours, once or twice a week, and give people advice. Where's ..."

"Free advice," Mitch interjected. "I can't even find time for Professor Nekrassov's work. I need an extra job ... a paid job ... Yuri. In case you haven't noticed, I have a wife and child to support."

"Tell Natasha to get a job."

Mitch snorted. Natasha had dropped out of school before Anja was born and spent her days harping on about things they couldn't afford. Hardly a day passed that they didn't hurl insults at each other. The fault was often his, he knew that. He was exhausted, and her constant whining pushed him over the edge.

Mitch's evening job at the *ryumochnaya* had ended, and he had tried to make up his lost earnings by seizing every chance of earning money on the side. His last job was hauling dry goods in a warehouse. He suspected the proceeds of the sale of the sacks of beans and flour he loaded onto a truck found their way into the pockets of the manager and some of the other staff. Mitch worried that he might be implicated in the scam. A year or so ago, the former director of the best-known food store in Moscow was executed for economic crimes. One morning last week, the *militsiya* stormed into the warehouse and carried out a random check to ensure people were in their place of work during working hours. Mitch, who had rung in sick to his office, hid behind a mound of sacks on the upper level. When he heard the stomp of boots on the staircase, he feared his heart would stop. After they left, he fled from the building. He never went back.

For Yuri, life was different. He graduated early and was now picking up lucrative cases. Mitch suspected that the successful outcomes of the trials Yuri was involved in were influenced by bribery and inside information. It was risky business, especially with recent Party attacks on corruption within the justice system. Although Mitch thought this was a step in the right direction, he worried about his friend. The public prosecutor in Kirgizia had been sentenced to death for soliciting bribes.

"Look at it this way," Yuri's voice cut into Mitch's thoughts, "you'd be doing the type of work you've always wanted—admittedly for free at the start—but you'd be getting a foot in the door in my office. When you've finished your internship, I may be able to fix it for you to join us."

Mitch shook his head. "I couldn't do your sort of work. It would stick in my gut to defend those scum."

"Wherever you work, you'll end up doing that."

"Natasha would never agree to me working for nothing."

"Don't tell her."

"Like she's not going to ask where I am!"

"Tell her … tell her it's a way of getting experience and earning more money later," Yuri urged. "Then she can have all the things she wants—the new refrigerator, jewellery, holidays. Those scum, as you call them, have influence with the right people. There's no end to the things you can get."

Mitch pondered for a few minutes. She might buy that story. And he didn't have to take the job at Yuri's office. In the meantime, he'd be doing something worthwhile.

"What happened to all your … what was it Natasha's father called them … fine ideals?"

Fine ideals? They belonged in another world. A world where he had vowed to stand up for people's rights. People like the Cherkasovs—Vanya, his father, and now Klavdiya. A couple of days ago, Tatiyana Ruslanovna's neighbour told him she had left. "Gone to Siberia to be closer to her husband," the woman whispered. "He's all she has left. I promised to keep a look out for the child in case she comes back." Mitch remained silent. Since his brush with the thug at the so-called employment agency, he had done some digging. There were many reports of young girls from poor families being lured to Greece, Italy, Turkey, and elsewhere, with the promise of well-paid jobs as child-minders, waitresses, or the like. He couldn't bear to think that Klavdiya had ended up in the prostitution racket. There wasn't anything he could do for Klavdiya, but maybe there were others out there he could help.

While Yuri was fetching more coffee, Mitch recalled the tales his father had told him of how Babushka Ira and Dedushka Dima had risked their lives in Petrograd helping others during the run-up to the Revolution. *And Dedushka paid with his life,* Mitch thought bitterly. Would that happen to him too? Didn't he just want a quiet life being happy with Natasha and Annushka? But would he ever be happy with Natasha? He knew the answer to that: the only way to keep her happy was to earn a lot of money. And the only way he could earn a lot of money would be to become like her father and thousands like him, who use any means of corruption or influence to get what they want.

But was he going to let his daughter grow up thinking her Papochka had compromised his principles, didn't care about people? By then he would be so caught up in the lifestyle Natasha loved, he wouldn't even remember he once had principles. He would have forgotten Vanya and the multitide of other Vanyas that he would never know.

Yuri put their cups down on the table. "I don't know how you drink this stuff." He pulled a small bottle of brandy out of his pocket and poured a liberal dose into each. "Well, Mitch, will you do it or not? It's just a few hours a week."

Mitch stared at the table, his eyes following the cracks in the wood, the deep indentations that must have been there before he was born. At times he wished he had never been born, or that he had been born in another time to another family. He took a gulp of his drink. "I'll give it a go," he said. "I'll tell Natasha tonight."

* * *

He didn't tell Natasha that evening. As he opened the door to the apartment, he heard the voice of his father-in-law. "Anja Yelena," Lyosha called. A reminder of yet another battle Mitch had lost—that of his daughter's name. Mitch dropped his bag onto a chair, pulled off his boots, hung his coat in the closet, and brushed snow off his hair with his fingers. "I'm coming to find you," Lyosha laughed. Mitch heard his daughter giggle and then she toddled through the doorway, elbows jabbing from side to side, body swaying unsteadily in her haste to hide from her Dedushka. She was wearing a red dress and matching shoes, none of which Mitch had seen before.

"Papochka ... Papochka," she called and ran toward him. Mitch bent down, gripped her under her arms, and swung her into the air. Her laughter, a mix of excitement and fear, was infectious, and he chuckled out loud. After a second or two, he lowered her onto one arm and rubbed her nose with his. "And what's my sweet girl been doing today?" Her answer was a wet kiss on his cheek.

"Anja, come and finish your tea. Mama has jelly." It was Natasha who spoke. She tightened the white ribbon that held Anja's mop of brown corkscrew curls off her face. "Where have you been?" she hissed, taking the child from Mitch. "I told you my parents were going to be here."

If she had, he had forgotten.

It was late when Yelena and Lyosha left. "Anja's gone off at last," Mitch said as he closed the hallway door softly.

"What a day!" Natasha sighed and kicked off her high-heeled black shoes. The tablecloth was coated with clumps of orange jelly; she gathered a few into a haphazard pile and then stooped to pick up cake crumbs from the rug.

"Leave it. I'll get up early and do it," Mitch offered. She straightened up and rubbed the small of her back with one hand. He put his arms around her and pulled her close; he could feel her heart beating through the tight-fitting, pink wool dress. "Why don't you run a bath," he murmured. "I'll open the bottle of wine your father brought." She drew away and he watched as she walked to the door. The brown leather belt accentuated her small waist and trim hips. Unlike many of her contemporaries, she hadn't let herself go after childbirth. *One advantage of her obsession with clothes,* he supposed.

She turned in the doorway and narrowed her eyes at him. "Don't be long."

He picked up Anja's cloth doll from where it was sprawled across one of the dining room chairs, wiped a smear of jelly from its face with his handkerchief, and carried it through to the kitchen, where he sat it on the tray on his daughter's chair at the table.

Outside, snow was still falling, and he could see the caretaker, Vyacheslav Ilyavich, bent almost in half, shovelling a mound of snow that had drifted across the entrance to the archway. *Poor sod! And I think I have a hard life.* During the time they had lived here, Mitch had become fond of Slava. He was always there when help was needed, moving furniture or other jobs Mitch couldn't manage on his own. He was astonished at the strength of the seemingly frail old man. One afternoon before Anja was born, Slava and Rodnina welcomed Mitch and Natasha into their home for tea. Natasha shifted uncomfortably in the armchair with its loose covering of faded fabric; her critical gaze took in the bed in the corner, the small table with its covering of oilcloth, and a wooden chair either side. Mitch felt strangely calm in the cramped room. Whatever the shortages and hardships outside, elderly Russians seemed to be able to instil a feeling of warmth in their homes.

Slava was now resting an arm on his shovel, a hand holding his back as he stretched. The old man looked up and waved. Mitch returned the greeting and then closed the curtains. He reached for the bottle of red wine, rummaged in a drawer for the corkscrew, pulled the cork out, and poured wine into two glasses. He thought back to his conversation with Yuri. He would have to tell Natasha about the *pro bono* work. But not tonight.

* * *

A week later, he knew he had left it too late to tell Natasha himself.

"And when were you going to tell me?" she yelled before he had the chance to take off his coat.

"Tell you what?"

"That you're working at that place where Yuri works. For nothing!" she threw at him. "Tell me it's not true, Mitch."

He didn't answer.

She shook her head. "How is it you can always find time for other people but never for Anja and me? Do other people count more than us? Is that how it is?"

"You know it isn't. Let's just sit down and talk. I'll ..."

"Talk? I didn't think we talked any longer. How do you think I felt having to learn from Tonya that you were working for free?" Her voice had risen to crescendo.

"Mamochka ... Mamochka," Anja whined as she toddled toward them.

Mitch stepped forward and bent down to pick her up, but her arms were already bound tightly around one of Natasha's legs.

"Leave her! I'll see to her." Natasha brushed his hands away and scooped Anja into her arms. "It's okay, baby. Mama's not cross with you, just that nasty Papa."

"Natasha! That's not fair!"

"Fair? You're a fine one to talk about what's fair." Her eyes blazed at him as she cradled the side of her daughter's head and snuggled it into her neck. "Shhhh, shhhh," she soothed and began to walk up and down the hallway. "I made out I already knew," she shot at Mitch as they came level with him. "My mother and Tonya's mother were there too."

Chort! Mitch could picture the imperious, all-knowing look on his mother-in-law's face.

"Can you imagine how humiliated I felt having someone tell me what my husband is up to?"

"It isn't like you think," he began.

"My father's as mad as hell with you," she cut him off. Anja stared at Mitch with an accusing eye as she held on to a strand of her mother's hair. "He says you'll be in trouble with the *militsiya*. One day you'll disappear, and we'll never hear of you again." She bit her lip, fighting back tears as she walked into the sitting room, put Anja down on the sofa, and sank into the seat beside her. "What are you thinking of? Don't you care about us?"

He shifted Anja to one side and sat down. "Of course I care." He tried to take Natasha's hand. She brushed him away.

"I gave up my career for you," she sniffed.

Mitch bit back words of dissent. "I know I should have told you," he said. "I didn't mean for you to find out like that. I knew you'd be upset." Natasha glared at him. "Justifiably upset," he added quickly. "But it isn't what you think. Doing this work," he swallowed the words *for free* "will put me in good stead with the people in Yuri's office. With any luck, Yuri will be able to persuade them to take me on when I've finished my three-year stint at the Bureau."

"And you expect me to believe that?"

"It's true," he protested. There was silence for a moment or two before he continued. "It'll be worth it. You'll see. I'll be earning a lot of money, and you can have all the things you want without us having to rely on your father for money."

"And what's wrong with that?" she snapped. "It gives him a lot of pleasure buying me things."

"But I want to look after you and Anja. How do you think I feel when he buys you things I can't afford?" She didn't reply. "I'll tell you how I feel. I feel like a fucking idiot!"

"Sledi za bazarom!"

"You'll never understand, not in a million years." He sighed loudly. "What's happened to you, Natasha? You used to want to help people, people like Mashen'ka and the other kids. Or have you forgotten them?"

"I don't want to hear about them," she interjected, twisting a handkerchief in her fingers. "It's always other people, never us!"

Anja was now climbing over Mitch's legs, reaching out to her mother. Her words, "Nasty Papochka, nasty Papochka," ran like a mantra through his head.

"Annushka, baby," he said, clasping her around her waist with one arm and rising awkwardly to his feet. She squirmed as he tried to hold her. Then she went stiff and held her breath. *"Khorosho! Khorosho!"* he said, lowering her onto her mother's lap. At the doorway he looked around and met Natasha's scowl.

CHAPTER TWENTY-THREE

LENINGRAD—SEPTEMBER 1986

The man was young, but his sunken eyes held the sorrows of an old man. Mitch and Yuri shifted forward in their chairs and leaned across the desk, struggling to hear his words.

"She ... she left ... a year ago." The man's shoulders hunched and he moved his head nervously from side to side, his eyes searching, as though fearing someone would creep up on him.

"Who? Who are you talking about?" Yuri's words sounded abrupt, and he paused for a moment before softening his tone. "We're here to help you, but we need to know what the problem is," he cajoled.

The man turned away, cuffing tears that brimmed in his eyes.

"Your name would help," Mitch murmured.

He looked at Mitch from under hooded lids and muttered, "Timochenko."

Mitch wondered what had happened to cause so much pain in one so young. He had been loitering in the shadows of the doorway when they arrived at Yuri's office. It was Saturday afternoon, and apart from the receptionist, who spent most of her time primping her hair, they were alone. "Take your time. There's only Yulia in the outside office. No one else will come in."

"My sister ... Anzhelika. She left a year ago." Timochenko gulped and shifted in his seat before continuing. "It was to have been her dream job. A waitress in a restaurant in Turkey."

Mitch closed his eyes for a moment, wishing he could shut out what he knew the young man was going to say.

"That's what the woman at the employment agency told her. She was so excited. She and her friend. They travelled together." The last three words were barely audible, and he paused to compose himself. "We warned her to be careful. We had heard stories of girls lured away from home, but she wouldn't listen. 'Stanislav, don't be an old worrier.' That's what she said. 'I have seen pictures of the restaurant. It is by the sea. Nastja and I will be able to go to the beach on our days off.'" A brief smile drifted across his face. "She had never been to a beach.

And we needed the money she would send home. My father is sick, and there is Mama and the young ones." Timochenko's chin sank on to his chest.

Mitch noticed the frayed collar of his shirt, the threadbare fabric of his jacket. After a few moments, Mitch broke the silence. "And you haven't seen her again."

Timochenko shook his head. "At first we waited for a letter. Nastja's mother visited us every week. They didn't hear either. After about two months, I went to the employment agency. They said they didn't have any record of either of them. Never heard of them. They said they never recruit girls that young ... she was fifteen."

Mitch felt a tightness in his chest.

"So you are trying to find her?" It was Yuri who spoke.

"We know where she is. A place called Antalya. Her friend, Nastja, came back three weeks ago. She told us that when they arrived there, the two of them and the other girls who had travelled with them were locked in a room. She said ..." His voice broke up and he pursed his lips in an effort to control himself. "She said they were guarded by men who threatened them if they didn't do what they were told. Nastja had cigarette burns on her arms. The men said that if they didn't submit to 'training' ..." He took a loud breath.

"Take your time," Mitch said.

"If they didn't submit to 'training,' their families would suffer."

"You want us to help get your sister back?"

"There was no restaurant. She's working in a ... a strip club. A brothel." Timochenko put his elbows on the desk, the fingers of both hands laced together, his knuckles white.

In the silence that followed, Mitch sought for words that wouldn't dash Timochenko's hopes. The smuggling rings were part of an international criminal network whose members grew fat on the proceeds of prostitution. Penalties for human trafficking were far less than those for smuggling drugs or cigarettes, and many law officers took bribes to turn a blind eye, arresting those who threatened to expose the racket, or beating them senseless. Since Vanya's sister, Klavdiya, disappeared, he hadn't dared let his mind dwell on the horror. And now, Anzhelika. Fifteen ... the same age as Klavdiya. Children. And how many others like them? He felt a coldness in his gut and could almost taste the fear of one so young forced to endure indescribable acts of sexual deviance, smell the rankness of the bodies smothering their innocence. He clenched his fists as he thought of his daughter's tiny body, the dark curls on her forehead. *If anyone did that to her, I'd kill them!*

"So where is this Nastja?" Yuri ventured.

"After she escaped, she hid here in the city. Her parents took me to see her. I barely recognized her. She was always such a beautiful girl, always laughing." His breath came in short, laboured bursts; his chest wheezed. "She told me that Anzhelika had been too frightened to go with her, to escape." He gripped his hands in his lap and looked down at them before continuing. "After we left, some people broke into the place where Nastja was hiding. When her father and I went back the next day, we found her. She was sprawled across the bed ..." His voice broke and he wrapped his arms around his body. Mitch pulled out a packet of cigarettes and lit one. He offered it to Timochenko. He shook his head.

Yulia's voice drifted through from the front office; it sounded as though she was gossiping with one of her friends on the telephone.

"Her throat ... it was cut." Timochenko's words were barely audible.

Mitch got to his feet. He paced back and forth. Once or twice he caught Yuri's eye but turned away quickly. This was something each of them had to decide for himself. A vision of Klavdiya came into his mind. It was one summer, and the sun picked out burnished copper tinges in her hair as she ran along the street toward him. An innocent child. *Has she ended up like Anzhelika? Nastja?* He took a long drag on the cigarette. "You realize we'd be taking a huge risk if we get involved."

"I don't have any money." Timochenko's words hung in the air.

"*Nyet! Nyet!* We don't ask for money. That's not the problem." Yuri's voice sounded strained.

"A friend of Nastja's mother ... she said you might be able to ..."

"Listen," Mitch interrupted, "these thugs have everything covered. *Militsiya*, immigration officials—they're all on their payroll. It's a dangerous organization."

"We could try to buy your sister back," ventured Yuri.

"With what?" Mitch snapped.

Yuri shrugged. "Look, why don't you leave it with us for a few days? We'll talk it over and see if there is any way we can help."

"I didn't know where else to go. I have to do something," Timochenko's voice trailed off.

"We'll see what we can do." Yuri stood up and walked around the desk. Timochenko got to his feet, pulled his jacket around his chest, and gripped it with the fingers of one hand. He looked first at Yuri and then at Mitch. Mitch turned away. "Come back the same time next week. I'm sure we can work something out," Yuri cajoled as he led Timochenko out.

"Are you crazy?" Mitch yelled when Yuri came back into the room. "We'd never get an extradition order through official channels. You know as well as I do that no one wants to get involved. Governments won't even acknowledge that this sort of thing goes on inside their borders."

Yuri shrugged. "What was I supposed to tell him? His sister's probably dead already?"

"And what difference is a week going to make?" Yuri didn't answer. "They're murderers, sadists."

"It's risky, but ..."

"It would be suicide to take on something like this."

"Are we going to give up without even trying?"

Mitch stabbed his cigarette out in the ashtray, remembering his encounter with the *vor* with the piercing eyes. "Yuri ... we can't take on the *mafiyosa, vory.* We can't." As he spoke, his inner voice nagged: *If you're scared, what must it be like for Klavdiya or Timochenko's sister?*

Yuri paced around the room and then stopped in front of where Mitch was slumped in a chair. "There must be an international organization that can help. We don't have to get directly involved, just find out if there's some group or other working on this sort of thing." Yuri waved a hand toward the doorway through which Timochenko had left. "We have to give him some hope."

Yuri's words were a jumble to Mitch, his mind a chaotic mix of conflicting thoughts. *Your first allegiance must be to Anja,* he told himself. *But can you just stand by and do nothing ... knowing this goes on?* He tried to blot out Natasha's father's words of warning: *One day you'll disappear and we'll never hear of you again.*

"What if it was Anja?"

"Leave her out of this!" Mitch yelled. He leapt to his feet and grabbed his jacket off the back of a chair in the corner. "It's not her!"

"But it could be one day. How would you feel then?"

"And what good will it do if I end up dead in the river ... trying to help people I don't know?"

"They're not just people. They're kids. Like yours."

Mitch shook his head. "I've too much to lose, Yuri."

"And they haven't? Don't they deserve a chance in life?

Mitch didn't answer. He needed to get away, to think things out on his own. "I have to go. I promised Natasha ..."

"Natasha! Natasha! Always Natasha!"

* * *

In the week that followed, Mitch was haunted by visions of young girls locked in rooms where no light could penetrate. At night, he awoke convinced he could hear their screams. In daylight, although the weather was warm for the time of year, a coldness chilled him to the core—a deep coldness he had not known until Babushka died and he had reached out and touched her as she lay in the coffin. He wished she was here now and he could explain his predicament. How could he ignore so much suffering? But what could he do without endangering his life and the lives of those he loved? One moment he was full of fight and determination, vowing to wipe the scum off the face of the earth. The next, his stomach felt hollow and his hands trembled. Babushka would have given him the courage to live with whatever decision he made.

To Natasha, he made the excuse of a stomach upset for his uneasiness and bad temper. There was no way he could tell her the real reason. She would make the decision for him, and he knew what that would be. Perhaps that was the answer. Get someone else to decide.

On Wednesday evening, Yuri drove Mitch to a *kafe* on the edge of the city. Professor Nekrassov was already seated at a corner table enveloped in a haze of smoke.

He looked up and for a moment his face didn't register he had seen them. His trademark red scarf was missing; his chin bore several days' growth. Mitch and Yuri pulled out chairs. The scraping noise jolted him out of his trance and he looked around, as if taking in his surroundings for the first time. "Ah! A problem. You wanted to talk to me about a problem," he slurred, squinting myopically at them. Then he pulled a bottle of vodka from his jacket pocket and took a swig. He offered it to them and shrugged when they both shook their heads. "Problems! We all have problems. Many, many problems. Life is full of problems. But first I will tell you about my problem. Not a little problem—not a little problem at all." The professor leaned forward; his chin almost touched the table. "My Borya. My dear Boris Konstantinovich. Like my brother he was." He looked from one to the other. "But now he is dead. Gone." The last words sounded heavy in his mouth.

"Tvoyu mat'!" Mitch blurted as he met Yuri's startled look.

The professor swayed, singing softly. Although his words were slurred, from what Mitch could make out he was singing one of the songs of the dissident Vlad Vysotsky; the songs Borya had sung on that never-to-be-forgotten evening.

"What happened to Borya?" Yuri's voice was no more than a whisper.

"The river. They said his body was found in the river. Suicide! That's what they said." The noise of the *kafe* whirled around. "His paintings—slashed, all of them. He would never have done that." He shook his head, pulled out the bottle, and took another swig.

"There was no note, no suicide note?" Mitch asked.

The professor snorted. "How could there be? He didn't know he was going to die."

Mitch swallowed hard. Yuri got to his feet. "I'll get some coffee."

"I warned him to be careful, but they got him in the end. Bastards!" The professor thumped the table. The buzz of conversation in the *kafe* hushed.

"Take it easy," Mitch urged in a low voice.

"Easy?" He grabbed Mitch's left wrist. "You tell me to take it easy when my friend has been murdered?" He shook his head and spat: *"Poshol ty!"*

Hardly a word was spoken during the time it took Mitch and Yuri to drink their coffee; each man stared at the black liquid as if it held the answer to his own dilemma. *Thank God he's quiet now,* Mitch thought to himself, watching the professor drain the bottle and light another cigarette. He thought about Boris Konstantinovich, his exuberance, the brightness of his paintings. *Surely someone like that doesn't commit suicide? Maybe he was murdered. But maybe it was the drink.*

"For me, it is over. *Zakonchenyy!*" The professor's voice cut through Mitch's thoughts. "But now, your problem. You said you had a problem you wanted to talk to me about."

Mitch and Yuri shook their heads. "*Nichego!* Nothing at all."

* * *

The following Saturday, Timochenko was pacing back and forth outside the office entrance when Mitch arrived. As soon as he saw Mitch, he hurried to his side. Mitch hesitated, his hands on the doorknob, pondering whether to tell Timochenko now. Their investigations had come up blank. There was no organization or overseas group able to negotiate a way through the maze of protection woven around the trafficking networks. In some countries, agencies ran so-called safe houses providing a modicum of security for victims who were able to escape their captors, but these were often raided and those running them beaten up or killed, and the girls dragged back to their lives of prostitution and misery. Yuri had reluctantly admitted there was nothing they could do. Mitch met Timochenko's anxious gaze. *We have to explain it to him properly; we owe him that,* he told himself as he opened the door. Timochenko followed him down the corridor.

Yuri was standing behind the desk. By the appearance of the ashtray, he had already worked his way through several cigarettes. He gestured to Timochenko to sit in the chair he had occupied last week.

Mitch closed the door, removed his jacket, folded it carefully, and laid it on the windowsill. *Why do I feel like a total shit?* he asked himself, avoiding the enquiring look Timochenko directed his way. Mitch lit a cigarette and stared at Yuri, willing him to be the first to speak.

"There's no easy way to say this." Yuri took a big breath, and then words tumbled out of his mouth: "There's nothing we can do. It's not that we don't want to help."

"You have to understand," Mitch added, "we can't take on these people. Not just the two of us. They're murderers. *Mafiyosa. Vory.*"

"And you're going to leave my sister with people like that, without even trying?" Timochenko's voice was loud and he got to his feet, hands gripping the edge of the desk.

"You have to understand," Mitch repeated.

"*Nyet*! You are lawyers. There must be some way. We have to get her back." Timochenko looked from one to the other, his hands now clenched into tight fists. "I beg you, please help her."

"Even if we got her back, she still wouldn't be safe. None of us would." Mitch leaned against the door, cigarette dangling from his mouth, trying to untangle the conflicting thoughts running through his head. *You have to think of Anja,* he told himself as he felt his resolve weaken.

Timochenko took a few steps around the desk toward Yuri. "I'll get money, do anything. Anything at all to get her back. Please. You have to …"

Yuri shook his head. "There's nothing …"

At that moment, the door burst open, slamming into Mitch's back and knocking him off balance. He sprawled forward and crashed into the desk. Stunned by the force with which he hit the wooden surface, he yelled "What …?" and turned to get up. A fist ground into his jaw. Hands gripped the top of his arms, hauling him upright. Then he was lifted off his feet and his back crashed into the bookcases that lined one side of the room. Books tumbled onto the floor. "What the hell?" Mitch shouted, kicking his legs and twisting his shoulders. His whole body jolted as he hit the bookcase again and was suspended there in a vice-like grip.

He stared down into the face of a man whose broad nose was squashed into his cheeks, one of which bore a jagged scar. The wide slit of a mouth opened. "*Zatknis!* Stay out of our business unless you want to be digging your own grave." The words were slow and deliberate. The eyes seemed to bore into Mitch's skin.

He flexed the muscles in his neck and shoulders in an effort to raise his arms. The grip tightened. Someone was shouting. It was Yuri. A man, who could have been the twin of this one, wearing a similar hooded jacket, had him in an armlock. His legs flailed behind him, kicking at his assailant. The scene seemed to play before Mitch in slow-motion. His arms felt as though they were going to break.

Then he saw him. Timochenko lying on the floor. Mitch tried to close his eyes, to block out what he saw, but they were locked wide open. Blood spilled from a gash on Timochenko's head, boots pounded into his ribs. The third man gave Timochenko another kick and then another. Mitch tried to shout. No sound came out. He looked away, staring down at his assailant, noticing what looked like a viper's head tattooed on the back of his hand. A moment later, the grip on Mitch's arms relaxed. He crumpled to the ground as his legs were kicked from under him. An excruciating pain went through the side of his head. Then nothing.

The pounding in Mitch's head obscured all sound. He curled his arms and legs into his body and lay still for several minutes. Then he drew the back of his right hand across his mouth and nose and stared at the blood on it. There were scuffling sounds, someone moving around. He reached out and grabbed a splintered chair leg.

"Mitch? Mitch? It's only me ... Yuri."

The words penetrated the fog in his head. "Yuri?" he croaked and pulled himself into a sitting position.

"You okay?" Yuri bent over him. Mitch dropped the chair leg and they both flinched as it clattered onto the floor. Yuri cursed and straightened up, one hand on his ribs.

Mitch struggled to his feet and staggered toward a chair that was lying on its side. The pounding in his head intensified as he bent down and hauled the chair upright; it wobbled when he sank onto the seat. "Have they gone?" he asked, prodding his left jaw gently with his fingers.

Yuri nodded.

"Where is he? Where's ... ?" Mitch looked around.

"Timochenko." Yuri was now leaning against the wall. "He's over there." His hand fluttered toward a corner of the room. "He's dead."

Mitch got up and wove an unsteady path through the debris littering the floor.

"Mitch, don't."

He stared at the body. The head was twisted to the side, the hair looked wet, congealed into clumps, and a trickle of blood ran from the ear down the neck. Mitch turned and groped his way into the corridor. He heaved, bending over, emptying the contents of his stomach. He felt Yuri's arm across his back. He heaved again. Bile trickled from his mouth and nose. Then, steadying himself with one hand on the wall, he followed Yuri along the corridor to the outer office. Light bathed the room. It looked just as it always did, except that the outside door was open and Yulia was not there. Yuri picked up the telephone receiver from the desk. There was no dial tone.

From the telephone booth at the corner, Yuri called the *militsiya*. He rarely used this booth, but today it didn't matter that the phone was bugged. Mitch's legs felt like jelly as he trailed Yuri back to the office. Outside the open door, they lit cigarettes and stood in silence. Mitch blotted out thoughts of Timochenko's mangled body and tried to recall even one feature of the young man's face as he had been in life. His thought process was frozen, locked solid. People walked by, floating in a haze.

"Let's go inside," Yuri urged, guiding Mitch through the doorway, where he slumped in Yulia's chair. The cigarette burned to his fingers, and Yuri took it from him and stabbed it out in the ashtray. "Mitch! You must pull yourself together. Do you hear me? The *militsiya* will be here soon. We have to get our story straight."

"We should have called the ambulance, a doctor. He may not be dead."

"They don't come more dead than that."

Yuri disappeared down the corridor. Drawers opened then closed.

"Take a swig of this." He unscrewed the cap of a small bottle of brandy. Mitch took a gulp and coughed. Snot dripped from his nose. He leaned forward, head in hands as he tried to stop the gulps that were now taking over his body.

"Paslushayte!" Yuri leaned across the desk and pulled Mitch's hands from his face. "Look at me, Mitch!" Mitch raised his head slowly. "You have to leave the talking to me. We can't tell them why Timochenko was here. If they ask, tell them you're my friend. You called in to see me." The wail of sirens pierced the air. "I'll say that one of Timochenko's relatives had been dismissed for stealing and he wanted me to ..."

"But we weren't going to help him." The words made Mitch feel worse. He wiped his eyes and then his nose with the back of his hand. He had let Timochenko down. The blast of sirens and doors slamming blotted out further thought. Yuri walked forward to speak to the *militsiya* officers, and the room was soon filled with grey uniforms and red-banded hats. Mitch felt strangely detached, as though it was all happening to someone else.

"What's wrong with this one?" Mitch looked up into the eyes of a *militsioner*.

"He's my friend. He was here when it happened."

"Can't he speak for himself?" the woman officer snapped.

"Poshol ty!" Mitch sneered.

"He's in a state of shock," Yuri interjected quickly and then inclined his head toward the corridor. "I don't think there's anything can be done for the one back there. We didn't know him. Just one of my clients," he babbled. "He wanted me to represent a relative who was dismissed for stealing from the place he worked."

The officers followed Yuri along the corridor.

A wave of sadness washed over Mitch, sadness not only for the dead man and his sister, but sadness that he, Mitch Galichin, wasn't even brave enough to speak his mind, tell them about Timochenko's sister. *I should have spoken up for them.* But even in his traumatized state, he knew it would be suicide. He thought of his daughter's sweet face, of her body still carrying the chubbiness of babyhood. He longed to be at home now, holding her. Tears coursed down his face. He cuffed them away, reached for the bottle, and gulped down a slug. Then his eyes followed the moving figures of two attendants as they carried the stretcher with the shrouded body to a waiting van. He followed. A crowd had gathered; their conversation faded as the stretcher slid into slots in the vehicle. Then the doors slammed and the van pulled away. Mitch watched until it was lost in the flow of traffic.

Back inside, he sat on the desk, fists clenched. His earlier lethargy turned to anger as the *militsiya* officers mingled around, chatting and laughing. "Bastards!" he cursed under his breath. *Don't they realize that a man has died here? A decent man.* He felt like tearing them apart limb by limb. The whole of his body began to tremble. He was a teenager again, railing against this corrupt society. *Get a grip of yourself,* he told himself as he fought to bite back words that threatened to escape from his lips. "You fucking bastards!" The voice was loud in his ears. Was it his? He held his breath, muscles tense, awaiting their reaction. The *militsiya* officers barely glanced at him as they laughed loudly and slapped each other on the back. Then they were gone. As the cars roared away, Mitch tried to still his trembling limbs, realizing how close he had come to shouting those words. By now, he could have been on his way to a dank prison cell, or a slab in the mortuary. No one would have known. He would have joined the countless ranks of the disappeared.

A moment or two later, Yuri and the two remaining officers came back into the room. One of them went straight out to the car. The other paused in front of Mitch. "I'll tell you what we've told your friend." He fixed Mitch with a steely gaze. "Forget what happened here, if you know what's good for you. *Ponimaete?*" Mitch nodded.

Alone again, Mitch and Yuri stared into the distance, passing the bottle from one to the other. Neither man spoke. Yuri tossed the empty bottle into the waste bin; the clang reverberated around the room.

Mitch noticed now that a bruise stained Yuri's left temple and cheekbone, and his lips were split. He had stayed calm and dealt with the *militsiya,* much as he dealt with whatever life threw at him. "Call your father. Ask him to come and get us." Yuri pressed a metal token into Mitch's hand.

Twenty minutes later Sergei arrived. "Look at the state of you!" he exclaimed. "What the hell's been going on? There's blood ..."

"It was a misunderstanding." Yuri's words sounded feeble.

"Papa, I'll explain everything later," Mitch cut in. "All we want now is to get out of here. Get cleaned up before I have to face Natasha."

Sergei looked more closely at the two of them. "You need to go to hospital," he said, his fingers gently prodding the bruise around Mitch's jaw and the lump on the side of his head.

"Hospital? You know what happens in those places? They'll tell you we stopped breathing."

When the trio arrived at the apartment, Sophia was in a state of panic. "Whatever's happened? Your faces!"

"It's okay. It looks worse than it is." Sergei's voice was firm.

"But who did it?"

"Never mind that now. You two sit in there," he gestured toward the sitting room; Mitch and Yuri did as he said and sank thankfully into armchairs. "Verochka Murmanevna, we'll need a bowl of water, some antiseptic, and cloths," Sergei instructed.

"But what happened? Who did it?" Sophia rubbed her hands in agitation.

"Later. I'll explain later," Sergei hissed.

Verochka bustled down the corridor to the kitchen. Two minutes later, she was back. "*Spasiba.* Put it down there," Sergei's tone was dismissive and, after a moment's hesitation, she left the room. Sergei closed the door behind her, and while Sophia dabbed agitatedly at both men's wounds with a cloth, he explained what Mitch and Yuri had told him.

"Oh, Mitch. Will you never learn?"

"We were telling him there was nothing we could do." Mitch winced and jerked his head away from his mother's ministrations.

"It scares me, the way you get involved in things."

"I wasn't involved," he snapped.

Sophia transferred her attentions to Yuri. "That looks painful," she dabbed at his temple. "You should go to hospital, both of you."

"We've been through all that. But just to make you happy, *lyubov' maya,* I'll call Anton Romanovich." Sergei turned to Yuri and explained. "He's a doctor, an old friend. He was at the wedding. Mitch and Natasha's."

Apart from a few grey streaks in his hair and beard, Anton Romanovich hadn't changed much since the day he had first been called to the Galichin home when six-year-old Mitch had measles. After examining both men and concluding that no bones were broken, he accepted the tea Sophia offered him. "The headaches and soreness should begin to subside in a few days. But if you become confused or lose consciousness, you must go to hospital." As he left, he urged them to stay out of trouble. "If you saw the sights I see every day ..."

Sergei phoned Natasha and explained that Mitch and Yuri had been involved in a scuffle. "Not their fault," he assured her, "they were innocent bystanders."

* * *

From the scowl on Natasha's face when he got home, Mitch knew she didn't believe the story. "You were at that place where Yuri works, weren't you?" she began. He hadn't the energy to confirm or deny her accusation. "Look at you!" She fixed him with a look of disgust. "You won't be satisfied until you're dead. *Imbetsil!*" she yelled.

"A bit of sympathy might ..."

"Sympathy? You expect sympathy from me?" she threw at him. "You've got responsibilities, and it's about time you thought about Anja and me."

"Is she sleeping?" he ventured.

"What do you care about her?" Natasha spat. "If you were worried about her, you wouldn't do such stupid things." The sitting room door slammed behind her.

Mitch lay down on the sofa. His jaw ached, and the thumping in his head had taken over the space around him. He couldn't think straight, couldn't put the sequence of the day's events together. They flashed through his mind like an old movie flickering in a jumble of frames. Then one frame stuck. It wouldn't move on. Timochenko's twisted body, the trickle of blood running from his ear down his neck.

CHAPTER TWENTY-FOUR
LENINGRAD—DECEMBER 1987

The fading light cast an unearthly pallor over the street as Mitch emerged from the courthouse. A hand gripped his arm and he turned. Artur Doubrovski smiled, revealing even teeth. "I knew I'd get off!" He threw back his head and laughed. Mitch bit back a cynical comment and muttered obsequious words of congratulations.

It stuck in his gut to defend people like Artur, who bought their phony innocence. But he needed to keep his job and at least have some hope of paying his debts. Since Timochenko's murder, he had cultivated the persona of a model Soviet citizen; he occasionally attended meetings of local Party cells, volunteered in supervising youth work groups, had been known to expound the virtues of the communist way of life, and accepted the holiday at a Black Sea resort to which he was entitled, hoping his misgivings didn't show.

President Gorbachev's moves toward a market economy and more open society early last year had filled Mitch with hope that he would soon no longer have to pay lip service to the tenets of this corrupt society; the Soviet Union would join the rest of the free world, where people made their own decisions and controlled their own lives. Now he wasn't so sure. The population was growing increasingly weary of constant shortages, and Gorbachev's modest attempts to democratize the Soviet political system had encountered serious resistance from government bureaucrats who were unwilling to relinquish control over the nation's economic life. Although the powers of the KGB (Committee for State Security) had been limited, the head of the organization was a key figure in undermining democratization, and people still feared a knock on the door in the still of night.

Despite Gorbachev's denouncement of "leaders who had become accomplices in criminal activities," crime syndicates had spread their nets and now controlled most strata of society, from Party officials to shopkeepers. But what could Mitch do about it without risking the safety of his family? And so today he had participated in the farce of another so-called trial. Before the judge delivered his verdict, Mitch had written the words "NOT GUILTY" on the top of his file.

He felt a modicum of pity for the judge, who like so many others was still dependent on local Party officials for appointment, housing, and other benefits. Once enmeshed in the web of corruption, there was only one way out!

From the top of the courthouse steps, Mitch watched Artur and his fur-coated, henna-haired wife get into a black Mercedes. The driver climbed into the front seat and the car roared away. "Look as though they own the place," Mitch muttered to himself. *I suppose they do.*

He joined the parade of heavily muffled figures weaving a haphazard path along the glacier of ice that passed for a sidewalk. On the corner, he rifled in his pocket, pulled out some coins, and dropped them into the jar an old woman held out. He waved away the small bar of soap she tried to press into his hand. As he looked at her careworn face, he wondered if in years to come, babushkas would still need to augment their meagre incomes by standing on freezing street corners, selling whatever they could get their hands on.

Is anyone free in this God-forsaken society? As he walked, he thought of Andrei Sakharov and other dissidents who had been released from exile. Like the rest of the population, their lives were still subject to the whims of what was still, in all but name, a totalitarian government. He recalled one of Babushka's habitual sayings in the aftermath of disaster: *"And the toiling masses continue to toil."*

Through the frost-streaked windows of a *kafe-konditerskaya,* Mitch glimpsed the blurred shapes of people hunched over tables. Inside he dropped his files onto a chair, took off his *shapka* and gloves, undid his coat, and ordered a coffee from the elderly waitress. "There's a piece of poppy seed cake left," she whispered. Mitch watched as she heaved her way to the back of the room, the bulk of her body wobbling precariously from side to side, each step seeming to require a gargantuan effort.

He dunked the stale cake into the coffee and thought about the coming weekend. On Sunday, there was to be a celebratory birthday lunch for Lyosha. With a bit of luck, Mitch would sit next to Pyotr Alekseevich, Natasha's brother. Petya was now married with two young children of his own, and he and Mitch were good friends. Petya had never again mentioned the warning he had given about Natasha's spending habits. There was no need to—they were clear for all to see. They should be able to get by on what Mitch earned—many people managed on less—but there was no way he could keep up with her excessive demands. He no longer had the energy to argue and said nothing when she came home with new clothes or trinkets bought with her father's money. They now lived in a state of uneasy truce, with the occasional night of erotic sex followed by weeks of her spurning his advances. Then the cycle started again. He was ashamed of how easily he succumbed—like a man with an addiction. He hated her almost as much as he hated himself, and vowed he would leave. But he couldn't walk out on Anja. She was the most important part of his life. Court decisions almost always awarded custody to the mother, and Anja would quickly become caught up in the Lipovskys materialistic world. He mustn't let that happen.

For months after that fateful afternoon when Timochenko was murdered, he feared *vory* lurked around every street corner and had avoided taking his daughter for walks, scared they would come after him and harm her. In his most paranoid moments, he was tormented by thoughts that they would whisk her away to some far-off land. *She's just a baby. They don't take girls that young,* he had reasoned. As time passed, fear faded. Guilt remained. He should have done something to defend Timochenko, help his sister—and Klavdiya.

When Mitch got up to pay, the waitress's hand brushed his—not the hard, calloused skin he expected; her skin was as soft as the crown of a baby's head.

* * *

On Sunday morning, the sky slid low overhead, and splinters of pale sunlight sliced across the covering of ice on the Neva. Mitch hurried along the towpath in the wake of three-year-old Anja. "Annushka! *Byt' ostorozhen,*" he cautioned. She stopped, looked around at him, and set off at a trot again.

It was cold, but the wind had dropped and he needed to clear his head before the horror of Lyosha's birthday celebration descended. As he watched the pink tassel of Anja's woollen hat bob up and down some way in front of him, he wished he could whisk her away to somewhere she could live a normal life. It was a forlorn wish. Although travel restrictions had been loosened, Natasha would never agree to leave and wouldn't let him take Anja on his own. He often thought of his early years in Montréal, when he and his mother had been close, happy. They had retained the sense of togetherness, but happiness had disappeared from both their lives. He often caught his mother staring into the distance, maybe thinking of what her life might have been. He blamed himself; without him, she might never have come to the Soviet Union. He had tried to explain this to her, but she brushed his concerns away, saying "Without you and Papa, my life would be nothing."

Anja had stopped now and was staring at something propped against a tree. Mitch broke into a run and as he drew level she asked, "Papochka? Is the man asleep?" He grabbed her hand and looked at the inert figure, unsure whether the man was asleep or dead. With the toe of his boot he prodded the sack covering the man's legs. The eyelids fluttered for a moment and then were still. Mitch noticed an empty bottle lying close by. "We'll leave him to sleep," he whispered and hurried Anja along the path.

Gorbachev's restrictive alcohol policy had led to an increase in home brewing, and Mitch guessed the bottle had contained Samogon. Mitch had avoided drinking the lethal substance since the evening at Boris Konstantinovich's apartment. Professor Nekrassov disappeared soon after Borya was murdered, and rumours circulated that he had fled to Finland, that he was living rough under an archway by the Neva, or that his body was found at a *dacha* outside the city. Mitch didn't know what to believe. Probably none of the tales. If he was a gambling man, he would bet that, like the man leaning against the tree, he had succumbed to Russia's battle with the bottle and was probably wandering aimlessly around the countryside, singing one of Vlad Vysotsky's songs. He thought fondly of the professor, picturing him with a bottle in hand, eyes glazed, steps unsteady, his voice intoning the dissident's words like a religious mantra. He almost envied him the freedom to go wherever the road led, with no responsibilities to weigh him down.

"Posmotrite," he said to his daughter now, and together they watched groups of people fishing through holes in the ice.

"Tell me the story, Papochka. The one about the people and the helicopters. *Pazhalusta ... pazhalusta,"* she pleaded.

She had heard that tale many times, but never tired of it. "Now, how does it go?" he joked, tweaking her nose with his gloved hand. "I know! It was a Sunday morning, just like today. There were six people. Four men and two women, I think." Anja nodded her head. "They were hungry and needed some fish for their supper, so they put on their warmest clothes and walked out on to the frozen river and dropped their fishing lines through holes they drilled in the ice. For a long time they didn't catch anything, not even one tiny fish." Mitch held a thumb and finger slightly apart in front of her face. "Then one person caught a fish and then another. And so it went until they had two fishes each."

"And then what happened?" Anja prompted. Her voice held all the wonder it had when Mitch first told her the story.

"Then they looked around. And would you believe that the piece of ice they were on had broken off from the rest?"

"What did they do?" Her voice was shrill.

"Well ... they ran around on the ice floe and shouted loudly, *Pamagite! Pamagite!*" As Mitch spoke, Anja stomped around in a circle. "They waved their hands, hoping someone on the shore would notice. But they were swept along toward the sea."

She stopped, hands in mid-air. "Someone did see them ... didn't they, Papochka?"

Mitch nodded his head. "An old man. He couldn't see them very well because of his bad eyes, but he heard them and hurried to the *militsiya* as fast as his crooked legs would carry him." Mitch hunched his shoulders, leaning on an imaginary walking cane. "And what did the *militsiya* do?" he croaked.

"They called out the helicopters!" Anja shouted triumphantly, raising her arms further up to the sky and giggling in anticipation of what she knew came next.

"And the helicopters hovered overhead, their rotor blades going around and around." He put his hands under her armpits, lifted her, and spun her around as fast as the slippery path allowed. "Until they were all rescued." He plonked her back down on the ground and laughed with her. "My, my, Annushka, you're getting a bit big for me to do that," he teased. He leaned against a wall, feigning exhaustion, and waited for his head to stop spinning.

"Can we go to the *kafe*? Please. Please."

"Race you there," he challenged half-heartedly, and the two of them slipped and slithered toward the lights of the *kafe-konditerskaya* at the top of the slope. Inside, condensation streaked the windows, shutting out all but the briefest glimpse of the world outside. As he watched Anja dip cookies into his glass of hot, sweet *sbiten'*, he wished they could stay in that warm cocoon forever.

CHAPTER TWENTY-FIVE

LENINGRAD—SEPTEMBER/ OCTOBER 1989

Mitch stared at his father, his mouth open wide. It was a full minute before the impact of what Sergei had said sunk in. "Papa, you can't mean that." His voice rose several octaves: "Surely they can do something."

Sergei leaned his elbows on the table and put his head in his hands.

Mitch got up from his chair and walked around to his father's side of the table. His arms and legs felt as though they didn't belong to him. "What exactly did the doctor say? Tell me."

Sergei straightened up and looked at Mitch. "He said ... he said the cancer is too far advanced." His bottom lip trembled. "There's nothing they can do."

"There must be. We can't just sit back and let it happen. It's Maman, for Christ sake!"

Shafts of sunlight cut across the cracked oilcloth on the table and streaked the faded chintz cover of the old armchair, where his mother usually sat sewing or repairing clothes to give them a few more months of wear. "Does she know?"

Sergei nodded.

Mitch looked at the door into the hallway. "I'll go in and see her," he said, trying to still the turmoil in his stomach.

"Leave her for a while. She's exhausted, so pale. I can't bear to see her like that." Sergei wiped tears from his cheeks with the fingers of one hand. "Oh, Mitch, what are we going to do without her?"

Mitch gulped. His father seemed old now; his eyes, usually alert and attentive, were dull, lifeless. "We won't have to be without her, Papa. We'll find something, someone who can help her. We can't just sit back and let it happen. We can't."

* * *

During the next three weeks, Mitch railed against the disease, masking his feelings of helplessness in a flurry of activity and following up on leads for what were claimed to be new treatments. But they weren't available for Sophia. His mother was apparently expendable to the Soviet system. Hospitals were short of medicines, and scarce resources were reserved for the productive workforce. An acquaintance knew of a doctor in Moscow who had access to foreign drugs. "These privileges never come without a price," Mitch was told. He swallowed his pride and asked Alekseĭ Aleksandrovich for a loan. "No problem," Lyosha laughed. "You are family, and families take care of each other. That's what I've been trying to make you understand for years." Mitch felt a tightening in his chest.

Sophia listened patiently as Mitch explained about the new drugs. She would have to go to a clinic in Moscow, but it would only be for a short while, just so that her condition could be monitored. "We'll see, *lyubov' maya*. We'll see," she said.

The following morning, Sergei appeared at Mitch's office. "Give the money back to Lyosha. It won't help her." He brushed away Mitch's objections. "The doctor here said the cancer has already spread to some internal organs. It's too late. The drugs will only weaken her and make her more vulnerable to infections."

Mitch felt his energy sap. His body ached with such an intensity that it took over his whole being. Part of him hoped he would be locked inside the pain forever so that he would never have to face reality.

"We have to be strong for her, son."

He watched from a window as Sergei crossed the road and walked along the footpath by the side of the river. Gone were the purposeful strides that Mitch always found difficult to match. *You must be strong for him as well,* he told himself as his father shuffled out of sight.

Sophia was fading before their eyes. Mitch scoured the stores for food items to tempt her to eat. *If she can just regain a bit of weight, she'll be okay,* he told himself as he stood for hours in lineups. President Gorbachev's plans for reconstruction had floundered, and even basic food items were rationed. *Perestroika* became a dirty word as queues got longer and longer and people angrier and angrier.

Mitch took Anja to see his mother every few days. A tinge of sadness washed over him as Sophia's face lit up when she saw her granddaughter. The two of them would settle on the sofa while Anja told Sophia everything that had happened since her last visit. Mitch was proud of his daughter. She seemed to sense that things had changed; she no longer angled for a walk in one of the parks and the ice cream that would inevitably be hers on the way home. Instead, she brought her favourite books and recited them by heart to her grandmother.

Today, Anja bounded into the room, hardly able to contain her excitement. "Babushka, look what I've brought you," she cried, thrusting a tiny, paper-wrapped parcel into her grandmother's lap.

"What is it?" Sophia blinked and tried to shake herself out of her drowsy state.

"It's a present for you. I bought it with my own money." The child's eyes were bright with anticipation as she shifted from one foot to the other, watching her grandmother unwrap the gift. "See, it has an 'S' on it ... for Sophia," Anja proclaimed, pointing to the pink initial embroidered in cross-stitches in the corner of the white handkerchief.

"So it does." Sophia's voice was a mere whisper. She leaned back on the pillows that supported her on the sofa.

"Don't you like it?"

"It's beautiful, my darling. *Spasiba*."

"You will come to my birthday party, won't you? It's next week. I'm going to be five, and I'll be having lots of presents." Anja leaned closer to her grandmother. "We could get one of those chairs with wheels, and I could push you."

Sophia's face contorted.

"Why don't you go with Dedushka and help him bring in the tea?" Mitch cajoled, his hands resting on Anja's shoulders as he propelled her toward the door. "I'm sure he has a treat for you hidden somewhere."

"I know where he hides things," she whispered gleefully and ran after her grandfather down the passageway.

Mitch tucked the woollen blanket around his mother's body. Although the temperature was unseasonably warm, for the past few days Sophia had complained of feeling cold. Mitch suspected the blanket was more to hide her emaciated body than for the warmth it might give. "Darling..." she hesitated for a moment. "I don't think you should bring her here anymore." The whites of her eyes shone like yellow beacons. "Best if she remembers me as I was." Sophia leaned her head back and closed her eyes. In that moment, as he looked at her jaundiced skin and sunken cheeks, Mitch accepted that his beloved mother was beyond help.

* * *

Two days before Anja's birthday, Mitch looked around the stark hospital ward. Mixed with the smell of disinfectant was an underlying odour of putrescence. It permeated everything, clinging to his clothes, his hair. It all seemed unreal, like a nightmare from which they would all wake up one day. His mother would be back home, and everything would be as it was before. There would be no white-coated doctors or nurses. No needles or tubes. The only smell would be the perfume she had always loved.

He pulled the curtains around the bed slightly apart and stood for a minute or so listening to his father reading aloud. His voice was low, hypnotic in its resonance:

> "To the secret, white house of yours,
> So gentle and quiet, we both
> Are walking in silence half-lost.
> And sweeter than all songs,
> Sung ever ..."[3]

Mitch's voice was little more than a murmur, in unison with his father's: "Are this dream, becoming the truth ..."

Sergei turned his head in acknowledgement, raised Sophia's hand to his lips, and kissed it before placing it gently on the counterpane. "You sit with her. I'll stretch my legs for a while," he said softly and handed the copy of Anna Akhmatova's poems to Mitch. Mitch sat down on the chair and opened the well-thumbed *samizdat* copy. In places, the carbon-type was scarcely visible, but he hardly needed to see the written words. How often had he heard his father reading those words aloud in the evenings when the three of them and Babushka had sat in the half-light? He leaned forward and rested his hand lightly on top of his mother's hand. One side of her face twitched and then was still. Every now and then she rambled, speaking softly in what Mitch took to be Yiddish or Hebrew. For the first time, he realized how painful it must have been for her not to be able to converse with anyone in the languages of her childhood and that he, her only child, could not share in the traditions and customs of her religion and way of life. She had done it all for him and his father. Why hadn't he ever spoken to her about it, thanked her? Tried to learn the languages of the

---

3 Along the Hard Crust of Deep Snows (1917), poem by Anna Akhmatova (1889-1966).

Hasidim? And now it was too late. She was slipping away from them with every moment that passed.

A few minutes later, she opened her eyes and looked at him. *"Ari,"* she murmured.

"What is it, Maman?" he asked and leaned farther forward.

"*Ari.* It was to be your Hebrew name." She closed her eyes. "Lion, you were always my lion. My ..." Her words trailed off as sleep overtook her.

Mitch sat quietly, wondering what his mother had meant. He tried to ignore the chorus of groans from the other patients, the rasping coughs, the thin voices calling out for a nurse, as he asked himself again the questions that had tormented him in the past few weeks. *Why did I cause them so much grief? Why couldn't I have been the son they always wanted? A good son ... a lion. Is that what she meant?* He thought back to that Sunday afternoon nearly six years ago when he told them Natasha was pregnant. The disappointment in his mother's eyes had been harder to bear than his father's anger. But if he had anything to be thankful for, it was the happiness his parents had watching Anja grow. His mother and Anja had a special rapport, finding pleasure in the simple things in life. The child brought out a softness in his father's nature, one Mitch had barely witnessed before. Despite her other grandparents' lavish presents, Anja's excitement always bubbled over at the prospect of a picnic in the country with Babushka Sophia and Dedushka Sergei. Now his mother would never know the young woman Anja would become.

Mitch waited for his mother's chest to rise once more so that he would know that at least for a moment he wouldn't have to face life without her. A few hours ago, when she had writhed in pain, he prayed that God would take her quickly. When his prayers were not answered, he sought within himself for the courage to help her. Alone with her, he had reached out a hand, willing himself to turn up the dose of diamorphine that the valve in her chest was administering. He had watched the doctor do it. If he could just turn it up high for a second or two there would be no more pain. He had turned away, hands trembling.

Now watching his mother in her drug-induced sleep, he wanted her to linger forever, so that she would always be the mother he loved, the mother who had gripped his hand and whispered encouraging words as the two of them shuffled closer to the fierce looking official on the immigration desk all those years ago.

"It's going to be all right," she had said over and over. As Mitch grew up, he realized the words had been as much for her benefit as his.

There was so much he needed to tell her. *"Ya lyublyu tebya, Maman,"* he began now, his voice a rasping whisper. "I'll always remember…" He paused and cradled her hand gently in his. "I'll always remember how you taught me to be tolerant of difference, to help people less fortunate, to smile at people on the street even if I didn't know them. 'You might be the only person who shows kindness toward them today. Not everyone has a loving family around them.' That's what you said."

The curtain opened slightly. "Is she …?" his father's tentative voice came to him.

"She's sleeping peacefully."

"You go," Sergei urged. "Natasha will be waiting. I'll sit with her a little longer."

Mitch gave his mother's hand a gentle squeeze and got up stiffly from the chair. He bent forward and brushed her cheek with his lips. Her skin looked clearer now and warmer. "I'll come back later," he said.

CHAPTER TWENTY-SIX
LENINGRAD–NOVEMBER 1989

Mitch cut the meat into even pieces, speared a chunk with his fork, and put it into his mouth.

"Mitch, dear, are you all right?"

He swallowed, rested his knife and fork on the plate, and met Vera Aleksandrovna Kishinevskaya's gaze. "I'm sorry. I was thinking about something. A case I'm working on," he lied. In truth, he had been trying to figure out how to fend off the people who were after him for money. The interest was piling up, and he felt as though he was being sucked into a deep abyss. He concealed a shiver, recalling the naked fear that gripped his body that morning. A man had suddenly appeared in front of his desk and, with one swipe of his hand, scattered files and books onto the floor. Mitch leapt to his feet, demanding to know what was going on. "The money!" the man yelled. "The boss gets nasty ... very nasty ... when people don't pay." Mitch stepped back quickly. His heartbeat thumped loudly. His cheeks flamed as the faces of his colleagues turned toward him.

"Ponimaete?" the man hissed. Mitch had nodded, unable to find his voice among the trembling within. "Two days, or I'll be back. I won't be so nice then." He grinned, leaned forward, took a drag on the cigarette he held in his hand, and blew a cloud of smoke into Mitch's eyes. "There is another way." His gravelly voice was lower now. "My boss pays his people well, particularly lawyers." He pulled a picture out of his pocket and held it in front of Mitch's face. Mitch blinked, trying to stop his eyes from smarting as he stared at the photograph. "Think about it. Your pretty little wife could have all the things she wants." The thug put the photograph back in his pocket and, narrowing his eyes at Mitch, growled *"Poslyezavtra!"* before lumbering away. The door slammed behind him, rattling the glass.

Fear mingled with humiliation had blocked Mitch's ears as he sank into his seat. He wrapped his arms around his upper body in an effort to get a grip on himself. After a few minutes, he took out a cigarette. His hands shook as he tried to light it. "Here!" He looked up into the face of Igor Mogilevich, the youngest and newest member of the Bureau, and quickly lit his cigarette from the lighter that flamed in Igor's hand. The young man gathered up the files and books from the floor and silently stacked them in neat piles on Mitch's desk. Mitch nodded his thanks before Igor walked back to his desk. The buzz in the office returned to normal, and Mitch took a drag on the cigarette, pulled a stack of paper toward him, and pretended to get on with his work. The only image in front of his eyes was the photograph of Natasha the man had thrust in front of him. *Where was it taken? How had it got into his hands?* Although Mitch had only a fleeting glimpse, it was definitely her—the hair, the way she held her head—but neither the clothes nor what he saw of the surroundings were familiar. Surely they wouldn't touch her? If they messed with her, they'd have Lyosha to contend with. *Oh, God ... Anja!* He had held his breath. The pounding of his heart blotted everything else out.

"Your mother always worried about you," Vera Alexandrovna's voice brought him back to the present. "You're working too hard; she was always telling you to slow down." She closed her eyes briefly, struggling with her emotions.

Mitch looked at her elegantly-arranged white hair, the finely-etched facial bone structure, slightly retroussé nose, and the pattern of lines around her mouth and eyes. *She reminds me so much of Maman,* he thought. This was the first time since his mother's death over a month ago that he allowed himself to remember what she had looked like. He had tucked her photographs into a drawer and hurriedly dismissed her from his mind as soon as her image threatened to break the brittle shell he had built around himself. Vera was right, he was working too hard. Working, working, working. It was the only way he could get through each day. Now as he looked at Vera Kishinevskaya, he allowed his mother back into his life.

He twisted the stem of his glass and looked around the room, his thoughts going back to the first time he visited Vera's home. He was probably about five years old, and on the way there, as he and his mother walked along Nevsky prospekt, she told him that he must be very polite and thank Vera properly when they left. "You remember the words I taught you?" The buildings towered above him as he tried to remember what he was supposed to say. Sophia pointed out churches of many different denominations, telling him that this had prompted the famous French writer, Alexander Dumas, to call the Nevsky "the street of religious tolerance." The young Mitch hadn't understood what she said nor appreciated the irony of her words both for the Soviet State's intolerance of religious idolatory or for his mother. Many years later, recalling the day in Montréal when she was turned away from her parents' home, the significance dawned on him.

But that long-ago winter's day, as he and his mother walked along the side of the *Yevropeiskaya* toward the Arts Square, Mitch let go of her hand and ran to the door of the hotel. Sophia grabbed his arm and pulled him back onto the sidewalk. "I want to go in," he wailed. "I'm cold!" After a moment or two, she bent down, pulled his hat further down over his ears, and told him gently, "You remember Papa told you that there are some places people like us can't go?" He hadn't answered. "Well, this is one of them," she said, her jaw set in her determined look.

That day in Vera's home, he had hunched in the corner of the couch, refusing to say a word to anyone. It wasn't until Lyuba, one of the people who shared Vera's apartment, held out a bag of candies to him that he got to his feet and grabbed two of his favourite 'Squirrels'.

"Your father? How is he coping?" Vera's voice cut into his thoughts.

"He's getting by. I usually have supper with him on Monday evenings. It's strange, as though she's gone out to the shops and we're waiting for her to come back." He gulped down a mouthful of wine and changed the subject. "What do you think will happen here now that the Berlin Wall has come down?"

"Who knows?" She shrugged.

"But Gorbachev? He seems to be supporting the dissolution of the Soviet bloc, the end of the Cold War." Mitch paused and leaned on the table, cradling one side of his head in his hand. "Is it just rhetoric, or is the Soviet hold on Eastern bloc countries finally coming to an end?" His mind went back to the images of East Germans standing triumphantly on top of the concrete structure that had kept them locked inside Soviet territory for nearly thirty years, dividing families and trampling on their human rights ... the people who had died attempting to escape to the West.

Vera shook her head. "Whatever happens, it won't make much difference to conditions here. I've seen it all before ... the promises of a brighter world ahead."

She's right. *We may not have a physical wall here, but the effect is the same,* Mitch thought sadly, wondering how long it would be before he and others like him could live within a free and democratic society. Would his Anja ever know what it is to be truly free?

Vera leaned toward him. "Take no notice of me, Mitch. I'm just a silly old woman."

"You'll never be that." He picked up his knife and fork again. Despite his myriad worries, he was enjoying the food. He hadn't tasted anything as good for a long time. Meat had almost vanished from the stores, along with milk, tea, coffee, and soap. Several times recently when he arrived home from work, his meal was congealing on the counter with a curt note from Natasha saying that Anja was staying with Lena and Lyosha for the night. He had questioned Natasha about her own whereabouts, who she was with. She always had a ready answer; he wasn't sure he believed her. And now there was the photograph. He swallowed the last of his food. "You haven't eaten much," he commented, noticing that the food on Vera's plate was hardly touched.

"I don't have much appetite. One of the penalties of old age," she smiled wistfully, "but with so many people hungry ..." She grabbed her cane. "Why don't we move to somewhere more comfortable?" she suggested. "I'm afraid I can't offer you any coffee."

"We still have wine to finish." Mitch picked up both glasses and put them on a small table between two armchairs.

Vera lowered herself down into one. "When your mother first came to Leningrad, things were difficult for her. She didn't feel she fit in here."

"I don't think she ever did." Mitch settled in the other chair and sipped his drink.

"There was a lot of bigotry. Some people shunned her. Ill-mannered, ridiculous people." Her words held the bitterness of a lifetime. "Why does everyone blame the Jews for the country's problems, see them as an ideological enemy? That ludicrous letter in *Sovetskaya Rossiya* last year. What was the woman thinking?" Vera Alexandrovna referred to a letter sent to the newspaper by Nina Andreeva, an obscure Leningrad communist, demanding the rehabilitation of Stalin's reputation and saying the country's woes were due to the Jewish element in the Party leadership. "Rehabilitation of Stalin's reputation? As a murderer? Is that what she meant? *Khuynya!*" Vera spat out the last word. "I always admired your mother. Her love for you and your father was so strong, she could overcome anything."

Except cancer. Mitch left the words unsaid. Thinking about it now, he realized how rich his parents' marriage had been. Perhaps he, too, wanted perfection.

But for most people, marriage wasn't like that. He only had to look at Lena and Lyosha. They were never totally honest with each other, paying lip-service to their supposed devotion while selfishly pursuing their own desires. Several times he had seen Lena with another man, and Lyosha had other dalliances—he had boasted of them to Mitch and Petya one night when he was the worse for drink. So could he really blame Natasha for the way she behaved, flitting from one desire to another? Even her relationships with so-called best friends were short-lived. She had long ago ceased to have anything to do with Marina Stepanovna, who had run the shelter for street kids and who now seemed to be the love of Mitch's friend Yuri Trubetskoy's life.

"I think I'll give your father a call and invite him to the ballet," Vera mused. "Maybe Mezentseva will be dancing."

"He won't be able to resist that," Mitch said absentmindedly, trying not to think of the thug who had burst into the office this morning. Everything was piling in on him. If only he could sleep, clear his head, he might be able to sort things out. During the past few months, hardly a night passed when his sleep wasn't disturbed by a nightmare. He ran through dark alleyways trying to escape from something—a threatening presence he could sense but not see, a hand he could feel but not see. He would burst into the light, in front of him a river, black and roiling, steaming as though a cauldron was deep below. At this point he would sometimes awake, bathed in sweat. Other nights, as he stared into the water, a woman appeared at his side. She held a baby in her arms. Then would come her piercing screams as a hidden force snatched her baby and tossed it, like garbage, into the river. Now every time he looked at the Neva, he imagined he could see tiny flailing limbs rising out of the water, out of the ice.

"Mitch, if something ... someone's worrying you, you can talk to me." Vera's voice intruded into his thoughts.

"It's nothing," he mumbled and drained the rest of his wine.

"If you're worried about money, I would be happy to lend you some."

No sense denying it—she knows. "It's just a temporary thing. I'll sort it out."

"I don't like to see you so worried. Won't you let me help?"

It would get the thug off my back, Mitch thought. But Vera was his father's friend, and he had no way of paying her back. "I'll sort it out," he repeated, checked his watch, and got to his feet. "I really must be getting back to work."

Leaning heavily on her cane, Vera walked with him into the hallway.

"Why don't you come and celebrate New Year's night with us?" Mitch suggested as he buttoned his overcoat.

"I would love to, dear. But New Year, that's for family."

"My father will be there, and you're part of the family. I know Maman looked upon you as a sister. Say you'll come." Vera smiled. "Anja can tell you about kindergarten. She chatters non-stop, and Natasha would love to see you." The last few words echoed in his mind. Whenever they were with Vera Alexandrovna, Natasha barely contained her dislike of the woman. In truth, Mitch knew she didn't care much for any of his family or friends, preferring the company of her so-called high-class friends. In her view, class was synonymous with money; he had long ago given up arguing that point with her. Vera Alexandrovna's quiet dignity was in stark contrast to the brashness of Natasha's friends. *It will be good for Papa,* he told himself now. "Please say you'll come."

She raised an eyebrow. "Well, if you're sure." Mitch nodded and pulled his *shapka* down over his ears. At the doorway, she added, "Whatever is worrying you, you know you can come to me."

He hesitated.

"Remember ... problems have a way of solving themselves."

Not this one, he sighed. *It's been with me for years.*

* * *

The following morning, Mitch went to Vera Alexandrovna's apartment and asked to borrow some money. She didn't ask why he needed such a large sum. Later that day, Leonid brought a paper-wrapped bundle of roubles to his office. Mitch breathed a sigh of relief. His Annushka would be safe.

CHAPTER TWENTY-SEVEN

LENINGRAD—DECEMBER 1990

Mitch leaned back in his office chair, yawned, and stretched. It was not yet 5:30, but everyone else had left. He lit a cigarette, took a couple of drags, picked up his pen, and started to work through the case notes for his stint in court tomorrow. There were a few points of law he needed to check, but if he worked quickly, he might be able to spend time with Anja before she went to bed. The telephone rang. He hesitated before answering.

"I knew you would forget!" Natasha began. When he didn't reply, she continued. "The concert! We're meeting ..."

"I haven't forgotten. I got held up here." He knocked the ash from the cigarette into the ashtray. "What time does it start?"

"I told you this morning," she said with an irritated sigh, "eight o'clock, but we're meeting Misha and Galina ..."

"Misha?" She hadn't mentioned Mikhail Victorovich Yagudin. Every time Mitch met Yagudin, he felt an involuntary tremor run down his spine and saw again Timochenko's twisted body. As a young man, Yagudin was known to be a member of the *vory v zakone,* and was now thought to be a *Sovetnik,* one of the older, experienced *vory* who act as counsellor to the underworld princes. "I told you I don't want you seeing him! The man's dangerous!"

"Dangerous?" Natasha laughed. "Misha's no more dangerous than ... than that old cat that silly old man Slava has."

"I told you, Natasha ..."

"You never like my friends. You're always finding fault with them."

Mitch sighed loudly. *What's the use?*

"We're meeting them—Misha and Galina—at Ket. In half an hour." The last four words were enunciated slowly, deliberately.

"Ket?"

"Yes, Ket. How many times do I have to say it?"

"You never told me we were going to Ket."

"I did. Everyone goes there."

"Natasha! We can't afford to go there!"

There was silence for a second or two. Then she said decisively: "It's all arranged."

Mitch bit back his anger. She had again manipulated him into an impossible situation. "What about Anja?"

"She's at Katya's. She's staying overnight, and I said you would take both girls to kindergarten in the morning ... as I don't have a car."

He let that remark go.

"Meet me at the restaurant," she snapped. The line went dead.

"Chort!" Mitch cursed and stared at the telephone receiver in his hand. He should call her back and say he wasn't going, but what was the use? Maybe she had told him—he tended not to listen to her whining. A quick count of his money confirmed what he already knew: he had nowhere near enough cash to eat at Ket. He could just not turn up, or arrive too late to eat or drink anything. But that would cause another scene. Either way, he was fucked.

At dinner the wine flowed. Mitch sipped his, his eyes scarcely looking away from Mikhail Victorovich Yagudin. His iron-grey hair was heavily oiled, one side of it swept back in a crisp wave. His face was angular, with heavy jawbones, his skin unblemished by age. As he talked, gold fillings glinted in his teeth. Mitch would bet that under the shirt and well-tailored suit his body was adorned with tattoos chronicling his criminal history. He looked down at his own crumpled suit—the only one he owned. As he looked up, Yagudin's eyes met his. Red wine slopped from Mitch's glass onto the white tablecloth.

Mitch ate in silence. The voices of the other three ran around in his head as they gossiped about people he neither knew nor wanted to know. *What the hell does Natasha see in people like them?* he asked himself, his gaze moving from Misha to Galina. Despite his objections, over the past few months, Natasha had been seeing a lot of them. *Or was it just Misha?* It occurred to him now that she spoke of him often. If she was to be believed, he was an expert on almost everything. He certainly knew how to charm women—a thinly veiled compliment here, a slightly risqué comment there. Natasha hung on his every word.

Mitch put down his knife and fork and answered an inane question from Galina Antonevna Ivanova. She was much younger than Misha and attractive in a strange sort of way. Her hennaed hair was severely cut; heavily made-up eyes bulged in an elfin face. Although Mitch didn't like her, he felt a certain sympathy for her. She looked like a waif caught in a storm. Any moment a gust of wind could sweep her away. There was no future for her with an asshole like Yagudin; *vory* never marry or have children. *Maybe she doesn't care.* That thought was quickly discredited as Galina scowled at Misha, whose arm was now along the back of Natasha's chair. Natasha smiled at him. He leaned in closer and whispered in her ear. She laughed coyly, whispered back, then drew away. For a few seconds, they gazed at each other. Then Misha picked up his glass and raised it in her direction.

Mitch gritted his teeth. *You're reading too much into it. She's always flirted with other men. It's the way she is.*

The top button of Natasha's royal blue jacket was open, revealing a sliver of black top across the line of her breasts. An oval brooch was pinned to the right jacket lapel. Mitch stared at it. The stone looked like an opal—a large opal.

"You must come and visit us at my *dacha* in Semiozerie," Misha urged, his hand moving to Natasha's shoulder. "Both of you," he added. Mitch glared at where Misha's fingers were now squeezing her arm. With a wry smile, Misha bellowed for another bottle of burgundy.

Sweat trickled down Mitch's back; he didn't dare think what a restaurant like Ket charged for that sort of wine, let alone the food. The pink walls and ornate furnishings crowded in on him, and he pushed his chair back noisily on the marble floor, excused himself, and stumbled to the washroom. Inside, he loosened his tie and leaned over the washbasin. For several moments, the backbeat of blood pulsing through his temples obscured thought. Then he sluiced cold water over his face, mopped it dry with a cloth from the pile at the side of the basin, and lit a cigarette. *You'll have to have it out with her,* he told himself as smoke drifted upward. *Ask her straight out if anything is going on between her and Yagudin. And Anja? I swear I'll kill him ... both of them ... if he goes anywhere near her.* He tightened his grip on the washbasin and breathed heavily, consumed by anger and fear.

It was some minutes before he was calm enough to go back to the table. "Misha's been telling me about the place they stayed at in Switzerland. It sounds nice," Natasha said.

Mitch fixed her with a steely look.

"You two should go." Mikhail Victorovich lit a cigar and puffed on it several times. "Better still, the next time we go, you must come along."

Mitch was spared the embarrassment of replying. Bowing low to Mikhail Victorovich, the waiter asked, "Would you like something for dessert?"

"I don't think we have time," Mitch began.

"We've time for a vodka or two," Misha interjected. The waiter quickly produced four glasses and a bottle of vodka. Misha gave the toast: *"Za vechnuyu druzhbu."* Mitch only mouthed the words.

His heart thumped in his chest as he wondered what the hell he should do when the bill appeared. He had been through several excuses in his head, each of which seemed equally lame. Then, with a grunt, Misha scraped back his chair and hauled himself to his feet. The manager appeared out of nowhere and led them to the front lobby, where staff waited with their coats. Yagudin's car was parked on the sidewalk outside the restaurant, and the driver quickly opened the rear passenger door. The manager bowed low to Misha and said he was honoured to have him visit his establishment.

At the end of the evening, Mitch poured himself a large drink and went over in his mind what he would say to Natasha. He had to know if anything was going on between her and Yagudin. It was eating him up inside. Glass in hand, he went into the bedroom. She was standing in front of the dressing table and taking off her earrings. Her jacket was on the bed. Mitch put down his glass, picked up the jacket, and looked closely at the brooch. She turned around and what could have been a flicker of panic washed across her face. "Where did you get it?" he asked, pointing a finger at the brooch.

"I ... I've had it a long time. It was my grandmother's."

"I don't remember it."

She shrugged, took the jacket from him, and hung it in the closet.

"I think you're lying."

"The way you drink," she looked at his glass, "it's a wonder you can remember your own name!"

"I'm not as blind as you think. I see things. Like tonight. With him ..."

She picked up a hairbrush and ran it through her hair. "I can't even enjoy being with friends, is that what you're saying?"

"A friend? Is that all he is? He looked more than that. The whispering in the restaurant, the ..."

"We were sharing a joke," she interjected. "That's what friends do."

"It looked more than that to me."

"That's what happens to drunks. They imagine things. See insects crawling up walls. Think they can fly." She laughed loudly. "The next thing you'll be saying is that I'm having an affair with that old man who lives down the corridor. You're pathetic!"

"And you're a whore!" he retorted.

* * *

The next morning, Mitch managed to ignore most of Natasha's barbed comments as they faced each other across the breakfast table. His head hurt like hell. *She's right,* he thought. His drinking habits were becoming a problem. Maybe he was imagining things. He didn't have any proof that there was anything going on between her and Yagudin. He had put two and two together and made what?

"Why can't we have two cars? Surely that's not too much to ask?" She pursued a well-worn path. "Misha said he can get us a Mercedes. He can arrange the permit too. It's easy."

"I bet it is. Why can't you get it into your head? I don't have the money." Until recently, not many women in the Soviet Union drove cars, let alone had their own vehicles.

"You have money for drink!"

He didn't have an answer to that. "I don't want anything to do with Misha or his stolen cars," he snapped.

"They're not stolen. He gets big discounts through his contacts."

"Discounts? Don't give me that. You know as well as I do that half the foreign cars here have been stolen."

"I don't know why you're so stubborn," the petulant voice came back at him. "You always spoil everything."

"Natasha, how much do you think I earn? We can hardly afford this place." He waved his right hand around, scattering crumbs from his half-eaten piece of bread.

Getting to her feet, she brushed the crumbs off the tablecloth into one cupped hand and threw them in the sink. "I'm getting a car, and there's nothing you can do about it!" She spat the words at him, her face close to his.

"I suppose you'll run to your father again."

She picked up her cup and saucer and put them in the sink.

"Look around outside. Most of the world is trying to scrape together enough money to exist, let alone complain because they don't have their own car. Or don't you notice the old women, the veterans, begging on street corners?" He gestured in the direction of the street. "Go look. They're probably out there now freezing to death trying to make enough money so they can eat today."

"I don't care about them," she shouted. "You care more about them than you do about me."

"How can you say that? I spend my whole life thinking about you and Anja."

She turned away and ran water into the sink. "Why shouldn't I have nice clothes, a decent car, and other things?" Mitch didn't answer. "It won't do those people out there any good if I go without."

Mitch got up from his chair and walked over to her. "I don't want your father to buy you ... us ... a car," he said, his hands on her shoulders. "I'll get you one, but not just yet."

She shrugged him off and walked to the other side of the room, wiping her hands on her skirt. "Can't you understand? I'm fed up driving around in that old thing you call a car. I'm ashamed to be seen in it. I hate it, and I hate you!" she yelled. Mitch opened his mouth to speak but she cut in. "And for your information, my father's not the only one with money." There was a note of triumph in her voice.

"What the hell do you mean?"

"Nothing." Her left eyelid twitched.

"You mean him ... Yagudin!"

She turned away. "I have other money. My mother ..."

"That's not what you meant." Mitch grabbed her arm and spun her around. "Tell me!"

"Get your hands off me," she shouted, pushing at his chest.

"Not until you tell me what you meant." He gripped her other arm.

"Let go! You're hurting."

"You didn't complain when that *zhopa* squeezed your arm last night!" Mitch glared at her and gripped her arms tighter. "Now tell me what you meant," he repeated.

She turned her head away and mumbled, "It's my mother. She's giving me some of the money Babushka left."

He let go of her arms. "Oh, your grandmother again!"

"It's Babushka's money. You don't begrudge me that, do you?" she whined, rubbing her arms.

"Well, if you already have the money, why do you keep going on at me about getting another car?"

"Because ... because I thought for once you might just manage to get me something I need. Is that too much to ask?"

He shook his head and walked out of the room.

"It's your fault we don't have enough money." Her piercing tones followed him. "Why don't you do what Misha does? You can make lots of money. He told you."

"I'm sick of hearing what that rat Yagudin does and doesn't do," Mitch yelled back at her. "It's Misha this! Misha that!" He pulled his coat out of the hall closet; the hanger clanged onto the floor. "I don't want to be mixed up in that sort of thing."

"It's all legitimate. There are always openings for lawyers in his business."

Mitch came back into the kitchen. "I bet there are. With his bent deals, lawyers must be overworked!" He put his coat on and took a couple of steps toward her. "It's him giving you the money."

She gave a nervous laugh and held the folded tablecloth in front of her body. "I told you it's my mother."

"If you're having ..."

"It's Babushka's money. Ask my mother." She shrugged her shoulders.

Mitch pointed a finger at her. "I'm warning you. If you let that thug anywhere near Anja, I swear ..."

"For God's sake, stop going on about it. Anja will be late for kindergarten." She turned, tucked the tablecloth into a drawer, and closed it with a bang.

Mitch stared at her back for a few seconds before stalking out of the room. In the hallway, he thrust his feet into his boots, picked up his car keys and briefcase, and slammed the front door behind him. A pulse throbbed in his temple as he headed for the stairs. *What the hell is she playing at?* He thought again of the way Yagudin had whispered in her ear, how she had smiled at him. He glanced back along the corridor. *I should get it out of her, make her admit it. She'll only deny it,* he told himself as he clattered down the stairs. In the entrance hall, he ignored the old woman who called to him from her chair in the corner. His anger propelled him along the path that skirted the courtyard, his boots sliding at odd angles on the slippery surface. He got into the front seat of the car, threw his briefcase onto the seat next to him, and started the engine. It spluttered several times before bursting into action and he sat for several minutes, the ice on the windows blotting out the world. Then he grabbed a scraper from the footwell in front of the passenger seat, got out, and began clearing the windows.

Why do I let her get away with it? he asked himself as he worked. *But what can I do? It will soon be New Year and Christmas, and Anja's excited about the parties. I can't spoil it for her.* Last year, he had drifted through the traditional celebrations, still raw from the loss of his mother. He had vowed that this year would be a magical time for Anja, with all the innocent happiness of a six-year-old. Inside the car, he revved the engine and pulled away. Vyacheslav, the caretaker, looked up from the side of a doorway where he was stowing garbage into bins and raised a hand in mock salute. As he drove past, Mitch's gaze was automatically drawn to Slava's wide grin, devoid of teeth, above his grey muffler. *He must be freezing,* he thought, and waved to the old man before driving through the archway and out to the street.

He shielded his eyes from the glare of the headlights of oncoming traffic. He hated these dark December days, when daylight didn't seep through until nearly 10:00 a.m. Not for the first time in the past year or so, he cursed Natasha's decision to send Anja to what she termed a more suitable kindergarten, close to her parents' home. The child had been happy at the one near their apartment, and Mitch couldn't get rid of the sneaking suspicion that the real reason behind the move was to give her ammunition for her campaign to have her own car.

The music on the radio played softly in the background, and it was some time before he realized that the program had changed and there was now a discussion about Foreign Minister Eduard Shevardnadze's resignation the previous day. In his turmoil over Natasha, he hadn't given the matter much thought. He listened for a few minutes and then snapped the radio off. *The whole damned country is lurching to disaster,* he thought angrily. The reforms that were supposed to transform the Soviet Union into a "free" market economy had floundered, and this winter even Mikhail Gorbachev's friends and advisers had begun to think the president had lost his way. Shevardnadze was now warning of an impending coup attempt and a dictatorship. The country was going back to its terrible past. Another great Russian experiment had failed.

What the hell do I care? My whole damn life's a mess. He mounted the sidewalk and made a right turn, cursing as a white Volga lurched toward him. He braked hard. "Can't anyone drive properly in this fucking city?" he shouted, banging the heels of his hands on the steering wheel.

Around the Vitebsky station, traffic slowed and heavily muffled figures wove between vehicles, puffs of white vapour where their breath had been. Mitch looked across at the outline of the majestic station building. As a child, he imagined it was a castle. He could almost hear his father's voice, long ago: "This was the station where the Tsar and his family used to board the train to *Tsarskoye Selo.*"

Ten minutes later, grainy ice crunched under his boots on the sidewalk outside the apartment building where Yelizaveta Artyemevskaya and her daughter lived. Two eager young faces peered at him through a frost-encrusted ground-floor window. He forced a smile and waved to them before pushing open the main door to the building. In what passed for a hallway, a film of ice coated the uneven paving slabs. The door of the apartment opened and he heard Anja's excited voice. "Papochka! Papochka!"

Inside, he closed the door quickly. "Have you had a good time?" he asked as he bent down and hugged her close.

"We had ice cream with chocolate sprinkles, and a feast … at midnight!" she declared, clasping her hands together in front of her mouth.

"It wasn't really midnight," her friend Katya confessed.

Mitch looked at the two girls. They couldn't be more different—in appearance, that is. Anja's unruly mop of shoulder-length, brown, corkscrew curls contrasted with Katya's silky blonde hair, which was plaited into one neat braid hanging down her back. Katya was given to plumpness; Anja didn't have any spare flesh. But both had dimples in their cheeks and shared the same childish sense of humour. As he looked at them, he said a silent prayer that they would always find fun in their lives.

"They've had a great time." Yelizaveta Artyemevskaya emerged from the kitchen. Through the open door, Mitch glimpsed a jumble of crockery littering the table. "How was your evening?" she asked.

"It was nice, thanks."

Liza smiled at him. She had the same long blonde hair as her daughter, but hers was held back either side of her face by shiny, black clips. Wisps of hair had escaped, giving her a slightly dishevelled appearance. She was leaning against the doorpost, and Mitch couldn't stop his eyes straying to the roundness of her breasts under the tight, red sweater or the way the black skirt clung to her hips.

"Come on, you two. We should be going," he said quickly. "Don't want to be late." He stooped to pick up the baby-blue overnight bag from its place by the front door; the hazel eyes of Anja's stuffed grey rabbit stared unblinkingly at him from its perch on top of the bag.

In the car, as they negotiated their way through the city streets, Mitch's thoughts were scattered. He was sure Natasha was lying about her relationship with Yagudin, the money, the brooch. Everything. The next moment, he doubted himself. *Maybe it's all in my mind.*

Snatches of the girls' chatter filtered through. "I don't believe you!" Katya's voice was indignant.

"It's true!" Anja asserted. "Papochka! Tell Katinka it's true."

Mitch gripped the steering wheel tightly, imagining Yagudin's fat fingers on Natasha's body. A chill ran through him as he wondered how many lives had been snuffed out by those fingers. Or maybe he didn't soil his own hands—others did the dirty work for him. Others like the burly man who had driven them from the restaurant to the theatre last night; Yagudin called him his driver, but he looked more like a thug.

"Papochka! It is true. Tell Katya."

Mitch looked in the rearview mirror and met his daughter's pleading look.

"Tell her, Papochka."

"Tell her what?"

"That Mama's getting a new car."

Mitch seethed inside and mumbled something through gritted teeth.

"There, I told you!" Anja said triumphantly. "It's going to be blue ... dark blue. And very shiny."

"What are you two doing at kindergarten today?" Mitch called over his shoulder some minutes later. "Anything exciting?"

"Boring stuff," they both chanted.

"Tomorrow, Mama and I are going out with Babushka Lena to choose a new dress for me. I'm going to wear it for their party," Anja announced. "Are you having a new dress for New Year, Katinka?"

Mitch took a sharp intake of breath. He knew that Katya's mother found it difficult to manage since her husband died earlier in the year. The likelihood of Katya getting a new dress was virtually nil. *I must stop Anja being obsessed with things like that. Get her away from Natasha and Lena's influence for a while. Show her you don't have to spend a lot of money to have fun.* He thought for a few moments. "Can you skate, Katya?"

"Papochka used to take me."

"Well, how about the three of us go skating in the New Year?"

"Mama can come too," Anja piped up.

Mitch took a noisy breath. "Maybe Katya's mother would like to come as well," he suggested as they pulled up outside the kindergarten gates. "Hurry, you're going to be late," he urged.

The two girls climbed out of the car, bags in hand. Anja slammed the car door and grabbed Katya's gloved hand.

Mitch leaned out of the window. *"Byt' ostorozhen!"* he cautioned as they slithered through the gap in the gates. The bell clanged. *"Ya lyublyu tebya,"* he said, almost to himself.

* * *

It was past five o'clock when Mitch returned to the office from the courthouse, and he spent the next half hour or so signing letters and responding to telephone calls. The voices of his colleagues droned in his head as they prepared to go home for the weekend. He stood up, rubbed the back of his neck, and leaned on the windowsill. Outside, snow fell on hurrying figures illuminated in the dim street lights, coating everything it touched.

His thoughts returned to long-ago Friday evenings when candlelight flickered over his mother's face as she chanted the blessing in Hebrew—the blessing that would be said in traditional Jewish families this evening. But they had not been a traditional Jewish family. He and his father had gone along with the charade. Mitch remembered now his mother's joy when his father had managed to find a somewhat battered menorah to replace the one in the trunk that had been lost in their move to Leningrad.

"I'm going now." The voice of Tamara Aleksandrevna, the typist, interrupted his reverie.

Mitch responded absentmindedly, turned from the window, and watched her disappear along the corridor. *Should I have married an ordinary woman like her?* he asked himself. Tamara's life appeared uncomplicated. She was efficient at her job, wore sensible clothes, and each evening returned to the apartment she and her husband and young son shared with his parents.

The office was empty now, and Mitch began to pace back and forth on the floorboards in front of his desk. He had done this many times over the years as he pondered this or that legal technicality, or how he was going to pay his debts. But today was different. If he didn't handle the situation with Natasha properly, it could screw up the whole of his life and Anja's.

* * *

At home that evening, he stared across the table at Natasha. He didn't know what he expected; she looked the same as ever. The outline of her nipples dimpled the fine white wool sweater she wore, and every now and then she tossed a lock of hair back off her face. He remembered that those were the things he first noticed about her all those years ago when she came into the lecture hall. *If only we could turn the clock back and make a better job of our marriage. Where has all the passion gone, the joy in being together?* She blamed him, and maybe she was right. Perhaps he should look for another job. He had been at the Bureau far beyond the three years demanded by the State. In truth, he was scared to make a move, scared of losing his secure job and plunging further into debt, scared of becoming enmeshed in corruption. Then there was the drink. He had been drinking heavily, particularly since his mother's death. It couldn't be much fun for Natasha watching him staggering around the apartment every evening. *If she is having an affair, perhaps it's been going on for some time and I've been too blind … or too drunk … to see.*

"Why do you keep staring at me?" Natasha's voice cut through his thoughts.

"Can't I even look at you now?" he retorted. His knife and fork clattered onto his plate.

"What's wrong with you?"

"My stomach hurts. Must be something I ate last night."

"Or what you drank!"

"Why are you always so bitter?"

She picked up some of the dishes from the table and put them on the counter. "Time for your bath, Annushka." Anja slid off her chair and followed her out of the room.

Mitch stood up. He really didn't feel well. He wished it were as simple as food or drink, he thought, as he walked over to the window and looked out. The snow had stopped, but the wind was whipping snowflakes from the roofs of parked cars. His eyes followed the swirling columns as they rose into the air and gathered momentum. Like the snow, his life seemed to be spinning out of control.

In the kitchen he squirted dishwashing soap into the bowl, filled it with hot water, and stood for a second or two with his hands and forearms in the suds before reaching for the first plate. His movements were slow, like a clockwork toy whose mechanical functions were winding down. After the last saucepan was dried and put away, he folded the cloth, hung it on the rack at the end of the counter, and went into the hallway.

He peeked around the corner of the bathroom door. Anja turned toward him, toothbrush in her mouth. He chuckled softly to himself as he looked at the curls that sprung out around her head. "Mama said you should tuck me into bed tonight. She has to call someone," she mumbled as she brushed her teeth.

He could make a good guess as to who she was calling. Anja turned off the tap, stood on tiptoe, and dropped her toothbrush into the holder on the wall. Mitch sat down on the edge of the bath and reached for a towel. He held out his arms to her, and she stood between his bent knees. "Look at you, *lyubov' maya,*" he said. "You've got toothpaste all around your mouth. You look like the clown at the circus." She giggled as he wiped her mouth with the towel. Her hair felt damp against his hand.

In her bedroom he switched on the bedside lamp. The base was in the shape of a little house; he and Natasha had bought it a few weeks after Anja was born, in the days when they were happy together. "You smell nice," he murmured as she scrambled into bed.

"I had bubbles."

"Well, it must be the bubbles then." He tucked the grey rabbit in beside her, pulled the quilt up to her chin, and sat on the side of the bed. It wasn't the bath foam that smelled nice—it was the warm smell of his own precious daughter. He turned his face away for a moment, swallowing back the wave of sadness that washed over him.

"Will you read me a story?"

"Read you a story?" His voice was a mere croak. "You usually read your own stories now."

"Pazhalusta ... Pazhalusta!"

"*Khorosho!* Just this once. Which one is it to be?"

"The Firebird!" she declared, pulling her arms free of the quilt and pointing to a book on the wooden chair at the side of the bedside table.

Mitch leaned over and picked it up. He could recite most of the Slavic folk tale of the orphan girl, Marushka, from memory; he had read it to her almost every night when she was very young. Now he took a deep breath and began. After a while, Anja's eyelids started to close, and it wasn't long before her long, dark eyelashes lay on her cheekbones. He continued reading for a while, his voice hardly more than a whisper. "The mischievous wind covered the feathers with grass and leaves, but nothing could rob them of their glowing rainbow colours." He closed the book, hugged it to his chest, got to his feet, and planted a kiss on her forehead. She stirred for a second and then turned on to her left side, her face buried in the rabbit. He ran his hand over the pink roof of the little house on the base of the bedside lamp, snapped the switch off, and tiptoed out of the room.

He listened outside the sitting room door; Natasha was still on the telephone. He was tempted to pick up the one in the hallway and eavesdrop, but she would hear the click, and he wasn't sure he really wanted to know. Instead, he grabbed the vodka bottle from the dining room cabinet and went through to the kitchen, where he poured himself a generous measure, swallowed it down, and sat at the table. He had to work out what to do. If he had it out with her, she would only lie. Then there would be a big row and Anja would wake up. He didn't want that. And did he really care what she did? Yagudin would tire of her before long, just as he seemed to be losing interest in Galina Antonevna. *If I ignore the whole thing, in a few months the affair—if that's what it is—will be over. If I confront her now, I'll risk losing Anja. She can fuck a different person every night for all I care!* he told himself. He gripped the neck of the bottle as realization washed through him. He really didn't care.

A few minutes later, he heard Natasha go into the bathroom and start running a bath. Cradling the bottle and glass in his arms, he decamped to the sitting room. The room was in darkness, and from the depths of the sofa he watched shadows of light and dark pass across the room. It was snowing again, and his eyes followed individual snowflakes as they danced and twirled in front of the window before being lost to sight. The vodka warmed him deep within. He felt he was floating, watching the man who used to be Mitchell Jakob Galichin drink himself to oblivion. It felt good, as though he had slipped into a comfortable room away from the world. Nothing mattered. He would end his days here with an everlastingly full bottle.

CHAPTER TWENTY-EIGHT

LENINGRAD—DECEMBER 1990

On Monday afternoon two weeks later, Mitch hurried back to the office. He had spent the past couple of hours at a People's Court, held in a former merchant's house, defending the fourteen-year-old son of a minor government official. The boy had gone on an alcohol-induced rampage, smashing windows at his school. In the pre-hearing interview, he had conducted himself with a brash air of superiority, treating the situation with a flippancy that irritated Mitch. Today, the bravado vanished. Awaiting the verdict, colour drained from his face; he sweated profusely and looked as though his legs would buckle under him. Mitch wasn't sure whether this was from fear of a harsh sentence or of his father's anger. The case was instigated at the father's insistence, to teach his son a lesson. Mitch had some sympathy for the boy and was thankful he didn't have a father like that. The boy was let off with a caution. Mitch wasn't under any illusion that his brilliant defence had led to the lenient verdict. As he left the court, he wondered how much money was in the envelope passed to the judge—to be shared with the two assessors, no doubt. Part of the farce that went by the name of justice in the Soviet Union.

As he walked, he cursed the fact that his car was off the road again. With the expense of the holiday festivities ahead, there was little chance he would have the money for the repairs any time soon. He thrust one of his hands into his overcoat pocket, berating himself for leaving his gloves in the office. His fingers touched something. He pulled out a piece of paper, unfolded it, and read:

> *Thursday evening. Seven. Lesnaya. Outside station. I have information. Remember Borya. If a friend appears suddenly ...*

He stopped in his tracks. *What the fuck? Borya? Boris Konstantinovich? It can't be. He's dead! Those words ... If a friend appears suddenly ... aren't they from a Vlad Vysotsky song?* Borya's voice ran through Mitch's head, the high-pitched tone from all those years ago. He stared at the note. There was something familiar about the handwriting. But whose was it? And what friend? It was written in pencil, the grubby paper torn from a cheap notebook. He turned it over. Nothing on the back. *Must be meant for someone else.* He looked down at his coat. There were many like it, and more than once he had taken the wrong one when leaving a public place. A search of his other pocket revealed a blue hair ribbon—Anja's—and the words on the note were too personal to be for anyone else. *Maybe it's been there for some time.* He dismissed the thought. On his way to the courthouse, he had switched his briefcase from hand to hand, warming first one hand and then the other inside his pockets. He would have found it then. So how did it get there?

He began to walk, his mind racing. *Could be from an informer*; dealings with them often held a hint of mystery. I have information. About Borya's murder? He looked at the note again and a more sinister thought hit him: *Mikhail Yagudin or one of his kontraktniki. Seven o'clock. It will be dark.* A ripple of fear ran through his body, and it was several moments before he could think rationally. *Get a grip of yourself,* he told himself firmly. *It has to be someone who knew about Boris Konstantinovich and the song. Professor Nekrassov? No ... he's dead by now or in a Samogon-induced stupor somewhere.* Then a more feasible explanation hit him. *Yuri! It's Yuri! He was in the same court today and could easily have secreted the note when the coat hung in the lobby. He's probably planning an evening carousing.* Mitch sighed. Marriage and impending fatherhood hadn't curbed Yuri's impetuous streak. *Why Lesnaya? What's he planning out there? If he thinks I'm going to spend an evening in a freezing kommunalka while he gets off with some sad young woman, he's gone too far this time,* he vowed, and screwed the note into a ball. He raised his arm to toss it away, hesitated, and put it back in his pocket.

* * *

At five o'clock on Thursday afternoon, Mitch sat at his office desk and read the note again. Yuri had denied any knowledge of it. Mitch didn't believe him. His friend's often repeated words came back to him: *You're too serious, Mitch. Take some time off and enjoy life.* Maybe he should. He deserved a break from the hell his life had become. He and Natasha hardly spoke, and when they did, they sniped at each other constantly. He should force the issue, get her to admit the truth about her and Yagudin. But there was Anja. He had to maintain some semblance of normality for her. Although what "normality" was in their household, was a dim memory. An evening carousing with Yuri might be just the tonic he needed. *Serve the bitch right!*

He would grab something to eat on his way to the Metro, and maybe a drink or two to set him up for the evening. Despite the government's efforts to restrict alcohol, it was still available—a tribute to the ingenuity of the Russian people. An icy wind whipped along the Nevsky and he walked quickly, shoulders hunched. An Intourist bus spilled an assortment of people, their brightly-colored clothing at odds with the crumbling grandeur of the buildings. Snatches of words carried on the wind as the tour guide tried to assemble her shivering brood into an orderly line. Mitch ducked into the restaurant ahead of them; he usually avoided tourist traps, but it was too cold to venture farther.

Seated at a corner table, he ordered a bowl of *Solyanka* and a brandy from a waiter dressed in the style of the Pushkin era. The waiter poured him a shot. On the far side of the room, the tour group shuffled to their seats. At the table next to Mitch, a party of six—three men and three women—burst into raucous laughter. *How long is it since I enjoyed myself like that?* he asked himself and drained the glass. *In my early student days before I met Natasha.* His life had become too serious, weighed down by a toxic mix of debt and fear. *Maybe tonight is the night to forget everything and enjoy whatever Yuri is planning.* He called for a refill, lit a cigarette, and sat back. A feeling stirred in his groin as he imagined what it would be like to be with another woman.

The spiciness of the *Solyanka* warmed him. A gypsy group in vibrant-colored costumes serenaded the bus party; the song was familiar, and the tension ebbed from his body as he hummed along. The diners at the next table took their leave—men hugging women, women hugging women, men slapping each other on the back, their faces flushed with alcohol and camaraderie. Mitch downed another drink and ordered a plate of *Khvorost,* Anja's favourite deep-fried biscuits drenched in honey and sugar. He felt a pang of guilt that he wasn't with her. *But where's the harm in enjoying myself? For one night.*

Twenty minutes or so later, he approached *Vosstaniya* Metro station. The evening air was icy, making it difficult to catch more than short gasps of breath, but the brandy and thoughts of the evening ahead warmed him. *You should do this more often.* The *pirozhok* rose majestically on top of the station building, and his thoughts drifted back to his first New Year in Leningrad. His father had told him that the *pirozhok* was called "The Little Pie." His parents had laughed loudly at his incredulous question: "Can you really eat it, Papa?" In his mind's eye he saw now the white lights of the festive tree dancing against the night sky, felt the firm grip of his parents' hands in his.

Inside the station, Mitch joined the throngs of people on the steep escalators. Because of the waterways in the city, platforms were built deep underground. Beneath illuminated ornate archways supported by stanchions of marble, he headed for the *Kirovsko/Vyborgskaya* line. Stalin had intended the stations to be "palaces for the people," and Mitch never ceased to marvel at the stunning architecture below ground. He had long ago given up trying to equate a man of such vision and sensitivity with the tyrant and psychopath Stalin was now known to have been.

In the subway car, he sat in a corner seat. A sea of open newspapers spread out before him as passengers scoured the classified advertisements looking for things to buy, rent, or exchange. Almost everything was in short supply. *Chernyshevskaya* and *Lenina* stations came and went, and Mitch's confidence began to ebb. *What if it isn't Yuri?* he taunted himself. *It may be a trap. I've not told anyone where I'm going.* At *Vyborgskaya,* the driver's cautionary announcement seemed like an omen: "*Ostorozhno. Dveri zakryvayutsyu.* Be careful. The doors are closing." *Lesnaya* was next. A check of his watch told him it was seven minutes past seven. He was late.

The train lurched and, with a screech of brakes, pulled into the station. The doors opened. Mitch stood back, letting others leave before him. The driver's announcement began again as Mitch stepped onto the platform. He waited, looking at the receding backs of the other passengers and searching for Yuri. A train pulled into the adjoining platform, and passengers spilled out. He was tempted to get on it, to go home and doze in the armchair. The train pulled away. The platform was almost empty. His footsteps echoed as he made his way to the escalator.

Outside the low station building, buses disgorged passengers. Lines of people waited, moving as one, bent toward the open doors, anxious for respite from the biting wind. Mitch paced alongside. Minutes passed and still no sign of Yuri. He leaned into the shelter of the building and lit a cigarette. A hand gripped his arm. "Remember me?"

Mitch spun around.

"Remember me?" the voice repeated.

The voice was strangely familiar. But the face? He scanned the sunken cheeks, the stubble on the chin. There was something about the eyes. Maybe not. "I don't think ..."

"The hair." The man's fingers tugged at the grey strands hanging below a knitted hat. "It was always shaved when I taught at the university."

"Professor?" Mitch searched the face for signs of the man he had known. "Professor Nekrassov?"

The other man grinned, revealing broken teeth.

"What happened to you? We thought you were ..."

"Dead!" The professor completed the sentence with relish. "The red bastards did their best!"

It really is him, Mitch thought, recalling how the professor's lectures were often peppered with profanities. The handwriting—of course, he had seen it many times scrawled across his law school papers. He offered the professor a cigarette. "Where have you been? What happened to you?"

He accepted the light Mitch offered and, leaning further into the shelter of the building, hissed, "We can't talk here."

"Why not? I'm ..."

"I'm going to take you to see someone." He wound a long, matted red scarf around his neck. "But it's better if we aren't seen together. Walk some way behind."

"Why the subterfuge?" Mitch asked, but the professor was already weaving his way between the waiting lines of people.

For a frail-looking man, he moved fast. At the corner of Kantemirovskaya ulitsa, Mitch caught sight of his woollen hat bobbing along in front of a group of people heading down Lesnoy prospekt. *So much for my evening of carousing,* he sighed as the wind howled across the road from the inky darkness of Karl Marx Park. On his left, faded anti-military-draft slogans adorned the pink and grey walls of the Bateninsky residential array. Mitch's father had brought him here years ago and explained that the 1930s buildings were erected for workers in factories on Vyborgsky side. He recalled now that the area's most famous resident was Leonid Nikolaev, who on a December day in 1934, walked to Smolny and gunned down Sergey Kirov, the Leningrad Party Secretary. Originally blamed on an anti-Stalinist cell, the assassination was the catalyst for five years of brutal purges throughout the country. It was now widely believed that Stalin himself was behind the murder.

Mitch had a moment of panic. *Where the hell's he gone?* He ran down a pathway between two buildings, boots slithering on the ice, and caught a glimpse of the tail end of a red scarf disappearing around a corner. His teeth chattered as he hurried after it. Sword-like icicles spilled from the fractured drainpipes of grime-bespattered buildings. Frozen laundry hung like petrified ghosts on balconies above. "Fuck!" he cursed aloud. "Where is he?" Mitch walked quickly to the end of the building, peering into doorways. At the corner, he scanned left and right.

"Down here!" The voice came from the depths of the frozen ground. "Make sure no one's following you."

Mitch peered between rusty pipes supporting a canopy over a flight of stone steps. A door at the bottom was partially open. A hand beckoned. He checked up and down the deserted footpath and then began to descend the steps. A gust of wind dislodged one of the loose iron sheets above his head. The clang startled him, and he slithered down the last few steps. The door opened wider and he was pulled inside.

Mitch squinted into the dimness within. He was in some sort of candle-lit cellar. "What's going on?"

"All in good time." The professor led him toward a table at the far side of the room. "First, you have to meet my dear friend."

Mitch's heartbeat raced wildly. *Not Borya, it can't be.*

A small man emerged from the shadows. As he came closer, Mitch saw a skeletal face; almost colourless eyes bulged above sharply-etched cheekbones. Wisps of hair sprouted from a conical-shaped skull. "Anatoly Vasilovich Savenkov," the man rasped.

Mitch nodded in acknowledgement.

The professor banged a bottle down on the table. "Something to warm us."

"Not Samogon! I'm not drinking that stuff."

"For you, we have the best vodka—*Sankt-Peterburg.*"

The bottle was still sealed, and Mitch looked at the label—not the best, but vodka.

"Tolya got it especially for you."

"I'll get the cups." Tolya shuffled toward the sink on the other side of the room; pipes clanged as he ran cups under a spluttering stream of water.

"Sit here." The professor wiped a hand across the seat of a wooden chair by the side of the table. Tolya handed Mitch a cup. Close-up, his skin looked yellow. *Like Maman's was toward the end,* Mitch thought to himself. As Tolya took his seat on the other side of the table, he began to wheeze. "It's the smoke." The professor gestured toward the small stove. "It's the only way we can keep warm."

"It's freezing in here," Mitch said. A stack of what looked like sawn-up floorboards was piled at the side of the stove. He remembered Babushka's tales of how she and his father used to scavenge for wood to burn in the *burzhuika* during the Siege. A haze of smoke hovered in the half-light.

The professor laid an arm across Tolya's back and spoke to him in a low voice. Mitch turned away, unwilling to intrude, and looked around the room. *How can anyone live here?* he asked himself. There was no natural light and, apart from a narrow bed along one wall, the chairs, and the table they were sitting at, no other furniture. *They must use the top of the burzhuika for cooking or heating water.* Mingled with the smell of smoke, Mitch detected an underlying odour of unwashed bodies. He looked now at the two men, their gentle actions, their concern. *In some ways, they have so much more than me, so much more than most people.* For all Natasha's extravagant ways, the apartment had never felt like home—not a home to be truly shared, where you loved and were loved in return.

Mitch broke the seal on the bottle, slurped vodka into his cup, downed the drink in one gulp, and poured another before pushing the bottle across the table toward Tolya. "It's good. The vodka. *Spasiba.*"

The liquid in the bottle gurgled as the professor poured some into the other cups. "We must toast good friends," he said and handed one to Tolya. *"Za vechnuyu druzhbu!"*

To eternal friendship, Mitch repeated to himself, still hardly believing that the professor had survived. "What happened after you left the university?"

The professor waved a dismissive hand. "That is not important. We have brought you here to hear Tolya's story." He turned and smiled encouragingly at his friend.

Tolya cleared his throat and began hesitantly: "I ... I was a police officer in Israel."

Mitch frowned. *This wizened man was once a member of one of the toughest police forces in the world?*

"You find it hard to believe?" Tolya looked levelly at him. "I was strong. I wrestled with men here at the Sports Club, the officers, *vory*. No one could beat me." A satisfied look passed across his face, and then he sighed loudly. "That was then. My wife, she wanted to go back to her family in Israel. We took our daughters with us and lived in Haifa. They are still there, and I am …" His words trailed off.

The professor patted Tolya's hand and then turned to Mitch. "You are wondering? A gay man—a *goluboi*? Married with children?" There was a note of sarcasm in his voice. "It happens. Sometimes, like Anatoly Vasilovich, we marry for love. It is possible to love men and women at the same time." A sad smile washed across his face. "Others marry to maintain an outward façade so no one suspects."

Tolya took up his story again: "In Haifa, I went to a party one night. My friends and I, we had too much to drink and, as men sometimes do, we ended up in a brothel."

It can't be happening again, it can't. Mitch shook his head, trying to shake out the image of Timochenko as he spoke of his sister all those years ago. His twisted body …

"I had never done anything like that before. I am not proud of it, but that is what happened," Tolya continued.

"He is a good man," the professor murmured.

"There was a girl. Very young. Younger than my daughters. But you must understand, I didn't touch her, didn't do anything to her. Just listened to her story." He held Mitch's gaze for several seconds. "She was from the Ukraine. She begged me to help her get back to her family. She said that when they weren't working, she and the other girls were locked in separate rooms so that they couldn't plan anything, talk about escaping. She was forced to have many men each day and night. Sometimes they were made to stand on the side of a road and pick up men. The pimp beat them if they didn't do what they were told. She had cigarette burns on her arms, bruises on her legs."

Mitch's heart thumped wildly. The words sounded like a death knell. He took a gulp of his drink, seeing again the sunken eyes of Timochenko, his gaunt face, his words so similar as he spoke of another young woman. "What … what did you do?" he heard himself ask.

"Nichego." Tolya sobbed quietly.

"Don't upset yourself." The professor handed him a grey-looking rag. "You did your best."

Mitch wondered what he would have done. It was heart-rending enough hearing tales second-hand, but seeing the despair in the eyes of a young girl as she told her story? He didn't know.

"I am not proud of myself," Tolya gulped. "Why did I go to a place like that? It's men like me …"

Mitch shifted in his seat, thinking guiltily of how he had relished the thought of spending the evening in drunken debauchery.

The professor continued Tolya's tale. "He didn't do anything at the time, but he thought a lot about the girl. About all the girls. He began to make enquiries about the people running the brothel, their contacts in the police force, border guards. One night, he was called to an incident on the edge of the city. He didn't go alone, but when he got there, the other policeman vanished. A car blocked the exit from the alleyway. Its headlights blinded him. He never saw his assailants. They left him to die."

The only noise was the dripping of the tap. Tolya sat in silence, head down, and it was a few moments before he spoke. "In the medical centre some days later, I was told by my superior officer that my contract had been cancelled. Immigration irregularities, he said. I had seven days to leave the country. My family … they stayed."

"I'm sorry for you," Mitch began. The words sounded inadequate. "But why are you telling me this?" His eyes were smarting from the smoke from the fire, and he ran the back of a hand across them.

"Tolya spent last winter sleeping outside. I found him and brought him here. He was very sick and rambled on about what had happened in Haifa, what is happening here. Living in the underbelly of society, people have stories to tell. Stories. Always stories. And names. We hear and see a lot, get to know who is really in charge in the city, who to avoid. We have places to hide, to watch." The professor glanced around. "Rat holes worse than this. We know who the people are, those who prey on innocence, selling young girls into sexual slavery. They give no thought to the human toll. *Den'gi! Den'gi! Den'gi!* That's what it's about. Money! So they can live in fancy houses, drive fancy cars, with fancy women!" He spat the last words out.

Mitch slopped vodka into his cup and gulped it down. *Don't listen to them,* he told himself. *It doesn't concern you. You have too much to lose.* "Everyone knows it happens. I've heard these tales before, and suffered for it! But believe me, there's nothing I can do. Nothing anyone ..."

"That's what everyone says. What I said," Tolya croaked. "We all make excuses."

"But now we have names." The professor got to his feet, took a penknife out of his coat pocket, and levered a brick out of the wall behind him. He pulled something out of the cavity and pushed the brick back in place. He snapped the knife shut, sat down, and extracted a sheaf of papers from the plastic bag he held in his hand.

"In here are the names of those running the rackets. You may know some of them." He placed the papers on the table. "There are also details of trafficking routes and those who take bribes. Government officials, *militsiya,* border guards."

"What do you expect me to do? Take on these people?" Mitch hunched his shoulders, shrinking into himself, feeling again the blows to his body, seeing the face so close to his, the jagged scar across the cheek. So vivid. The memory of that day hadn't faded. It still held the power to send him into paroxysms of fear. His hands trembled.

"It has to start somewhere, somehow," the professor urged.

"Not with me. Look for someone else. Someone with a death wish!"

The professor ignored his comments. "They make big money. More than you or I could earn in a lifetime. But at what cost?"

"You're not listening!" Mitch's voice was loud now. "I can't get involved." Despite the cold, he was sweating.

"The cost is the lives of young girls." The professor pushed the papers across the table toward Mitch. "Some of their names are in there, and the places where they are held."

Mitch avoided the accusing looks directed his way as he tried not to think of Vanya's sister, Klavdiya—the summer day when sunlight burnished her hair as she ran toward him. The last time he saw her.

"How old is your daughter?" Tolya's voice cut through his thoughts. "Six? Seven?" Mitch didn't answer. "In a few years, she could be one of their victims."

"I won't let it happen. Not to her!"

"How are you going to stop it? She'll be walking along a street and someone—maybe someone she knows and trusts—will lure her away to some far-off place." The professor paused for a moment. "They'll take away her passport and convince her that if she runs away, she'll be sent to prison for being in the country illegally. If she goes to the police," his laugh sounded manic, "she'll be back in the brothel before she knows it!"

Mitch swallowed bile that had risen in his throat.

"The girls, they are sold on to other pimps. Even when they are pregnant, there is no let-up. There are men who pay twice as much for sex with pregnant women. And the babies? Abandoned or thrown off balconies or into rivers, as their mothers are when they are no longer useful. Do you condone that?" the professor asked Mitch.

"Zatknis'!" Mitch spat, trying to block out the nightmare that plagued him—the limbs of babies reaching up out of the Neva. "Why won't you listen to me? There's nothing I can do!"

"It could be your daughter, your granddaughter." Tolya wheezed and was soon bent double. The rag was now spattered with blood.

Mitch pulled his handkerchief out of his pocket and pushed it across the table, the whiteness of the fabric luminous in the subterranean gloom. His mouth was dry and he poured himself another drink and threw it down his throat. Both men's eyes were now on him. "Why me? Why don't you tell your story to someone else?" As he spoke, he heard his mother's voice: *Why shouldn't it be you, Mitch?* Those words had always been her response when, as a child, he whined about some trivial injustice. *This is different,* he told himself now.

"Can you imagine what it's like to live in fear of your life? Every day, year after year." It was the professor who spoke.

"Why don't you do something about it yourselves?"

"Us? They're going to believe us?" The professor laughed loudly; the noise reverberated around the room. He gulped down the vodka from Tolya's cup, went over to the sink, drew some water, and held the cup to Tolya's lips. "But coming from someone like you, that would be different."

Mitch pulled out his cigarettes, took one himself, and offered them across the table. Tolya shook his head; Mitch lit the professor's cigarette and then his own. "You've already told me what happened to Tolya. And you expect me to put myself in the same position?"

"There won't be any danger to you," the professor said. "We have a plan ... one that will be difficult to trace back to you."

Mitch snorted loudly. "And how do I know the information is genuine?"

"You have my word for it," the professor said solemnly.

"*Nyet!* It's too risky. I can't get involved." Mitch made a big play of checking his watch, got to his feet, and buttoned his coat. "I have to go."

"Please. Listen to our plan. That's all we ask. Then you can go," Tolya pleaded. "Go home to your wife and daughter. Your happy family."

If only you knew. Mitch sat down again.

The professor reached for the papers. "We want you to go to London ..."

"You can't be serious!" Mitch looked at both men. Their gaze was unflinching. "London? How am I supposed to manage that?"

"There are conferences. Gatherings of lawyers. Things are easier now. People like you can leave the country."

"And what would I do when I got there?"

"Newspapers. The newspapers there print stories, stories like this. They aren't censored or run by the government. You give the information to them."

"Why don't you send the papers to them. There must be ways."

"You think they wouldn't be intercepted before they left the country?" The three men sat in silence for some moments before the professor spoke again. "The people in London, they will need some sort of personal contact with the informant. Know they can trust him. A lawyer ... like you."

"You make it sound easy," Mitch scoffed. "And what if they found out it was me? The *mafiyosa ... vory*? What do you propose I do to protect myself, my family?"

"That would be part of the deal. Anonymity for you."

"You're crazy! Those people have informers everywhere. They'd find out."

"Aren't those young girls worth the risk? There are thousands of them. Maybe more."

Mitch looked away, biting his lip.

"Think of their families. How must they feel not knowing ... imagining, dreading?"

What if I do it and something happens to me? One life to save many? Strangely, he didn't care about himself. It was Anja. Who would protect her if he wasn't around? *But what if when she's older ... ? Don't even think about it!* he cautioned himself. *She's safe at the moment, that's the important thing.* "I can't. I can't do ..."

Tolya cut in. "So you're going to continue your comfortable life knowing that every minute of the day, young girls are being raped, tortured, murdered, while some pimp gets rich on the proceeds?" He breathed noisily.

"Please. Take the papers and think about it." The professor put the papers back in the plastic bag and slid it across the table toward Mitch.

"You're not listening to me!" With a swipe of his hand, Mitch knocked the bag onto the floor. "I don't want anything to do with it. I can't!" He shoved his chair back and got to his feet. He had to get out of this place. "I've already seen one person murdered for trying to help one of these girls."

"Whatever happened to the decent young man I taught all those years ago?"

"He grew up. Got a life. One he doesn't want to lose."

"You disappoint me." Professor Nekrassov bent down and picked up the plastic bag. "You used to have principles. Principles worth fighting for. Now look at you!" He sneered.

The room started to close in on Mitch. His vision clouded, and the walls tilted at odd angles. He ground his cigarette out on the floor, grabbed his *shapka* and gloves, and stumbled to the door.

"Go! Run, you coward!" Was that the professor's voice, or was it Mitch's own voice in his head? He didn't know. He jammed the *shapka* on his head, wrenched the door open, and slammed it behind him. Outside, he went quickly up the steps. The wind had dropped and freezing fog cloaked the area, shrouding him with every step. Already he was lost. *Go! Run, you coward!* the words followed him. He heard a door open and quickened his pace. Footsteps followed him and he began to run, weaving around blindly as though the hounds of hell were after him. The noise of his footsteps filled the space around him and drummed in his ears, clattering like hoof beats. He skidded to a halt and groped his way along the side of a building, the hoof beats deafening now. Cowering against a wall, he pressed his hands to his ears and slid to the ground. He was again the terrified child beneath the statue of the Bronze Horseman in Senate Square, waiting for the hooves to crush him. It was some moments before the noise faded and he leaned back, relaxing his arms, the only sound now his own laboured breath.

With trembling hands, he lit a cigarette, took several drags, and waited until the thumping of his heart settled into a calmer rhythm. *What's the matter with you? You're going crazy!* It was years since he had thought about that rearing horse. He avoided Senate Square whenever he could, but this was something else. What was he scared of? Those two old men? How could they hurt him? Tolya looked as though he wasn't long for this world, and the Professor not much better. Waves of pity washed through him now as he thought of the two of them living in that awful place, the tenderness they had shown each other. He got stiffly to his feet and blew breath onto his frozen hands. Where were his gloves? He stumbled back to the footpath, scanning the ground, searching for them. A shape approached through the fog. Mitch shrank further into his overcoat, gripping the lapels tight around his throat.

"I've been looking everywhere for you. You shouldn't have rushed off like that." Professor Nekrassov held out the rolled-up bag containing the papers. "Please take them. We have no one else to give them to." He grabbed Mitch's coat, thrust the papers into his pocket, turned on his heel, and was swallowed up in the gloom.

CHAPTER TWENTY-NINE
LENINGRAD—JANUARY 1991

Natasha looked at herself in the full-length mirror, hands resting on her hips. The fine silk of the purple dress, cinched in at the waist, emphasised her shapely figure. Faint traces of a smile softened her mouth. Diamonds dangled from her ears; the pear-shaped stones glinted in the light from the wall sconces. Her right hand caressed the matching necklace where it rested above the plunging neckline, revealing just enough of her breasts. A tremor ran through her body. *Enough to tantalize.* Tonight her senses tingled; her whole being pulsated. She bent down to adjust the straps of her black high-heeled shoes, turning her feet this way and that. Straightening up, she ran her fingers through strands of hair, pulling them forward onto her cheeks.

Satisfied, she walked to the console table at the far side of the sitting room, grasped the neck of the champagne bottle, lifted it out of the ice bucket, and tested the coolness of the bottle with the tips of her fingers before grinding it back between the chunks of ice. Two crystal glasses gleamed from their resting place on a silver tray. She ran her fingers over the table's matched Circassian walnut veneers and traced the brass mouldings on the front of the centre drawer—two sphinxes, their tails extending magically into luxuriant flowering plants. The table was a wedding gift from Vera Kishinevskaya. She frowned. When Vera and Mitch were together, it was as though the two of them inhabited a private world in which Natasha had no place. She had tried to rationalize her feelings. It couldn't be jealousy, not with a woman Vera's age. But what did she care? Tonight, Mitch was in Moscow.

Tonight belonged to her and Misha. He made her feel special. He was exciting, moved at a fast pace, knew how to enjoy himself. Over the past weeks, she feared Mitch would confront her with what he suspected. She had nearly blurted everything out. But Misha insisted they wait. When the time was right, he would set her and Anja up in a beautiful apartment, and they would want for nothing. They would travel abroad, stay in the best hotels. There would be someone to look after Anja. "Don't I love her as my own daughter?" His lawyers would fix the divorce and custody of the child. Of course, he would have to get rid of Galina

Antonevna. "She puts up with my dalliances, my flirtations, as long as it doesn't affect her lifestyle. But we have to be careful. She could make things difficult for me … my business activities," he said. Natasha brushed off his explanation. As long as she could be with him, nothing else mattered. Sometimes not even Anja.

For years, Natasha had dominated the men around her, taking delight in bending them to her will, making them worship her, bestowing favours on them now and again. But with Misha it was different. He oozed power and authority. People took notice of him. When he touched her, an unfamiliar feeling of submission washed through her, exciting her. Sometimes he teased her, running his hands over her body until she begged him to come into her. He would shake his head and say she had to earn it. Then he would be rough, even brutal. She enjoyed the physical pain, the way he possessed her. At other times, he was gentle and caressing. The uncertainty increased her sense of desire. He always rewarded her. Now her hands went automatically to the diamond necklace, and she relived again the time he had taken her to his *dacha* in Semiozerie. A storm was brewing and, when rain lashed against the windows, he opened the full-length doors to the garden and took her hand. Outside, he licked rain off her naked skin as streaks of lightning flashed across the sky illuminating the tattoos on his body. The noise of the wind and claps of thunder added to the intensity of their lovemaking. Afterwards, he carried her inside the house and laid her in front of the fire. Covered with his jacket, she breathed in the smell of the man whose very being could make her tremble with longing. She had slept, and when she awoke, the necklace was wound around her fingers. The earrings came later.

Now she picked up a framed photograph. It was taken outside the church on their wedding day. Mitch looked young, a mere boy. He was a virgin, and she had guided his fumbling, enjoying the sense of power and sexual superiority. In an odd way, she had loved him. But not the all-consuming passion she felt for Misha. He was a powerful opiate, one which she couldn't do without. Mitch had been more compliant, easy to dominate. She had defied her father's wishes, manipulating him too until he agreed to their marriage. On their wedding day, a thrill ran through her body when she saw the stricken look on her father's face. She was powerful indeed. At times now she felt a sadness for lost times—times when Mitch had talked to her in soft tones that spoke of love and concern. He could pluck sunshine out of a cloudy day. But the sunshine had faded and she was bored with him and the way he expected her to exist. She needed nice things, fun in her life, and was tired of his constant whining that they didn't have money. And why didn't they have money? Because he wouldn't do what everyone else had done from time immemorial. They bribed people, or turned a blind eye to some scam to get a better job, a larger apartment. That was how people lived—everyone except Mitch and his damned principles. She pulled out a drawer and dropped the picture inside.

The peal of the telephone startled her. Her stomach fluttered and she pressed it lightly through the silk of her dress as she walked across the room. *"Da?"*

"Mamochka, is that you?"

"Yes, it's me, Anja."

"I wanted to say goodnight. We've had *syrniki* and *kefir.*"

"That was nice," Natasha replied, shifting her position so that she could see into the courtyard. The big black Mercedes was just emerging from the archway. She thought of Misha, the strength in his body, and the way he would remove her dress, her underwear, admire her perfect figure. She breathed in, savouring the stirrings of desire.

"And we dressed up in Katya's mother's clothes. I had red shoes and …"

"That's nice," Natasha's distracted voice interrupted Anja's flow. "You go to sleep now and I'll give you a call in the morning before you go to school."

"Will you be all right on your own?" The child's concern belied her tender age.

"Mama will be fine."

Natasha replaced the receiver. *Tomorrow will be Anja's,* she resolved as she walked into the hallway.

CHAPTER THIRTY

LENINGRAD–JANUARY 1991

"Why don't you take Anja to buy her new shoes? She knows where we get them," Natasha urged.

It was Saturday afternoon, two days after Mitch had returned from Moscow. "You could come too," he responded. "Make an afternoon of it. Stop for tea or an ice cream somewhere."

Anja's face lit up at the mention of ice cream. "Can we Mama? Please?"

"*Nyet.* Not today. I'm going to Eugenia and Sasha's."

It was on the tip of Mitch's tongue to ask who the hell Eugenia and Sasha were. He swallowed the words, knowing she would launch into a diatribe, at the end of which he would be made to feel guilty that he couldn't recall her so-called friends. If they existed.

In the hallway, Natasha put on her fur coat and zipped her long boots. "There's the remains of yesterday's meal in the fridge," she threw over her shoulder to Mitch as she headed to the front door. "I won't need anything. Eugenia is cooking a big meal."

I bet she is! Mitch thought to himself.

"Can I come with you?" Anja trailed behind her.

Natasha turned and stooped to kiss the top of her daughter's head. "Not today. There won't be any children there," she said firmly, ignoring the child's wails.

"Natasha!" The door slammed behind her. Mitch stared at it.

"Why wouldn't she take me?" Anja sidled up to him.

"There's nothing to cry about." He bent down and gathered her into his arms. "We can still go for ice cream. *Khorosho?*"

She nodded.

"You go and get ready while I clean up in the kitchen." He gave her a gentle push.

From the kitchen window, he watched Natasha brushing snow off her new blue Mercedes. *She's going with him, she must be.* It had only stopped snowing an hour ago, and she wouldn't normally venture out until the roads were clear. He had to do something. But how could he follow her with Anja there? He had thought about getting someone else to do it but wasn't sure he really wanted proof. "Lying bitch!" he cursed under his breath as she got into the car.

Some minutes later, Anja's plaintive voice came from the kitchen doorway: "When will Mama be back?"

It went through his mind that if she didn't come back, it would solve his problems. He would have custody of Anja, clear his debts, and the two of them would be happy together. Maybe ask his father to live with them.

"When will she be back?"

"Later," he muttered, drying his hands on a towel.

"Can we go and sing with the snow?"

Since his daughter had first started to walk, he had taken her out in fresh snow and made up silly songs, which they both sang out loud. It was the last thing he felt like doing today, but he had to make an effort for her sake. And it might stop him from thinking about Natasha and that bastard. "Why don't we go to the gardens? The snow will be deep there. Then, after we've bought your shoes, we'll go to *Yeliseev's*. They may have chocolate," he tempted.

"And we have to get Mama a gift for her birthday."

"*Da*. A gift for Mama."

An hour or so later, Mitch pulled open the door of the shoe shop. A bell clanged and he ushered Anja inside. The interior of the shop was dimly lit, and a female assistant glanced up from where she was kneeling in front of the window, tying a young boy's shoe laces. The boy and a woman—who was probably his grandmother—were the only other customers. Mitch and Anja stamped their feet on the doormat; clumps of snow spilled off their boots. He looked around, remembering the times his mother had brought him here. The room was smaller than it seemed to his young eyes all those years ago. The straight line of upright chairs in front of the shelves on either side of the room were lined up much as they were before. The worn brown linoleum looked vaguely familiar, but maybe not. "It hasn't changed much," he whispered.

Anja looked up at him, her cheeks blotched red from the wind. "Mama always takes me to the store where Babushka's friend works. They have special shoes there."

"I'm sure we'll find something nice here," Mitch cajoled as they walked forward together. He scanned the shelves. Although still limited, there was a greater variety of colours and styles now. In his day, there were only lace-up shoes in two colours: black and brown. An assistant approached. She was tall and thin and dressed in a plain green dress.

Fifteen minutes later, boxes littered the floor in front of where Mitch and Anja sat. Anja turned away, gripping the vertical bars of the chair with both hands. "I don't like horrible black shoes. I want red shoes. Mama said I could have them."

"You need shoes for kindergarten," Mitch insisted. Anja pouted. He sighed loudly and asked the assistant, "Do you have any red?"

"I think we have a couple of pairs in her size."

Anja loved the first red pair she tried and paraded back and forth on the linoleum, never taking her eyes from the shiny shoes with the strap across. Mitch looked at the price on the box. It was more than he had expected, but prices had spiralled out of control since Mikhail Sergeyevich's bungled efforts to decentralize the Soviet economy. Anja skipped over to where Mitch was sitting and beamed at him.

Outside, the wind whipped eddies of snowflakes into the air as they joined the throng of people crossing the street at the traffic lights. Anja's feet slipped from under her, and Mitch yanked at her arm. The bag holding her new red shoes swayed in her hand as he pulled her upright and helped her over a pile of snow heaped alongside the curb.

They walked in silence, Mitch pondering how he was going to manage until he got paid again. They had spent far too much at New Year, and the car repairs cost more than he anticipated. Now the shoes.

"Papa! Papa!" Anja shrieked. "There's Mamochka and Dyadya Mikhail." She wriggled free of his grasp.

He stopped in his tracks and looked where her finger was pointing. Natasha ... and Mikhail Yagudin. They were standing in the shadow of an archway on the other side of the street. Yagudin had his arm around her. Blood pounded noisily in Mitch's temples. He gaped at them, rooted to the spot. At that moment a black car pulled up and a man in a dark overcoat got out of the driver's side and hurried around the back of the car.

"That's Boris, Papa. He's nice. He took me to Katya's when you were away."

Mitch tried to move forward, to take a step into the road, to run across the street and confront them. He was transfixed, his hands gripped into tight fists, every nerve in his body taut. He couldn't move.

"Boris let me play with all the things in the back of the car. They have real drinks in there," Anja jabbered. "Quickly, Papa. Let's go and see them." She waved a hand frantically and pulled at Mitch's wrist. "Mama! Mama!" Her voice was lost in the siren of a *militsiya* vehicle careening in and out of traffic.

"Nyet! Nyet!" Mitch heard his own voice, far away.

"They've gone," Anja wailed.

He stared across the street to the place where Natasha and Yagudin had stood.

"I wanted to show Mamochka my new shoes."

His head felt as though it was going to burst. A feeling of disgust washed through him. Disgust for them and for himself. How could they do that? And how could he have stood there and watched them? He should have pulled her away. Punched him! The street was strangely quiet now, the only sound the crunching of boots in the snow.

"Papa! Papa! What's wrong?" Anja tugged on his arm again and again. "Papochka ..."

"Chto-to ne tak?" The woman's voice jolted him out of his trance.

He pulled his *shapka* off and threw it onto the ground.

"It's Papochka," Anja cried. "He's gone all funny."

Mitch opened his mouth to speak. His lips were numb. He couldn't form the words. After a moment, he reached out and took his daughter's hand. "It ... it's okay," he stammered, a vacant expression on his face.

The woman picked up his hat and held it out to him. A frown creased her forehead. *"Chto s vami?"*

"I didn't feel well ... dizzy." Mitch managed a weak smile. "I'm okay now."

"If you're sure." She started to walk away and then turned and hesitated. "The little girl?"

"She's fine."

The woman went on her way.

"Did I do something wrong?" Anja asked in a small voice.

He shook his head, trying to rein in his emotions. "Papa's fine now. Let's go home."

"What about Mama's gift? And the chocolate?"

"Another day. We'll get the chocolate another day."

* * *

About nine o'clock that evening, Mitch closed Anja's bedroom door quietly. Unsettled by the events of the day, it had taken a long while for her to go to sleep. He poured himself a drink and took it into the bedroom he shared with Natasha. Her clothes were scattered on the floor, draped over a chair. He had long ago ceased tidying up after her. He picked up a dress and looked at the label: *Zaitsev*. The name sounded vaguely familiar. Where had he heard it? After a moment, it came back to him. "Zaits*ev ... the Red Dior."* She had thrust a glossy magazine in front of him. "The dress. So elegant. Don't you think so, Mitch?" He had barely glanced at the picture, certain that a dress like that would cost more than most people earned in several months. Now he dropped the dress onto the floor where he had found it and began searching the dressing table drawers. He didn't know what he was looking for or why he was bothering. He had enough proof of what was going on. He had seen them together. *Lying bitch!*

He pulled a magazine off the pile on Natasha's bedside table and began leafing through it, shaking his head at the pomposity of it all. He thought of his mother, the way she had mended her clothes, making them last. "This will do for another year," had been her stock phrase as she darned an already thin jacket or winter coat. He dropped the magazine back onto the heap. As he did so, something fell down behind the table.

He leaned over and grasped a small, grey velvet box. He clicked it open. It was the opal brooch—the one she said had belonged to her grandmother. In gold lettering on the dark blue satin lining was the inscription, *Staeli-Frieden, Zurich. Zurich? What was it Yagudin said that evening at Ket? "The next time we go to Switzerland, you must come with us."*

"Bitch!" Mitch cursed loudly. "I knew it!" He threw the box hard against the wall.

Two hours later, he heard Natasha's key in the lock. The front door closed. He took a deep breath, put down his glass, got out of the armchair, and walked across the darkened sitting room.

"Did you and Anja have a good time?" she asked brightly as he came into the hallway.

"You slut!" he said slowly, deliberately.

She paused for a moment and then turned and reached into the closet.

He grabbed her arm, pulled her toward him, wrenched the coat out of her hands, and threw it on the floor. "How dare you! We saw you with that ... that ..." He spat the words in her face and gripped her other arm hard.

"Let go of me." Her voice was low and deliberate as she twisted her upper body in an effort to loosen his grip. He began to shake her. A look of fear passed across her face. "Stop it!" she yelled, kicking him in the shin. He winced. Hatred built up within him. He slapped her hard across her left cheek. She reeled backwards, knocking against a table. The lamp on it swayed. "You bastard!" she shouted.

He still had her by one arm and dragged her into their bedroom and threw her onto the bed. His shoulders rose and fell as he tried to calm himself. "Stay where you are!" he commanded and closed the door.

"And who are you to tell me what to do?" she said, getting slowly to her feet and inching around the bed, away from him.

"I'm your husband, that's who I am. Or have you forgotten?" He fought to control the trembling in his body.

"Some husband you are. You can't even take care of your family," she taunted.

"I'm warning you." He pointed a finger at her. "Stay away from that bastard!"

"If you're talking about Misha, he's more of a man than you'll ever be!"

He moved around the bed. "He's a *vor!* A vicious sadist!" He spat the words out. "You let him anywhere near Anja, and I swear ..."

"You'll what?" she sneered. "Anja likes him. She has fun with him. He ..."

"Keep him away from her!" Mitch interjected, coming closer and jabbing his finger against her chest.

"And what's the big man going to do about it?"

At that moment, Mitch lost it. Like a man possessed, he grabbed her hair in one hand and twisted her head toward him. Then both hands went to her throat. Power coursed through his fingers. She struggled. He pressed harder, harder. It felt good. Her eyes bulged and strange noises came from her mouth. He stared at her. She went limp, her eyes rolled back in her head. An instant later, he came to his senses and let go. She dropped onto the bed.

He backed away, the only noise now the sound of his breathing. He turned, groped blindly for the dressing table, and gripped the edges with both hands. *God! What have I done?* The room was spinning. He closed his eyes and tightened his grip. When he looked again, he didn't recognize the face with the wild eyes staring back at him in the mirror. He shifted his gaze. He could see Natasha's reflection in the glass. She wasn't moving. A feeling of dread washed through him and he turned around slowly. As he did, she rolled on to her side, drew her legs up to her body, and coughed.

"Thank God." He let out a noisy breath. "Natasha," he murmured. "I'm sorry. I don't know ..."

"Sorry? Is that all you can say?" Her voice was hoarse. She shifted away from him and sat up, one hand at her throat.

Mitch took a step toward her.

"Stay away from me, you maniac!" She coughed and moved farther away.

Energy drained from his body. A cold chill gripped the pit of his stomach. *You nearly killed her.*

She started to get up. "Don't come near me," she warned, swiping his hands away as he reached out to help her. "Get out of here!"

His legs felt like stone.

"Get out! I don't want you here, you brute!"

"I can't leave Anja, she's ..."

"You're not going anywhere near her." She staggered past him and yanked the door open. "Get out!"

"Natasha, please," he pleaded, "you know I'd never do anything to hurt her. She's all I live for."

"You're not going anywhere near her," she repeated, stumbling into the hallway.

"I can't. I can't leave her." He sank down onto the bed and put his head in his hands.

"We're finished!" She bent down, unzipped one of her boots, and threw it through the doorway, narrowly missing his head. The other boot fell short of where he sat. "You're despicable!"

He stared at his fingers, curled again as they had been around her neck. All the anger of the past few years had spilled out. He had totally lost control. *What sort of monster are you?* he asked himself, thinking of the thrill that ran through his body, how he had enjoyed the feeling of power. A sob rose in his throat, and his whole body shook. Some minutes later, he ran a hand across his cheeks and straightened up. She was talking to someone on the telephone. On shaky legs, he made his way into the hallway. She put the receiver down. "My mother's on her way." She tried to clear her throat. "You're damned lucky my father isn't home."

"Natasha, please." He walked toward her. "I'm sorry. So sorry."

"Sorry won't get you anywhere. I want you out of here!" she said and disappeared into the kitchen.

In the sitting room he leaned on the desk, trying to think of what to do. *You've played right into her hands. How could you have been so stupid? Now you're the one at fault.* He poured a drink and gulped it down. *Thank God Anja didn't wake up.* He picked up the phone and dialled. "I'll explain when I get there," he said, stopping his father's flow of questions.

Natasha was now standing in front of Anja's bedroom door.

"Can't we just talk about this?" he began in a low voice.

She brought her right hand from behind her back. She was holding a long kitchen knife.

"For Christ's sake, Natasha, there's no need for that. All I want to do is talk."

"So what was that before?" she said, her left hand rubbing her throat, a look of contempt on her face. "Can't you get it into your stupid head? I have nothing to say to you."

They glared at each other in silence. Then he turned, went into the bedroom, and threw some things into an overnight bag. He zipped it up, carried it into the hallway, dropped it onto the floor, and turned toward Anja's door. Natasha was there before him.

"Let me talk to her. Please."

"After what you did, you're not going anywhere near her." She waved the knife in front of his face.

"For Christ's sake! She's my daughter. I can't just walk out and leave her. I love her."

"Get out of here before I call the *militsiya*." Her look was venomous. "You want her to see them take you away?"

His shoulders sagged as he walked to the closet, kicking the fur coat away. He pulled his coat out and put it on. "I'll call you tomorrow," he said and jammed his feet into his boots.

"I've nothing to say to you."

"We have to talk. About Anja. I need to see her, to explain."

"Explain what? That you tried to strangle her mother?"

"Don't think you can stop me from seeing her." He moved closer until his face was level with hers. The tip of the knife touched his neck. "I'll fight you in the courts if I have to. Tell them what a slut ..."

There was a loud knocking on the door. A look of relief passed over Natasha's face. "That's my mother."

Mitch looked at the door of Anja's room. Then he picked up his briefcase and bag and opened the front door. He almost knocked Lena off her feet as he barged past.

"What's going on?" she began.

"Ask your whore of a daughter!" he threw over his shoulder. At the stairwell, he paused and looked back. Anja came into the corridor, rubbing her eyes. She looked first at Natasha and then at her grandmother.

"Annushka!" Mitch called.

"Papa! Where are you going?" She took two steps toward him. Natasha yanked her back.

"Papa will be back soon. You mustn't worry ..."

Lena pushed Anja inside the apartment.

"You keep him away from her!" Mitch yelled at Natasha. The door slammed.

PART FOUR

CHAPTER THIRTY-ONE

LENINGRAD—JANUARY/ FEBRUARY 1991

Some hours later, Mitch stared at the ceiling of the bedroom in his father's apartment—his bedroom before he married. He replayed the scene with Natasha over and over in his head, wishing he hadn't done it. Wishing he could turn back the clock. He felt as though someone had gouged out his stomach.

He slid his legs over the edge of the bed, reached for his cigarettes and lighter, and walked over to one of the windows. Swishing the curtains back, he flopped down onto the wide windowsill. Outside, pale lamplight pooled on the snow. An image of Anja came into his mind; she was lying on her side, her face buried in the grey rabbit, tousled curls springing out in all directions. He swallowed hard. He should have taken a chance, grabbed her and vanished into the night. But he knew he couldn't have done that. *Whatever happens,* he told himself, *she mustn't be upset. None of this is her fault.*

How had he allowed himself to lose control? In that one moment, it was as though he was possessed, compelled to do something to make Natasha come to her senses. Anything. He clenched his fists now thinking of her and Yagudin standing on the other side of the road. Anja's chatter in the background: *Boris took me to Katya's.* He felt again the strength, the pliability, as his fingers pressed into Natasha's throat.

Hours passed, lost to him in a sea of disbelief, grief. Tapping noises roused him from his stupor. The bedroom door opened. *"Khorosho?"* his father asked. Mitch stared vacantly at him. "Come and have breakfast. You'll feel better with food inside you."

"It'll take more than food ..." his voice trailed off.

"We need to talk."

Last night when his father questioned him, Mitch said he needed to get away for a few days, that was all. Now looking at his father's careworn face, he wondered how he could burden him with more problems. Since Sophia's death, Sergei wore the mantle of a lost soul—searching, never finding.

"Your old dressing gown is in the cupboard. It doesn't look as though you brought much with you." Sergei's voice cut through his thoughts.

Some minutes later, Mitch slid into the chair opposite his father at the kitchen table. Sergei nudged Mitch's coffee cup toward him. "What's this about? What's going on?" Mitch didn't answer. "It's all right. Anastasia's gone. She spends Sundays with her family."

In truth, it wasn't the possible presence of Anastasia that worried him. His father's new housekeeper appeared far less interested in family business than Verochka Murmanevna had been. He didn't know where to start. When he did, he felt as if he was speaking about someone else. The person he had once been didn't try to strangle his wife. "I don't know what came over me, Papa. I couldn't stop. I wanted to kill her."

Sergei leaned an elbow on the table and rubbed his unshaven chin with the fingers of his other hand. "Don't blame yourself. She pushed you into it." He gave Mitch a sympathetic look. "Any other man would have done something drastic years ago. All that business with her parents interfering in your life."

"I can't blame her," Mitch countered, taking a gulp of coffee.

"Why not? She deceived you."

"I shouldn't have lost my temper. It was unforgivable. If Anja had come in while I ..." He looked down at his hands.

Sergei twisted sideways in his chair, reached for a cloth, and lifted the coffee pot off the stove. "What will you do?" he asked, topping up Mitch's cup.

"I'll go there this morning."

"Leave it a couple of days. Let things calm down."

"I can't. Anja will be wondering where I am."

* * *

Just before eleven that morning, Mitch parked the car in his usual space in the courtyard. *"Chort!"* he cursed out loud—Natasha's car wasn't there. Inside the building, he took the stairs two at a time, put his key in the front door, and pushed it open. "Anyone here?" His voice drifted into the silence. He shivered; the place felt damp, not like a home at all. In the kitchen, he put his hands around the coffee pot. It was cold. *If she's taken Anja to be with him, I'll ... I'll ... Take it easy,* he told himself. *They're probably with Lena.*

In Anja's room, the bed covers were pushed back, the imprint of her head blotched the pillow. Her nightdress wasn't there; the backs of her *tapochki* peeped out from under the bed, where he'd put them last night. It was as though she had been spirited away. He picked up the slippers and sank down on to the bed, cradling them in his arms, rocking gently back and forth. Some moments later, he tucked them back where he found them and opened the cupboard—most of Anja's clothes seemed to be there.

In the sitting room, he poured a slug of brandy. From the armchair he watched the roadway. After nearly an hour, he realized waiting was futile. If he telephoned Natasha at her parents' home, the likelihood of speaking to her was remote. And he didn't want them involved any more than they were already. He and Natasha would sort this out. *If it means being with Anja, I'll put up with anything,* he vowed, taking a pad of paper and a pen out of the desk drawer. He had to be careful what he put. After several false starts, he tore the sheets of paper up, put the pieces in his pocket, and wrote, *Sorry I walked out. We have to talk. Call me at my father's apartment, please.* It stuck in his throat to apologize, but he had been wrong in what he did and, if a bit of grovelling would ensure he could be with his daughter, then so be it. The next note he wrote was to Anja:

> *Annushka, my darling,*
> *Papa is staying with Dedushka for a few days, so you're not to worry.*
> *Remember that Papa loves you very much.*
> *Be good for Mama.*
> *I'll be home soon.*

Under his name he put a row of kisses and drew a funny face—the one that always made her giggle. Then he folded the sheet of paper in half and tucked it inside the bag she took to kindergarten.

It took a few minutes to gather up enough clothes and toiletries to see him through the next few days. He closed the front door behind him.

At regular intervals throughout the day, he called the apartment. Either Natasha wasn't there or she wasn't answering. At 9:30 p.m., he rang her parents' number. The housekeeper answered. As Mitch was trying to persuade her to get Natasha to the phone, Lyosha came on the line and shouted a string of expletives.

"Listen," Mitch interrupted.

"*Nyet!* You listen to me! She doesn't want anything to do with you ever again. Stay away from her and Anja!" The line went dead.

"How dare he! How dare he forbid me to see my own daughter!" Mitch slammed the receiver back on its rest. A pulse throbbed in his temple.

Sergei looked up from the newspaper he was reading and nodded his head knowingly. Mitch dialled Natasha's brother's number.

"Where are you?" Petya asked.

"My father's place. You heard what happened?"

"We were round at my parents' this afternoon." He snorted loudly. "Christ, Mitch, you made a mess of her neck. The bruises. Papa's lawyer's seen her already. They've taken pictures. What the hell were you thinking?"

"I don't know. Everything built up inside me."

"They're angry, really angry."

"I know. I just spoke to your father. Or rather he spoke to me." Petya didn't comment. "Is Anja all right?"

"She's okay. A bit quiet."

"Can I ask a favour?" Mitch continued quickly. "Would you speak to Natasha for me?"

"And say what?"

"Tell her I'm sorry. That I'm willing to put up with her seeing Yagudin ..." He paused for a moment, taking in the impact of what he had said. "But I must see Anja. If that's the only way, I'll have to do it." The last sentence was spoken softly, as if to himself.

"It won't help, Mitch. Not at the moment."

"I can't just leave it."

After a moment's hesitation, Petya said, "I'll see what I can do. Maybe take her to lunch or something."

"Spasiba."

"I'm not promising anything. I don't like what you did, but with all the crap she's given you over the years ..."

In the days that followed, Mitch's nerves were stretched to breaking point. It was Thursday before Petya had the chance to talk to Natasha in private. "You're not going to like it, Mitch," he reported. "She said ... she said she'd see you in hell before she'd let you anywhere near Anja!" Petya breathed out noisily.

"Why am I being made to look the fucking villain? She's the one who's been carrying on with that ... that vermin."

"You can't deny she has a good case. The evidence is there. Her neck."

"I should have finished the damned job!"

"And then where would you be? In the *Kresty,* awaiting trial."

"*Ya znayu. Ya znayu.* I feel so damned helpless. I want to kick everything in sight."

"At least she's not living with Yagudin." Petya paused and then added, "I probably shouldn't tell you this, but she may be taking Anja back to the apartment at the weekend. Sounded as though she was fed up with things where she is."

"I'll go and see them there."

"Let things settle down, Mitch. Get back to normal for a few weeks."

"Normal? I can't even see my own daughter!"

"So you're going to go barging in and have another row? Upset Anja? You need to calm down."

Mitch knew Petya was right. If he had learned anything at all from the mess his clients got themselves into, it was that most situations escalate out of control when anger takes over. Surely he had learned that lesson, if nothing else. He had to be careful, not give her any more ammunition. "I'll give it a few days," he agreed reluctantly.

"Go there during the day while Anja isn't home. And don't lose your temper!"

* * *

On Monday morning, instead of driving to work, Mitch parked the car in a side street near Anja's kindergarten and hovered in the shadows of an archway from where he could see the gate. A few minutes later, Natasha's car drew into the curb. She got out and opened the passenger door. Mitch craned his neck to see his daughter. He caught his breath and tears welled in his eyes as Anja ran through the open gate, her satchel bouncing on her back. Halfway across the yard, she stopped and waved to Natasha. As he stood there, an idea came to him: he would go into the building, say there was an emergency at home and that Anja was needed. No one could stop him. He was her father, after all. They would go somewhere far away where they weren't known. But as he watched her filing through the doorway with the other children, he knew he couldn't do it.

How could he take her away from everything she knew? What sort of life would they have? He was sure to get caught. What would happen to her then?

Natasha was now driving away. He ran back to his car; it juddered into action and he pulled around the corner with a squeal of tires. He lost sight of her at an intersection and prayed she was going home and not to her parents. Parking the car along the street from the apartment building, he ran through the archway into the courtyard and was relieved to see her car in its usual place. At the apartment door, he hesitated, wondering whether he should knock. *It's still your damned home,* he told himself and put his key in the lock. It wouldn't turn. He tried again. *She's changed the fucking lock!* He rattled the door handle. "Natasha," he called. "Open the door! *Pazhalusta.*" He listened. Banged the door hard with his fist. "Open the fucking door! I know you're in there." He lit a cigarette and took a couple of drags. "We need to talk. Please let me in," he pleaded, speaking just loud enough to be heard. "I promise I won't do anything. I'll never hurt you again."

"Otstan'!" her voice came from the other side of the door. "If you don't go, I'll call the *militsiya*."

"We have to talk. About Anja. I need to see her. Just a couple of hours with her. You can be there too. Surely you won't deny me that."

"Poshol ty!"

"You can see him ... Yagudin. I won't stop you." He threw the cigarette onto the floor and ground it with the toe of his boot. "We can go on as we were. I'll give you money for you and Anja. Anything you want."

"Anything I want! Well, that's new!"

He leaned against the door. "Let me in, please." All he heard was the click of her heels as she walked away from him. Then loud music began. "I'll wait here all day if I have to," he shouted. "You have to come out some time."

He sat outside the door for over an hour. By then, his teeth were chattering and he was chilled to the bone. A door opened farther along the corridor and Mitch scrambled to his feet and made for the stairwell. In the courtyard, he looked up. She watched from the apartment window.

* * *

In the week that followed, he couldn't concentrate on his work. On Friday morning, his boss called him into his office. "Do you have a problem?" he asked before Mitch had the chance to sit down. Mitch held on to the back of a chair. It felt as though he had the burdens of the world on his shoulders. "What happened in the Babadjanov case? You nearly lost that one. What were you thinking?"

Mitch's mind was a blank. *"Izvinite,"* he mumbled and stared at Anton Nikolaiovich Golubkhov, as though seeing him for the first time. Had his hair always been grey? His jacket was open, the buttons of his shirt stretched across the expanse of his belly.

"What's the matter with you?"

The tone of voice snapped Mitch from his trance. "I'm sorry," he repeated. "I've got some problems at home."

"If you don't concentrate on your work, you'll have one more problem." Anton Nikolaiovich pointed a finger at Mitch. "Another performance like that and you're out! Understand?"

* * *

After work that evening, Mitch and Yuri sat at their usual table in the corner of the *kafe* on Liteynyy prospekt. Mitch's thoughts wandered as Yuri enthused about the wonders of his week-old son. "His eyes are the palest blue imaginable. And his hair ..." Yuri stopped talking and looked at his friend. "You're not listening, are you?"

"*Prastite!* What did you say?"

"I asked if you were listening, but obviously you're not," Yuri responded. "You've got to snap out of this, make a new life. Look at you! When was the last time you shaved?"

"It's easy for you to talk." Mitch slumped down in the chair.

"You have to face the fact that Natasha isn't going to have you back. Agreed?"

Mitch nodded, almost imperceptibly.

"If you lose your job, you won't have any chance of providing for Anja." Mitch didn't respond. "What you need to do is earn more money, clear your debts, and prove to the Court that you are a responsible father. They'll at least give you access rights."

Mitch nodded desultorily.

"Don't just sit there nodding your head. Do something about it. Move on!" Yuri took a gulp of his coffee. "Do what I did and get a job in a co-operative. There's money to be made now."

"I know you're right, Yura, but I don't seem to be able to concentrate on anything. All I can think of is being with Anja."

"And that's going to happen with you like this?"

"If you want to know the truth, I can't bear to think Anja could be happy without me." Mitch stirred his coffee slowly. "I must be a bad father. Surely, if I love her, I should want her to be happy."

"Of course you love her. Same as I love my son." Yuri's face creased into a satisfied smile. "It'll work out. Natasha will come round. Let you see the kid. Give it time."

"Time? Don't you think I've given it enough time? It's been more than two weeks now. It kills me to think of that thug being anywhere near Anja. That's what I can't take."

"It doesn't sound as though he is. You've already said that Natasha's not with him—at least, not living with him."

"That doesn't mean she's not still seeing him."

Yuri scratched his head. "You could initiate divorce proceedings. You don't need a reason. You can do it after a month and apply for access rights to your child."

"*Nyet!* I don't want it to come to divorce. Natasha and I can sort it out." Mitch stared into his coffee cup, as though it held the answer to his problems.

"I know it's difficult. I can understand you don't want a man like that, or any man, near your daughter. But try looking at it another way."

"What other way? How else am I supposed to look at it?" Mitch snapped.

"All I'm trying to say is that if he's really fond of Natasha, he'll make sure no harm comes to her or Anja. That sort always look after their own."

"She's not his! The fucking asshole!"

They finished their coffee in silence.

* * *

Three days later, Mitch stood in his usual spot opposite Anja's kindergarten. He did this most weekday mornings now in the hope that one day Katya's mother might be the one to drop Anja off with her own daughter. Yelizaveta Artyemevskaya wouldn't deny him a few minutes with his daughter. Each day, he feared seeing the big black Mercedes with Boris at the wheel. What would he do then? But apart from one morning when Lena escorted Anja to the door, it was always Natasha.

Today he watched her kissing Anja goodbye. As he did every day, he sent an air kiss winging across the yard to his daughter. Then he lit a cigarette, savouring the brief glimpse he'd had of her.

"What the hell do you think you're doing?" Natasha was standing in front of him. "I've seen you here before. What are you playing at?"

"For Christ's sake, Natasha. You can't deny me looking at her."

"As long as that's all you do. I don't want you upsetting her, do you hear?"

"Of course I damn well hear. The last thing in the world I want is for her to be upset." They glared at one another for a moment, and Mitch silently cautioned himself not to lose his temper. He ground out his cigarette. "We have to talk," he began in a low voice, "this has gone on for long enough."

"When will you get it through your thick skull? You're not having anything to do with her. Nothing at all!" she yelled. "I'm filing for divorce. You'll be hearing from my lawyer!" she spat at him.

Mitch felt as though he had been kicked in the gut. "No, Natasha! Please. Don't do that! We can still make a go of it. Give me a chance." He put his hands out instinctively toward her.

"Don't touch me!" She backed away.

"Khorosho! Khorosho!" he said. "I'm not touching you."

"If I know you've been anywhere near Anja, you'll be in trouble. Big trouble." She glared at him, turned quickly on her heel, and dashed into the road. There was a squeal of brakes and a car skidded to a halt inches from her.

The driver wound down his window and shouted. "What the hell are you doing, woman?"

Mitch bit back the thought that in that instant his troubles might have been over. Natasha was now on the other side of the street, and he ran across the road and grabbed the edge of the car door as she tried to close it. "Natasha, please ... listen to me."

"Stay away from her," she said as she tugged at the door, "or you'll be sorry."

"What are you going to do? Set your thug of a boyfriend on to me?" She scowled at him and he let go of the door. She slammed it shut, started the car, and turned the wheel quickly. He jumped out of the way and watched the car disappear around the corner.

A horn blasted from behind. "You going to stand there all day?" Mitch stared blankly at the driver whose path he was blocking.

CHAPTER THIRTY-TWO

LENINGRAD–MARCH/APRIL 1991

The mournful sound of a Russian ballad echoed in the underground tunnel as Mitch walked from the Metro station. The accordion player looked hopefully from one passerby to the next, his body swaying as he drew the squeezebox in and out. Mitch climbed the steps to the street; the music was lost in the hum of traffic. Needles of snow spat in his face as he walked. His boots were leaking, his feet cold and wet. He'd given up on his car for a while.

It was over four weeks since Natasha told him she was filing for divorce. He hadn't heard anything from her lawyer, and was now convinced she was lying. Mitch was playing for time, hoping she would come to her senses and allow him to see Anja. He had cut his alcohol consumption, was concentrating on his job, and last week received rare words of praise from his boss. He had begun to save money to rent an apartment of his own, somewhere for Anja to visit and maybe stay now and again, and had called in a favour from an ex-client who claimed he could procure a small place close to her school ... at a price.

Now in the dimly lit entrance hall to the Bureau, he stamped his feet, trying to bring life back into his frozen toes. Then he took off his *shapka,* brushed snow from his overcoat, and climbed the stairs to the second floor. In the corridor, a man approached. "Mitchell Jakob Galichin?"

Mitch nodded. "You have an appointment?"

The man shook his head. "I have to give you this." He thrust a large envelope into Mitch's hand.

Mitch looked at it. "What? What's this?"

"It's from your ex-wife's lawyer."

"My what?"

"Your ex-wife. The one who's just divorced you. You've forgotten?"

Mitch's mouth fell open.

"It's in there. The court decision." The man pointed to the envelope.

"There must be ..."

"I think you'll find it in order."

"There must be some mistake. She hasn't filed for divorce."

"Notice was served on you."

"What notice? When?"

"Your memory not so good?" A smirk spread across his face and he turned and headed for the stairs.

"Come back here you, you …" The man had gone. Mitch stared after him for a moment and then stumbled to his desk and with trembling hands tore the envelope open and pulled out a document. He went over the words once, twice, unable to comprehend; it was as if it was the first time he had seen such phrases strung together. Reality set in. He gasped and sank down onto the chair. A judgement had been passed granting Natasha a divorce … *on the grounds of the irretrievable breakdown of the marriage. And custody of Anja!* The blood drained from his body. *The father is deprived of his parental rights to exclude him from all issues relating to the child, who has made her preference known to the Department of Guardianship and Curatorship that she wishes to live with her mother. In the opinion of the Court, the father's aggressive behaviour would negatively impact the physical or psychological development of the child.* His vision blurred, and it was some moments before the words on the page regained a semblance of order. The document was dated a month ago and certified with the Apostille of the Justice Directorate of the City of Leningrad. The statutory period had passed. It was final. He slumped forward in the chair, a loud pounding in his head. *She knew! The bitch knew! This was already going through when we met outside the school.* But how could it be? He hadn't signed anything. He hadn't agreed to a divorce. "Fucking bitch!" He banged a fist on the desk. "How could I have been so stupid?"

"Is something the matter?" He looked up into the pale blue eyes of Tamara Aleksandrevna, the typist.

"My wife. She's divorced me." He breathed heavily and spoke in short gasps. "My Anja. I knew nothing about it."

"Can she do that?"

"She can if her fucking father pays," he said through gritted teeth. His words summed up the passage of their marriage.

"Money, that's what it is. The same thing happened to my husband's cousin. She …" Tamara Aleksandrevna's voice droned on.

Mitch read again the words on the judgement. *Aggressive behaviour.* He couldn't argue with that. Her neck. He had hung himself. How could he have been so stupid? He didn't care about her. It was Anja. He had deluded himself, believing he was the one constant in his child's life. *Bastards! Why did they have to make her say it?* From the age of ten, the court had an obligation to seek the child's opinion; although Anja was underage, she had been interviewed by someone from the Department of Guardianship and Curatorship and deemed capable of formulating an opinion. "How could she do that to her?"

Tamara Aleksandrevna paused in mid-sentence. "*Prastite.* Was it something I said? I didn't mean ..."

Mitch stared at her. Her image froze, as if he was looking at a photograph.

* * *

Half an hour or so later, he arrived at his father's apartment. Sergei came out of the kitchen, a cup of coffee in his hand. "Mitch? What are you doing back here?"

Mitch went into the sitting room, snow dripping from his coat and *shapka,* boots shedding clumps of slush where he walked.

"What's wrong? Has something happened?" His father hurried after him. "Not Anja? Tell me nothing's happened to her!" He spoke quickly.

Mitch shook his head.

"You haven't lost your job?" Sergei put his cup down onto a side table.

"It's Natasha. The bitch! She's divorced me!"

"What do you mean?"

"She's divorced me, Papa. Don't you understand?"

"She can't have."

Mitch reached for his briefcase, opened it, took the envelope out, and threw it onto the table. "Read that!" He slumped down into a chair. Energy drained from his body. Every bone and muscle ached.

Sergei looked quizzically at Mitch, picked up the envelope and pulled out the papers. He read the first page. "Surely you didn't sign anything?" Mitch shook his head. "She must have forged your signature."

"She's welcome to a divorce." Mitch sat up. "It's a relief to be rid of her. But Anja ... Read the rest of it. It seems I'm a bad father."

Sergei spluttered and cursed as he read. "You can't let this go. You have to challenge it, Mitch."

"Don't worry. There's no way she's getting away with this."

"Have you been to see this ..." Sergei searched for the lawyer's name in the documents. "Obolensky?"

"Believe me, I could smash his face in."

"You didn't?"

"*Nyet.* Apart from having someone to take my anger out on, it wouldn't achieve anything. I have to play her at her own game. Bribe someone if necessary. Provide evidence that she's an unfit mother. I don't care what it takes. Anything ..."

"You have to be careful, Mitch. You can't falsify evidence."

"Like she did, you mean?"

"We need to think about this. Plan our moves."

Mitch sat in brooding silence as Sergei read through the document again.

"Do you think Anja really said that ... that she prefers to live with Natasha?" Mitch asked.

"I'm sure it's all lies, Mitch. You know as well as I do how manipulative Natasha can be. She probably told Anja all sorts of tales about you, or promised her some treat. You can't blame the child."

"I don't."

"You're absolutely certain you didn't sign anything agreeing to a divorce?"

"You think I wouldn't remember?"

"That's not what I meant. But if we can prove your signature is a forgery, we can turn it to our advantage."

"Do a deal, you mean?"

"We'll need to handle it carefully."

* * *

An hour later, Mitch and Sergei sat opposite Natasha's lawyer. He was a thickset man. His suit jacket hung on him as though it had been made for an even larger frame; his shirt collar was so tight, it seemed it would pierce his throat. He shifted uncomfortably in his chair, loosened his tie, and undid the top button of his shirt when Mitch demanded to see the paper he was supposed to have signed agreeing to a divorce. Then he rummaged in a drawer, pulled out a folder, extracted a document, and slid it across the desk. "Your signature," he said, turning the paper around and pointing a finger at the bottom of the page.

Mitch stared at the signature. It was a good forgery and, if he didn't know better, he would swear he had signed it himself. Sergei picked it up. His gaze strayed from the signature to the lawyer several times before placing the paper back on the desk in front of Mitch.

"As you can see, the document bears your signature."

"I could take this to a handwriting expert and have you struck off," Mitch spat.

The man laughed loudly. "And what good would that do you? Your ex-wife had ample evidence of your behaviour."

"Forget her! It's not the divorce. He's welcome to her!" His voice was loud now, the fingers of his hands splayed on the desk, as if to get to his feet. "You can tell that to the stinking swine who pays you! Got that, asshole?"

Sergei put a steadying hand on Mitch's arm and addressed the other man. "You can tell your client that my son will be appealing this decision," he began.

"And charging her ... and you ... with forgery, unless she lets me see my daughter," Mitch spat.

* * *

The following afternoon, Mitch was jotting down notes after a meeting with a client. The telephone rang. Still writing, he reached out a hand and lifted the receiver. "Natasha called," his father said.

Mitch dropped the pen. "What did she want?"

"Good news." Sergei spoke quickly. "She's going to let you see Anja."

"Are you sure ... that's what she said?"

His father laughed. "Once a week. You can see her once a week."

Mitch let out a loud yell and looked around. His colleagues were looking expectantly at him. "I can see Anja!" A cheer went around the office. "What was that, Papa?"

"I said, I have to be there too. I'm sorry, Mitch, she won't have it any other way."

"It's okay. I don't mind. You must miss her too."

"I only have one granddaughter." Neither man spoke for several moments. "She said it has to be on an unofficial basis for the time being. Then if it goes okay, she'll apply to have the ban rescinded."

Mitch leaned an elbow on the desk. "Do you think she's up to something? Maybe have me arrested for breaching the order?"

"I don't know, but it's the only chance you have, at least for now."

"When? When can I see her?"

"Saturday morning. We have to pick her up at the apartment at ten o'clock."

Time dragged. Every time the telephone rang, Mitch feared Natasha had changed her mind. He still wasn't convinced it wasn't a trap. He had been over it in his mind time and time again. But he had to take the chance. On Friday evening, Mitch and Sergei were in a jubilant mood. For the past few weeks, as if by unwritten agreement, neither man had spoken of times past, their conversation restricted to mundane, everyday matters. Tonight, they shared happy memories of Anja and spoke openly about Sophia for the first time since her death. "Do you remember when the four of us were on holiday at Yalta, Papa? And Maman …" Mitch started to laugh. "She mistook that man on the beach for someone she used to know. Then he followed her around. She couldn't get rid of him."

Sergei raised his eyebrows. "Did we ever tell you what we found out about him?"

Mitch shook his head and chewed on a tough piece of chicken.

"He was a member of the Politburo. We saw his picture in the newspaper. He must have slipped away from his minders for a while."

A vision of his daughter flashed across Mitch's mind. "Do you remember how Anja stood in front of him with her hands on her hips? She was so little then." He swallowed hard. "She had on her pink plastic shoes."

"I think she must have scared him off, because he scurried away across the rocks." Sergei laughed loudly. "Another drink?"

* * *

The next morning, Sergei manoeuvred his car into a parking space in the courtyard of the apartment building. They were early and sat in silence for several minutes, each consumed in his own thoughts. Mitch looked up at the windows of the apartment. He thought he saw his daughter's face, but maybe it was his imagination. At five minutes to ten, the two men entered the building. "I won't be long," Sergei said as he got into the elevator.

Natasha had made it clear she wouldn't allow Mitch in the apartment, so he paced around the dimly lit hallway, checking his watch, each minute seeming like an age. Thank God the nosy old woman wasn't in her usual position doing her knitting. He couldn't handle an inquisition from her or her friend as to why he didn't live there anymore. A clanging started in the elevator shaft. Louder now. He held his breath. Although not particularly a religious man, he prayed Anja would be with his father, not daring to think what he would do if she wasn't. With a thud, it arrived on the ground floor. The door opened. "Papa! Papa!" She launched herself into his arms and he whirled her around and around, laughing and hugging her. They came to a stop and he smothered her face with kisses then buried his face in her hair. She smelled so good. He lowered her to the floor and looked at her. His Anja. She was here with him. He thanked the gods above.

"Well, what's it to be, Annushka?" Sergei asked, his arm around Mitch's shoulder as they walked to the car. "Where shall we go?"

"Pushkin! Can we go to Pushkin?" She looked expectantly from father to grandfather and back again. "Please, Papa. We used to go there with Babushka."

"Pushkin it is." Mitch opened the back door of the car.

Anja climbed in and grinned at him, deepening the dimples in her cheeks. "We could have ice cream."

He laughed and closed the door. As they pulled away, he resisted the urge to see if Natasha was at the window. Instead, he turned and smiled at Anja in the back seat. His precious daughter was here and the sun was shining. What more could he want?

During the drive to Pushkin, Mitch checked several times to make sure no one was following them. As they left the city behind, he relaxed and their voices filled the car as they sang Anja's favourite songs. At times, it was just Anja who kept the verses going. "May there always be sunshine," she piped. Mitch leaned back in his seat, listening to the sweet sound and wishing this journey could go on forever; the three of them could glide off to another life in another place. She was into the chorus now: "May there always be Mama."

Sergei pulled the car into the side of the road outside the Alexander Park and they climbed out. Anja fidgeted as Mitch tucked her red woollen scarf inside her white quilted coat, put her hat on and pulled it down over her ears. Inside the entrance gate, she ran up the incline to the Palace and skipped around, waiting for the two men to catch up. "Can we go to see the big birds on the bridge?"

"Okay, but watch the paths. They may be slippery. Mama will be cross with me if I take you home with a broken leg, won't she?" Mitch grinned.

Anja shrugged. "She's always cross with you. She said you don't love me anymore."

Mitch felt as though he had been knocked sideways. "Of course I love you," he gasped. Tears pricked his eyes and he bent down, his face level with Anja's. "Don't you ever believe I don't love you."

"But you didn't come to see me."

"That was because Mama wouldn't let me see you. Not because I don't love you."

"Leave it, Mitch."

He felt his father's hand grip his shoulder. Mitch pulled his daughter closer and whispered, "I will always love you. Always and forever."

"Now where are these birds you want to see?" Sergei urged. "I'm getting cold standing around here."

Mitch straightened up. "Annushka can lead the way. She knows where they are."

They followed her along winding paths through the hauntingly beautiful, frost-encrusted park. "She's only a child, Mitch. Don't let it spoil the day."

"I know." Mitch's eyes were firmly fixed on the small, white-coated figure bobbing ahead of them.

"Do you ever wonder what must have been going through the minds of the Tsar and his family during their last summer here, while they rode and had picnics in the park? He must have known their days were numbered."

"He was naïve, Papa, believing that the Russian people would never abandon their traditions, their history." They walked in silence for a while. "Hopefully, the children didn't suspect what was in store for them."

"The children. You have to protect the children," Sergei murmured almost to himself.

Anja was now dancing up and down on one of the Chinese bridges across the canal. "Papochka! Papochka! I found the birds," she shouted and pointed triumphantly at the giant stone vultures above an ornamental arch. Mitch and Sergei grinned at each other and hurried to join her.

On the walk back through the park, Mitch's thoughts strayed to the times he had come here with his mother. She told him that the place instilled in her an aura of serenity, somewhere you could connect with Russia's spiritual past. He had never understood how a place so closely linked with the last violent breaths of a dying empire and dynasty could evoke such feelings. Today, as a shaft of sunlight streamed through frost-covered branches of trees and enveloped Anja in a kaleidoscope of colours, he thought he knew what she meant.

They stopped in the shadow of the ruined gothic chapel. "A watchman used to live in a tiny little room at the base of the tower. Did you know that, Anja?" Sergei asked.

She shook her head. "Mama said one day we're going to live in a big, big house!" she declared. "Will you be there too, Papa?"

Mitch's throat constricted.

* * *

Weekdays dragged as Mitch counted the hours until he could see his daughter again. On Friday evenings now, he joined his colleagues from the office in one bar or another, drinking and talking over the events of the week. In the company of men, he began to feel a camaraderie and lightness of spirit he hadn't felt for years, burdened as he had been with Natasha's constant demands. Maybe this was the best his life was going to get, drifting through the week, anticipating a few brief hours of happiness with Anja.

Natasha still hadn't had the access ban rescinded. It had been over four weeks now, and he dreaded that she might stop him from seeing his daughter. Last night, the thought had niggled at the back of his mind, quelling the childlike excitement he usually felt as Saturday morning approached. He had downed one drink after another and smiled stiltedly at his friends' ribald jokes. After an hour or so, the smoke-filled atmosphere in the bar had begun to press down on him. He had to get out, try to clear his head. "Must be a woman. Why else would you leave before we've finished the bottle?" his friends speculated noisily when he got up to leave. As he walked to the Metro station, he told himself to stop worrying and just enjoy being with Anja. He had accepted that he would always be on the periphery of his daughter's life, but to be cut out for good ... that would be more than he could take.

Natasha still held the upper hand, controlling almost everything in his life. He had abandoned thoughts of getting somewhere of his own to live—when he had run the idea past her on the telephone, she was adamant that she wouldn't allow the child to be alone with him. He had tried to reason, pleading that Anja could at least spend one night at his father's home. She wouldn't budge. He swallowed angry words, fearful that an outburst would inflame the already sensitive situation. He attempted to get his money back from the former client to whom he had paid a bribe to secure an apartment near Anja's school. The man's wife had come to the door, two small children clinging to her skirt, and told him that her husband had left the city. Maybe she was telling the truth.

On Saturday morning, torrential rain soaked Mitch and his father as they ran from the car to the apartment building. Mitch waited; at this time, his emotions were always in turmoil as he dreaded the possibility his father might emerge alone from the elevator. But the gods were with him and he dashed forward to scoop his daughter into his arms.

They spent the morning at a museum that Anja's friend Katya had visited. When they came out, the rain had stopped and the temperature risen. Anja paused in front of a woman who was drying tables and chairs at an outdoor *kafe* and looked expectantly at her father and grandfather.

Sergei grinned. "What's it to be this week, Annushka? Chocolate sprinkles?"

Ice cream in hand, she settled on Mitch's lap and giggled as he wiped a blob off her chin. He hugged her close. "Tomorrow, we're going to Dyadya Mikhail's birthday party. Mama says there will be lots of people and a big cake. You should come, Papa."

Mitch shuddered.

"It's at his *dacha*. There's a big room there, and it's full of toys, just for me. A dolls' house too."

"Prekrati eto!" Mitch heard himself utter. "I don't want to hear about Dyadya Mikhail. You're not to see him!" He tightened his grip around Anja's waist.

"You're hurting me, Papa." She tried to wriggle free and dropped her ice cream.

"Mitch! Let her go!" His father's voice snapped Mitch out of his trance. Sergei pulled Anja to her feet. "We have to get back. Anastasia will have our lunch ready."

"What did I do, Papa?" Anja wailed.

"Nichego, nichego," he murmured.

"My ice cream!" She pointed at the floor.

Back at Sergei's apartment, Anastasia set out the lunch on a rug on the sitting room floor. Anja seemed to have forgotten Mitch's outburst. "Let's pretend we're having a picnic by the canal, like we used to with Babushka," she suggested. Anja and Mitch sat cross-legged on the rug, munching sandwiches and talking about the imaginary things that floated past; Sergei opted for the comfort of an armchair.

After they had eaten, Mitch flopped onto the sofa and patted the place next to him. She curled her legs under her body and leaned against him. He put his arm around her. "How about I read you a story?"

She looked up at him, a frown wrinkling her forehead. "You said I was too old to be read to."

"Just this once, as a special treat." He kissed the top of her head. "What's it to be? I'm sure we still have some of your books here."

"*The Firebird*. Can we have *The Firebird*?"

Mitch laughed—he had known this was the story she would choose.

Sergei rose from his chair, scratched his head, and said, "I think we might have that."

"You do! You do! Babushka used to read it to me when I was little. I know where it is." Anja scrambled to her feet. Mitch and Sergei listened to the sound of her footsteps running along the hallway.

"You have to be careful, Mitch. No more outbursts. It's upsetting her."

"I know, Papa. I know." He sighed loudly. "But I can't bear to think of that beast anywhere near her."

"Here it is!" She burst back into the room. "It still has Babushka's marker in my favourite part."

As Mitch read, she snuggled closer. His voice began to crack as he said the familiar words: "... feather after feather floated down on meadow and forest."

* * *

The following Saturday morning, the sun shone as the three of them set out in Mitch's car, heading to Pushkin again. "Mama says we should buy me a new dress today," Anja piped up from the back seat.

"We'll do that later," Mitch replied, mentally checking how much money he had left after paying for the car repair and reducing his other debts. He could always borrow some from his father until he got paid in a few days' time.

"I shall wear the dress for Polya's party tomorrow. It's going to be in a restaurant."

"Who's Polya?" Mitch asked, reflecting that there were now parts of his daughter's life he knew nothing about.

"Polya. Polina Kornilova. We're going to have ..."

"There's something wrong with the car," Mitch cut in. There was a loud clanging noise and black smoke billowed out behind them.

"Mama's car is much nicer. Why don't you get one like that, Papa?"

"This one's fine," he snapped. He pulled the car into the side of the road, got out, and slammed the door.

The car wasn't fine. After twenty minutes or so of trying to sort out the problem, grease smeared his hands and clothes.

"Why don't we call Boris, Papa? He's Dyadya Mikhail's driver. His car never breaks down," Anja declared, dancing around on the sidewalk. "It's fun! He has lots of drinks …"

"Zatknis'!" Mitch barked. "I'm sick of hearing about fucking Dyadya Mikhail!" He rummaged in the back of the car for a rag with which to clean his hands.

"Mama says it's bad to say those words."

Sergei took Anja's hand. "I'm cold. How about some hot chocolate? There's a *kafe* along here." They walked away.

Mitch went in search of a phone kiosk from which to call the mechanic who was supposed to have repaired the car. He cursed himself for losing his temper. *Why do you do it? Do you want her to hate you*? He tried to enjoy each minute with her, but she seemed to be slipping away from him.

Sometime later, they stood on the side of the road and watched the mechanic drive the car away, a cloud of smoke in its wake.

Anja looked up at Mitch expectantly. "Are we going to Pushkin now?"

"*Nyet!* We can't go to Pushkin without the car. It's too far."

"But you said we could." She stamped her foot.

"I know what I said, but things have changed, and we can't go."

"We can get my new dress." Her bottom lip trembled. "You promised."

Late afternoon, as their cab pulled into the courtyard at the apartment building, Anja rummaged in the bag she was clutching. "I can't wait to show it to Mama. It's the nicest dress I've ever had."

Mitch recalled the way she had paraded around the store, twirling this way and that, thin red ribbons swirling from the waistband, the white sailor collar covering her narrow shoulders. The dress was more than he could afford, but he was past caring. He had spent most of his adult life worrying about money, and where had it got him?

Anja got out of the cab. "Polya will be so jealous," she said. A satisfied smile washed across her face.

Mitch slammed the door. He wished she wouldn't talk like that.

"Hurry, Annushka. We're late already," Sergei urged.

Mitch bent down and hugged her. She struggled free and ran after her grandfather. The bag swung at her side.

CHAPTER THIRTY-THREE

LENINGRAD—APRIL 1991

The following Saturday morning, Mitch tried to still his feeling of foreboding as he scanned up and down the street outside Natasha's apartment building, praying that her car would come into view and that Anja would be with her. The car hadn't been in its usual place in the courtyard, nor were there any lights in the windows of the apartment when he and his father arrived. "Anja's probably been staying overnight with one of her friends, and Natasha's gone to pick her up. But I'll go up and see if they're there," his father had said as he got into the elevator. That was over ten minutes ago. *What the hell's she playing at?* Mitch cursed, stepping into the road and looking again. Then he threw his cigarette down and dashed back through the archway. As he emerged into the courtyard, the entrance door opened. Sergei and Slava, the caretaker, came out. Mitch caught his breath and ran toward them. "Where is she? Where's my daughter?" he yelled.

Slava shook his head. "They've gone."

"Where? Where have they gone?"

"I don't know. Thursday, your wife, she put suitcase in car. I ask if she going away. She tell me mind own business."

"Anja? Was Anja with her?"

"My wife, Rodnina. You remember her?"

"Da! Da!"

"Later, she saw them, your wife and little girl. They drive off ..."

"Natasha came back on her own," Sergei interrupted, "but Slava said she left again yesterday evening."

"I knew she'd pull a stunt like this," Mitch muttered.

"Izvinite, izvinite." Slava apologized, wringing his hands together.

"It's not your fault." Sergei put a hand on the old man's arm.

Mitch rummaged in his jacket pockets, pulled out a scrap of paper and a pen, and, with trembling hand, scribbled some numbers down. "These are my phone numbers, my office and home." He handed the paper to Slava. "If you see either of them, call me straight away."

"I will. I tell Rodnina too." Slava's face relaxed into a weak smile, revealing gums naked of teeth, as Sergei pressed some money into his palm.

Mitch and Sergei got into the car. "Where do we begin to look?" Sergei gave a loud sigh and pulled away.

"Natasha's parents. Let's hope they're there." Mitch cursed himself silently for not finding out from Anja where Yagudin lived. "Can't you go any faster?" he urged his father, leaning forward in the seat and drumming his fingers on the front panelling.

At the entrance gates to the Lipovskys building, the guard stepped out of the gatehouse and informed them that the Lipovskys had gone away. "On Thursday."

Mitch clambered out of the car, took out his money, and began to count some notes. "Was anyone else with them?"

"The little girl. Their *vnuchka*."

"Did they say where they were going or when they would be back?" He counted out more money, praying silently that he didn't run out.

"Their driver ... he said he took them to the airport."

Mitch caught his breath. "The driver. Did he know where they went? What flight they were on?"

"Nyet." A long blast of a car horn came from behind. "You have to move," the guard said, easing the money out of Mitch's hand.

Sergei manoeuvred his car into the side of the road, switched off the engine, got out, and rushed over to where Mitch was now staring across the compound. "Where the hell have they taken her?" he cried, gripping the iron railings.

"She won't come to any harm, not with her grandparents. They love her the same as we do," Sergei placated.

"They don't love her. She's just a possession to them, like everything else. They've done this to stop me from seeing her."

"At least we know she's not with Yagudin," Sergei began.

"You don't know that. He may have been on the same flight, or they've taken her somewhere to meet up with Natasha and him. *Ublyudok!*" Mitch shook the railings. The guard approached.

Sergei hustled Mitch back into the car. "I've got a friend, an old informant, who works at Pulkovo. I'll call him and ask him to check the flight manifests and find out where they went."

Several hours later, Sergei's friend called back. Mitch paced around the room while his father spoke to the man. "Where did they go?" Mitch hissed. "Was he with them?"

Sergei replaced the receiver. "Barcelona. Lipovsky was on a business visa."

"Barcelona! What the hell are they doing taking my child to Spain without my permission?" He banged his right fist hard into his left palm. "And why would Natasha let them?"

"There's no record of Natasha or Yagudin on any of the passenger lists. That's something to be thankful for." Sergei picked up his glass and gulped his drink.

Mitch let out a pent-up breath and stopped pacing.

"He's going to check the inbound flights for the next few weeks and ..."

"The next few weeks? They have to come back before then! I can't go on like this, not knowing." Mitch paced back and forth again and then grabbed the telephone receiver. "I'm going to call Petya, see if he knows anything."

Petya claimed he didn't have a contact number for his parents in Spain nor did he know when they were coming back. "The whole fucking family's closing ranks," Mitch cursed as he slammed the receiver down.

That evening, he borrowed his father's car and drove to the home of Yelizaveta Artyemevskaya, the mother of Anja's friend Katya.

"We knew nothing about it until yesterday when Katya's teacher told the children that Anja has gone away with her grandparents," Liza explained.

"For how long? Did she say?"

She shook her head.

"Has Natasha said anything?"

"*Nyet.* I've hardly spoken to her, not since the trouble between the two of you. She wouldn't let Anja come to Katya's birthday party. Made some excuse. Both girls were really upset." She took a bottle of red wine from a cupboard and held it out to Mitch. He nodded, looking around and thinking of the times he had been here to collect his daughter or drop her off. It always looked so normal, so inviting. He stooped down and picked up a red ribbon, still tied in a bow. *Anja has one like that. Could it be?* He cradled it in his hands.

"Do you know where they've gone?" Liza asked, pouring wine into both glasses and indicating a chair at the kitchen table.

"Barcelona. They left on Thursday." Mitch sat down, gripping the ribbon in one hand as he gulped a mouthful of wine.

"Natasha. I saw her yesterday, coming out of Passazh." Liza took a sip of her drink. "She was with him."

Before Mitch could stop himself, great wrenching sobs came from somewhere deep in his throat. *"Izvinite, izvinite,"* he gasped.

Liza put an arm around his shoulders. "It'll be all right. She'll be back. You'll see."

"At least Anja's not with him," spilled out as an involuntary cry of anguish.

"Mama! Mama! What's wrong?"

Liza held her arms out to her daughter, who was now standing in the doorway. "Anja's Papa. He's missing her."

"Does my Papa miss me too?" Katya snuggled into her mother's body.

"Papa misses you more than anything in the world," Liza comforted, "just like we miss him."

Mitch pulled out a handkerchief, wiped his eyes, and blew his nose. "I'm sorry, Liza. I didn't mean to upset you and Katya."

Katya looked at the ribbon he was holding. Mitch gave her a weak smile and placed it in her hand. "Anja has one just like it," he muttered and took a gulp of wine.

Katya was now sitting on her mother's lap at the table; her long blonde hair tumbled over her white nightdress. "Will Annushka be back soon?" she asked.

He couldn't find his voice.

* * *

A week went by. There was no news from Sergei's friend at the airport. Each evening and on the weekend, Mitch loitered outside the apartment building, waiting for Natasha to come home. His throat was raw, but still he smoked cigarette after cigarette. He seldom ate, sometimes picking at pie or a salami sandwich. He arose early on weekday mornings, took the Metro to the apartment building and, even though her car wasn't there, pounded on the apartment door, hoping she may have come back during the night.

On Wednesday afternoon of the second week, as he was leaving the office to attend a pre-trial meeting with a client, Tamara Aleksandrevna called to him. "There is a phone call. A man. He won't give his name. He says he must speak with you."

Mitch hurried to Tamara's desk and grabbed the receiver from where it rested on top of a pile of documents. *"Allo."*

"She's here," Slava said in a hoarse whisper. "Come quickly."

Mitch slammed the phone down and ran toward the stairs. "Wait! Wait! Your briefcase," Tamara Aleksandrevna called, but Mitch had more important things on his mind.

Outside, he dashed into the road and flagged down a *chastniki*—one of the private cars that operate as unofficial cabs—signalling with a V sign to indicate double fare. "I'm in a hurry, a big hurry. There's extra money in it for you on top of the double fare," he promised the young driver. He quickly counted his cash as the car pulled away. They careened through the streets, at times mounting the sidewalk and scattering pedestrians to get around other vehicles. "Stop here!" Mitch shouted, and the car squealed to a halt on the road outside Natasha's apartment building. He thrust money into the driver's hand, got out, and dashed through the archway. Natasha's car was still there. Inside, he took the stairs two at a time. Outside the apartment, he paused to regain his breath and calm himself. He had to handle this properly. He knocked on the door. His heart thumped wildly as he heard footsteps inside. The door opened slightly. He pushed his weight against it, stepped inside, and slammed it shut. Natasha stumbled back against the wall. "You? You can't come in here," she hissed. There was a wild look in her eyes.

Mitch walked swiftly along the corridor, peering into rooms. They were empty. In Anja's room, he paused. Her bed was made up, but her grey rabbit was not in its place on her pillow. He opened the door of the cupboard. Apart from the clothes she wore for kindergarten, the only things that hung there were some dresses—too small now, too precious to discard.

"What the hell do you think you're doing?" Natasha's voice came from the doorway.

Mitch closed the cupboard door and turned to face her. "Why did you have to send her away?" His voice was low, as though not wanting to disturb the air in the room.

"She's with my parents. She's quite safe." Natasha edged away from him and into the corridor.

"Why?" Mitch threw out his hands in despair and followed her. "Things were going well."

"No, they weren't. She was upset. She didn't want to see you anymore. You were always cross with her, she said."

"That's not true, Natasha."

"So now you're saying she's a liar."

Mitch shook his head.

"The remarks about Misha. She told me."

"Maybe I said a few things, but she was happy being with me on those Saturdays."

"She wasn't. She was very unsettled, crying all the time."

"That's because she wants us to be together. A proper family."

"You don't understand, do you? You were pulling her away from the life she knows, where she is happy."

"So you've sent her away ... to a country she doesn't know!" Mitch jeered. "She belongs with us, Natasha. The two of us."

She shook her head. "You're no longer part of her life or mine. If you want her to be happy, leave us alone. Both of us."

"I can't do that. I love her. I can't bear ..." They glared at each other. "When will she be back?"

"You're not to try to see her."

"Please, Natasha, just a few hours each week. That's all I'm asking." She turned her back on him and walked into the hallway. "I promise I won't say anything about Yagudin or you. Just let me see her."

"It's better for her to be with me, my family, her friends."

"And him?" Blood pulsed noisily in Mitch's temple. "I swear, if ..."

"You'll do what?" She fingered her throat and narrowed her eyes at him. "If you go anywhere near her, I'll have you arrested ..."

"For what?" Mitch cut in. "Breaching the access order? You think my signature on the divorce papers will stand up in court?"

"How about child molestation?"

His mouth dropped open, and it was a moment or two before he was able to speak. "Child molestation? Anja? You can't be serious!"

"Just watch me!" she laughed.

He looked at her, aghast. "You know I'd never touch her. For Christ's sake!" There was a loud buzzing in his ears, and he leaned back against the wall, willing himself to stay upright. His lips were numb as he struggled to form words. He felt as though his tongue was choking him. "You … you're crazy!" he tried to say. The words sounded jumbled together.

She smirked.

He took two steps toward her and then gripped the side of the hall table, trying to calm his breathing. "You would sink that low?" He shook his head. "You can't really think I'd do something like that? Not to Anja?" His voice sounded odd, not his at all. She said nothing. "Natasha, tell me … nobody's touched her. Please."

She grinned. "She'll say whatever I want her to say."

"You disgusting bitch!" His voice was loud; the buzzing cleared in his head. "You'd put your own daughter … our daughter … through all that just to get back at me."

"Try me."

"Your fucking boyfriend. It's him. The bastard!"

"That's not how I'll tell it!" she smirked. "I'll make sure you rot in the *Kresty*!"

"You tell him to keep his filthy hands off her!" Mitch lurched forward and grabbed her arm, shouting, "If he's been anywhere near her, I'll fucking kill him!"

"Let go!" She struggled and pushed him hard.

He staggered back.

"You come anywhere near either of us, and I swear I'll see you in prison."

"You're evil," he muttered through clenched teeth.

"I want you to leave," she spat, shoved past him and pulled the front door open. "Now!"

"Don't worry, I'm going. I wouldn't soil my hands with a scheming bitch like you!"

* * *

That evening, Mitch told Sergei haltingly of Natasha's allegation that he had sexually molested Anja. It was almost too awful to put into words. "She said what?" his father spluttered.

"Don't make me say it again!"

Sergei stared at him, as though measuring up a stranger.

"You think I did it!"

"*Nyet.* Of course I don't. But why would she make something like that up?" He got up from the armchair. "Tell me exactly what she said."

"She said ... she said if I went anywhere near Anja, she'd have me arrested for ..." Mitch's voice broke up.

"I always knew that woman was evil, but this beats everything!" Sergei exploded, his face turning from red to crimson. "If I get my hands on the lying bitch ..."

"You're to stay away from her, Papa. The situation's bad enough without you barging in there."

Sergei's face contorted as he struggled to control his anger, and it was some moments before he asked, "What are you going to do? Challenge it in court?"

"I can't put Anja through that. I've seen enough young people under cross-examination. You know what it's like, what they go through. There'd be a physical examination, questions. She'd end up scarred for life."

"You can't let it go."

"I'll think of something, but taking it to court isn't the answer. You know as well as I do that with a large enough bribe and threats of physical violence from Yagudin's henchmen, medical reports would be tampered with, so-called witnesses produced."

"Do you think someone else has done it ... done something to her?" Sergei's voice was little more than a whisper. "Him?"

"I don't know, but I'm fucking well going to find out!" Mitch took a gulp of his drink. "The thought of anyone doing that to her ... it screws me up, makes me sick inside."

"She's lying. She must be."

"I damn well hope she is." Mitch closed his eyes for a moment. "But how am I going to prove it without involving Anja? Tell me that, Papa."

"Surely, if Natasha's father knew, he wouldn't let anyone get away with it."

"Forget Lyosha!" Mitch retorted. "If ..."

"You may not like the man," Sergei interrupted, "but he dotes on Anja. If he thought something like that had happened, he'd make sure whoever did it wasn't capable of going near another child—or woman, for that matter!"

"If anything has happened to her, I'll personally wipe out whoever's done it!"

"Maybe that's why Lyosha and Lena have taken her away," Sergei muttered. "Maybe they knew."

In the early morning hours, Mitch paced around his bedroom, hands screwed into tight fists. Natasha's words spun around and around in his head: *Child molestation ... I'll have you arrested. She's lying,* he told himself again and again.

It's a ploy to keep me away from Anja. He thought of her frail body, her vulnerability, her innocence. Surely if Yagudin had done anything like that to her, she wouldn't want to go to his *dacha,* to his birthday party. It didn't make sense. If only he could be sure Natasha had made the whole thing up.

He lit a cigarette and went into the sitting room. One shot of vodka followed another. He picked up a framed photograph of his daughter. A shaft of early morning light picked out her curly hair, pale complexion, the sprinkling of freckles across the bridge of her nose, the dimples in her cheeks. He gulped back tears as he looked at her trusting face. He had to find out. If only he could find some way to go to Barcelona, find her, and take her away somewhere. Ask her gently if anyone had ever done anything to her. It would be difficult finding the right words, but he must. "Oh, Annushka," he gulped.

There was a knocking on the door. Mitch got quickly to his feet and went into the hallway. *Who the hell can it be at this time?* He didn't dare think of the obvious. The knock so many people dread. He looked through the spyhole in the door. A man and a woman. The man raised his hand and thumped again. As Mitch went to open the door, his father came out of his bedroom, hastily fastening his dressing gown. "Leave it, Mitch. I'll see to it."

"But what if ... ?"

"Go back to bed," Sergei snapped.

Mitch walked slowly back to his room. Once inside, he left the door slightly ajar. An uneasy feeling gripped his stomach. His father's voice was low as he ushered the man and woman into the hallway and checked the corridor before closing the door. *What the hell's going on?* Mitch wondered, trying to make out what was being said. "I told you ... you're not to come here." *Papa obviously knows them, but who are they?* The other man seemed agitated as he pleaded. "We didn't know where else to go ... there was no one ... not at the address ..." The rest of his words were lost as Sergei guided them into the sitting room. The door closed.

Mitch shut his bedroom door and leaned back against it. Had he seen the man and woman before? He didn't think so. His thoughts drifted back to a similar incident some years ago. He must have been fifteen or so. His father was talking to someone in the hallway. Mitch had got off his chair at the table, but before he got to the door, Babushka had closed it and told Mitch to mind his own business and finish his meal. "I haven't spent all day cooking for you to leave the food to go cold," she'd admonished.

CHAPTER THIRTY-FOUR
LENINGRAD—MAY 1991

Three weeks had passed since Natasha uttered the words that shattered Mitch's world. Three weeks in which his sleep was plagued by a terrifying nightmare. It was always the same. Anja's screams of "Papa! Papa! *Pamagite! Pamagite!*" faded as she was dragged down a dark alleyway. His heart thumped loudly as he ran after her, shouting, "Papa's here! Papa's here!" He clawed frantically at the assailant's back. Searing heat burnt his hands, but still he clawed. "Run, Anja! Run!" Mitch yelled as she broke free. The figure turned around. Folds of white skin hung where the face should have been. Mitch recoiled and stared in horror as the figure swayed from side to side. A cool wind whirled around Mitch, stronger and stronger, colder and colder as the figure moved faster and faster. The air was icy now, the figure gyrating out of control. Mitch drew his arms around his body, teeth chattering. Suddenly, the wind dropped, and a deathly quiet descended. "Anja!" Mitch yelled. "Anja ...?" Twisting around and around he called her name over and over. He came to a stop, teetering on the edge of a deep chasm that had opened up where the figure had been. He stared into black emptiness.

"Anja! Anja!" Mitch couldn't tell whether he shouted the words or if they were merely in his head. He jolted bolt upright in bed, drenched in sweat, breathing heavily, gripping the bedclothes. Untangling his hands, he held them in front of his face, searching for burns. There was nothing. Time and time again he tried to convince himself that Anja wasn't in the dark chasm of his dreams. She was safe in Barcelona with her grandparents. But would she ever be safe without him to protect her?

On rare moments when a glimmer of hope seeped through, he imagined Natasha confessing she had made everything up. Glimpses of joyous times he would have with his daughter flickered through his mind; there would be no doubts to sour their lives, and the sun would shine on everything they did together. Then he was gripped again by fear.

Natasha's brother, Petya, told him to ignore Natasha's allegation. "Anja sexually molested? *Khuynya!* She's lying. She always does when she can't get her own way. You should know that by now, Mitch."

The darkness still hovered.

There was no news from Sergei's friend at the airport, nor from Yelizaveta Artyemevskaya, who had promised to let him know if Anja appeared back at school.

At work, he moved like an automaton through his daily routine. He stayed late, sitting at his desk, drinking and trying to conjure up his daughter's face, her voice, her laugh, out of the fog clogging his brain.

He had given up questioning his father about his night-time visitors. "Don't you have enough problems of your own to worry about?" was always Sergei's response.

Often, too disturbed to sleep, Mitch paced the streets until dawn, slipping in and out of shadows, avoiding the patrols stepped-up in the wake of recent unrest in the country. The government was running scared. Relaxation of state price controls caused many goods and services to rise by as much as 1,000 per cent, and an estimated fifty million Russian workers had joined in protest strikes. Boris Yeltsin, Chairman of the Russian parliament, had denounced communism, urging speeding up of reforms and calling for Gorbachev's resignation. In Europe, Soviet post-war domination was ending. The Communist Party was taking its last gasps. Wasn't this what Mitch had wanted? Yearned for? Now it hardly mattered.

At first when he'd arrived back at his father's home from his nocturnal walks, Sergei was waiting for him, a pot of coffee on the stove, a hug taking the place of words. A rare closeness developed between the two men. Mitch found comfort in a sense of stability, at least in one area of his life, that had been missing since his mother died. He realized that during his early childhood years in Montréal, he and his mother had formed a lasting bond that his father had never been able to penetrate.

But as days drifted past and Mitch sank further into despair, his father's patience ebbed. Coolness crept back into their relationship. "Get on with your life," Sergei snapped. "Fight for the child." Mitch could only look back, for that was where Anja was.

This morning, the streets were quiet as he crouched at the side of the Panteleimonovsky Bridge—the bridge where he had waited for Natasha on their first date. He stared at the water and, as on that long-ago day, watched white *cheryomukha* blossoms drift past. He wondered where his life would have taken him if she hadn't turned up. Maybe he would have married an ordinary girl who loved him and was content with a simple life. There would have been no Anja but other children who bore the looks and temperament of both parents. He stared into the water and let unashamed tears flow.

Around 7:00 a.m., he found himself outside the *kafe* he and Vanya frequented as teenagers. The green paint on the door was now scarcely visible and bore remnants of posters of events long past. Inside, as he sipped weak coffee, his mind drifted back to the pledge he and Vanya had made in this place. Their words were solemn as they vowed to fight for the silent armies of people who, by virtue of their beliefs or the colour of their skin, were condemned to live in the shadows. It had seemed easy then.

He thought guiltily of Professor Nekrassov and Tolya in their subterranean hovel. He should check on them, take food, a bottle of vodka, seek medical help for Tolya. It was months since the professor had foisted the papers on him. He should return them.

The papers! Fuck! Where the hell are they? He closed his eyes and tried to reconstruct that freezing December night. He must have gone home and put them somewhere. But where? In those few weeks before he attacked Natasha, he had been eaten up with suspicion about her and Yagudin. Everything else passed him by, like a silent movie playing to an empty theatre. He had barely functioned. But where did he put the papers?

* * *

He left work early that afternoon and spent a frantic twenty minutes or so ransacking his bedroom at his father's apartment. *The papers must be here somewhere,* he told himself, searching under his bed for the second time. *They can't have vanished.* He had been wearing his winter overcoat; the professor had rolled the papers up and put them in a pocket. They weren't there anymore, so where were they? A hot sweat came over him. *Damn! If I've left them in the apartment, I'll have to get in there somehow.*

He lit a cigarette and paced back and forth. *Think! Think!* he counselled himself. *When you went home that night, you wouldn't have left them around for Natasha to find.* He flopped down on the bed and tried to picture himself entering the apartment. *You would have hung up your coat in the hall closet. Could you have put them in there?* He got to his feet and stubbed out the cigarette. *The bag!*

That's what I did. I put them in the bag. He grabbed the bag from the bottom of the armoire. He was pretty sure he emptied it when he brought the rest of his belongings from the apartment. Now he turned the bag upside down, shook it, and banged his hand on the bottom. Nothing.

He looked up to the top of the armoire and climbed onto a chair. His hands found a cardboard box. A cloud of dust wafted over him as he hauled it down. Kneeling on the floor, he took the items out one by one. They were some of his childhood treasures. Looking at them now, it dawned on him that these weren't items he treasured but things his mother had kept in remembrance of the young, innocent boy he used to be in the days when their lives were simpler and worries revolved around having enough to eat. He picked up a book—the one his father had bought him not long after Mitch arrived in Leningrad—and flipped through the pages, remembering how Timur, the boy in the title, had formed a secret club with his friends to do chores and favours for families whose men were away serving in the Soviet Army. The patriotic tale was the start of his indoctrination into the lies that were the Soviet State. He snapped the book shut and rummaged through the rest of the contents of the box: miniature toy soldiers dressed in army uniforms, rockets, tanks, books with smiling, rosy-cheeked children on the covers. He slid the box back into place and ran a hand over the top of the armoire. His fingers touched something and he stood on tiptoe, trying to grasp whatever it was. A moment later, he pulled out a plastic bag. The papers! *How the fuck did they get there?*

He sat on the side of the bed, cradling the papers in his hands, thinking back to that evening in the freezing cellar. "In a few years, your daughter could be one of their victims," Tolya had said. Mitch had dismissed the old man's taunts, secure in the knowledge that Anja was safe. But was she? His hands shook as he took out the sheaf of papers. Did he really want to know what was in them? He began to read.

Sometime later, he lit another cigarette and walked over to the window. He felt cold and empty inside, sick to his stomach as he thought of what he had read. Young girls who had disappeared, many not heard of again, others found battered, bloated from drowning, throats cut. It was almost exclusively focused on the Leningrad sphere of the trafficking operations, written in a variety of handwriting, unintelligible in places. But how did he know the information was genuine? He leafed through the first section again:

Antonina Sichinava. Left home in Novgorod for job as healthcare worker in Milan, Italy. April 1987. Aged 17. Last seen in January 1988 working in strip club.

Olesya Tolstaya. Leningrad. Aged 16. Worked as hostess at Beogradske night club, Osijek, Croatia. Not heard of since March 1989.

Dariya Yadova, Leningrad. Went to Cyprus to work as translator. October 1988. Aged 19. Worked at Kolinia Cabaret, a known nightspot providing cover for prostitution. December 1989, escaped and went to police. Body found in park same day.

Irina Gabashvili. Originally from Tbilisi, Georgia. Came to Leningrad to attend university, but went to Jaffa, Israel, to work as hotel chambermaid. Aged 18. April 1988, found on road outside city. Throat cut.

Tamara Sharapova. Borovichi. January 1989. Aged 15. Recruited to work as children's nurse in Palermo, Sicily. October 1989, body found on railway track.

Fifteen! Mitch shivered. *Anja will be seven this year. In just a few years* ... He didn't let his thoughts go further.

Dina Ivanovna ... Lyudmila Terashkova ... Olga Akhatova ... Kosovo ... Beirut ... London ... Istanbul ... the lists went on and on, page after page. Many as young as fourteen. Bile rose in Mitch's throat as he forced himself to read again the atrocities they had suffered, and many were still suffering. The names were grouped together under the so-called employment agencies that recruited them. One was the place he had gone looking for Klavdiya. Her name wasn't listed. She was fifteen when she disappeared and would have been twenty now. Looking at the lists of girls and what happened to them, he realized his thoughts of her were in the past tense.

He turned from the window, took a drag on the cigarette, and began to read again the names of those running the operations. Many were familiar and not unexpected. There were always rumours circulating around the city of corruption in high places, Party and government officials, *militsiya,* people on the take—it was part of life. But this was different. If the papers were to be believed, the magnitude of the operations and global reach were far greater than he could have imagined. There were details of trafficking routes, money-laundering operations, contacts. The racketeers' influence also extended into legitimate sectors of the economy and government. A few were his ex-clients.

One page contained a caveat:

> *Lower echelons of organizations not allowed to know who leaders are. Vory superiors—Tsar or Pakhan—control cells through a Brigadier. With restrictions on access to leadership, network organizations tend to be fluid, highly adaptable and resistant to disruption. As a result of gangland wars, those who control the regional operations change constantly, and it is difficult to ensure the accuracy of information at any given time.*

At the end:

> *Information obtained in the past six weeks indicates that a turf war is taking place between rival cells for control of the Leningrad sphere of operations.* It was dated November 20th, 1990—two weeks or so before he had last seen Professor Nekrassov.

Where did they get all this? Mitch wondered. It was a few moments before he felt the heat of the burned-down cigarette on his fingers. He dropped it into the ashtray and sank down onto a chair.

Time passed. He heard his father in the hallway talking to Anastasia, the woman who cooked and cleaned for him. Mitch got to his feet, put the papers back in the plastic bag, rolled it up, and tucked it in his jacket pocket.

He ate a hurried meal with his father, hardly tasting the food, his mind in turmoil. Still chewing, he slid his chair back and excused himself, saying he was going out to meet a friend. "Nice to see you taking an interest in life again," Sergei mumbled as he cut another slice of bread.

* * *

Later, as Mitch headed along Lesnoy prospekt, he thought of the evening he had sped along this same street, trying to keep the professor's bobbing woollen hat in sight. The anti-military-draft slogans were still visible on the walls of the Bateninsky buildings, but unlike that winter night when the wind had howled across the inky darkness of Karl Marx Park, a gentle breeze rustled the trees. He stepped around a group of people standing on the corner of an alleyway. Their banter followed him as he hurried along the pathway between two buildings.

Everything looked different in the bright evening light, and he squinted, uncertain whether he was on the right path. Some minutes later, he spotted the iron canopy over the steps to the basement, scurried down them and banged on the door. No response. He banged harder. A voice came from behind him. *"On ushel!"* Mitch spun around. A face gazed down at him through a gap in the rusty pipes supporting the canopy. "If you're looking for the professor, he's gone."

Mitch climbed the steps two at a time. "Gone where?"

The man's hair was matted, his face encrusted with grime, his sweater and pants stained. The appearance didn't match the cultured voice. "Under the railway bridge." He took a couple of steps toward Mitch and pointed in the direction of Lesnoy prospekt.

Mitch edged away.

"You can usually find him there in the evening."

"His friend Tolya? Is he there too?"

"*Mertvyy!* Up there with the angels, if you believe all that bullshit."

A few minutes later, Mitch stood under the railway bridge over Lesnoy prospekt. Apart from an old woman poking through garbage with a stick, there was no one around. He headed down the side of the bridge, searching for evidence of someone living rough: bundled clothes, bedding. Only the smoldering remnants of a fire. Back at the bridge, he paced back and forth on the pathway. A trolley clattered past, and Mitch looked up, watching its poles negotiate the wooden panels attached to the underside of the bridge. "The wood. It stops the electrical wires from touching the metal," a voice rasped in his ear.

Mitch turned around and stammered: "I … I was looking for you".

"I heard."

"Where are you living?"

"Here and there." The professor pulled a bottle of vodka out of his pocket and took a swig.

"Tolya. I'm sorry about Tolya." Mitch sought for words.

The professor took another swig. His face was even more gaunt than before. He looked at Mitch with vacant eyes; tears dribbled down his cheeks. Mitch kicked a stone against the wall.

"Let's walk for a while." The professor tucked the bottle into a pocket and began to shuffle down Lesnoy. Mitch walked in silence at his side, past the pink and white building housing the swimming pool of the Army's Sports Club.

"The papers. I looked at them," Mitch began.

"You took your time."

"I know. I've had some problems. My daughter." Mitch's throat tightened. "Where did you get the information?"

"Tolya. He knew a lot of people. Some had been involved in the trafficking racket, some not. Many of them talked to salve their own consciences, I suspect."

"How do you know they're telling the truth and not just pointing a finger at others to save themselves?"

"Tolya, he'd known most of them for years. He trusted them. Like him, some had spoken out—and paid the price. Jobs lost, families victimised. Why wouldn't I believe them?"

"You met them?"

He nodded, pulled the bottle out of his pocket and offered it to Mitch.

He waved it away. As they walked, he tried to sieve through his muddled thoughts. *What do I have to lose? Even if Anja comes back, the odds of Natasha letting me see her are nil. She's evil enough to go through with her threats. I can't put Anja through that—the questioning, examination, investigation.* He shivered. *Maybe she's better off without me. I bring her nothing but grief.*

The professor stopped walking and looked across the street at the Military Sport Institute. Mitch paused too, lit a cigarette, and gazed unseeing at the frieze above the entrance. "I'm not promising anything, but before I decide whether or not I can help, I'll need to meet some of these informers," he said.

"Give me a few days." They walked on.

"Don't give them my name. Tell them … tell them I'm an ex-colleague from the university doing research for an academic paper."

"You'll have to meet them individually. They won't want anyone else there." The professor turned toward Mitch and stared levelly at him, eyes still brimming with tears. "Tolya was brave. I owe it to him. I have to do something."

"If I get involved in this, it'll be for my own reasons," Mitch snapped.

The professor rambled on as though he hadn't heard. He spoke of Tolya's last days, how he had tried to soothe him as he writhed in agony. "Makes me think the Soviets were right when they banned religion. He was a good man, so what sort of God made him suffer like that?"

Mitch thought back to the last days of his mother's life, when she had muttered in what he and his father took to be Yiddish or Hebrew, seemingly speaking to her parents. Mitch had felt her slipping away to a place closed to him, where spiritualism sustained her. "Some find solace in religion," he said.

"Khuynya!" The professor cursed and took another swig from the bottle. "*Religiya!* Just another way to control the masses."

They paused alongside the wall separating Lesnoy from the railway track. A train thundered past, and the professor cursed loudly. "This whole shit country's a criminal swamp." He drained the bottle and threw it against a tree. "The bastards in authority are no better than *vory!"*

"Careful what you say," Mitch warned, checking there was no one within earshot.

"Me? What do I have to lose?" he scoffed loudly. The train had gone and his voice pierced the silence.

"So when can I meet these people?" Mitch's voice was low.

"*Voskresen'ye.* Come to the old place—where Tolya and I used to live. Give me your telephone number. I'll call you."

Mitch scribbled his father's number on a scrap of paper and slipped it into the professor's jacket pocket. "How do I know I can trust them? That it's not a setup?"

"You don't."

* * *

On Sunday afternoon, Mitch parked his father's car some distance from where he was to meet the professor. He was early and paced around the Bateninsky residential array, trying to calm the lurching feeling in his stomach. Since seeing the professor again, his mind had flipped from determination to hear what these people had to say, to the thought that he need not turn up at all. *Let someone else put their neck on the block.* But this was something he had to do. He'd just listen, not make any promises. He had concealed the papers beneath the lining in his briefcase, but now, as he traversed the walkways between the shabby buildings, the case felt like a ticking time bomb. Never a smart dresser, today he felt embarrassingly well kempt amid the tattered laundry hanging from balconies cluttered with the detritus of people's lives. A group of young boys jeered at him from their perch on an iron railing, and a fleeting thought crossed his mind: *If they grab the briefcase, the problem will be theirs, not mine.* He walked on. At the top of the steps leading to the professor's former "home," he took a couple of drags on his cigarette, tossed it away, and began the descent.

At his knock, the door opened and the professor ushered him inside. The room was lit by candles; their tallow smell hung in the air. Mitch peered through the gloom and sniffed, trying to identify a deeper, more pungent odour.

"The first one will be here soon." The professor slopped vodka into two cups and handed one to Mitch. "It might take a while. They only agreed to come if we were going to be alone." He swigged his drink and poured himself a refill. "Not everyone could make it ... they were out of the city."

"I hope this isn't a waste of time." Mitch examined the label on the bottle before taking a mouthful of his drink.

"What else do you do on a Sunday afternoon?"

There was a rustle in the corner. Mitch flinched. The professor laughed. "*Krysy!* Not the human kind!"

Mitch sat down and put his feet on the rungs of the chair, trying to ignore the rats. "I assume I can make notes?" He opened his briefcase, pulled out a notebook and pen, and retrieved the bottle of vodka he had brought.

The professor clasped it to his chest. "No names, though. They don't want that. I'll give you those later." He put the bottle down, slurped his drink, and leaned across the table. "Think about it, Mitch. This problem ... it's only going to get worse. The Cold War has ended, and now the Soviet Empire is crumbling. If we thought the Soviets were corrupt, we haven't seen anything yet. Weakened states attract criminal organizations. Freedom of movement means borders are easier to cross. Fertile ground for expanding illicit trafficking."

"You sound as though you're giving one of your lectures," Mitch snorted.

"It's the sort of lecture I always wanted to give. Not those meaningless words approved by the censor."

"You were never that convincing."

"Not to you. I always had the feeling you knew what I really wanted to say."

"Look where it got us!" Mitch waved his hand around the room.

"I'd rather live in a place like this and have a clear conscience."

The door opened; the candles flickered. A short brawny man dressed in a black tracksuit stepped inside and closed the door quickly. A whiff of sweat and cologne came with him. He swivelled his cropped head from side to side and peered into the gloom, checking that no one lurked in the shadows. "There's only us and the rats." The professor gestured toward the corner of the room where scuffling noises could still be heard.

"Anton Arturovich." The man held out a hand to the professor. It was the first time Mitch had heard him addressed by his given names—it hadn't occurred to him that he had any. "I'm not sure I should be doing this. I've done enough damage. My family ..." the man's gravelly voice trailed off. He hunched his shoulders; his head sank further into his bulky neck.

"It's only a research project. Your name won't be mentioned," Mitch encouraged.

"Davayte vyp'em." The professor got to his feet, retrieved another cup and poured. The man gulped the drink down.

During the course of the next half an hour or so, the man's story emerged. He had been in the Army, a champion wrestler, a man proud of his achievements. He had travelled to several countries, won some trophies, and was feted by his superiors. After a match in Germany, he had gone on a tour of clubs with friends. In one, a skimpily-clad young woman performed a sensual dance. Men in the audience called out to her, boasting of their sexual prowess and conjecturing about what they would do to her later. He had joined in, excited by her body, the way she moved. As she gyrated in front of him, he leaned forward to touch her between her legs, as several others had done. The look of fear that passed across her face brought back images of terrified mothers clutching their children to their skirts as his Army unit patrolled the streets of Kabul. He withdrew his hand quickly. The following evening, he went back to the club. This time as she danced, he looked not at her body but at her face. It still had the chubbiness of childhood. "I arranged to have sex with her, but when it came to it, I couldn't. She was fifteen. It would have been like fucking my own daughter." The professor replenished their drinks, and the man stared at his cup for some moments before continuing. "She asked me to help her. She came from a village, close to my parents' village, the place where I went to school. I might even have known her father, her mother. Who knows? They may ..."

"What did you do?" Mitch cut in.

"She said she was fourteen when she was taken. Rural villages are easy picking for traffickers. More virgins than in the cities, the girls more susceptible to being seduced by promises of a better life. They pay more for virgins, you know. Men like us."

Mitch bit back a barbed response.

"She and the other girls lived in the cellar at the brothel. She hadn't been outside the building since she arrived. They were scared, all of them. Their documents had been confiscated by the pimp. They were in the country illegally and would be put in prison if anyone knew—that's what he told them. One girl escaped. The next time they saw her, the cross she had always worn around her neck was wound around her lifeless hand."

When he returned to his Army unit, he couldn't get the girl out of his mind. On his next visit to Germany, he sought her out at the club. This time he made notes, getting her to recount every detail of how she came to be there: the employment people who had first approached her, the route they had taken, border crossings, anything or anyone she could recall. She had spoken in frightened whispers, relaying what she remembered and what others had told her. He didn't go back to the brothel again, fearing it might throw suspicion on her. He began to make enquiries, using coercion, sometimes brute strength, to extract information for the dossier he compiled. "I don't like some of the things I did, but they were necessary."

"Did you find the girl's family. Tell them where she was?" Mitch ventured.

He shook his head, drained the last of his drink, and got to his feet. "There's nothing more I can tell you. Anton Arturovich has it all."

"He's still scared," the professor said after the door closed.

"He wouldn't say what happened."

"He tried to make the information public but was warned off by his superiors. His family received threats. He caved in. Not as tough as he looks."

"Similar story to Tolya's ..."

"Nyet!" the professor snapped. "My Tolya—he did something about it."

"I meant the sport ... the wrestling."

"That man, Konstantin Romanovich Aleshkovsky ..." The professor paused while Mitch wrote the name down. "He'll live with his nightmares for the rest of his life."

Tolya lost his. Mitch kept that thought to himself.

There followed three more men, their arrival and departure spaced to retain anonymity.

The first, a former border guard, had received threats as to what would happen to him if he didn't co-operate with the traffickers. He had spent time in a psychiatric facility, haunted by the procession of young girls he'd sent to their doom. "I didn't know they were being trafficked, not at first," he excused himself. His eyes bore the look of a tormented soul.

The same look was evident in the next man, who had worked in the Office of Visas and Registration. "One day, I recognized the picture on an application. My friend's sixteen-year-old daughter. Her innocent face looked out at me. But I had to do it ... issue the visa. I would have lost my job. She went to Turkey." He broke down as he told them that four years later, the girl came back. They had finished with her. She looked like an old woman. She had been forced to have sex with hundreds of men to pay off the "debt" she owed the traffickers. "I couldn't look at her father, couldn't bear to hear his words." He paused for a few moments, trying to control his emotions. "She had two babies while she was there. They were taken from her."

For a while, he continued co-operating with the traffickers and accepting their money. He began to drink heavily, imagining the girls in the pictures were talking to him, pleading with him to save them. He couldn't get their voices out of his head. But still he put the official stamp on the papers. At night, the girls began to invade his dreams. They stared at him, red heat seering into his eye sockets until he could see no more. "I was desperate, couldn't live with myself. I had to do something to get out, so I made out I was sick, couldn't work. It was the only way." His family lost their home; his wife took the children to live with her parents. "There's nothing left for me to lose."

Mitch felt a sudden affinity with the man. "You did the right thing."

"One evening, I sought out my friend, the girl's father. I had been drinking all day and the voices in my head told me I must tell him ... tell him I was the one."

Mitch grimaced. "What did he do?"

"He took me into their home, sobered me up. If you hadn't done it—that was what he said—someone else would. Can you believe that?"

Mitch didn't answer. He knew he wouldn't have been so charitable if the victim had been Anja.

"Everything and everyone is for sale in this fucking country!" the man cursed.

"He gave Tolya the names of the people involved," the professor added. "The girl, she was too scared to say much. But now that has changed. She has AIDS."

The rats stopped scuffling.

"They can't hurt her anymore." The man began to sob and waved away the drink the professor offered. "Her family, they are good people. They allow me to live with them."

After the man left, realization came to Mitch that there were many victims, not just the girls and their families. Lives ruined, hopes dashed. For what? Greed!

As the next man entered the room, a chill rippled down Mitch's spine. There were tattoos on the back of his hands.

The professor pulled out a chair, but the man looked around and headed to the toilet. "There's no water," the professor called after him. Mitch knew now where the smell was coming from.

"He's one of them," Mitch hissed. *"A vor!"*

"He was, but not anymore. You can trust him."

The man was still fastening his pants when he came back into the room. He poured himself a drink, swigged it down, and sat on the chair next to Mitch. Mitch shifted away a bit. "You scared?"

"Nyet."

The man laughed. "I was one of them when I was younger." He ran a hand over his bald head. "Didn't have the stomach for it. Got out while I could."

"He now runs a legitimate business," the professor confirmed.

"Not as much money in it, but I sleep at night. I have a wife now. She was one of them—one of the girls. Beautiful." His hands followed the imaginary curves of her body.

"I get the picture," Mitch spat.

"I was in prison for a while. Young and stupid. *Vory* rule is total in those places, and youngsters are soon initiated into the code. It becomes their family. Lower classes like me never knew who the *Pakhan* was. Those who did were scared to whisper his name." He paused and lit a cigarette. Mitch lit one, too. "When I got out, I was involved in petty scams, nothing too rough. One day, a friend came to me. He owed me a favour and said he had this girl who was being trafficked to Bosnia in a few days. Maybe you'd like to have some fun with her first, he offered. She's not a virgin. Worth a lot of money, virgins." He paused and took a drag on his cigarette. "She was beautiful. I wanted her for myself, so I offered him money. I didn't have enough, so she went to Bosnia. I couldn't stop thinking about her. Then a man I knew, an older *vory,* asked me to take over one of his legitimate businesses. Run it for him. 'You are just the man I need, tough, smart, intelligent.'" He puffed out his chest. "I did well. Made us both a lot of money, but still I kept thinking of the girl.

"Two years passed, and I wondered if she was still alive. Some of them don't last, you know." The words fell into the silence. "I decided to find her. Friends told me I was a fool. 'Why would you want someone who has been with hundreds of men, maybe infected?' they asked. I used my contacts, went there, and tracked her down. She wasn't as beautiful as she had been. Not so popular, so I was able to buy her. I told the pimp I was starting my own operation. There was more demand than he could handle. I gave him a good price, and there were plenty more where she came from." Mitch flinched. "It was difficult at first when she came back. She was frightened of everyone. Diseased, too. Nothing that couldn't be cured, so I sent her to a medical facility. Now, she is my wife."

"*Vory* never marry."

"I told you," he snapped. "I left that behind long ago. I have a legitimate business. Two children. My daughter, when I look at her, I know I must protect her—with my life, if necessary. The tales my wife told me were terrible. I knew it was bad, but not like that. So that is why I gave Anatoly Vasilovich the information. It's all there. It's all true. When I look at my wife, I'm ashamed I could ever have associated with *prestupniki* who would do such things." Mitch's feelings toward the man softened. "Nobody must know it was me. I owe it to my wife. She's a good woman, didn't deserve to be used like that. None of them do." He got to his feet, poured another slug of vodka, and threw it down his throat. "You should get that toilet fixed," was his parting shot.

"That's a brave man," the professor commented. "Takes courage to do what he did."

"How do we know we can trust him? Maybe the mob are using him."

"Did you look in his eyes?" As the professor spoke, Mitch realized he had been too scared of the man, or maybe the reputation of the *vory,* to make eye contact with him. "You can tell a lot by people's eyes. He's an honest man." Mitch opened his mouth to protest. "Believe me, he is. He learned his lesson. He bought out the owner of the business and now has to pay protection money himself. Ironic, isn't it?" the professor chuckled.

Divine retribution, Mitch thought to himself. He had heard stories of business owners who refused to pay and were made to dig their own graves, sometimes buried up to their necks and forced to watch their wives or girlfriends raped. He had wondered how he would react.

"Now I have to take you to meet someone. Do you have a car?"

Mitch nodded. The professor pocketed the vodka bottle and they walked out into the sunlight, leaving the rats to their own devices.

"Nice car," the professor remarked as he sank into the front passenger seat.

"My father's. Mine keeps breaking down."

As Mitch drove, the professor commented about people he knew, places they passed. Mitch's mind churned. He had to keep a clear head and not be swayed by emotion. The *vor's* words kept coming back to him: *My daughter, when I look at her, I know I have to protect her— with my life, if necessary.*

They wove in and out of traffic on Svetlanovskaya Square, past the Radio Engineering Technical School and a huge billboard proclaiming, "At the smell of gas call 04." An old man on a bicycle, laden with what looked like his worldly possessions, wobbled as they cut in front of him and headed down a side street. Mitch looked in the mirror; the man gesticulated angrily at them. On they went past a scattering of old houses.

"The man we are going to see, he's the father of one of the girls on the list." The professor peered around, checking street signs. "This is it, down here toward the railway track." They drove along the dirt road, passing newly built wooden homes interspersed with ramshackle shacks and old properties. "Here! Just beyond this shed."

Mitch stopped the car and they both got out. The professor headed along the side of the road. Mitch wandered over to the shed. Its walls were held together by timbers criss-crossed at odd angles; an intricately carved trim decorated the space between walls and corrugated roof. The door was propped open and he looked inside—an oil stove, a chair, and a bed heaped with coats. The heap moved. Mitch hurried after the professor and caught up with him on the path through the tangled garden of a house. "You sure this is the right place?" Mitch asked, noticing the boarded-up windows.

They stooped under the limbs of a gnarled tree and rapped on the front door. It opened and a man wearing a dark blue shirt and brown pants stepped out. His hair was snowy white. His face widened into a grin as he gripped the professor's hand.

"Maxim Vladimirovich!" The professor paused, unsure whether to reveal Mitch's name. Mitch stepped forward and took the other man's hand. "The professor's good friend," he said, looking into vivid-green eyes.

The other man nodded his head knowingly. "Come in. We'll go through to the back of the house. It's lighter there." As they followed him along a dark corridor, he explained, "I've had to seal the windows at the front. The young boys, they roam the area smashing things. No discipline." Mitch grimaced, wondering if his father's car would still be intact when they came out. The room they entered was bright. Two windows framed a garden where flowers tumbled in colorful profusion. Mitch gazed at the peaceful wilderness. When he turned around, he noticed a woman lying on a bed along the side of the room; she stared out of a window, unblinking. "My wife. She looks all the time for Dariya, our daughter," Maxim explained, tucking a red and white quilt over her lower body. "I'll fetch tea," he said.

Mitch put his briefcase on the floor and picked up a framed photograph from a side table. A lump rose in his throat. The smile, the dimples in her cheeks, the riot of dark curls tumbling around her face—the girl looked like an older version of Anja. "That's Dariya. She was our only one," the man said as he put a laden tray down on the table. Mitch put the photograph back where he had found it.

As they sipped tea and nibbled *vatrushka,* Mitch's thoughts went back to when Babushka had made the little cream cheese buns when he was young. *If only she were here now, she would tell me what I should do.* He thought of his Dedushka. Although Mitch had never known his grandfather, Babushka had brought him to life in the tales she told of a good man who was not afraid to stand up for his beliefs.

Maxim began to relate his daughter's story. She was nineteen when she left home over two years ago to work as a translator in Turkish-controlled Northern Cyprus. "Such a bright girl. She had a natural gift for languages. My wife," he nodded toward the bed, "she was ill and needed specialist treatment. It was more than we could afford. Then one day Dariya came home. She was bubbling over with excitement. There was the chance of a good job. 'I can earn enough to pay for your treatment, Mamochka,' she said. 'Then, when you're better, we can all go on holiday, maybe to the Black Sea.' It was typical of her, always thinking of others, never herself." He took a gulp of tea before continuing. "We didn't hear from her. We didn't worry too much at first. She's having a good time doing something she enjoys, we told ourselves. But weeks passed and there was still no word. We knew there was something wrong. It was unlike her. If she was ever away from home for more than a couple of days, she always sent a message, sent us her love. She was a good daughter." He closed his eyes for a second or two. "I went to the recruitment agency and, after making enquiries, they said she had sent a message to them via their agent in Cyprus. She was very busy and would write soon. That wasn't like her. I should have known it was a lie, should have gone to Cyprus myself and found her. After a while, the people at the agency here told me not to bother them again; it wasn't their fault if our daughter didn't write."

The girl's mother was now waving a hand agitatedly toward the garden. "She thinks it's her, come home," Maxim explained. He got to his feet and comforted his wife. "It's hard for her. She hasn't spoken since the day we were told," he said in a low voice.

"What happened?" Mitch asked.

"The *militsiya,* they came here to tell us our daughter was dead. Her body had been found by a gardener in a park." He sat down in the chair.

It came back to Mitch now. He remembered her from the papers—a name on a list. Now as he looked around, he saw again the human tragedy, the remnants of lives ruined.

"No one does anything to stop it. The government, the police, here, there, they're all in on it, all guilty," Maxim continued. "I went there, to Cyprus. Friends collected money for my fare, paid bribes for an exit visa. I had to see for myself, speak to people, find out what happened to her. The police said witnesses told them she had been at a party, had too much to drink, and wandered off. I asked for the names of the witnesses, but they wouldn't give them to me." He shook his head. "There were no witnesses. No party."

"Was there an investigation?" Mitch asked.

Maxim laughed softly. "They said there had been, tried to persuade me to go back home. Threatened me. But I hadn't gone all that way to be scared off. I found out where she had worked and made my way there. The road is lined with nightclubs, one after another. Concrete buildings, no windows. There it was, a flashing neon sign with dancing girls: 'Kolinia Cabaret.' To think our Dasha ended up in a place like that." His voice broke and it was some moments before he continued. "I was angry, but I went inside, pretended to be a customer. The girl they gave me was young, sixteen. She had bruises on her body. I told her to put her clothes back on. I wasn't going to hurt her. I just wanted to know what happened to my daughter. She kept looking anxiously toward the door as she told me, hesitantly, what she knew. It seems Dariya got away, but the police found her and handed her straight back to the nightclub owner. That was the day her body was found."

Mitch glanced across to the girl's mother. She seemed to be sleeping now. "Did you bring your daughter's body back?"

"She had been cremated." Maxim's face contorted with grief. "I think we need something stronger than tea." He got to his feet, pulled a bottle and three glasses out of a cabinet, and poured three shots of vodka.

"What about the other girl, the one you were with at the nightclub? Did you find out who she was?" Mitch asked.

"I did. I found her parents here in the city and told them where she was. I walked away wondering if it would have been better to have left them in ignorance. What can they do? What can any of us do?"

The professor raised his eyebrows as he looked at Mitch.

When they got up to leave, the mother raised an arm again, pointing to the spot in the garden where she imagined her dead daughter was approaching, coming home. Then she turned and fixed Mitch with a crooked smile. Her eyes followed him to the doorway.

They were both quiet on the drive back. Shadows lengthened and pale evening light cast an unearthly aura on buildings and streets. It would soon be the time of the *Belyye Nochi* when there is no darkness and the Leningrad sky is bathed in mother-of-pearl luminosity—a magical time to look forward to, a time when not even birds sleep. Now there was no magic. Mitch couldn't get the thought of Dariya's parents out of his mind, condemned to spend the rest of their lives imagining what their daughter had gone through, how abandoned she must have felt at the hands of her murderers.

He brought the car to a halt on Lesnoy prospekt under the railway bridge that the professor now called home. He lit a cigarette, passed it to the professor, and then lit one for himself. He took a drag, exhaled, and watched smoke curl in front of his face. "I'll need to know the names of the *vory* superiors running the operation here."

"It'll cost money," the professor responded.

"I'll get it. Let me know what you need." In his mind, Mitch imagined Dariya's mother's smile widen into a grin. The professor opened the door a crack. "You have to find somewhere to live," Mitch began.

"It's not necessary. What does an old man like me matter?"

"You matter a lot ... people like you."

As Mitch drove away, he reflected on the part the professor had played in his life. He was the first person, maybe the only one, to know what went on in his inner soul.

CHAPTER THIRTY-FIVE

LENINGRAD—MAY 1991

For two days Mitch agonized over whether to tell his father about the papers and what he planned to do. If anything went wrong and the *vory* or *mafiyosa* discovered who had leaked the information, his father's life could also be in danger. *There's no way around it. He has to know.*

On his way home from work, Mitch stood in line for almost an hour outside a store, waiting to buy a bottle of brandy. The line moved slowly forward. He was tempted to go straight home but told himself that tonight of all nights he needed the courage that alcohol brought. A tram clanged past, and a young man hissed in Mitch's ear: "Benzin?" Mitch shook his head. *"Dvadtsat' litrov? Deshovyy,"* the man tempted. Mitch waved him away and watched as he drifted along the waiting line, stopping here and there, seeking someone on whom to unload his illicit fuel. Three elderly men in front of Mitch bought glasses of *Kvass* from a street vendor. Between gulps, they spoke in theatrical whispers, cursing Gorbachev for his soft approach with the Baltic Republics. "He's giving it away. Everything we fought for," said one. "He's doing what Adolf Hitler failed to do. Bringing the Soviet Union to its knees." Three heads nodded in unison. "Yeltsin. He's the one to get us out of the mire."

Half an hour later, Mitch let himself into the apartment. He listened. It was quiet. Usually at this time of day, his father was in the kitchen listening to the radio. Mitch opened the kitchen door. Anastasia was slumped at the table, an empty vodka bottle and glass in front of her. A lock of grey hair had strayed from the normally neat bun at the back of her head and hung over the side of her face. She looked up; her cheeks were flushed, her eyes red rimmed. "Anastasia? *Chto-to ne tak?*" Mitch extinguished the gas under a pot that was boiling over on the stove. "My father?"

"Your father?" She squinted at him myopically.

"Where's my father?"

"Him? He's in the sh … sh …" She hiccupped. "Sitting room."

Mitch rushed into the sitting room and let out a thankful sigh. His father was asleep in a chair, his chest rising and falling rhythmically, his spectacles on the end of his nose, a newspaper perched precariously on his knees. "Papa!" He shook his arm gently. "Papa!"

Sergei flinched. "What? What?" The newspaper fluttered to the floor.

Mitch bent down and picked it up. "It's me, Papa."

"Mitch?" Sergei blinked and looked around, trying to focus his eyes. "I must have dropped off." He struggled to sit up.

"What's wrong with her?" Mitch tipped his head in the direction of the kitchen.

"Don't ask!" Sergei took off his spectacles and placed them on the arm of the chair. "While I was out this afternoon, she had a telephone call to say her brother had died. When I got back, she'd been at the drink!" Mitch tossed the newspaper onto the side table, retrieved his briefcase from the hallway, and took out the bottle he had bought. "We'll have to hide it from her," Sergei snorted. He got to his feet, took two glasses from the cupboard, poured a generous measure into each, and handed one to Mitch. "I told her she should go to her family, but she's insisting on cooking supper."

"You should look for someone else to help out." Mitch dropped his jacket onto the sofa and swigged his drink. "You don't need this sort of aggravation."

"Anastasia and I ... we rub along okay most of the time."

Mitch pondered whether now was the time to broach the subject of the papers. With all this upset, it was tempting to leave it, but there would never be the right time.

"Sit down. I don't think we'll be eating any time soon," Sergei said.

Mitch's heart thumped wildly as he took the papers out of his briefcase. "Papa," he said and gulped the brandy, "there's something I have to show you." He looked down at the papers. "I'd like you to look at these."

"What? What are they?" Sergei put on his spectacles and took the papers from Mitch.

"Read them, please." His stomach churned as he leaned forward in the chair, hands clasped together, watching his father's expression as he read.

Several minutes passed. Sergei looked up at Mitch, his eyes narrowed, his jaw set. He folded the papers.

"You haven't finished ..."

"I've seen enough!"

"It's shocking. What do you ..." Mitch began.

"What do I think?" Sergei looked levelly at his son. "The best thing you can do with these is destroy them."

"I can't do that!"

"Are you crazy? Destroy them, for Christ's sake, or I will!" He twisted the papers in both hands as though to tear them.

Mitch leapt to his feet, grabbed his father's wrist, and levered the papers out of his grasp.

"Where did you get them?"

"It doesn't matter where I got them." Mitch was now leaning against his father's desk on the far side of the room.

"Haven't you enough trouble without looking for more?" Sergei struggled out of the chair and came toward him.

"I know you're right, but ..." He felt his father's warm breath on his face.

"Destroy them or destroy yourself and all of us!"

The words held the menace Mitch knew to be the truth. He barged past his father, rolled the papers up, tucked them into his jacket pocket, walked quickly into the hallway, and hung the jacket in the closet. "Someone has to take a stand," he began as he came back into the room. "I can't sit by any longer and know all this is going on. It could be Anja in a few years."

"So you're going to write your own death sentence ... and probably mine ... for the sake of people you don't know?" Sergei's voice was loud. "What about Anja then?"

"I've lost her anyway," Mitch countered.

Sergei opened his mouth to respond.

"I'm going now." Anastasia was standing just inside the doorway. She was dressed in a dark grey coat, a black scarf around her head, stockings wrinkled at the ankles. The flush from her cheeks had disappeared, and the paleness of her skin accentuated the red rims around her eyes.

Sergei struggled to regain his composure. "Are you sure you're okay?"

"Don't worry about me," she slurred, "it's yourselves you should be worrying about. All this shouting!"

"Just a disagreement. You know what we're like," Sergei muttered in a valiant attempt to adopt a lighter note.

"Like a couple of children, the two of you!" She adjusted her headscarf and, with a disapproving look, shuffled out of the room. "Your meal's in the oven," she called.

The two men glared at each other in silence until the front door closed.

"You're a fool!" Sergei spat. "You can't take on these people. You know as well as I do that the KGB is in league with the *mafiyosa, vory*. They're the ones running the rackets."

Mitch lit a cigarette. "I know all that. But I can't ignore it any longer. It's like a cancer eating into everything."

"Leave it to governments. They can fix it by increasing the penalties for trafficking."

"As if that's going to happen!"

"Let Gurov have a crack at them." Sergei referred to Alexander Gurov, newly appointed Chief of the Organized Crime Control Department.

"He'll end up like the rest, forced out when he gets too close to those on the take in the bureaucracy."

"Wait and see. Give him a chance."

"And how many girls are going to disappear, or spend their lives in fear, while all this happens? While we wait and see!"

"So you're going to throw away your own life and jeopardize your child's future for ..."

"It won't come to that. Not if I'm careful."

"Careful!" Sergei spluttered. "You make it sound as though you're playing some adolescent game." He took a couple of steps toward Mitch. "These people are murderers. They'd think nothing of ..."

"You think I don't know that? Imagine what those girls go through. Not knowing if they're going to live or die, from one day to the next!"

"You don't know them. Names on paper, that's all they are."

Mitch turned away from his father and stared out of the window. He thought of Dariya's mother, locked in her silent world, waiting for her dead daughter to come home. "Papa, I have to do it."

"It's insane!" Sergei's face was puce.

Mitch turned to face him. "This is all I can do for Anja. Try to rid the world of vermin like them." His voice was low.

"And write your death warrant!" Sergei sank down into a chair.

"Anja's better off without me."

"If you thought that, you'd have left Natasha long ago." Sergei leaned forward. "*Pazhalusta,* Mitch. I beg you. Don't do it."

"And live with myself knowing I was a coward, a failure?"

"Better than a dead hero!" Silence followed Sergei's words. "It's not cowardice. You can't fight this on your own. No one can. It's suicidal." When Mitch didn't reply, Sergei continued: "You're just like your grandfather. He was murdered because he put other people first."

"Ya znayu."

"I grew up never knowing my father. Do you want that to happen to Anja?"

"Would you rather she ended up like one of those girls?"

"Of course I wouldn't." Sergei shook his head slowly. "You must have a low opinion of me ..." his words trailed off. He reached in his pocket, pulled out a handkerchief, and mopped his face.

"It's not about you or me, Papa."

"Try telling that to the *vory* when they come knocking at my door."

"It won't come to that," Mitch said with a certainty he was far from feeling.

"So now I'm going to be forced out of my home. The only place I feel close to your mother ..."

"No one's forcing you out of your home."

"If you go through with this, do you think I'll feel safe here, waiting for a knock on the door? It'll be like Stalinist times. The great terror all over again!"

"If you're scared, imagine how it must be for those girls. You read what they do to them."

"I know what they do to informers!" The distant sound of sirens pierced the silence that followed Sergei's words.

Mitch perched on the arm of the sofa. "Papa, I met the parents of one of the murdered girls. Their lives are ruined. The mother hasn't spoken since the police told them their daughter was dead. I can't ignore other people's suffering any longer. If you knew the nightmares I have ..."

"You'll have worse nightmares if the *vory* are after you."

"They don't have to know it was me."

"If you believe that, you're more of a fool than I thought!"

Mitch got to his feet, jabbed his cigarette into the ashtray, and ground it out.

"I didn't mean that, Mitch. You know I didn't." Sergei struggled out of his chair and came toward Mitch, one arm outstretched.

"What do I have to do to make you believe in me, Papa? Nothing I've ever done has been enough."

Sergei gripped Mitch's left arm. "Is this to make me proud of you?"

Mitch pulled the hand away. "I have to do it for me. Not for anyone else. For me!" He thumped his chest with his fist.

"Do you think I want to lose you too?" Sergei's voice broke up.

Mitch turned away from him, breathing heavily, as he sought for words. A few moments later he spun around to face his father. "Papa, I have to do this."

Sergei sank down into the armchair.

"I'll make sure it can't be traced back to me … or you. I promise."

"And how are you going to manage that?" Sergei shook his head. "You never face reality, Mitch. The whole of your life …"

"Face reality? That's exactly what I'm trying to do." Mitch threw out his arms in despair, and it was a moment before he continued. "Papa. I've thought it all out. I'm going to give the information to a newspaper in London."

"London? And how are you going to get there?" His father's tone was cynical.

"There's a legal conference. I'm trying to arrange …"

"And what happens after they print the information? Where will you go then?"

"My name won't be brought into it. No one …"

"You can't be that innocent!" Sergei rolled his eyes heavenward.

"Haven't you always told me to stand up for what I think is right in the world?"

Sergei picked up his glass.

"That the good man always wins in the end. Isn't that what you said?" Mitch went on.

"That was just talk. Look around you, Mitch. The good man doesn't often win. He's the one who ends up in … in a shallow grave!"

It was a moment or two before Mitch could bring himself to speak again. "Things are changing. In a few weeks, we'll get to vote for the first time ever."

"And you think just because we put a mark on a paper, the bureaucrats are suddenly going to find they have a conscience and tackle these people?"

"I thought you told me to leave it to governments. Gurov'll fix it!" Mitch's laugh was bitter. Sergei glared at him and Mitch blurted the first thing that came into his head: "There's talk again of freedom of the press." He knew this was ridiculous as the words left his mouth.

"Freedom of the press! Don't make me laugh!" Sergei banged his glass on the table and mopped his brow. "That will never happen. Only last week a good friend of Vladimir Timofeyev, a journalist, was assassinated for writing about KGB involvement with the *mafiyosa*. You know as well as I do the number of businessmen, bankers, *militsiya* ... and lawyers ... who've been arrested for—what was it, you said—taking a stand?" he sneered. "Mark my words, those truly responsible will never come to trial. You get involved in this, Mitch, and you'll end up dead!"

Mitch couldn't disguise the tremor that ran through his body.

Sergei blew his nose noisily and wiped his eyes with the handkerchief. "Please ... don't do this. Let it go. For your mother if for no one else."

"That's not fair. You know I've never done anything to hurt either of you."

"No one can hurt her now." His father sounded defeated. "I thought you had more sense, Mitch, after that other time."

Mitch looked at him; he saw an old man tired with life.

"Do us all a favour. Destroy those papers and tell whoever gave them to you that you're not interested."

Mitch was sweating now, the glimmer of a headache beginning to nag. "I need some air," he said. In the hallway, he grabbed his jacket. "I'll be back later," he called and slammed the front door behind him.

Outside, a wind had got up; he hunched his shoulders and bent his body into it. He hated leaving his father on his own, and pictured him eating his supper, empty chairs around the table.

In a nearby bar, Mitch ordered a brandy and gulped it back. Leaving the glass on the counter, he put his hand in his pocket, pulled out an assortment of loose change, extracted a metal token, and fed it into the telephone in the corner of the room. "Yuri, any chance you can meet me, say in half an hour?" After a moment's hesitation, Yuri agreed. "Tell Marina I'll make it up to her," Mitch promised, gave him details of where he was and put the receiver down.

The buzz of lively chatter in the bar was interspersed with loud, deep-throated laughter. Mitch downed three drinks and was slumped at a corner table when Yuri arrived. "*Khorosho?*" He gave Mitch a friendly punch on the shoulder.

He looked up. "*Izvinite!* I was miles away."

"You looked as if you wished you were miles away," Yuri replied. He sauntered over to the counter and came back with another glass and a bottle.

"Thanks for coming out. I needed someone to talk to."

"I was glad to get out." Yuri filled both glasses. "Fedya's going through one of those phases where he screams as soon as we put him to bed. It's been going on for weeks."

"Anja was the same."

Yuri shifted his chair closer. "You look awful."

"Thanks," Mitch sniffed.

"What are friends for?" He leaned closer to Mitch. "What's the problem?"

Mitch scratched the side of his face agitatedly and then pulled the papers out of his pocket, unrolled them, and lay them on the table. "I need to show you these."

"What are they?"

"You don't have to read them." He placed a hand on top of them. "I'll understand if you don't want to be implicated."

"Why the mystery?" Yuri slid the papers out. As he skimmed the pages, his expression changed from puzzlement to open-mouthed horror. He breathed out noisily and pushed the papers back across the table to Mitch. "Where the shit did you get them?" His tone was low.

"It's better if you don't know."

Yuri slopped more brandy into their glasses and gulped his back.

"Yuri, I know you can't get involved—with Marina, Fedya, and the new baby any minute."

"Too fucking right!" he said quickly. "You're not seriously thinking of taking on those people?" Mitch didn't answer. "You can't be. It's madness," Yuri concluded, licking the fingers of his right hand where drink had spilled on them.

"*Ya znayu.* But I have to do something. I can't ignore it any longer." Mitch shifted closer toward Yuri. "And it's only going to get worse with borders opening up. It was bad enough when Timochenko ..."

"And look what happened to him!" Yuri's voice was little more than a whisper. "You can't do it, Mitch. Let someone else end up as target practice. You've got too much to lose."

"I've nothing to lose," Mitch said calmly. "The only thing I can do for Anja now is to make sure nothing like that ever happens to her." He picked up his drink and gulped it back. "I can tell you one thing," he said as the glass clattered on to the table, "I'm going to nail those bastards!"

"Keep your voice down!" Yuri hissed and looked around quickly. "We can't talk here." He drained his glass, got to his feet, stuffed the bottle into his jacket pocket, and beckoned to Mitch to follow him outside. Mitch picked up the papers and scurried after him.

The two walked in silence for some minutes until they came to an area shaded by trees at the side of one of the canals.

Yuri took a swig from the bottle and passed it to Mitch. "You don't know what you're taking on, Mitch. Believe me. This isn't some petty financial scam. This is a network of hardened criminals. Life's cheap to them." Yuri bit his lip before continuing. "You'll start something you won't be able to finish. You'll end up lying dead at the side of the road, and the *militsiya* will put it down as a common street murder and fit someone up for it. They do it all the time. You know that."

"That could be Anja in a few years' time. She could be one of those girls."

"You get rid of the scum running the rackets now, and others will step into their shoes. And all you'll get for your trouble is a bullet in the back or your head bashed in."

Mitch took another swig from the bottle.

"What's wrong with you? You seem bent on suicide," Yuri railed. "You know as well as I do that it's useless to try to nail them in the courts. Leaking it to the press won't work either. No one will touch it." Yuri shuddered, recalling a rumour he heard last week: the severed head of a young newspaper hack had been found in a cardboard box on a construction site. "Take it from me, Mitch, you'll never win against these people." When Mitch didn't respond, Yuri grabbed his arm and spoke, his face inches from Mitch's. "Listen to me. You can't do this. There are people here in the city who will make sure they find you, wherever you hide."

"You're being over-dramatic!" Mitch struggled, trying to free himself from Yuri's grasp.

"I've had dealings with these people ... inside dealings. I've seen what they do to people who betray them."

"You've worked with them?" Mitch spat, yanking Yuri's arm away.

"I was forced into it. They had something on me. Something that happened years ago."

"How could you?" Mitch stared at his friend.

"They threatened my mother, my sister. It was brutal." A shudder ran through his body.

"I didn't think you'd stoop that low."

"I'm not proud of what I did." Yuri looked away.

"So now I know where the money comes from. The fancy suits, the car, the apartment," Mitch sneered.

"Not anymore! It's finished." Yuri lit a cigarette.

Mitch's hands trembled as he lit his own cigarette. He felt as though he had been punched in the gut. Yuri, of all people. "So now I suppose you're going to inform on me!" There was a note of fear in Mitch's voice.

"I haven't sunk that low!" Yuri took a couple of paces toward Mitch and looked him in the eye. "You have my word, Mitch. I'd never betray you. You've always been like a brother to me."

As Mitch stared into Yuri's eyes, he thought of the times they had spent together—the good and the bad. Yuri had never let him down, always been there. That afternoon when Timochenko was murdered, Yuri was the one who had kept his head, handled the *militsiya.*

"Believe me, Mitch. I've paid my debt to those scum. They'll get nothing more from me."

Mitch took a drag on his cigarette.

"Are you still going through with it?" Yuri asked.

"I've made up my mind. Nothing will change it." Mitch gulped a mouthful of brandy, wiped his mouth with the back of his hand, and passed the bottle to Yuri. "I've done nothing with my life. What do I have to show for it? A failed marriage, a daughter who I can't ..." His voice broke.

"You can't think like that, Mitch. Things could change. You shouldn't give up."

The two men stood for several minutes, drinking and smoking in silence. Then Mitch rasped, "Yuri, I need money."

"So now I have to give you money so you can get yourself killed?" Yuri tossed his cigarette butt into the canal.

"It's probably their money anyway," Mitch scoffed. "I need it to pay for more information."

"What are you going to do with it—all this information?"

Mitch opened his mouth to speak then stopped.

"I swear you have nothing to fear from me, Mitch." Yuri's voice was low as he went on. "On Fedya's life."

Mitch paced back and forth and then turned to face Yuri. "*Khorosho.* I'll tell you," he began, "I'm going to London. I'll give the information to a newspaper there. Let them publish it."

"You'd better make damned sure no one traces it back to you."

"Anonymity. That'll be part of the deal."

Yuri looked levelly at Mitch before he spoke again. "Look, I know someone who has a contact in one of the national newspapers in London." He paused for a moment. "Though why the fuck I'm telling you, I don't know."

Mitch dropped his cigarette. "Who is he? Tell me!"

"Calm down! For Christ's sake! You're going to do it anyway, so I might as well tell you." Yuri let out a loud sigh and took a swig from the bottle before continuing. "Some time ago, the people in London were trying to sniff out who's behind the human trafficking rackets this end. It's a big problem there. Girls from Russia, the Ukraine, Georgia. My friend asked me what I knew. He'd heard I'd had dealings with some of those people here in the city."

"Can you find out if they're still interested?" Yuri didn't respond. "Please, Yuri, I need to know before Sunday. I have to meet the person who gave me the papers."

"I'll see what I can do," Yuri looked at his watch.

"And the money?"

"Let me know how much you need." He thrust the bottle into Mitch's hand. "I won't let you down, Mitch. Fool that I am!"

CHAPTER THIRTY-SIX
LENINGRAD—MAY 1991

By Friday evening, the tension between Mitch and his father stood like an unassailable wall. They sat on either side of the kitchen table and ate their meal; neither man spoke.

Mitch chased a piece of meat around his plate with his fork and came to a decision. *Tomorrow, I must look for somewhere else to live.* Despite his assurances to his father, Mitch was far from sure that, if things went wrong, the thugs wouldn't come looking for him here. In the past few days, he had begun to think someone was following him. He had tried to rationalize his suspicions, telling himself it was all in his imagination, but he wasn't convinced. Last night before going to bed, he had looked out of the sitting room window. In the shadow of the doorway of the building opposite, he thought he saw something move. He drew back from the window and then looked cautiously around the edge of the curtain. There it was again. As he watched, it took on the shape of a human head, in front of it what looked like the glow from a lighted cigarette.

It will be safer for Papa if I live somewhere else. He didn't qualify for an apartment through official channels and, as it wouldn't make sense to share with anyone, it would have to be in one of the rundown buildings scheduled for redevelopment, where short-term unofficial lets were sometimes available. Short-term. Was that how he thought of his life now?

* * *

On Saturday morning, he awoke early. Anastasia was already in the kitchen preparing breakfast. He poured himself a cup of coffee and drank it standing up, staring blankly out of the window. Then he rinsed the cup under the tap and left it to drain. "Tell my father I'll be back this afternoon," he said to her.

"You've not had your breakfast."

"I'll get something later."

"What about your lunch?" she asked. But Mitch had already left the room.

All morning he traipsed around the less salubrious parts of the city, seeking out notices on advertisement boards and asking around. The places he saw were dumps, not fit for human beings. One room was in the building where Vanya and his family had lived. Mitch stood outside, his mind going back to the night he had searched for his friend. He didn't go in.

Around noon, he bought a couple of sausages on sticks from a toothless babushka in a kiosk, kicked away empty beer bottles from the ground in front of a bench, sat down, and ate the sausages. Needing something to boost his spirits, he headed into a bar and downed two shots of vodka. A casual conversation with the bartender revealed there were empty rooms in a building around the corner. "Not much of a place. It's coming down at the end of the year. There's an old woman. Friend of my mother. Second floor. Twenty-three. She'll know what's available. Tell her Anton Valentinovich sent you."

Outside the apartment building, Mitch looked up. The ornate carvings, a holdover from Tsarist times, looked out of place against the crumbling plaster-work. He pushed open the heavy wooden entrance door and squinted, adjusting his eyes to the dimness within. Dust particles floated in a rasp of light coming from a window part way up the staircase. Hardly any of the doors on the second floor had numbers, and he breathed a sigh of relief when he came to one on which "23" was scrawled in chalk. He rapped on it with his knuckles, and after a moment, a voice came from within. *"Kto tam?"*

"I've come about a room. Anton Valentinovich sent me."

A bolt slid back and the door creaked open. Before him stood a grey-haired woman. The top of her head was level with Mitch's shoulder; her brown skirt reached to her ankles, and she clasped the edges of a grey cardigan around her chest. She looked him up and down. "There's an apartment on this floor. Wait there. I'll get the key," she said in a thick Georgian dialect. One elbow protruded from a hole in the cardigan as she hobbled down the hallway. It seemed an age before she reappeared, clutching two large keys. "The other side of the corridor," she explained, turning one of the keys in the lock on her door.

Although the apartment was bigger than others he had seen, like the rest, plaster flaked off walls, electrical sockets hung at crazy angles, and what looked like centuries of grime pitted paintwork and floors. It was cold too. "Takes a while to warm up," the old woman said, as though reading his thoughts. In the sitting room, she pulled the curtains back and coughed, fighting off the shower of dust the movement stirred. "Not much of a view," she cackled, revealing gaps in yellow teeth. Mitch looked through the cracked window onto the blank wall of the adjacent building. "But the neighbours are nice. You don't have to worry about anyone in this building. Decent people who've fallen on hard times," she shrugged.

"Haven't we all."

"Just you ... is it?"

Mitch nodded.

"I can give it a clean for you," she tempted and held out a hand. "Marta Basilashvili."

"Mitch Galichin." He took her calloused hand in his. "From Georgia?"

"Da."

"Terrible thing, the earthquake. Did you know anyone ... ?"

"My brother. He was lucky. Pulled out of the wreckage. Most of my family left years ago. Why we come here?" She shook her head. "And now they say the earthquake is Georgia getting what it deserves for voting for independence. Nasty people here."

"Not everyone."

She smiled. "The kitchen. Through here." She opened a door the other side of the hallway, and Mitch followed her along a narrow passageway. "Good spot for storing food, if you can find any," she said, waving a hand at the barren shelves lining the walls on either side. They emerged into a room not much bigger than the one they had just passed through. It had a rust-splattered stove, a deep sink, and a couple of low cupboards. Light crept in through the dirt-encrusted window. Mitch leaned on the windowsill and looked down to the street below. A group of people walked past on the opposite sidewalk. One of them stopped and gestured to a small child to hurry—the man scooped the child into his arms and ran to catch up with the group.

Back in the sitting room, Mitch sat on a wooden chair at a table against the wall. His nose twitched; the place smelled musty. And the bathroom. He wrinkled his nose, remembering the pungent smell—as though an animal had decayed there. That would have to be sorted out. *You're not going to find anything else,* he reasoned. The old woman seemed nice and the furniture, such as it was, came with the apartment. He could always pick up a few more bits at the *commissione,* the consignment store where those without money or influence were forced to shop. "How much is this?"

She shrugged. "No one pays rent anymore. That way, we're unofficial and they can get us out. So long as you slip the caretaker a few roubles for the gas and electricity, and a bottle or two every week, he won't tell anyone you're here. But you'll have to find somewhere else by the end of the year."

"Okay. I'll take it."

* * *

The following afternoon, he met the professor and handed him the money Yuri had loaned him. "It's a lot of money," Mitch said. He hadn't any idea how he was going to pay it back but found a perverse sense of satisfaction in the thought that he may be using the thugs' own money against them. "Are you sure you can trust your informant?"

"You have my word for it."

"If I'm going to put my life on the line, I need to know."

"Why would I lie? I'm getting nothing out of it."

"I'm not accusing you of lying. I need to be sure." If he was unsure of Yuri, how could he trust anyone?

"My informant has a score to settle with the *Pakhan* … the boss. This," he said as he waved the envelope containing the money, "ensures his safe passage out of the country."

"And who ensures my safe passage?" Mitch's voice contained an element of cynicism.

"I'll be here next Sunday," the Professor wheezed, "with the information."

"You'd better be. I'm leaving for London on Tuesday of next week."

"You'll have it. Have you contacted anyone in London?"

Mitch nodded. "One of the newspapers. They're interested." He pointed at the envelope. "You'd better put that out of sight."

The professor stuffed it into the inside pocket of his jacket and shuffled away.

* * *

Mitch moved into the apartment the following evening, although *moved* was hardly the right word for transporting one bag of clothes and three boxes of things his father declared he no longer needed. His own car was back on the road again, and he fobbed off Sergei's request to come to the apartment with him. "Later, Papa. When I have it sorted out."

"That area isn't good, Mitch. I don't know why you have to go. We were getting along okay. Apart from the other matter."

Mitch ignored the comment. "I'll still come to see you, have a meal now and again." As he drove away, he swallowed a lump in his throat. His father looked abandoned standing at the side of the road.

A pungent, acidic smell assailed Mitch's nostrils when he opened the door of the apartment. He dumped the box he was carrying onto a chair and threw the windows wide open. *Whatever did she use to clean the place?* he wondered. He put his head around the bathroom door. The previous stench had gone. In the kitchen, Marta had left a pot of watery soup and half a loaf of bread; Mitch sniffed them both to make sure they had escaped her decontamination regime. Then he retrieved a battered metal coffee pot from a cupboard, took off the lid, and held the pot under an iron tap whose label held the promise of hot water. He turned it on. It shook violently and then cold water splurged out in gushes, hitting the coffee pot and cascading down the front of his shirt. "Shit!" he cursed, turning the tap off quickly and dropping the pot into the sink.

Before going to bed, he sat in the only armchair and shifted a cushion to one side to cover a spring poking through the fabric. Despite closing the windows and putting on a thick sweater, he was cold. Good thing he would be gone by winter—although quite what he meant by "gone," he didn't dare think. He poured himself a drink, lit a cigarette, and looked around. *Is this what you've come to?* he asked himself. *It's scarcely better than the hovel where the professor and Tolya had lived. At least there aren't any rats—nothing could survive the old woman's efforts!*

Where had it all gone wrong? He had worked hard and been a good husband and father, or so he thought. Perhaps Natasha was right. Maybe he should have tried to earn more money. But it wouldn't have made any difference. Whatever he gave her, she always wanted more. His gaze lingered on the picture on top of the corner cupboard—his father must have tucked it into one of the boxes. It was taken at the May Day parade last year. He and Natasha were on either side of Anja, who was clutching a large red crêpe paper flower and waving a flag. They looked happy. He stubbed out his cigarette, got out of the chair, and picked up the photo in its frame. "Annushka, my darling," he choked. "Where are you?" he pleaded, willing her image to answer him. If only he could see her, hold her, know she was all right. He slumped back down in the armchair and continued to stare at the picture.

* * *

The following Saturday morning, Mitch awoke late. Wrapped in his old dressing gown, he stumbled into the kitchen, shivering. The temperature outside had warmed that past week, but none of the heat had seeped through the fabric of the building. He fiddled with the control on the iron radiator and thumped it hard in exasperation. Shaking his now sore hand, he twisted his head from side to side and gradually straightened his shoulders. Mornings had never been his best time. He needed to go into the office—he had a mountain of case notes to write before he left for London on Tuesday, and he still needed to convince his boss that he was serious about work and worth the bureaucratic hassle and expense of a trip abroad.

He tipped grounds from the coffee pot into the brown plastic bucket that served as a waste bin, filled the pot over the stained sink, plopped two meagre spoonfuls of coffee into it, and stood it on the stove. A quick turn of a tap and gas hissed out. Its pungent smell overwhelmed all others, and Mitch lit a match quickly. The gas ignited with a bang, and flames licked around the base of the pot.

He opened a cupboard; it held a knob of bread, two eggs, a packet of butter, sugar (from his father's small stock), a carton of orange juice concentrate, and a plastic-wrapped package of *Pelmeni.* He shook thick dregs of orange juice into a glass and, from three paces, tossed the empty carton into the bucket. Then he pulled out the plug of rag that held the window in place and opened it. Perched on the window ledge, he lit a cigarette, enjoying the warm breeze and going over in his mind what he still had to do before going to London. He must call on his father and pick up his old Canadian passport—the one he had as a child—his birth certificate and maybe that of his mother. He hoped they were still in the wooden box where she had kept them. An image came to him of her sitting on the bed, the contents of the box strewn around as she lingered over each official document, a finger tracing the names, the pictures. He must have been quite young then and had bounded onto the bed, causing her to gather everything together and put it back in the box. He had craned his neck, watching her conceal it in the darkness at the back of a cupboard. Now he needed those documents as evidence of his citizenship to produce to the Canadian authorities in London, where he hoped to get a new passport. Although if the bureaucratic process ground as slowly as in the Soviet Union, he was doomed to fail.

And there was still the translation of the professor's dossier to complete. He could hardly expect the newspaper people in London to be fluent in Russian. He remembered now how he and Babushka had spoken secretly in English, enjoying the subterfuge in direct defiance of his father's order: "If the boy is going to survive here, he must speak Russian … and only Russian!" Not for the first time in his life, Mitch was thankful for Babushka's fearless example. He wondered what she would think of him now.

His thoughts were interrupted by a persistent banging on the door. "I'm on my way, Marta Nikolayevna," he called. It hadn't taken long for he and Marta Basilashvili to shed the more formal use of their names. He had come to recognize her distinctive pounding on the door and was intrigued as to how a frail, bird-like creature could produce such a powerful sound. He slid the bolt back and, before the door was fully open, she shuffled in.

"When are you going to give that up?" She frowned at the cigarette dangling from his lips. Her battered black shoes clattered on the cracked linoleum as she headed to the sitting room and pulled back the curtains.

"Kofe?" He called from the doorway. "Sugar? You haven't given that up yet?"

"Sugar is better for you than cigarettes," she shouted authoritatively. "You have to watch the gas pipes. They fracture. One day you light cigarette and 'Pouff!' we go up in smoke!" she cackled and wriggled her way into the armchair, between the law books that seemed to have multiplied since Mitch moved in. He handed her a mug of coffee and set his glass of orange juice on the table. "Eat your breakfast. Don't mind me, dear," she instructed as he came through from the kitchen carrying his own coffee. He stubbed his cigarette out in the ashtray, sat down, tore the bread apart, scraped butter on to one piece, and began to eat.

"What are you doing this afternoon?" Marta Nikolayevna pulled a couple of books out from the side of the chair. They hit the floor with a thud.

"Nichego," Mitch mumbled, his mouth full of bread. He nodded in the direction of the books. "I have some reading to do."

She shook her head. "You can't spend all your time in here, a young man like you. A couple of my friends and I are getting together for tea at my place. We've invited Mariya Kornyevskaya, the young woman who lives downstairs. She has a daughter. Alina, that's her name. About seven or eight, I think. You must have seen her. Pretty girl. Red hair like her mother. We don't know what happened to the father. He's never been around."

Mitch smiled. He had gotten used to the speed with which Marta spoke, as if she was paid by the word and the end of her allotted conversation time was rapidly approaching. "I think I know who you mean." He had been behind the mother and daughter as they came out of the building yesterday. The child was about Anja's height—skinny, too. She had skipped along the street, and a gut-wrenching feeling of longing for his own daughter had washed over Mitch. He had quickened his pace to get past them and, as he drew level, the mother turned her head toward him. Flaming red hair framed an elfin face aswarm with brown freckles the size of pinpricks.

* * *

That afternoon, Mitch and Mariya Kornyevskaya sat on adjacent rickety chairs at Marta Nikolayevna's table. It was covered with a cloth embroidered with red stitches, broken in places. On it stood an assortment of mismatched china. Alina was in the kitchen helping Marta and her two friends set out the cakes they had made.

"They seem to be spending a long while in the kitchen," Mariya whispered. Her green eyes sparkled with amusement.

Mitch grinned. The three old women had nudged each other conspiratorially as they hustled Alina into the kitchen with them, leaving Mitch and Mariya alone. He supposed it was irresistible for them to plot to bring the two of them together. *She's attractive in an odd sort of way,* he thought to himself, noticing how several freckles had almost merged together across the bridge of her nose.

"They look like triplets in their identical print dresses," Mariya chuckled.

"Reminds me of a Chekhov play," Mitch offered. "Do you think they were called Olga, Masha, and Irina in another life?"

They stifled their laughter as Alina burst through the doorway. "Mamochka, you should see what they've made." She slid into the seat next to her mother. "I know what I'm going to have." She put her elbows on the table, her face alive with anticipation.

For an hour or so, Mitch forgot his problems as he laughed at Marta and her friends' anecdotes about various tenants who had come and gone in the past few years. "How long have you lived here?" he asked Mariya.

"The beginning of last winter."

"It was after Papa left." Alina bit her lip and stared at her plate.

Mitch looked at her. "Aren't you going to eat the last cake, Alina?" he cajoled.

She looked up and put her head on one side. "Could I, Mama?"

"I'm not the one to ask."

"Of course you can, *dorogaya dyevushka.*" The three elderly women sitting in a row on the opposite side of the table spoke as one and nodded their heads in unison.

Mitch covered his mouth with a hand, and Mariya leaned down, pretending to pick something up from the floor, to conceal their mirth.

Having composed himself, Mitch leaned back in his chair and watched Alina lick the white icing off the top of the cake. He thought of the time he and his parents had taken Anja to the *kafe-konditerskaya* she had chosen for a treat for her third or fourth birthday. Her eyes had sparkled and her dimples deepened as the waitress placed the plate of pastries in front of them. Long tails of the white ribbon that held her hair in place had trailed on the table as she knelt on the chair and tried to decide which cake to eat first. Mitch had reached out his hand to take the one with pink icing, the one he guessed she was coveting. Her bottom lip trembled; her brow puckered into a frown. He had laughed and moved his hand away slowly to select an uninspiring looking cake from the other side of the plate. She had giggled as her fingers grasped the pink-festooned prize.

"Mitch?" Mariya's voice cut into his thoughts.

He looked around. The three old ladies were looking expectantly at him.

"Larissa Feodorevna was asking what you think about the presidential election next month," Mariya prompted.

"I don't think it'll make much difference whoever's in power," he said, tracing a line of stitching on the cloth with a fingertip. "They're all corrupt."

"At least we get to have a say in it. It's never happened before, so that must ..." Larissa began.

"And you think they'll let the likes of us vote?" Marta interrupted. "We're not even supposed to be living here."

"Yeltsin must be better than Gorbachev. He's made a real mess of the country. We were better off with Stalin."

"Larissa Feodorevna! What are you saying?" Marta banged the table hard with a fist, rattling the cups in their saucers. "All those people he murdered!"

Alina buried her head in her mother's lap as the women continued to argue.

"It will be nice if they restore the city's name, though," the woman on Marta's left, whose name Mitch couldn't recall, piped up. "St. Petersburg. Much better than Leningrad." She had hit on something on which they could all agree.

"You mentioned you were at the State University, Mitch. Did Anatoly Sobchak teach there then?" Mariya referred to one of the candidates in the forthcoming first democratic election for the post of mayor.

"He did. His lectures were quite amusing." Mitch laughed at the memory and then explained: "He often made mildly anti-government comments."

"And got away with it?"

"Seemed to. We were all scared to agree with him, though. He was friendly with one of the administrators—Vladimir Putin, ex-KGB."

"Ex-nothing!" Marta spat. "Once KGB, always KGB." No one disagreed with that. "How old is your daughter?" she asked as she refilled Mitch's cup.

"She's six and a half."

"The same as me." Alina sat up straight in her chair. "What's her name?"

"Anja. Anja Yelena."

"Yelena? Doesn't she have a patronymic?"

"Nyet."

"Why not? That's silly!"

"Alinochka!" Mariya scolded.

"But everyone has one." A puzzled look creased the child's brow. "Mine's Artyomovna. When I'm big, everyone will call me Alina Artyomovna." There was a tinge of pride in her voice. "And Papa, he was called Artyom Fyodorovich. That's right, isn't it, Mama?"

"It's rude to question people."

"Where I came from, people don't use patronymics."

Mariya fixed him with a smile. "Where was that?"

"Canada."

The three old ladies exchanged glances, and Marta remarked: "You don't sound Canadian."

"Marta Nikolayevna! You've never met a Canadian," Larissa said indignantly.

"And what's he?" Marta gestured toward Mitch and glared at her friend.

"Does she live with you?" Alina's insistent voice cut in.

He shook his head. "She lives with her mother."

"Just like me," Alina declared and popped the last crumbs of cake into her mouth.

"You must bring her along the next time we get together." Marta fixed him with a steady gaze.

"She'd like that," he mumbled and was relieved when the conversation moved on to the problems of the sporadic water and electricity supply in the building.

"You wait until winter," Marta Nikolayevna warned. "You'll be lucky if you get any hot water. And the heating ... it goes off for days."

"I hope you have warm blankets." Mariya fumbled in a pocket for a handkerchief and wiped smears of icing from Alina's face. "Sit still," she urged as the child wriggled in her seat.

Marta scraped her chair back and pulled a bottle of wine out of a cupboard. Larissa fetched glasses from the kitchen. "Georgian, the best there is!" Marta declared with pride as she pushed two full glasses across the table to Mitch and Mariya.

Mitch forced himself to swallow a mouthful; Georgian wines were too sweet for his taste.

An hour or so and two bottles later, Mitch, Mariya, and Alina left. Outside Mitch's door, they paused. "We'll have to get together sometime. Maybe coffee?" he ventured.

"No more wine!" Mariya laughed and held the side of her head.

CHAPTER THIRTY-SEVEN

LENINGRAD—MAY 1991

The next afternoon, Mitch paced back and forth at the base of the railway bridge over Lesnoy prospekt for almost an hour. He kicked a stone, berating himself for having trusted the professor with so much money. *Chort! He's probably been drunk all week!* The stone ricocheted with a clang off a metal girder. Then a more sinister thought struck him: the whole thing was a trap and the professor walked right into it! He stopped walking, heart racing, and held on to one of the supports of the bridge. *Surely not.* Surely the old man would have known, or at least suspected, if something was amiss. And it couldn't be Yuri—Mitch hadn't told him the identity of his informant. Unless someone had followed him. He looked up and down the street again and then checked his watch. *I'll give him another ten minutes. If he isn't here by then, I'll go and look for him.* But apart from the old place where he and Tolya had lived, Mitch hadn't a clue where to look.

The ten minutes were almost up when he saw the professor weaving in and out of the trees, edging a path. "Where the hell have you been?" Mitch yelled, walking quickly toward him. The professor staggered and cannoned into a tree. *Drunk again! I knew it!* Mitch broke into a run. "I thought you weren't coming!" He gripped the old man by an arm.

"I said I'd be here," the professor rasped, bent double and taking noisy gasps of breath. "I've been sick."

"Sounds as though you still are," Mitch said, regretting his initial assumption and abrupt tone. He put an arm across the other man's back, gently levered him upright, and walked him slowly toward a yellow-painted door, at the side of which was a bin. He tipped the contents out, turned the bin over, and lowered the professor onto it.

"Prastite," the old man apologized, his voice barely a whisper, his face ashen.

"Take your time; there's no hurry." Mitch pulled a small bottle of brandy out of his pocket and removed the cap. "Here, this'll help." A few swigs later, some of the professor's colour returned. "Have you seen a doctor?" Mitch asked, knowing what the answer would be.

The old man gave a weak smile and fumbled in his pockets. "This is what you need." He pressed a folded sheet of paper into Mitch's hand. "Sorry I was late. It took me longer than I thought to walk here."

Mitch put the paper in his own pocket without looking at it. "You're not still sleeping outside, are you?"

The old man shrugged. "What does it matter?"

"It matters to me," Mitch said. "All those years ago, you were the one person who believed I could make a difference to people. Everyone else just dismissed it as ... what was it they said ... my fine ideals?"

The professor hacked and spat into a filthy handkerchief. "Maybe that was all it was for all of us."

"Not anymore!" Mitch lit a cigarette, took a few drags, pinched it out with the tips of his fingers, and put it back in the packet. "When was the last time you had anything to eat?"

"I'm not hungry."

"You're coming home with me," Mitch said, wondering at the stupidity of his own words. "No arguments. Just for a few days. There's an old woman there; I'm sure she'll be glad to sort you out."

"I don't need sorting out. Not by an old woman!" The professor's tone was indignant.

Back at the apartment building, the professor gasped and wheezed up the staircase. Mitch feared he wouldn't make it. *What the hell are you doing?* he asked himself as he opened the apartment door and manoeuvred the old man along the passageway. *The last thing you need is a corpse on your hands!* "Nice place you have here," the professor rasped before a coughing fit overtook him.

Later, having devoured hunks of bread smothered in butter and Marta Nikolayevna's runny home-made jam, washed down with copious mugs of strong tea, he slept soundly in Mitch's bed, snoring rhythmically. Mitch looked at him and shook his head. "What the hell am I going to do with you while I'm in England?"

No nearer an answer, he settled in the armchair in the sitting room, a slug of vodka by his side, and unfolded the paper the professor had given him. It was a roughly-drawn organization chart. He stared at it, his eyes like beams transfixed on the name at the top, his brain unable to absorb what he read. Blood drained from his body. Then the paper slipped through his fingers and fluttered to the floor. He reached for the glass. Lifting it shakily to his lips, he took a mouthful and tried to swallow. Vodka spilled out in an arc. A stain spread across his pants. He watched it, seemingly detached as though it was seeping through to some other person's leg.

A snapshot flashed in front of his eyes: Natasha and Yagudin standing on the other side of the street. Anja—pointing, shrieking, "Mamochka ... Dyadya Mikhail". It ran like a black movie, over and over. Then the picture changed. His daughter ran toward them. Yagudin took her hand.

Mitch's hands balled into tight fists. He squeezed harder and harder until his fingernails punctured his palms. Then he sprang to his feet and paced around the room, cursing loudly. "Fucking bastard! I knew it! I knew it was him!" There was a note of triumph in his voice. Reaching down, he picked the paper up. At the top of the chart, the name of the *Pakhan:* Mikhail Victorovich Yagudin. "I'll see you rot in hell! You bastard!" Mitch cursed through gritted teeth. Because of his age, everyone assumed Yagudin was no longer an active member of the *vory* but just a *Sovetnik,* an older, experienced *vor,* revered for his violent past, a counsellor to the underworld princes. "*Ublyudok!* You didn't fool me." Now Mitch had all the proof he needed. No more doubt. No more hesitation. There was an icy coldness in the pit of his stomach, and he threw a shot of vodka down his throat, trying to dislodge the picture of Anja still in his mind. "Mikhail fucking Yagudin! I'll nail you, you fucking bastard! Make sure you never go near my daughter or anyone else's daughter again!"

With trembling hands, he picked up the photo frame, pulled the picture out, and tore it down one side. "You let that animal near our daughter," he railed at Natasha's tattered image as though she was in the room. "*Bitch! Bitch!* Devil incarnate!" Holding the flame of his cigarette lighter to one edge, he watched as she shrivelled and blackened. Then he dropped the charred pieces into the ashtray and held the remains of the photograph up to his face. *How did it come to this, my sweetie?* Anja smiled back at him. Her mouth seemed to move, but no sound came from it. He whispered: "Papa will protect you. I swear." Silent tears washed his face.

He gave thanks again that Anja was in Spain with her grandparents. Although he was sure some of Lyosha's business transactions in the art world weren't legitimate, his scams were far removed from the horrendous crimes and human misery in which scum like Yagudin trade. He needed to move fast and make sure he nailed the bastard before Anja came back.

Some hours later, he slept.

* * *

He awoke with a start, a crick in his neck, and looked around. Reality flooded in. He pulled himself upright in the armchair, reached for the paper, and studied the spidery handwriting. *It wasn't a dream.* He felt strangely calm as he folded the paper, got to his feet, and placed it with the others under the inside lining of his briefcase.

Sitting at the table and smoking his first cigarette of the day, he listened. Apart from the clanging of pipes, which was a fixture in the building, there was no other sound. Then he remembered. *Christ! The professor!* He jumped to his feet. *Govno! I hope nothing's happened to him.* Leaving the cigarette in the ashtray, he headed to the bedroom. He hesitated outside the door. *What if he's dead?* He pushed the door open and walked hesitantly toward the bed. Relief flooded through him—the old man was asleep. To be certain it wasn't anything more permanent, he leaned over and put a hand in front of the professor's mouth; his breath was warm.

An hour or so later, Mitch scribbled a note and left it on the table. Then, briefcase in hand, he knocked on the door of Marta Nikolayevna's apartment. "You're early," she commented as she let him in.

"I have a favour to ask." Not waiting for her response, he went on. "One of my old professors is sick. He was living on the streets, so I brought him back here for a few days while he recovers."

"You want me to make sure he's okay while you're out," she nodded knowingly.

"If you could. But ... there's one thing. He smells. Really smells."

"He wouldn't be the first man I've seen in that state," she cackled. "You won't recognize him when Larissa Feodorevna and I have finished with him."

"But ..."

"Get off to work," she said, shooing him into the corridor.

Professor Nekrassov, you don't know what you're in for! he chuckled to himself as he hurried toward the stairwell.

* * *

It was late afternoon by the time Mitch finished checking and double-checking the files on his outstanding cases and briefed a colleague on two that were scheduled to be heard that week. He dialled the office number for Petya, Natasha's brother. After a few loaded questions from Mitch, Petya admitted that his parents weren't happy with Natasha's relationship with Yagudin. "They wanted to get Anja away. For a while."

"Any idea when they're coming back?" Mitch ventured, trying to sound casual.

"A couple of weeks, I think. I'll let you know if I hear anything." Just as Mitch was about to ring off, Petya added, "Natasha's stupid allegation … the sexual molestation. My father said it's just her being vindictive. He's sure Anja's fine. Nothing happened to her."

An hour or so later, Mitch sat across the table from his father. He hadn't intended staying for a meal, but Sergei had tempted him. "You'll be helping me out. She cooks far too much, and I end up having to eat it day after day." Mitch looked at the droop of his father's shoulders, the solitary place setting, and reached for cutlery out of the drawer.

For several minutes, the only sounds were the scrape of knives and forks on plates, the slurp of wine. Then the two men's eyes met. Mitch swallowed a lump in his throat as he saw that his father's eyes were brimming with tears. "This is nice," Mitch smiled.

"She's not a bad cook." Sergei brushed his cheeks with the back of a hand.

"I meant the two of us … being together."

"It's how it should be, what your mother would have wanted." Sergei's voice had a huskiness to it.

Mitch took a gulp of wine. "She always worried what would happen to the two of us if she wasn't around. She's probably up there," he said, raising his eyes to the ceiling, "wishing she could come down here and tell us not to be such stubborn fools!"

"We're too much alike for our own good." Sergei wiped a smear of sauce from his lips. "Why don't you come back here to live, Mitch? I'll take my chances …"

"*Nyet.* Not yet. Maybe later, when all this is over." Sergei opened his mouth to protest, but Mitch hushed him. "Papa, you must listen." He put down his knife and fork and leaned his elbows on the table, his face now only inches from his father's. "The trafficking racket … I know who's heading it."

"I don't want to hear about it." The expression on Sergei's face changed, as though a mask slid down.

"You will when I tell you who it is!" Mitch launched straight into his tale.

"You're absolutely sure?" Sergei asked as Mitch finished.

"I am, but even if I wasn't, for Anja's sake I'd have to act on the information."

"Lyosha and Lena must have known what Yagudin was mixed up in. It makes sense now that they would want to get Anja out of the way."

"Petya as much as admitted it."

"And Natasha's allegation that …" Sergei hesitated before continuing, "that Anja has been molested. Did Lyosha say anything about that?"

"He's sure she's lying." Mitch took a gulp of his drink. "Evil bitch!"

Sergei sat back in his chair and looked levelly at his son. "I've been a fool, Mitch. I should have been more supportive, helped you. If only I'd realized."

"You weren't to know."

"Don't make excuses for me. I should have trusted your instincts."

"Don't blame yourself. Based on my past behaviour …"

Sergei waved Mitch's protestation away. "I dread to think what might have happened to Anja if you hadn't found out." An involuntary shudder ran through Sergei's body, and it was some moments before he spoke again. "You know, it's difficult for a father to admit that sometimes his son is right and he is wrong."

"That's in the past. It's the future that matters now."

"Let me go. Let me go to London, be the one to leak the information to the press."

"No, Papa. This is something I have to do."

"But my life's nearly over."

"You've got years left in you yet."

He shrugged his shoulders. "Your mother always said I'd live to be an old man."

"Get it right. A cantankerous old man is what she said!" Mitch grinned.

"I'm only sorry she didn't live to see how true her words were." Neither man spoke for a few moments. "But one thing I know—she would have wanted me to do this for you and for Anja."

"I can't let you."

"You have to." Sergei took a gulp of wine before continuing. "I have to make it up to you."

"For what?"

"For bringing you and your mother here. All these years, watching her suffer. She hated it here, you know."

Mitch was silent.

"She lost all her joy in life. All because of me." He sighed loudly. "Sitting here on my own these past few weeks, I've cursed myself for being so selfish, told myself how different your lives would have been in Montréal."

"But we couldn't have been happy there without you."

"And were you happy here, Mitch? Either of you?"

Mitch couldn't bring himself to answer the question directly. "Maman loved you, and I had two loving parents. Not many people can say that." The only sound was the tick of the kitchen clock. "We make our own lives, Papa. It wasn't all your fault. I have to take some of the blame."

"Please, Mitch, just let me do this one thing for you. Let me go to London."

Mitch shook his head.

"That's what parents do—protect their children."

"That's why I must do it, Papa. It has to be me."

* * *

It was late when Mitch got back to his apartment. Except for the remains of the professor's breakfast, there was no sign of him. Mitch dropped his briefcase onto the chair and made his way along the corridor to Marta Nikolayevna's door. Loud voices and laughter came from within, and it was a while before he could make anyone hear. Marta's steps were unsteady as she led him into the kitchen, where the professor was holding court, glass in hand, regaling Marta's wide-eyed friends with his tales.

"Don't believe anything he tells you!" Mitch quipped. He was relieved to see the professor looked better. The flushed cheeks were more likely from the drink—there were a number of empty bottles scattered around. But apart from the coughing and wheezing, he bore little resemblance to the man Mitch had struggled up the stairs with yesterday. He was freshly shaved, his skin and hair positively shone, and he was dressed in different clothes. "They were my late husband's ... my Arkady's," Larissa Feodorevna declared proudly when Mitch commented on them.

"You should have told me about these ladies," the Professor slurred, "not kept them to yourself."

"I didn't know you were into ladies!"

"These ladies are different. *Krasivya.*" The three old women beamed. "Don't you worry about me while you're away. I'm going to stay here with Marta Nikolayevna. She's going to look after me."

Marta refilled his glass and gave his shoulder a pat before turning to Mitch. "You don't have to concern yourself about him. With three women around, he'll live like the Tsar!"

"I hope he doesn't end up like the Tsar," Mitch mumbled to himself on his way out.

PART FIVE

CHAPTER THIRTY-EIGHT

LONDON, ENGLAND—MAY 1991

Mitch peered through the aircraft window, shielding his eyes from the sun's glare as it formed a kaleidoscope of colours filtering through threadlike cracks in the plexiglass. His thoughts drifted back to the long flight from Montréal to Moscow as a child, when he feared that a rampaging giant wielding a big hammer lurked outside ready to smash the window and send them to their doom. He could almost hear his mother's gentle voice telling him that not even a huge giant could smash them.

Now he watched Leningrad disappear as the aircraft climbed higher and lurched through cloud. A few moments later, they emerged into blue sky. Shafts of sunlight illuminated the white fluffy clouds below, reminding Mitch of a depiction of heaven he had once seen. A feeling of peace washed through him; he felt close to his mother up here. He sat back in his seat and closed his eyes, wishing he could fly around in limbo and never have to face the reality of what his life had become. He thought of his father, of all he had lost, and Anja and her childish innocence. It would be tempting never to go back to the Soviet Union. Anja and Sergei would join him in some far-off land, and they would live in a house filled with laughter, never fearing a knock on the door. In the evenings there would be comfortable silences, gently fading light, Anja tucked safely in bed, the flickering flames of a fire reflected on the walls, his father asleep in an armchair.

Mitch's dreamlike state ended abruptly as the man sitting next to him attempted to get out of his seat, twisting this way and that, trying to manoeuvre his large frame through the pitifully narrow gap. He flopped back into his seat, breathed heavily for a few moments, then gripped the back of the seat in front, arms stretched to their full extent, his stomach a giant balloon encased in bold blue and white striped fabric. The woman sitting in the seat in front was lifting a glass to her lips when the man, with a gigantic effort, heaved himself upright. The unfortunate woman tipped back in her seat and then catapulted forward. Her drink, complete with a wedge of lemon, cascaded into the air. The perpetrator straightened his clothes and shuffled toward the rear of the plane.

Mitch lit a cigarette and watched the mopping-up operations. Then he turned the plastic catch on the back of the seat in front; the tray table crashed down at a crazy angle. Supporting one edge with his knee, he began to sort through his conference papers, idly ticking off seminars he might attend. The newspaper people in London had arranged for one of their investigative crime reporters, who was also a lawyer, to attend part of the conference. When he got to his hotel, Mitch was to await instructions. It was beginning to take on the characteristics of a spy novel. As a ten-year-old, he had driven his mother to despair, weaving stories that they were being followed by an American agent who was trying to steal nuclear secrets that Mitch had hidden in the lining of his jacket—secrets that would change the whole course of the world. Those fears were all too real now. The paranoia he had felt during the last few days was still with him. In the cab to the airport, he had checked behind to make sure no one was following. Even here in the relative anonymity of the aircraft cabin, he scrutinized the passengers around him, wondering if he was being tailed. He could now rule out his immediate neighbour—even the most inept amateur sleuth wouldn't have drawn attention to himself like that!

If you're going to go through with this, you must get a grip of yourself, he told himself firmly. *You haven't done anything. Not yet.* He leaned over, caught the arm of a stewardess and asked for a vodka. He ignored the supercilious look she directed his way and began to leaf through the list of workshops: Patent Law and Intellectual Property; Legal Protection of Computer Programmes and Databases. *And, how about this one?* he asked himself cynically: *Search and Seizure; The Thin Line between Legal or Illegal Probable Cause.*

"This your first visit to England?" Mitch's neighbour thumped back into his seat.

Mitch hesitated, tempted to pretend he didn't understand English. He shook his head. "I was there before."

"Great country."

Mitch turned away and looked out of the window, noticing in the distance the silver shape of an aircraft going in the opposite direction. He prayed that Anja wasn't on it. He had to get everything underway before she came back.

He yawned loudly, put the conference schedule back into the folder, and turned his thoughts to what he must do when he arrived in London. With a bit of luck, he would be able to get to the Canadian High Commission in Trafalgar

Square before they closed. He didn't know how long it would take to get a new passport—hopefully, he could persuade someone that he must have it before returning to the Soviet Union. The passport was a precautionary measure, one he hoped he'd never need. Then there was the call from the newspaper. What if he was out when it came? Despite their assurance of anonymity, what if someone talked? It was impossible to ensure that no one would be open to bribes from the criminal fraternity. Then what? The questions whirled around and around in his head. Where the hell was his drink?

"Going on holiday?" came from the adjacent seat.

"Nyet."

"Business?"

"Conference." Mitch stubbed his cigarette out.

"What sort of conference?"

"Legal."

"You a lawyer?"

Mitch didn't answer.

"I heard a great joke the other day. You'll love it." The man continued without waiting for Mitch's response: "How do you save a drowning lawyer?"

Mitch stiffened in his seat.

"Take your foot off his head!" The man heaved with laughter.

A cold shiver coursed through Mitch's body. He pulled his cigarettes and lighter from his shirt pocket, and it was some moments before his hands were steady enough to light one.

"You a nervous traveller?" the man asked.

"Poshol ty!" Mitch swore at him. From the amiable look on the man's face, he didn't understand Russian. The stewardess handed Mitch his drink. He gulped it straight down and asked for another.

"You okay, mate? It was just a joke."

Mitch stared out of the window. Below, a river snaked through the countryside; its waters glinted like sparkling jewels. An image came back to him. Their honeymoon. Natasha walked along the edge of the sea; gentle waves broke in cascades around her ankles. She turned and smiled at him. At that moment, he had loved her more than he had ever thought possible. What a fool he'd been.

An hour or so later, as the aircraft wheels juddered on to the tarmac at Heathrow Airport, he drained the last dregs from the glass he had secreted out of sight of the eagle-eyed stewardess. He cursed himself for having drunk so much—if ever he needed to keep a clear head, it was now. The engines screamed in reverse thrust mode and the plane slowed. It came to its final stop at the gate, and all at once the cabin was filled with the noise of people getting to their feet, and overhead lockers opening. Mitch sat still, watching the activity outside, where workers were already throwing an assortment of parcels and suitcases onto a baggage truck. He felt his neighbour struggle out of his seat. Mitch didn't get up until the passengers were moving in a steady line.

That evening, he swished the curtains across the window at the small hotel on Eastbourne Terrace and sank down into the only armchair, his hand instinctively searching for a protruding spring. His gaze took in the pristine pale-green walls and gleaming white paint. *No flaking plaster or rotting woodwork here. Warm, too.* He leaned back in the chair, his mind going over his visit to the passport office that afternoon. Numbed by travel and vodka, he had joined a line, shuffling slowly in step with others, scraping his suitcase along the floor. People around him complained volubly about wasting their lives queueing. Mitch realized that like most Soviet citizens, he had become inured to waiting in line. Lines operate like social clubs, a place to catch up with gossip and rumours, to curse politicians in whispers. Today, when it was his turn, the assistant behind the glass screen had informed him politely that he was in the wrong place, and that the section he needed was now closed for the day. "Try again tomorrow morning," he advised. On the way to the hotel, Mitch ate a hurried meal in a bistro close to Paddington Station, anxious not to miss the telephone call from the newspaper; he needed to at least know the name of their lawyer who would be at the conference. Assuming they would meet somewhere away from the conference venue, he had stopped at a store and bought a London street map.

Doubts were now beginning to creep back in. *You don't have to do this,* he told himself. *It's not too late to pull out.* Twice, he took his suitcase from the closet. Both times, he thought of his daughter, of the vulnerable young woman she would be in a few years' time, and of the unknown numbers of young girls—each someone's daughter—who at that moment were living in fear, their bodies violated to fill the pockets of scum like Yagudin. He put the suitcase back.

Taking the coffee jug into the bathroom, he filled it with water then set it to brew. While it gurgled and spewed steam, he paced around the room, pausing now and again to stare at the telephone, willing it to ring. *Maybe they've had second thoughts and aren't going to run the story.* How would he feel then? He would have let Anja down—not only her, but the uncountable young women who would soon become victims if he didn't do something to stop it. His thoughts went back to the Sunday afternoon in that sad house, and Dariya's mother lying under the red and white quilt, waiting for the daughter who would never come home. He mustn't fail.

In the early hours of the morning, the telephone rang insistently. Mitch shot up in bed, at a loss to know where he was. He gaped at the telephone for a second or two before picking up the receiver. *"Allo."*

"Mr. Galichin. Is that Mr. Mitchell Galichin?" It was a female voice.

"Da."

"Sorry I couldn't call earlier, a problem ..."

"A problem?"

"Here at the newspaper." She called out an instruction to someone before continuing. "Just wanted to give you my name ... Ruth Shelby ... so we can look out for one another at the conference."

"Okay."

"Have to dash. Things are crazy here."

"See you ..." He was speaking to himself.

* * *

After breakfast at the hotel, Mitch trailed back to Trafalgar Square. It was a bright day and the sunshine seemed to have quelled his feeling of paranoia. He was first in line but had to wait some time before the passport office opened. He thrust his old passport under the gap in the glass and explained that he wanted to renew it.

"You need to make an appointment and fill in an application form," the clerk advised.

"How do I do that?"

"The forms are over there on the counter," the clerk waved a hand toward the far wall, "and go to the end desk to make an appointment."

A few minutes later, Mitch stood on the sidewalk outside. *What a waste of time,* he sighed. The earliest appointment was Monday morning, too late to be of any use. He must be on the plane on Saturday; his visa was only valid for a day either side of the conference dates. To stay longer would make his boss and the Soviet authorities suspicious of what had kept him in London. And there was always the possibility that Anja had returned while he was away. He couldn't risk it. He checked his watch. He would have to hurry if he was to make it to the conference in time to register. He skirted quickly around Trafalgar Square, dismissing from his mind the memories of when he and Natasha walked hand in hand here on their honeymoon, and joined the gaggle of well-dressed people heading to Charing Cross station.

He made it to the conference venue with only minutes to spare and thrust his letter of confirmation in front of the dark-haired woman behind the desk. "Ah, Mr. Galichin from Leningrad," she said, fixing him with a friendly smile. Mitch took the folder she handed him and scanned the names on the scattering of badges that remained on the desk. Ruth Shelby's wasn't among them. He pinned his badge on his jacket lapel, ran a hand through his hair, and headed toward the double doors the woman indicated.

After the introductory session, Mitch joined the other participants in the break-out room, where coffee and biscuits were served. He gauged there must be well over a hundred lawyers milling around, at least a third of whom were women. He tucked his folder under his arm, poured himself a cup of black coffee, stirred sugar into it, put two biscuits in the saucer, and began to drift around. By the time he located Ruth, the break was almost over. She was what his mother would have called "striking," with cream skin, high cheekbones, and a slightly retroussé nose beneath sleek black hair that was plaited into a thick braid which curled around the front of her neck. She was talking to an older man, and, as she spoke, her hand stroked the end of the braid. Mitch strolled past for the second time; she turned her head slightly, her gaze moving from his badge to his face for the briefest moment. Then she looked away. He drained the dregs of his coffee and headed to his seminar.

At lunchtime, he filled his plate from the buffet table and took his seat at a round table, already occupied by two men. They were soon joined by three women, one of whom Mitch was relieved to see was Ruth. When they made their introductions, she gave no hint of recognition. Later, she leaned across the table and peered with dark, brooding eyes at Mitch's badge. "Leningrad. A real Russian!" was all she said before turning to resume her conversation with "Gerald Poynton, Baker & Neve, Manchester," as his badge revealed.

In the last seminar of the day, Mitch sat in the back row. As the lecturer was about to begin, Ruth Shelby entered the room, scanned the crowd, and slipped into a seat on the end of a row some way in front of Mitch. She joined in the lively exchange of views and ideas. Mitch would have liked to have done the same. The subject was interesting and one which could be useful if he ever left the Soviet Union and practised law in a country where there was such a thing as unfettered justice. He remained silent, unsure of his command of English and not wishing to draw attention to himself.

"A few of us are going to the pub along the road for a drink," the young man sitting next to him said as the session wrapped-up. "Why don't you join us? Red Lion, you can't miss it." Mitch mumbled his thanks, saying he had to make a phone call and might join them after that. He stuffed the conference material into his briefcase, all the time watching Ruth out of the corner of an eye. She was now on the edge of a knot of people shuffling to the back of the room. Mitch made his way slowly to the end of his row and stepped into the aisle. As they filed through the doorway, he found himself alongside her. "Did you find it interesting?" she asked, turning her head slightly toward him. His mumbled reply was lost in the commotion as small groups broke off from the crowd and called to others to join them. "I made a few notes you might find useful." Ruth pressed a folded sheet of paper into his hand. He turned to thank her, but she had melted into the crowd.

Inside a stall in the washroom, he unfolded the paper. "Tonight, 9:00 p.m." was written at the top, followed by directions to an address in somewhere called Fountain Court. He scanned the page. At the bottom was the name Basil Shelby, QC, and the instruction to ring the bell. *Shelby? Must be one of her relatives,* he thought as he folded the paper and tucked it in the inside pocket of his jacket. Unclipping his badge, he put it in his pocket and washed his hands.

* * *

Two hours or so later, Mitch emerged from Temple station onto Victoria Embankment. Traffic thundered along the road, allowing only snatched glimpses of the River Thames and the buildings on the opposite bank. It was a warm evening and, after the stifling atmosphere of the Tube, he let the light breeze waft over him, cooling the sweat that had beaded on his forehead. He checked the directions: "Facing the river, walk to your left. Then take a left turn into Middle Temple Lane." He looked at his watch—even allowing for getting lost, there was loads of time before he was to meet Ruth. He had left the pub earlier than intended; the noise level was unbearable and the ribald, sometimes lewd, banter irritating.

Along the Embankment, someone brushed past. Mitch shrank back, heart pounding. *Get a grip,* he told himself firmly and followed in their wake. As he walked, he went over in his mind what he would say if anyone stopped him. He should have an excuse for being there, maybe make out he had got out at the wrong station and was now hopelessly lost. Then he remembered where he was—London, not Leningrad. He walked with almost a spring in his step.

It was still light, a grey-tinged hue unlike the luminosity that turned Leningrad into an almost fairytale place at this time of the year. *How deceptive light can be,* he mused as he turned into Middle Temple Lane. The directions led him through a warren of lanes, courtyards, and gardens. If his meeting with Ruth wasn't looming, he might have enjoyed the walk. It was quiet here, no footsteps followed, no shadowy figures lurked. It was difficult to imagine that in the middle of a bustling, noisy city, somewhere so peaceful existed. *What is this place?* he wondered, looking around at the brick buildings, the tall, narrow windows, and the black-painted railings. Here and there, red and mauve flowers spilled out of windowboxes. He craned his neck to read the inscription on a brass plate next to a black-painted door. Under the name was written, "Barrister at Law." Mitch recalled an article he had read. No ordinary lawyers graced these buildings. These were the elite of the legal profession, working in higher courts. He looked up at the building. Somewhere up there, a skilled legal mind was working on a case for the defence or prosecution, a case that would have a fair hearing in a court untainted by corruption.

A few people walked quickly past, heads down, some with red or blue cloth bags slung over their shoulders or clasped in their hands. In Fountain Court, he sat on one of a number of benches around the periphery, trying to still his churning stomach. *Soon it will be over ... at least this part,* he told himself. A few yards away, a fountain danced beneath a canopy of bright green leaves hanging from trees with gnarled trunks. Apart from the trickle of water and the twitter of birds, it was quiet. Not a human sound to be heard. He leaned back, brief-case on his lap, inhaling the atmosphere. If things had been different, he might have worked in a place like this, hurried home to a loving wife. A clock began to strike. He counted, and on the stroke of nine, got to his feet and walked quickly across the square to the building that bore an array of plaques, one of which announced, 'Basil Shelby, Q.C., Barrister at Law'.

He pressed the bell. *No going back now.* When the door opened, he did a double take. This Ruth Shelby looked different than the woman with the neatly plaited hair and smart, pale-grey fitted skirt and jacket of earlier. Her hair now hung loose in long waves, cascading over a black chiffon blouse that floated above blue jeans. "Come on in, Mitch," she urged, closing the door behind him. "Everyone's gone. We'll go through to my father's chambers."

Mitch followed her along a narrow passageway, glancing into offices whose walls were lined with bookcases, desks stacked with huge tomes, and sheaves of paper. There was a musty scent, as though remnants of past legal cases and precedents contained in the books percolated the air.

Ruth opened a door at the end of the corridor and they entered a room that was larger than the others, the centrepiece of which was a huge desk. "It's not usually like this," she said, running a hand over the almost clear surface. "My father. He's in Bermuda leading the prosecution in a murder trial." Mitch peered at the spines of legal books in the bookcase. "His clerk waits for Daddy to go away and then gives the place a good blitz. Wish he would come and do the same to the apartment!"

"You and your father live together?" Mitch asked.

"We do. And we're both packrats," she laughed.

"Your mother ..."

"They're no longer together." A brief look of sadness washed over her face. "How about a drink before we start?"

"Please."

"The old man only runs to single malt," she said. Seeing the puzzled look on Mitch's face, she explained. "It's whisky." She half-filled two glasses, handed one to Mitch, and flopped down into her father's chair.

Mitch sat the other side of the desk, briefcase on the floor at his side, and pulled out his cigarettes and lighter. "Do you mind?"

She pushed a crystal ashtray toward him and brushed away the cigarette he offered. "One heavy smoker in the family's enough."

Mitch took a sip from his glass and tried to hide a grimace.

"It's a bit of an acquired taste." She laughed and took a mouthful of her own drink. "Let's get started."

"Before we go any further, I need some sort of assurance from you that no one will know it was me who gave you the information."

She leaned back in the chair and looked at him for a few seconds. "If you're asking for a cast-iron guarantee, I can't give it to you."

"But you have to understand—it's important no one knows it was me. I have family ..."

"All I can say is that if your name becomes known, it won't be from me or anyone else at the paper," she interjected. "That's not how we work."

"Look, I'm putting my life on the line here."

"Aren't we all?"

Mitch took a long drag on the cigarette.

"You have to trust us." Ruth looked him squarely in the eyes. "You'll be what we call an undisclosed source."

"What choice do I have?" Mitch muttered almost to himself.

Several drinks and cigarettes later, Mitch had told Ruth everything he knew. Some of the names and situations were familiar to her. Yagudin's name was new. "This is good stuff, Mitch. Just what we needed to fill in the gaps, tie the whole thing together." She paused for a moment and then asked, "Have you ever met him ... this Yagudin?"

Mitch felt heat rising up his neck and into his cheeks. "He ... he knows my wife," he blurted and then corrected himself. "Ex-wife." He cursed inwardly. *Why did you say that?*

Ruth narrowed her eyes at him. "This isn't some sort of vendetta is it?"

Mitch shook his head. "No. I've been working on this for weeks. I only found out it was him a few days ago."

"Only, if it was, we wouldn't touch it."

"It isn't."

She narrowed her eyes at him. "What sort of money are you looking for?"

"Money?"

"When people bring information like this to us, they expect some sort of payback."

"This isn't about money," Mitch protested.

"Then what is it?"

"It's a long story."

"I've got all night." She leaned back in the chair and leafed through the papers again.

Mitch got slowly to his feet and walked over to the window. "My friend's sister. She was fifteen when they took her." He lit a cigarette. It was dark outside, and he could just make out the black shape of a tree, to the side of which a light shone in a window. "The girl's mother, she needed the money. That's how the racket operates. They prey on the poor, the most vulnerable. But they're not the only victims." He turned to face her and pointed at the papers. "Some of the men in there, the ones who got involved in the racket ... for whatever reason ... they're victims too. They live in fear. Lives ruined. Parted from their children."

"Tell me something, Mitch. Do you have children?"

"A daughter."

"And this ... this Yagudin. He's a friend of your wife, you said."

"Ex-wife!" The cigarette dangled from Mitch's lips.

"And you still say this isn't a vendetta?" She fixed him with a steely look.

"If you put it like that ..." Panic streaked through his body. *If they decide not to go ahead, what am I going to do? There's no one else.* "Look, I wouldn't be much of a father if I wasn't worried about my daughter. But it isn't just about her. I've met the families of some of these girls—girls who've been murdered or disappeared without trace." He stubbed his cigarette out in the ashtray on the desk and leaned toward her. "Believe me, I wish it didn't have to be me. I'd like nothing more than to go home to Leningrad and forget I ever found out about all this." He took a deep breath. "But I can't. Something has to be done to stop the racket, bring these people to justice, give governments a wake-up call." To his own ears, his voice was surprisingly calm. "I can't ignore it any longer."

For a while, the only noise was the ticking of a clock. "Okay. Let's get on with it," Ruth said.

Mitch said a silent prayer of thanks.

"Now let me fill you in on how I'm going to approach this," she began. Hardly pausing for breath, she told him that the main focus of her story was to be a young woman ("We'll call her Elena") who had been enticed from her home in a village outside Leningrad and was now in hiding in England. "A friend of the girl's mother approached the kid one day with the offer of a job here in London. The woman worked for a recruitment agency, a front, one of those in your dossier." She thumbed through the papers and pointed to the name of the agency that sent Klavdiya and Dariya to their doom. "Coming from her mother's friend, how could the girl and her mother not trust her?"

"A familiar tale," Mitch said.

"We'll also need to use some of the personal stories in your notes. Two girls in particular ... the one who went to Cyprus as a translator, and the girl with AIDS." Mitch opened his mouth to protest, but she cut in. "We won't name them, but as they were recruited by the same people, it will back-up the main story, show Elena wasn't a one-off, emphasize the evil this Yagudin trades in. The girl with AIDS? Well, she's as good as dead, so that will show that even if the girls escape, the misery still goes on."

"I see your point," Mitch concurred, "as long as they or their families aren't identified. They've suffered enough."

Ruth rambled on, flitting from one point to another in quick succession, outlining how she would connect the stories to ram home the point that human trafficking is a huge international crime respecting no borders. At times Mitch found it difficult to follow her drift, but he was mesmerised by the passion with which she spoke and her ability to translate bold facts into a story that brought the horror to life.

"Now, this girl, here ... Olga Akhatova." She pointed to one of the names on the translated version of the professor's lists. "She ended up in the same brothel as Elena. They were smuggled through the same route. And this one here ..." Before Mitch had the chance to identify which girl she meant, she was off on another tack, speaking aloud the thoughts that buzzed in her head. "Yes, that will work, linking all three, showing how the web spreads out. And the girl who went to Milan ..." Her eyes scanned the lists. "I thought so! She and Olga Akhatova both came from Novgorod. Same age. I'll start with a description of rosy-cheeked girls on their way to school. Maybe they went to the same one. Elena will know the sort of things Soviet schoolgirls talk about—their hopes, their dreams. Then switch to how they ended up: strip clubs, brothels, scared faces plastered with makeup, young bodies violated, families waiting for letters that don't come, corpses on roads, railway tracks."

When she finally finished, neither spoke for a minute or so. Then Mitch said, "Those girls you mentioned ... you can't use their names, especially the ones that may still be alive."

"I know where to draw the line, Mitch." She reached for the bottle and dribbled what was left into his glass.

"But do you really need to use a real person? This Elena. Even though it's not her real name, they'll know who she is by putting the facts together."

"Let me tell you something about this business, Mitch. Readers like the human touch, someone to pity, a person with a tragic history on which to pin their grief. It's sad," she sighed, "but that's the way it is."

"But the girl? Even if she's in hiding, what about her family in Russia? That's how these people operate. They tell the girls that if they don't co-operate, their families will suffer."

"Elena was an only child. She has no family now. Her father was killed in an accident some years ago, and after they took the girl, the mother ... well the mother gave up, wasted away."

"Another victim!" There was no note of triumph in Mitch's voice. "But what will happen to Elena?"

"She'll get a new identity, a new home, somewhere far from here. She's learning English and, with a financial settlement from the newspaper, she has some hope of salvaging a life of sorts."

"Which is more than most," Mitch concurred.

"So there we have it!" She drummed her fingers on the desk. "Anything else you need to know?"

"How long before the article is published?"

"Weeks. Maybe longer. Facts have to be checked. Your translation verified. Then our legal team ... of which I'm a part ... will go over it all with a fine tooth comb."

"But we have to nail these bastards before ..." Mitch stopped. He had been about to say "before Anja comes back." *You have to play this carefully,* he cautioned himself. He could bluster about the number of girls who would be enmeshed in the sex trade while the facts were checked, but she was too astute to swallow that without looking for a deeper, more personal reason.

"Believe me, Mitch, I want to get names out there, expose the bastards, but it's more than my job's worth not to follow procedures."

Mitch rubbed the side of his face.

"If you take it to another newspaper, you'll be faced with the same problem."

There was no answer to that. "But there's to be no reference to my name. I have to protect my daughter, my father."

"The only name on the article will be mine."

"Yours? Isn't that dangerous?"

"It wouldn't be the first time I've been threatened. We have to hope that once we name names, they won't be in the position to intimidate anyone." She began to gather the papers together. "The story will be syndicated, so it will reach a massive readership, and our contacts on the ground in the Soviet Union will make sure it's picked up there by the media."

"Let's hope they have the guts to run it," Mitch murmured. "It's not easy for them. The government's clamping down on the press again. You don't know from one day to the next what's going to happen."

"Not surprisingly, with the calls for independence in the Baltic States, the people there are showing a keen interest in anything that puts their Soviet masters in a bad light." She laughed. "So we're sure of some coverage there."

"Latvians, Lithuanians, Estonians ... many of them have family and friends in the Soviet Union. It won't take long for news to filter through," Mitch supplied.

Ruth folded the papers. "I'll need to keep these, the originals and your translation."

"I'm glad to be rid of them," he muttered.

She pulled a brown envelope out of a drawer in her father's desk, put the papers inside, and sealed it. Then she went to the bookcase, ran her fingers along a row, pulled two huge tomes halfway out, dropped the envelope behind them, and slid the books back in place.

"What if anyone takes the books out? They'll find them," Mitch said.

"They've got to get past Henry first!"

"Henry?"

"My father's clerk. He's like a rottweiler!" Seeing the puzzled look on Mitch's face, she explained. "A rather large, fierce dog. Seriously, no one ... apart from me ... would dare enter this inner sanctum when Henry's around. It would be easier to evade the Swiss Guard at the Vatican!"

Mitch laughed and drained his glass, wondering whether it was the whisky or the relief of no longer having the papers in his possession that made him feel light-headed.

"I'll pick them up tomorrow. I need to get working on the story, but I can't risk taking them with me tonight." She checked her watch, grabbed a leather jacket from a coat stand, and shrugged into it. "I have to meet someone in Soho. That's where a lot of these girls are forced to work, where they pick up clients. Why don't you come along?" When Mitch looked hesitant, she said, "Up to you."

He agreed, somewhat reluctantly.

"I'll leave these on Henry's desk with a note saying I brought a friend back here for a drink. That'll get him wondering," Ruth chuckled, tucking the empty bottle under an arm and picking up the glasses. "He'll replace the Macallan. It'll be our little secret. I've known him since I was a little girl. He used to spoil me then. Still does."

Outside, Ruth turned a key in the lock on the front door and explained, "We'll walk through to The Strand and grab a cab."

Their footsteps echoed as they walked across the square. There was no one else around, and Mitch felt strangely safe here, as though he was in a secret world, one he didn't want to leave.

As they emerged onto The Strand, Ruth pointed out a sprawling stone building on the other side of the street. "The Royal Courts of Justice."

"Royal? What sort of cases do they hear there?" Mitch asked.

"The High Court deals mostly with civil disputes. The really serious criminal cases—the sort my father handles—are heard in Crown Court. Then there's the Court of Appeal. That's there too."

Mitch's gaze scanned the spire, the turrets, the elaborate carvings.

"It's really impressive inside," Ruth elaborated. "If you can make time, it's worth a visit. Apart from private family cases, anyone is allowed to watch trials free of charge. Come and go as you like."

"Maybe another time," Mitch said. "It would be refreshing to see real justice in action!"

Ruth stepped into the road and hailed a cab. "Windmill Theatre!" she told the driver.

"Theatre?" Mitch queried when they were seated. "It's nearly midnight."

"It's no longer a theatre, but everyone still calls it that. It's a landmark. A nightclub now. Lap dancing, I think, is its most recent incarnation, or maybe it's transformed yet again." Noticing Mitch's expression, she nudged his elbow and laughed. "We're not going in."

Mitch watched the lights of traffic speeding toward them. There were still a lot of people on the street. A couple waited at traffic lights; the man held a sleeping child in his arms. Mitch thought of the times he had felt Anja's head snuggled into his neck as he carried her home.

"You have to admire these chaps," Ruth said, indicating the driver, who had just made a sharp turn into a dimly lit side street. "They know all the shortcuts in the city." At that moment, the cab lurched to a halt. The driver blasted the horn, leaned out of the window, and cursed loudly at a pedestrian stumbling across the road. "Soho's an interesting area," Ruth continued as they pulled away. "Used to be a respectable place, family restaurants, shops. Normal people going about their lives. Then unsavoury elements moved in, and the theatre started putting on non-stop revues with near-naked women. Some people were scandalized, but others looked on it as a form of art."

"Art?" Mitch grimaced.

"Yes, surprisingly enough, art! You see, the women weren't allowed to move, making tableaus that some viewed as beautiful pictures. Even in wartime, through air raids, the shows went on. Nothing stopped them. "We never close" was their motto. Apparently, long queues formed early each morning, and there was a stampede to get into the front rows of the theatre."

"Didn't the government close them down?"

"Far from it. The shows were seen almost as part of the war effort, a welcome release for servicemen from the horrors of battle."

"What about the women? It sounds like an earlier form of what's going on now."

"This was quite different. The women were well paid, well looked after. Better than working in a munitions factory," she shrugged. "Maybe they were happy to give pleasure to young men who may have been going to their death in the front lines. Who knows?"

They travelled in silence for some minutes and then she turned to Mitch. "We're almost there. Leave me to pay the cabbie. You get out your side, melt into the crowd outside the theatre. There's usually a gaggle of men loitering there. When you see me go past, follow some distance behind. A few people around here know who I am and what I do, so it's best we're not seen together." She leaned forward, looked at the meter, took some money out of a purse, and then cautioned: "Don't speak to any of the women. Their pimps will be watching. They don't miss a thing."

Mitch nodded his head in acknowledgement.

"When you've seen enough, go home. Get some sleep. You look as though you could do with it."

"Will I see you again?"

"When do you leave?"

"Saturday. The morning flight."

"I'll call you at your hotel tomorrow evening," she said as the cab pulled into the side of the road.

Mitch climbed out, clutching his briefcase, and for a few seconds he was dazzled by the bright lights on the theatre facade on the other side of the street. Then he dodged between two moving cars and stood on the sidewalk, facing the theatre doors. From there he could see the cab's reflection in the glass. As it pulled away, Ruth crossed the street and, not glancing his way, breezed past. Mitch counted to ten and then turned briskly on his heel. As he did so, he collided with a man. For a moment, he was sure his heart stopped. "Sorry, mate," the man apologized, a good-natured look on his face. "Not going in?"

Mitch shook his head and hurriedly joined the trickle of people, mostly men, strolling along the sidewalk. He craned his neck, searching for Ruth. He spotted her and settled into a measured pace some way behind. She led him past girls posing outside nightclubs, in shop doorways, on street corners, hands enticingly placed on hips, their faces locked in the same frozen smile. Mitch swallowed back the waves of pity that threatened to overwhelm him. As he drew level with each girl, he asked in a low voice: *"Otkuda vy?"* He caught his breath. "Minsk." The dark-haired girl had seemed to speak without moving her red-painted lips. He looked into her eyes. Despite the heavy makeup around them, they were dull, lifeless. He felt the light touch of her hand on his arm. As he moved away, he wondered if he had imagined her softly spoken plea: *"Pazhalusta ... pamagite."*

CHAPTER THIRTY-NINE
LENINGRAD–JUNE 1991

The girl from Minsk. Her red-painted lips and heavily made-up eyes haunted Mitch's dreams and gave a terrifying twist to his paranoia of what would happen when the newspaper article was published. Each night, he felt her hand locked in his as they fled their pursuers—pursuers whose featureless faces shone like headlights in the darkness. The high wall at the end of the cobbled street ... the feel of warm breath on the back of his neck as he lifted the girl higher and higher. When he could no longer see her, he turned around. Light blinded him. This was when he always awoke, shielding his eyes from the glare—breathless, soaked in sweat.

By day, when fear threatened to overcome him, his inner voice intoned a caution: *Act normal; no one will suspect.* How did he used to act? Maybe he had always imagined someone was stalking him, chasing him into an alleyway where he smelled death.

Before leaving England, he had made a last-ditch attempt to get Ruth to commit to a more definite timeframe than her vague reference to "weeks." "Impossible," she said. He pressed her to at least leave a message with his father as soon as she had a publication date, to which she had responded, "You'll be taking a chance. Your father's phone may be tapped." Mitch was all too aware of the risks but he had to know, so they agreed on a short, innocuous message Ruth would say to Sergei. "The article will probably appear on a Saturday," Ruth had gone on to say. "Weekends are when exposés have most impact. Couples reading the newspaper over breakfast, the comfortable scene scorched by realization that this could happen to their daughter, their granddaughter. You know how it goes, Mitch." He knew only too well.

On this Tuesday evening, Sergei looked at his son sitting on the other side of the kitchen table, taking in the black smudges under Mitch's eyes, the frown lines creasing his forehead, the desultory way he shifted his food around the plate. Oh, how he wished he could turn back the clock and give Mitch the life he would have had in Montréal. For the love he and Sophia shared, his wife and child had paid a hefty price. And now? He wasn't worried about himself. He would be happy never to have to face another day without her. But he must stay strong, protect Mitch and Anja. They were all he had left.

As he toyed with his food, Mitch's mind went over his visit to Yuri and Marina's apartment yesterday evening—a visit he had tried to avoid. Yuri averted his eyes when Mitch looked at him; the easy camaraderie they had shared was gone. Mitch felt only cold suspicion. Marina, unaware of the tension, recounted tales of the exploits of their two-year-old son, Fedya. Mitch had forced himself to laugh. He liked Marina and felt bad about the way Natasha had rejected her. But Yuri? He was the wild card.

"You don't think Yuri would inform on you, do you Mitch?" Sergei asked now, as though reading his son's thoughts.

"Not deliberately," he replied, with a confidence he was far from feeling. "But the mob forced him into it once by threatening his family. Think about it, Papa. Now he has more to lose. Faced with a choice between me, and Marina and his children ..."

"But you've known each other for years."

Mitch put down his knife and fork. "I don't seem to have much appetite," he apologized. Bile rose in his throat, and he took a gulp of wine and swallowed it down, wondering how much longer he could live with this uncertainty. Whatever the outcome, he just wanted to get it over.

"The professor. Do you trust him?"

"With my life!"

Sergei frowned. "And the newspaper in London. No one there will talk?"

"I don't think it's likely. Very few people there know where the information came from. Ruth and I were careful not to be seen together."

"That may be, but you still need to be prepared for the worst."

The worst! The words sent a chill through Mitch's body. "They may come looking for you too, Papa."

Sergei got to his feet, gathered the remnants of the meal together, and stacked them on the counter.

"You have to face facts," Mitch urged. "If they find out it's me, you're a target too."

Sergei filled the coffee pot.

"And there's Anja. I have to ..."

"Forget Anja for the moment," Sergei cut in. "First, we have to decide what you're going to do." He lit the gas under the coffee pot and sat down. "Now let's assume Yagudin and his people find out it was you ..."

"How will we know that they know?" In a quaking voice, Mitch answered his own question: "We won't. Not until they come looking for us."

"Which is precisely why we have to act now. When the article is published in London, you'll need to lie low somewhere until the lot of them are behind bars. It may only be for a few days."

"But if I disappear, it will arouse suspicion."

"Not if we plan it carefully."

"I don't know."

"You've hardly taken any holiday since all this started. Surely they wouldn't object if you told them you're expecting your daughter to come home and you're hoping to spend time with her. You'll have to keep it flexible, so that you can go at short notice." When Mitch didn't respond, Sergei went on. "Please, Mitch. Do it for me."

"You've thought it all out."

"I've thought of little else."

"I'm not going without you, Papa!"

"Don't worry about me. I'll hunker down at Vera Alexandrovna's place. She's always asking me to stay. She gets frustrated with Leonid and Lyuba," he said, referring to the couple who shared Vera's apartment. "Their hearing's not so good."

"But ..." Mitch tried to interrupt.

"Vera and I ... we'll listen to music, talk over old times. You know what we're like," Sergei forced a laugh. He hated lying to his son. Weeks ago, Sergei had resolved that he must stay in his own apartment, whatever happened. It was the only way he would know if anyone was looking for Mitch. Vera would call the apartment every day, and if there was a problem, she knew what to do. They had it all worked out. He had made her promise.

"I'd be happier if we were together," Mitch said.

"We will be. Later. Now, listen, I've come up with a plan I think will work. Vera has a *dacha* in Lyubin, out on the Novgorod road. You could stay there until the heat dies down."

"A *dacha*? I've never heard her mention it. Did Maman know?"

"Da."

"Why did you never take her there? You know how much she longed for fresh air, a break from the city."

"It was difficult. The *dacha* ... " Sergei sought for words. "It's used for other people, when the need arises."

"What do you mean? What need?"

"Nothing! I've already said too much."

"But if I go there, I need to know what's going on," Mitch protested.

"It's better if you don't. It could put other people's lives in jeopardy." Sergei got up from his seat, grabbed a cloth, lifted the coffee pot off the stove, and poured it into the cups.

Mitch stirred a scant spoonful of sugar into his. Was it possible? Vera, who always looked as though a puff of wind would blow her over—was she really mixed up in something ... something dangerous? He thought guiltily of the money he still owed her. "I can't impose on her," he mumbled. "I already ..."

"If you're feeling guilty about the money you owe her, forget it! It's been taken care of."

Mitch's shoulders slumped. "I didn't know you ..."

"You've had more than enough to deal with," Sergei cut in. "And what's money when family's involved?"

"What did you do to be cursed with a son like me?" Mitch slumped down in the chair.

"Stop talking like that!" Sergei snapped. "If you want the truth ... I'm proud of you. I know I'm not good at saying it, but not many people would have the guts to do what you're doing."

"I'm beginning to wonder if I can go through with it. It scares the shit out of me!"

"*Khuynya!* We're in this together, Mitch. So long as we keep our heads, we can do it." Sergei took a gulp of coffee. "This place you're living in ... you still don't have a phone there?"

Mitch shook his head.

"What if I need to get hold of you at weekends?"

"I'll call you a couple of times a day."

"You said I could come ..."

"I haven't had time to sort things out, Papa, with all this going on."

Sergei looked at his son for a moment or two and then changed the subject. "Now, what about Anja? Any news from Petya?"

"Nothing new. Lyosha's still having problems getting export licences for some of the paintings he wants to bring out of Spain."

"Can you trust him? Petya, I mean."

Mitch shrugged and took a gulp of coffee. "Anything from your contact at Pulkovo?"

"Not yet, but he'll let me know as soon as their names are on the incoming passenger lists."

"What happens if he's away? He can't work seven days a week, surely?"

"Someone else checks. It's all taken care of. But if Anja comes back before Yagudin's out of the way, we'll need to get her out of the city."

"I've been thinking about that. The only real possibility is Yelizaveta Artyemevskaya, Katya's mother." Mitch went on to outline his plan. "The difficulty will be getting Natasha to agree."

* * *

As soon as Mitch got to his office the next morning, he picked up the phone and dialled. After going through the pleasantries, he said, "Liza, there's something I need to talk to you about."

"There's nothing wrong with Anja, is there, Mitch? We were worried. She's been away so long."

"As far as I know, she's okay. There's been a hitch with Lipovsky's business deals in Spain."

"Katya really misses her, you know."

"That's what I want to talk to you about, Liza. An idea I'd like your help with."

"What is it?"

"I'd rather not tell you over the phone. Will you be home this evening?"

"This evening and every evening. Why don't you come and have a meal with us? I'm badly in need of adult conversation!"

"If you put it like that, then yes, I'd love to." Despite his sadness, on the few occasions he had visited Liza's apartment since Anja left, he felt close to his daughter, as if the walls had absorbed a trace of her childish chatter, her giggle, the smell of her hair.

That afternoon, one of his colleagues whispered to him that a consignment of vodka was being unloaded at the store around the corner from the Bureau. Mitch checked he had enough money and sped off. He secured two bottles.

In the early evening, one bottle sat on the front passenger seat of his car. The other bottle he had dropped off at Marta Nikolayevna's, and by now was probably half empty. As Mitch drove, he marvelled at the change in the professor since moving in with Marta. The company of the old women and their joy in life had revealed a side of him that Mitch had never seen. The quiet, serious demeanour had all but disappeared, and a sometimes deprecating sense of humour had emerged. Before Mitch left, the three women were arguing volubly about the possible outcome of today's election to choose the first President of the Russian Federation. The professor had winked at Mitch, risen to his feet, and tapped the table with his glass. The women hushed, the professor cleared his throat and began in a serious voice: "But my good ladies. We should look at this another way." The three women leaned forward in their seats, eagerly awaiting his words of wisdom. "Let us assume it's a landslide for Boris Yeltsin. Everyone's predicting it, so that is probably how it will be. And hasn't the good comrade promised that if he is elected and prices continue to increase ... as they undoubtedly will ... he will put his head on the railtrack? Isn't that what he said?" Three heads nodded. "Now, none of us is stupid enough to think that Yeltsin can halt spiralling prices. So I put it to you, isn't this an efficient way to dispose of politicians?" The women seemed stunned for a few moments, and then the professor dissolved into loud guffaws, which quickly had him wheezing.

Marta had jumped to her feet, undone the cap on the bottle of vodka, slopped some into the professor's glass, and held it to his lips. "Anton Arturovich, you're incorrigible!" she scolded. "There was I believing that was what you really think."

"And what makes you think it isn't?" the professor spluttered.

That evening, as Mitch parked the car outside Liza's apartment, he looked up at the window where his daughter had always waited, eager to catch the first sight of him. Tonight, there was no impish grin, no cheery wave. Liza opened the door, and for a few moments, he let his body lose itself in the comfort of her hug. He smelled the faint odour of sandalwood, felt the softness of her body, her long blonde hair against his face. A hand tugged at his arm. "Tell Anja to come back soon. Before school starts," Katya demanded. The two girls would be starting school in September. "If she doesn't, I'll probably have to sit next to a nasty boy!"

Liza laughed softly, relinquished her hold on Mitch, and hustled her daughter into the kitchen.

After their meal, Mitch sat at the table smoking a cigarette and listening to Katya's pleading voice coming from the bedroom as she tried to cajole her mother into letting her stay up. "*Pazhalusta, Mamochka.* Just a few more minutes," she begged. Mitch took a drag on the cigarette. He would give anything to hear his daughter say those familiar words.

"Always the same plea," Liza laughed as she came back into the room and closed the door. "Just a few more minutes," she mimicked and then sat down. "Now what was it you wanted to talk about?"

Mitch poured vodka into their glasses. "When Anja gets back, I'd like to get her out of the city for a while."

"Surely when she comes home she'll want to be with Natasha and her friends."

"That's part of it, Liza. She must be missing her friends, particularly Katya. You know how close they are. And after all that time with her grandparents, she needs to have some fun with kids her own age."

Liza fixed him with a penetrating look. "And what's the other part?"

"What other part?"

"You said 'that's part of it,' Mitch. So what's the other reason? I don't think you'd be thinking of sending Anja out of the city without a very good reason, not when she's been away so long. At least in the city you have a chance of seeing her. Spying on her, as Natasha put it."

"Spying! Is that what she said?" He ground the cigarette around and around in the ashtray until the butt bent in half. "You're right, there is something else behind it."

"It's him, isn't it? Yagudin!"

Mitch nodded.

"I know it's difficult, Mitch, but you'll have to accept it some time."

"I'll never accept it!" he snapped. "Not when my daughter's safety's at stake."

Careful, the voice in his head intoned.

"What do you mean?"

"*Izvinite,* Liza. I can't go into details. All I'm asking for is your help."

She sipped her drink.

Mitch leaned across the table toward her. "You mentioned when I was here some time ago that Katya is going to stay with your husband's parents for a few weeks this summer, somewhere outside the city."

"Novgorod. They live in Novgorod."

Lyubin, out on the Novgorod Road. His father's words ran through Mitch's head.

"Do you think there's any way you could persuade Natasha to let Anja go with Katya, supposing she's back from Spain by then?"

Liza grimaced.

"I wouldn't ask, Liza, but I don't want him anywhere near her."

"Why?" When he didn't answer, she continued in a slow, deliberate voice. "Mitch, if you're asking me, or Mstislav's parents, to take responsibility for Anja, then we have to know what's going on."

He lit another cigarette. "I don't trust him. Not near my daughter!"

"Is he violent? Did he do something to her?" Liza's eyes were wide.

"I don't know, but I'm not going to take that chance. If you thought he'd done something to Katya, you'd feel the same."

"I'd strangle the bastard!" She wrung her hands together. "But what makes you think he might have? Did Anja say something?"

"*Nyet.* Not Anja."

"Who then?"

"Natasha ..." Mitch sought for words. "Natasha said that if I tried to see Anja, she'd have me arrested for child molestation."

Liza stared at Mitch with horror-struck eyes. "Child molestation? You?"

Mitch nodded.

"But you didn't. Surely ..."

"Of course I fucking didn't! You know me better than that."

Liza let out a noisy breath. "I'm sorry, Mitch. It was such a shock. I didn't know what to think."

"Neither did I."

"But why? Why would Natasha say something like that?"

"You know how vindictive she is, lashing out at people when she can't get her own way."

"But her own daughter?"

"I knew she was lying about me, but then I got to thinking. Could it be someone else? Maybe it was him."

"Yagudin? You don't really think ... ?"

"I don't know what to think."

"Surely if Natasha thought he'd done something like that, she'd see him in hell before she let him near Anja."

"I've given up trying to figure out what Natasha would or wouldn't do."

"Maybe she asked her parents to take Anja with them to get her out of his way."

"Maybe." Mitch sighed loudly.

"But you don't know for certain anyone's done anything to Anja," Liza reasoned. "Do Natasha's parents know what she said?"

"Lyosha says he's sure nothing like that happened. Just Natasha lashing out."

"Do you believe that, Mitch?"

"I want to, but ..." He leaned an elbow on the table, cradling the side of his head in his hand. "Would you risk it if it was Katya?"

She shook her head. "But even if she goes with Katya to Novgorod, she has to come home some time. You can't ..."

"I'll cross that bridge when I come to it." Mitch drained his glass. "If necessary, I'll have to ask Natasha's parents to let her live with them for a while, until I can get to the bottom of what's going on."

Liza pushed her glass toward Mitch. He refilled both glasses. It seemed an age before she looked up and said, "I'll do it."

"You will? *Spasiba. Spasiba,*" Mitch grinned. "I can't tell you what that means to me."

"I don't know how the hell I'm going to persuade Natasha to let Anja go, though."

"You wouldn't be lying if you said Katya's missing her. And I'm sure Anja would jump at the chance of being with Katya again. They'll have fun."

"I suppose I could tell Natasha that Katya's grandparents have suggested she bring a friend ... and naturally Katya wanted Anja."

"One thing, Liza," Mitch cautioned, "when you're speaking to Natasha, don't let on I've told you. Don't mention me at all! She has to think it's your idea."

She nodded understandingly.

The two of them then talked of practicalities. Katya was due to leave for Novgorod in a little over two weeks, but Liza was sure that could be changed to tie in with whatever date Anja came back to the city.

"How are you planning to get Katya to Novgorod?" Mitch asked.

"Her grandparents. They always pick her up and bring her back in their car. Bit of an old wreck, but it usually makes it."

"Whatever you do, Liza, don't let Yagudin or his driver take them."

"You think I'm crazy?"

It was late when Mitch drove home. He felt bad not telling Liza the whole truth, but he couldn't risk it. At least she'd agreed to help. Although there was no certainty the plan would work, he had to take the chance. If it did, maybe he could get his father to visit Anja in Novgorod—the access ban didn't apply to him. *You might even drive there yourself,* he pondered. *Just a glimpse, that's all.*

He slowed the car and gazed at the Peter and Paul Fortress on the opposite bank of the Neva. The golden angel holding a cross atop its gilded spire reached up like a beacon of hope in the mysterious twilight of the *Belyye Nochi.*

That night, the dream didn't come.

CHAPTER FORTY

LENINGRAD–LATE JULY 1991

"*Voskresen'ye.* They're coming home on Sunday," Petya blurted.

Mitch gripped the telephone receiver. *"Oni yest'?"* His voice was little more than a whisper.

"The problem with the export licences has been fixed. Sunday is the first flight they can get on."

Two days! Mitch caught his breath. *Anja will be back in two days.*

"You still there, Mitch?"

"*Prastite.* It took me by surprise. She's been away so long ..." his voice trailed off.

"Mitch, don't try to see her. I'm only telling you because ..." He paused for a moment. "Because whatever Natasha says, you have a right to know."

"I appreciate it, Petya."

"Anyway, Anja won't be in the city for ..."

"What do you mean?" Mitch interrupted.

"She's going to Novgorod."

"Novgorod! Why the hell is she going there?" Mitch hoped his tone was convincing. "Not with him!"

"*Nyet,* not with him!" Petya snapped. "She's going with Katya, her friend. Her grandparents live there, and Katya's mother asked Natasha if Anja could go."

"So she's sending her away again."

"She's not sending her ... Anja wants to go."

"When? When's she going?"

"Soon, I think." When Mitch didn't comment, Petya urged, "Don't tell Natasha I told you."

"I haven't spoken to her for months," was all Mitch said.

After putting the receiver down, he sat for several minutes twirling a pen with his fingers. The noises of the office whirled around. He did not hear them. His mind was full of thoughts of how different things would be if Anja was coming back to a normal family—the excitement of meeting her at the airport, hugging her close, her happy chatter on the way home. He dropped the pen onto the desk and dialled his father's number.

"I'll check it out with my contact at Pulkovo tomorrow evening," Sergei said. "The passenger manifest might be available then."

"I'm pretty sure Petya's telling the truth," Mitch mused. "No benefit for him to lie."

"Why don't you come and spend the night here tomorrow? I don't like to think of you on your own all weekend."

"I won't be. There's a woman ..."

"A woman!" Sergei cut in. "I don't think ..."

"It's not like that, Papa. She lives in the same building, that's all. We're taking her daughter out for the day."

"Don't get involved, Mitch."

"I'm not!"

"You could come here later."

"If it makes you happier, I'll drive over for supper and stay the night."

"I'll get Anastasia to cook something special for our meal, and then on Sunday ..."

"If this is your way of making sure I don't go to the airport, you needn't bother. I'm not going to jeopardize things now."

"It's not about that at all." Sergei's tone was indignant. "I get lonely too."

Mitch checked his watch. "Papa, I have to go. I'm due in court."

As soon as Mitch replaced the receiver, the telephone rang. It was Liza. "You've heard Anja's coming home?"

"Petya just called."

"Natasha, she wants me to arrange for the two girls to go to Novgorod on Monday morning. She said she has to leave later in the week herself."

"Probably going off somewhere with him," Mitch muttered.

"I don't think so. When I tried to find out where she was going, she was a bit evasive. I had the feeling she was making an excuse," Liza said. "It got me thinking you may be right, Mitch. What you said about him. Maybe she doesn't want him near Anja."

* * *

The next morning, the professor let Mitch into Marta Nikolayevna's apartment and asked in a low voice, "Any news from London?"

Mitch shook his head. "I hope it's soon. I can't take much more of this uncertainty."

"What are you talking about out there?" Marta called from the kitchen.

"She's wrapping food for you to take with you, in case you get hungry," the professor laughed as he led Mitch down the corridor. "If I stay here much longer, I'll be round like a pig!"

"*Ay-yay-yay!* Anton Arturovich! If you keep on like that, you'll be on short rations!" The tender look Marta gave the professor belied her tone.

"You shouldn't have gone to all this trouble." Mitch's gaze took in two packages neatly wrapped in white cloth and tied with string, lined up on the table.

"Don't deny me this pleasure," Marta said. "Like having a family again ..." her voice broke up.

Behind her back, the professor shook his head at Mitch, warning him not to pursue the matter.

"I really appreciate it." Mitch put an arm around Marta's shoulders and held her. "Mariya and Alina will too."

"It's nothing," she shrugged him off.

"Why don't you come with us? Both of you. It's a lovely day."

"We have something to do today." She wiped the back of a hand over her eyes, picked up a canvas bag, put the food packages inside, and handed it to Mitch. "Don't go losing the bag," she admonished and began to gather up the breakfast dishes that littered the table.

The professor trailed Mitch to the front door. "We're going to the church to light candles," he whispered. "It's the anniversary of the day her two grandsons were killed ... in Afghanistan. Same day. Same grenade."

As Mitch walked away, it occurred to him that although his own life was complicated, he had much for which to be thankful. Anja was coming back, and for a while she would be safe in Novgorod.

* * *

On the way out of the city, Mitch wove in and out of traffic, praying the car wouldn't break down or run out of gas. Fuel was in short supply, and he had paid an exorbitant price for a can of the stuff. He glanced sideways at Mariya and then at Alina in the rearview mirror. The smiles on their faces told him it was worth it.

The radio announcer's voice droned on about the document *A Word to the People* published in *Sovetskaya Rossiya* last Tuesday. Signed by twelve public figures, it railed against current conditions in the Soviet Union, where prices had risen by more than 50 per cent in the first half of the year, and factories were closing. Although the Soviet President and General Secretary of the Communist Party, Mikhail Gorbachev, had dismantled many of the totalitarian aspects of the Soviet state, there was virtually no private enterprise to replace it. Boris Yeltsin, the recently freely-elected President of the Russian Soviet Federative Socialist Republic, was continuing to gain in popularity with his clarion call to Russia to get up off her knees. "Do you think Yeltsin can pull it off?" Mitch asked Mariya.

She squeezed his arm gently and said, "Let's pretend we live somewhere else, just for today, shall we?"

He laughed and turned off the radio.

The rest of the drive was a delight, with Mariya chatting about the joy of being out of the city and excitedly pointing out sights to Alina—places and things Mitch had never noticed before. They stopped in Sestroretskiy Kurort and threw pebbles into the water. Mariya reminisced about her father's grandiose plans to one day build a house here. "He would invite his friends—artists, poets, writers—to share the house. A refuge for them, was what he said."

"Is he an artist?" Mitch ventured.

"A poet. He died five years ago." She looked around, caught her breath, and ran over to a patch of grass just behind the beach. "This is where it was to be ... I'm sure it is." She beckoned Mitch toward her. "The porch—right here, overlooking the wild roses." She turned on her heel and took several measured strides, as though pacing out the length of the porch. "There would be comfortable chairs. Like him, most of his friends were in poor health. The Gulag." Her voice was low as she uttered the last words. "He said they would soon get well with fresh air and good food. It was as simple as that."

"Your father ... it sounds as though he was a good person. I wish I could have met him."

She looked Mitch up and down. "You know, I think he would have liked you." Her smile broadened into a grin.

Later, the sun was warm on Mitch's back as he spread the blanket out on the sand at Repino. Mariya, walking back up the beach, called to him: "Just breathe that air. You can smell the pines." The faded fabric of her dress clung to her slender legs with every step she took. "Thank you for bringing us here, Mitch. Alina has hardly ever been out of the city. It's lovely to be able to show her the places I used to know."

Mitch looked down to the edge of the water where Alina was jumping from stone to stone. He narrowed his eyes, and a shiver ran through his body. From this distance, she could be Anja.

"Now, what's in these parcels Marta Nikolayevna packed for us?" Mariya's voice broke into his thoughts. She leaned down and unwrapped one of the packages. "Salmon sandwiches. The woman's a magician!"

"A sorceress!" Mitch laughed, opening two bottles of beer. "I'm sorry we don't have glasses."

"My Artyom Fyodorovich," she said as she closed her eyes briefly, "he used to say it tasted better out of a bottle."

Mitch swallowed back the urge to ask what had happened to her husband. Despite the cheerful demeanour she displayed to the world, there seemed to be an aura of sadness around her.

She knelt on the blanket, untied the other food parcel, laid out sandwiches and hardboiled eggs, and took the bottle he handed her. Shielding her eyes from the sun, she gazed around. "It's beautiful, Mitch. So bright and sparkling."

Mitch took a couple of steps toward her. "Where will you and Alina go ... when you have to leave your apartment?" he asked hesitantly.

"An old friend of my father. She said we can squeeze in with her. It will be good for Alina to grow up with a substitute Babushka around."

His heart lurched; she looked so young and vulnerable. *If only ...* he thought to himself. He reached out a hand to help her up. She clambered to her feet and held out her arms to Alina, who was running toward them.

CHAPTER FORTY-ONE
LENINGRAD

THURSDAY, AUGUST 15, 1991

Mitch turned over in bed and buried his face in the pillow, blocking out a chink of light leaking through the gap in the curtains. His mouth was dry, and his head felt as though it didn't belong to him. *What day is it?* he wondered, trying to dredge the answer from the numbed fragments of his brain. Snatches of his father's voice ran around in his head: "*Anja? ... she's having a great time ... spoilt by Katya's grandparents.*" Memory flooded back. Yesterday was Wednesday, the day Sergei drove to Novgorod to visit Anja. How could he have forgotten? Over supper, Mitch had plied his father with questions: Did she look well? Has she grown? What was she wearing? What did they eat? Where does she sleep? What was the house like? Was there a garden? Sergei had answered in as much detail as he could remember. Now, instead of having to make up an image of her in his mind, Mitch could colour in the details. He pictured her waking up in the bed with the pink coverlet. Later, she and Katya would take turns riding the green bicycle around the garden. Katya's Babushka would call them in when lunch was ready. His father had skirted around Mitch's concerns that Anja had forgotten he had ever been part of her life. "She isn't pining for you, Mitch. But then, you wouldn't want her to, would you?"

Mitch raised his head slowly now, brought his left wrist close to his face, and checked his watch. "*Tvoyu mat'!*" he cursed. The thought of having to withstand another tirade from his boss was enough to make him throw back the bedclothes and swing his feet to the floor.

In the kitchen, he ignited the gas under the coffee pot, lit a cigarette, and, as he did every day, told himself that today would be the day the telephone call would come from London. It had to. He couldn't go on like this much longer. Fear stalked him day and night—fear that Yagudin already knew he had informed on him. He had tried to rationalize these thoughts, telling himself that if that was the case, he would already be lying on a slab in the mortuary. The thought brought little comfort as he leaned now against the edge of the window jamb and peered at the street below. People hurried by, some with small children gripped by the hand. It looked normal, but who could tell? Assassins come in many guises. It was now ten weeks since he had given Ruth the information. *What if something has happened to her, or the newspaper has decided not to print?* Could he just go on with his life, knowing what he knew? How would he ever make sure his daughter was safe? He wouldn't allow himself to calculate how many young women had gone to their doom while the lawyers at the newspaper verified facts—women like the one he could see now, her dark hair blowing in the wind. He wanted to reach out and grab her, to look into her eyes and warn her: "Be careful. Stay close to your family." Instead, all he could do was watch her teetering progress, her steps impeded by the height of her heels, the tightness of her skirt. *Maybe I should risk a call to London.*

Each evening as he hurried home from the Metro, he resolved that tonight would be the night he wouldn't drink. Some evenings several hours passed before he reached for the bottle. He had tried putting it out of sight, but even behind closed cupboard doors, it beckoned. He needed the numbness alcohol brought. It was the only way he could slip into the warm, secret place where nothing could harm him or his daughter. The curse of drink—maybe he was more Russian than he cared to admit.

He turned from the window, emptied last night's cold coffee out of a mug, extinguished the gas, picked up the pot, and refilled the mug. A frantic search of the cupboards produced not one grain of sugar; he had meant to try to buy some yesterday. The lukewarm liquid slid down his throat untasted, and then he put the mug back on the counter, ground the cigarette out in a saucer, and went into the bathroom. He stared at the face in the mirror. *Is that really me?* He touched the darkened skin lying in folds beneath bloodshot eyes and lifted a lock of lank hair. With a fingernail, he chipped off a hardened splodge of shaving soap from the decaying surface of the glass. Then he filled the washbasin with tepid water, plunged his head into it, and lathered his hair with soap.

Forty minutes later, Mitch slid silently into the chair behind his desk, took a file out of a drawer, picked up a pen, and began to leaf quickly through page after page of depositions—to an observer, hopefully giving the impression he had been hard at work for hours. After a while, he looked up and met the amused gaze of Sasha Smirnov. "He's in court this morning," the young man laughed.

"*Zhopa!* Why the fuck didn't you tell me?" Mitch aimed his pen in Sasha's direction.

Catching the pen nimbly, the other man retorted, "I haven't seen you work so hard for weeks. It was impressive."

It was lunchtime when the call came. Mitch was alone in the office. "She called." His father's voice was low. "Saturday. It's going to be Saturday."

"That's the day after tomorrow."

"She tried to get me yesterday."

The two men were silent for several moments and then spoke simultaneously: *"Chort!"* Mitch gasped; "You know what you must do," his father said.

Mitch tried to speak again, but his throat constricted.

"Come here this evening. We'll talk then," Sergei said.

Mitch dropped the receiver onto its cradle He bent down, pulled the remnants of a bottle of brandy out of a drawer and gulped some back. Over the past few weeks, he had told himself he just wanted to get the whole thing over. But now the time had come, he wished he could turn back the clock. *Just a few more days, that's all I need.* His shoulders slumped and he leaned his elbows on the desk, buried his face in his hands and told himself to stay calm. *Act normally. It's the only way to get through.* With trembling hands, he reached again for the bottle and drained the dregs. *One step at a time. One day at a time. Don't think about tomorrow.*

That afternoon, after sitting through a pre-trial meeting in which he stumbled over words and had difficulty remembering the basis of his defence, Mitch showed the client out and asked Tamara Aleksandrevna to cancel his last appointment of the day.

"I have things to do," he explained. "My daughter ... she's home, and I'm taking some deferred holiday. Just a week."

"It will be nice if you can spend time with her before school starts."

Mitch managed a weak smile. "I'll be in tomorrow to clear up the rest of my work. If anyone calls about the Asimov case next week, Glubonin is handling it. He has the file."

Outside, he stood for a few moments in the shadow of the doorway. His head throbbed and, despite the heat, the pit of his stomach felt like ice. Maybe if he walked for a while he could get his thoughts together, think about what he had to do.

An hour or so later, outside the Sheremetev Palace, he gripped the lapels of his jacket across his chest, warding off another shiver, and then hurried into the seclusion of the courtyard. He looked up, trying to remember which were the windows of the rooms once occupied by the poet Anna Akhmatova. His mother had pointed them out many times. He had never understood how she found comfort in Akhmatova's tragic verses. He leaned against a wall, lit a cigarette, and inhaled deeply in an effort to mask the remembered odour of putrescence in the hospital ward where his mother spent her last days. He heard again his father's voice as he read from the well-thumbed *samizdat* sheets: *The mountains bow before this anguish/The great river does not flow ...* [4]

Evolving out of grief for her son's imprisonment during the Yezhov terror, and officially silenced for more than fifteen years, Akhmatova had composed this, her most famous poem, in fragments, which were distributed among friends to memorize. Now as Mitch stared at the blank windows, he thought of the men and women who throughout history had defied the might of the Soviet State. Artists, writers, poets—like Mariya's father and his friends—who had suffered but never given in. Had they known the same gut-wrenching fear that gripped his own stomach? Had they plumbed the depths of despair, searching for the courage to go on? They confronted a much larger force. There was no escape for them. He took another drag on the cigarette, ground out the butt with his heel, and walked back onto Liteynyy prospekt.

---

4 'Dedication,' part of poem cycle for the work 'Requiem,' written between 1935 and 1961 by Anna Akhmatova (1889-1966).

CHAPTER FORTY-TWO
LENINGRAD

SATURDAY, AUGUST 17, 1991

Mitch poured gas into the tank, screwed the cap back on, and stowed the empty can in the car alongside two full cans. With fuel in short supply, he was now in the habit of siphoning the tank every time he left the car parked for any length of time. His bag was already stowed, as was a box of food and drink. He did a final check of his pockets: key to the *dacha,* Vera's directions, money, and enough cigarettes to last a few days.

In the early morning silence, he leaned on the hood of the car, lit a cigarette, and looked around the deserted street. Surely he would be as safe here in the apartment building as anywhere? Not even his father knew the address. Despite the crumbling concrete, peeling paint, sporadic water supply, and smell from the garbage heaped against the wall of the building, this place was the closest he'd felt to a real home since he and Natasha were married. He thought of the professor and Marta Nikolayevna, of the joy this seemingly mismatched pair found in each other's company. At least he could be proud of bringing them together. And Mariya Kornyevskaya. His eyes strayed to the window of her apartment. He imagined her asleep in bed, Alina by her side. *Maybe it's best to go—safer for everyone if you're not here for a while. You promised Papa.*

He drove slowly. The newspapers had hardly hit the streets in London, and it would be hours, if not days, before the story filtered through. After the strain of the past few weeks, he needed to wind down, clear the chaos in his head, if that was possible. He turned off the main thoroughfare and headed along the river embankment. A small boat loaded with cardboard boxes sped along the *Neva,* keeping pace with the car for some distance. As the boat headed under *Most Leytenanta Shmidta,* Mitch turned into a side street and followed the circuitous route he always took to avoid driving near Senate Square. One day he would confront his fear of the rearing statue of the Bronze Horseman—the edifice that had inhabited his nightmares since childhood. Today wasn't the day.

On Bolshaya Morskaya ulitsa he pulled the car into the side of the road and turned off the engine. Saying a silent prayer that no one would steal the fuel or his supply of food and drink, he locked the car, walked back to the main thoroughfare, and headed through the gardens toward the imposing facade of St. Isaac's Cathedral. Vendors were setting up stalls alongside the sidewalk; he brushed away hands offering bars of soap, plastic handbags, and cheap jewellery. Inside the cathedral, he stood in the shadows, breathing in the smell of incense and allowing himself to relish the hushed atmosphere. High above stood images of the apostles and evangelists. During communist times, the building was home to an atheist museum, but since last year, services were held on religious holidays. Later in the day, the cathedral would be busy accepting the prayers of the faithful. Now only a scattering of worshippers knelt on the steps before the royal doors—some with heads bowed, others gazing at the three rows of icons. Beyond these, the stained-glass window depicted Jesus in a scarlet robe. Mitch knelt. Like his Dedushka, who Babushka told him had worshipped here in the dark days of 1917, the safety of his family—Anja and his father—dominated his prayers. He intoned silently the words that, as a young child, he heard Babushka whisper before she got into bed in the room they shared: *Through the prayers of our holy Father, Lord Jesus Christ our God, have mercy upon us and save us ...* She told him that if he mentioned the words to anyone, *Baba Yaga* would whisk him off to live in her hut that stands on chicken legs.

He remembered now his mother's face, her eyes closed, as she bowed her head in silent prayer each morning all those years ago. She had gripped his four-year-old shoulders and made him promise that when they got to Russia, he would never mention the prayer to anyone. It was their secret. The young Mitch loved secrets. It was only as a teenager he discovered she had been saying to herself the words of the *Amidah*, the blessings silently intoned by *Hasidim* at the start of each day. He also realized she had hidden her faith, knowing it would bring retribution on her family. Now as he looked up to the silver dove in the cupola, he prayed that somewhere up there she was free to embrace the tenets of her faith unhindered.

Outside, a party of tourists straggled on the steps, listening to their guide relate the tale of the young British architect who designed the cathedral. A fortune teller prophesied he would die after the building was finished. Their laughter rang in the air when they heard it took forty years to build. Mitch shivered as he walked down the steps. He knew the ending to that story.

He was relieved to see that the fuel cans and food were still inside the car. It spluttered into life and, after a moment or two, the needle on the fuel gauge hovered where it had been before. On the way out of the city, he drove past familiar sights, remembering how excited he was on that long-ago day when he and his mother arrived in Leningrad. It was after Vanya's death that he began to fear the might of the Soviet State. The imposing buildings took on a sinister form, towering over him, shutting out the rest of the world—a world he was forbidden to join. But now as he drove along Moskovskiy prospekt, an unfamiliar fondness for Peter's city washed over him. This was where Anja was born. He allowed his mind to wander, conjuring up wistful images of the two of them walking the city streets again, tramping through snow, skating in the park and, on a bright, sunny day like today, eating a picnic by the water. When doubts crept in, he told himself to stay positive and believe the happy times would happen when the nightmare is over. *Anja is what it's all about.*

As he turned onto the Novgorod road, an idea built in his mind. *Keep driving ... past Lyuban ... you can be with Anja in a few hours.* It was tempting, but he told himself there would be time for that later, when Yagudin was out of the way. Then, somehow, he would persuade Natasha to let him see his daughter again.

The traffic slowed. There was a checkpoint ahead. *What if they're looking for me? Someone talked. Yuri?* He cautioned himself to stay calm; he had gotten away with it so far, and it was unlikely that anything had changed in the past few hours. As he approached the booth, a *militsiya* officer stepped out. Mitch held his breath. The officer waved him on and held up a hand in front of the car behind. Mitch looked neither left nor right, just straight ahead.

On the outskirts of Lyuban he stopped the car in front of a mustard and white painted *dacha* and checked the directions Vera Kishinevskaya had given him. From there, it wasn't long to the side road she said he should take. He passed empty fields and tracks veering off toward unseen places. Just as he was beginning to think he had taken the wrong turn, he came upon a turquoise-painted *dacha,* partially hidden by a tall hedge. There were no other houses in sight, and it was the right colour, so it must be the one. The wooden gates creaked as he opened them wide. He waited, half expecting an irate tirade to come from the house, but all he heard was the chittering of birds from the vine winding its way up the front wall. He drove the car through the gateway, parked it behind a shed out of sight of the road, and closed the gates. In the back garden he glanced around, breathing in the heady scent of flowers. Pink hollyhocks fringed the fence. Yellow umbrellas of blossom atop sinewy stems of dill stood guard over a neglected vegetable patch, where the leaves of what might once have been lettuce flopped in wilted heaps on the ground. Mitch kicked the dirt with the toe of a shoe and sank down onto a wooden bench, welcoming the chance to sit for a few moments in that peaceful place, so far removed from the chaos his life had become. He gazed at the rusty water pump, the gardening tools abandoned by the side, and the remnants of past attempts at growing flowers or vegetables piled in a fermenting heap in a corner.

Inside the house, the air smelled musty, unused. He pulled back the curtains and threw open the window. Sunlight fell on simple appliances and well-used furniture crowding the small kitchen. He breathed more easily here, safe in this secret little world, a place where he could step back from his life and become someone else. He wondered if the other people who sought refuge here had felt the same. A quick inspection revealed a small sitting room at the front of the house, and upstairs a bedroom and bathroom. The bed looked tempting, but he went back down the stairs and unloaded the car.

Later, he wandered into the garden, pulled up the lettuce, tossed them on to the compost heap, and looked out across the fields. He would have been happy in a place like this, where life was simple, where he could have taught his daughter to appreciate the truly good things the world has to offer. Instead, what had he done? Blundered through marriage, fighting off constantly mounting debts. He had thought he was a good husband and father. *If only things had been different.* He lit a cigarette and inhaled deeply. His thoughts strayed to Mariya Kornyevskaya. She and Alina would be sitting together at the table covered with the bright yellow cloth. Their meal would be simple: black radish or fish with bread, a glass of *Kvass* for Mariya, a mug of milk for Alina. *Maybe, when all this is over, I'll bring them here with Anja.* The thought comforted him as he went back inside the *dacha* to prepare his solitary meal.

As night drew in, he settled into the armchair in the kitchen and opened a book, a brandy bottle on the table by his side. Tonight, his consumption must be carefully rationed. An hour or so and two drinks passed. He put the book down and searched his mind, trying to remember what he had read. He jerked upright.

Listened. *What was that? There it is again.* A tapping sound. It was coming from the front of the house. He crept through to the sitting room and peeked around the edge of the closed curtains. In the moonlight, fronds of brittle vine waved in front of the window-pane. As he watched, a gust of wind took hold of the gnarled branches and flung them against the window. He walked back into the kitchen and poured another drink.

SUNDAY, AUGUST 18, 1991

In the early hours of the morning, Mitch awoke with a start, the acrid smell of smoke in his nostrils. He clambered out of bed and ran down the stairs, through the sitting room, and into the kitchen. He found nothing—no smoke, no smell, no flames. Back in the bedroom, he flopped on to the pillows. The dream had been so vivid. Flames rose into the London sky, filling the air with choking smoke. Ruth's face illuminated in an orange glow. She leaned out of the window and tossed the squirming body of a girl toward the ground. The girl's skirt billowed out like a parachute, and for a moment she was suspended in mid-air. Mitch had rushed forward, arms open to catch her. As he touched her, she melted in the heat.

He listened to the steady beat of rain on the tin roof and tried to rid his mind of the images. In the past few weeks, in his more desperate moments when fear of what might happen took hold, part of him hoped the newspaper building would burn down. There would be no story, no fear of retribution. But then he thought of the people who worked there, their families, the girls in the brothels, and the parents who mourned. *The story must be out there now. There's no going back.* He looked upward in the half-light, following the shapes of water stains on the ceiling. *Whatever's going to happen, let it happen soon,* he pleaded silently and closed his eyes.

When he awoke again, the patter of rain had stopped. He got out of bed, pulled his sweater on over his pajamas, moved an edge of a curtain to one side, and peered out. No sign of anyone. The sun was breaking through and a veil of mist hovered above the field on the other side of the road. Downstairs, he cut bread and waited for coffee to brew. His mind drifted back to long ago Sunday mornings when he was growing up: bratwurst sizzling in the pan, Babushka tapping the back of his hand as he tried to grab a piece before it was ready.

All morning, he paced around the house, sat in the armchair, and paced around again. And so the hours passed. The sense of calm he felt yesterday had washed away with the rain. He needed to know what was happening, whether anyone had connected him with the story. It was the uncertainty he couldn't stand. He turned on the radio. Making no sense of the incessant babble, he snapped it off. He picked a book off the shelf by the stove, leafed through it, and put it back.

Sweat trickled down the back of his neck. The kitchen was like an oven. He opened the door and sat on the damp garden bench, grateful for the cooling breeze. He rolled his shirtsleeves up to his elbows, an unlit cigarette between his lips, closed his eyes, and imagined sitting here for the rest of his life. He would drift off into the long sleep of the dead. By the time his rotting remains were found, the sunshine would have gone and icy winds would chill the ground. *Will they wonder who I was, or will I be consigned to an unmarked grave, a victim of a careless life?*

Something creaked. His eyes shot open. There was a thud. The cigarette fell from his lips as he scrambled to his feet. *Get inside. Lock the door.* The fingers of his left hand gripped the outside of the door post.

"Anyone there?" a voice rasped.

Mitch froze. A figure came into view. Not the sinister figure he feared. Before him stood an old woman dressed in a heavy coat. Strings of grey hair stuck out from the edges of her black headscarf. She came toward him, head nodding incessantly. He breathed more easily.

"Do you live here?" she demanded, head still nodding.

"I … I'm staying here," he began, and cautioned himself to say no more.

She stared at him. He shifted from one foot to the other. "Flowers. Nice flowers," she said, her face now close to his. A trickle of saliva ran down her chin between two coarse whiskers. She grinned at him, and he took a step into the doorway. Then she began to wave her hands above her head and turn around and around in circles. She stumbled and stepped out of one of her boots — men's boots, too big for her. Mitch grabbed one of her arms and steadied her; she stared at him with unfocused eyes, a confused expression on her face. Then the head started nodding again.

A wave of compassion overcame his initial fear. "You should be going home," he urged.

She looked down at her bootless foot.

You have to get rid of her. What if someone comes looking for her? He let go of her arm, grabbed the boot with one hand and her bare ankle with the other, and jammed her foot into it. Then he took her gently by one arm and guided her around the side of the house.

"Bicycle!" she cried. "My bicycle!"

It was lying on the ground by the side of the open gate. Mitch pulled it upright and held it until she clasped the handlebars.

"Spasiba." She fixed him with a puzzled look, wheeled the bicycle through the open gate, and got on. He watched as she wobbled up the road, head still nodding. "What a nice young man, what a nice young man," she shouted to no one in particular.

He closed the gate, hurried back inside the house, locked the door, and stood with his back leaning on it, one hand grasping the doorknob. *The old crone seems harmless, but what if she tells someone I'm here?* He cautioned himself to stay calm. *You're safer here than anywhere. The old woman obviously has a mental problem, and the odds of anyone believing her are slim. She's probably forgotten about you already,* he told himself, moving to the kitchen window and closing the curtains. He slumped in the armchair in the gloom. He ate nothing but drank plenty. It was almost six o'clock when he dragged himself from his stupor, lit a cigarette, and snapped on the radio. For a moment or two, he couldn't make sense of what the announcer was saying. He moved closer and turned up the volume. *A coup? Gorbachev kidnapped? What are they talking about? They must have got it wrong.* There had been repeated warnings of a plot against Gorbachev, but who would do such a thing?

A chill ran through Mitch's body. The story the newscaster related held all the horror of Stalinist times. A knock at the door of the President's Crimea *dacha* ... a top KGB official enters ... telephone lines dead. Valery Boldin, Gorbachev's own chief of staff, acting on behalf of the so-called State Committee of Emergency, had demanded the President declare a state of emergency and authorize reform measures. If not, Vice President Gennady Yanayev would take control. *Is Russia's flirtation with democracy over?*

Although the President's plans for *Perestroika* and *Glasnost* had gone off track, he was the best chance the country had ever had. *What will happen now? A return to the totalitarianism and chaotic centralised planning that made Russians little more than serfs? Would the military take over? The KGB?* "Shit!" Mitch stubbed the cigarette out. "There'll be a ban on publication," he gasped. "There's bound to be. Any hope that the media will have the guts to print my story will vanish. All my efforts … for nothing!" He gripped the edge of the table with both hands. *With the country in chaos, Yagudin will evade prosecution, slip under the net, free to carry on his trade in misery. And Anja?* He mustn't let anything happen to her. *At least she's relatively safe for the time being in Novgorod with Katya's grandparents. That's something to be thankful for,* he comforted himself. But his father? What would happen to him if there was trouble in the city? He paced from the kitchen to the sitting room and back again, running his fingers through his hair. Thoughts whirred around and around in his head until he couldn't make sense of anything.

Later, as the sun was going down, he stood in the garden and watched the sky change from red to indigo to black. The colours matched his mood. He thought of Dariya's mother, waiting for her long-dead daughter to come home. Of Ruth and the girl she called Elena, risking their lives to expose the racket. He owed a debt to all of them. And Anja? Tears welled in his eyes as he thought of his daughter. If for no one else, for her sake he had to make sure Yagudin was out of the way. And even without the threat of Yagudin hovering, what sort of life would Anja—or Alina, or Katya, or any of the soon-to-be young women he saw on the street every day—have in a country that lurched from one crisis to another?

He flopped down on to the bench and stared into the blackness. The scent of flowers seemed to have increased in the dampness of night. He shivered; the smell reminded him of the graveyard where Babushka was buried. *What would she do?* The answer to that was easy. Protect her family. That was the most important thing in life. That was what she always told him. Apart from his father, Anja was his only family. Surely it wouldn't be wrong if he took them to a place where his father could spend the rest of his life in peace, and Anja could blossom in a nurturing environment, where her every movement wasn't monitored, where there was no need for an internal passport or to beg permission to go away from home for more than a few days. *Is that too much to ask?* Vera Kishinevskaya must know how to go about it, get them all out of this hellhole. A long-suppressed longing for his daughter washed through him. Whatever Natasha said, he needed to see her. Just a glimpse. *Tomorrow,* he promised himself. *Tomorrow, I will drive to Novgorod.*

The thought spurred him into action. Inside the house, he checked his watch, grabbed his jacket and car keys. He drove slowly back to the main road. There was a store on the corner, on the outside wall of which was a telephone booth. He pulled into the side of the road and let the car idle for a while. Illuminated in the lights from the storefront, a group of people bunched together. Their talk would be about the coup. How it might affect their families. Their remarks guarded. Conditioned by centuries of distrust, where neighbour informed on neighbour, Russians still found it hard to reveal their true feelings in public. They, or their parents, lived through the German occupation of this area and Stalin's rule, where people disappeared for uttering the most innocent remark.

Mitch turned off the engine and got out of the car. The group turned as one to stare at him. He tried to walk with an air of nonchalance, but his gait was erratic. Reaching the booth, he fumbled in his pocket for a metal token and the slip of paper on which he had written Vera Kishinevskaya's number. He fed the token into the telephone, dialled the number, and waited, praying Leonid didn't answer. The old man was almost deaf, and Mitch didn't want to have to shout. The group of people were now huddled together again, and Mitch spoke quickly when he heard Vera's voice. "Vera. My father. I need to speak to him."

"He ... he isn't here. Not at the moment."

"What do you mean?"

"He had to go back ... he forgot something."

"He has been staying with you, hasn't he?" Mitch asked. "He promised he would." She didn't answer. "I'll call him at home," he snapped.

"Before you hang up," she said, "I had Leonid pick up the newspaper from a friend at the British Embassy. It's really damning. There's a picture of him ... Yagudin ... on the front page."

"That's there, not here, Vera. With all the confusion around the coup, there's bound to be a ban on publication. It's all been a waste ..."

"Don't give up yet. No one knows how things will turn out here, and the article will have drawn attention to their operations in England and elsewhere." Her voice held a note of hope. "There's no mention in the newspaper of where the information came from."

Mitch breathed a sigh of relief. Ruth had kept her word.

"Your friend called. He said the talk on the street isn't good."

Mitch took a sharp intake of breath. She was talking about the professor, to whom Mitch had given Vera's number in case he had anything to report.

"They're out there. Threatening anyone who might have talked. He said there's also a rumour that there's infighting at the top. Suspecting one another."

"Let's hope they do us all a favour and eliminate him themselves," Mitch hissed.

"Your friend said to tell you he's going away ... taking his friend with him. Just a precaution. They'll be at the place he took you to one Sunday. He said you would know where that was."

At least someone has some sense, Mitch thought to himself, relieved that the professor and Marta would be out of harm's way. "Did you tell my father about this?"

"Yes."

"He shouldn't be on his own. What's he thinking of?"

"He wouldn't listen to me," Vera murmured. "You know how stubborn he is."

"I'll call him."

Mitch inserted another token and dialled his father's number. It seemed an age before he answered. "Why are you there? You promised ..."

"I forgot my spectacles," Sergei blurted.

A truck thundered past on the main road, and Mitch leaned further into the booth and muttered through gritted teeth, "You're lying! You never went there."

It was a few seconds before Sergei spoke. "Someone has to be here. Otherwise, how will we know if anyone comes here looking?"

"And what if they come?" Mitch didn't allow himself to answer his own question.

"*Ya znayu.* But sometimes parents have to do things for their children. You should know that."

"You have to get out of there. Tonight!"

"It's not safe out there, Mitch. You heard about Gorbachev?"

"I heard it on the radio."

"Who knows what will happen?"

"Which is why you should do as you promised."

"I'll see what the situation is tomorrow," Sergei said and changed the subject quickly. "I just had a call from Anastasia. She's at her sister's house. She said people on the street are saying Gorbachev's been taken to a gulag. Just like when Stalin ..."

Mitch felt a tap on his right shoulder. He stiffened and turned his head slowly.

"The telephone," the young man hissed.

Mitch gulped. "I'll only be a minute."

The man took a few steps back, his legs firmly planted, arms wrapped across his chest, and stared at Mitch.

"I have to go, Papa. Someone needs to use the telephone."

"Vera ... did she tell you about the newspaper?"

"She did. I don't know what good it will do with all this going on." Mitch could now feel the heat of the man's breath on the back of his neck. "Papa, listen to me. Tomorrow, you must do as you promised."

"I will."

"And whatever you do, don't answer the door. Not to anyone." Mitch's voice was little more than a whisper. He put the phone down, brushed past the young man, and hurried to the car.

Back at the *dacha,* he poured himself a drink, gulped it down, and poured another. From what the professor said, it didn't sound as though Yagudin knew who had informed on him. Maybe he could risk going back and checking on his father. There were bound to be roadblocks on the major routes into the city, but he could take the quieter roads.

He turned on the radio. Reports were now coming in that thousands of troops were heading for Moscow, Leningrad, and the Baltics. He leaned on the kitchen table, wondering what he should do. At least Anja was safe for the moment, but what about Mariya and Alina? The announcer's voice cut into his thoughts: "Unconfirmed reports allege that Boldin and his co-conspirators are in possession of Gorbachev's black box, the briefcase containing the codes to launch all nuclear weapons throughout the country."

Mitch held his head in his hands. "Shit! What will become of us?"

CHAPTER FORTY-THREE

LYUBAN/NOVGOROD/LENINGRAD

MONDAY, AUGUST 19, 1991

Mitch stood in the kitchen doorway of the *dacha* and watched pale streaks of dawn brush the sky. His bag was packed and stowed in the car, but it was too early to leave—a car on the road at 6:00 a.m. might arouse suspicion. In the kitchen, he put the coffee pot on the stove and cut a slice of bread. He twirled the dial on the radio in the hope of hearing some news. All the stations were broadcasting patriotic music. When the coffee was ready, he poured some into a mug and pulled a chair up to the kitchen table. The butter was a runny pool, and he daubed some on the bread and lit a cigarette.

The music stopped. Silence. Mitch's shoulder muscles tensed. *Surely they haven't taken all the stations off the air,* he wondered, his fingers on the radio dial. Then a voice boomed out: "TASS is reporting that Vice President Gennady Yanayev has assumed command ... Gorbachev has serious health problems and can no longer govern." *Health problems? Would they dare assassinate him with the whole world watching?* The voice continued: "Strikes and demonstrations are banned, and all media is under official control."

"Govno!" Mitch banged a fist on the table, rattling the crockery. "I knew it! I fucking knew it!" Any chance of getting the article in print here had vanished. He felt drained, as though his whole life had been geared toward this one moment, this moment of abject failure. *By the time the media ban is lifted, the story will be old news.* If only he had found the courage to expose Yagudin himself, plastered the city with posters showing the bastard's face, telling people what he was doing, the lives he was ruining. He jolted upright. Why hadn't he thought of that before? He could still do it. *And when the country gets back into some semblance of order—if it ever does—the new regime may clamp down on corruption and bring scum like Yagudin to justice.* He shook his head. *Who are you fooling?* The music on the radio pushed through his mind like a dirge.

After a moment or two, he got to his feet, snapped the radio off, picked up his mug of coffee, and stepped into the garden. His mind raced. If he couldn't fix Yagudin for a while, he had to get Anja away from him. Soon. In a couple of weeks, school would start, and she would have to go back to the city. He couldn't risk leaving her with Natasha. He had to act fast, get her right away, out of the country. That was the only way he could be sure she was safe. His father had told him that Vera Kishinevskaya arranged forged passports and passage out of the country for people she had hidden in this house. When he got back to the city, he would ask her to set things in motion for the three of them. It would be difficult to persuade his father to leave, but he had to; he couldn't leave him behind. First, he must drive to Novgorod and look around the outside of Katya's grandparents' house. Then, when everything was ready to go, he would know the location of the house and garden and the route to get Anja away from the area quickly. A brief smile washed across his face—he might even catch a glimpse of her today.

The thought spurred him into action. It was still early, but if he didn't do something soon, he'd go crazy. He'd risk being stopped. He rinsed the dishes and, after making sure everything was switched off in the house, locked the door and reversed the car out onto the road. As he shut the gates he paused and gazed across the empty fields, the chittering of birds filling his mind.

There was a trickle of traffic on the main road, and he tucked himself in between a van and a car. He checked the rearview mirror; the car behind turned off outside the village. All seemed normal. Kilometre followed kilometre. Traffic increased. The closer Mitch got to Novgorod, the more edgy and nervous he felt. Maybe it was too risky. What if Anja saw him and told Natasha? He would lose his chance to get her away. And what if he was stopped by the *militsiya?* A truck ahead belched black fumes, and Mitch dropped back, peering around the side of the vehicle, scanning the road ahead for tell-tale signs of a roadblock. *What are you afraid of?* he asked himself. *Tell the truth. Your daughter is staying with a friend and you're going to visit her. That's all you have to say.*

Some time later, the domes of the Cathedral of St. Sophia rose in the distance, below which were the formidable walls of the Kremlin. Mitch's mind went back to the time his parents brought him here when he was about eight-years-old. The red brick walls of the fortress towered above them as his father recounted that the first stone of the original walls was laid on the body of a living child. "Where's your sense, telling him such a scary story?" his mother snapped. "Now he'll have nightmares about it!" His father retaliated: "You can't shield the boy from reality. He has to toughen up, learn to deal with these things. This is a hard country. Brutal things happen." *How right he was,* Mitch thought now as he crossed the bridge over the Volkhov River.

He followed the signs for the Yurev Monastery, the blue and silver onion domes of which he could see clearly now. His father said that Katya's grandparents' home was near the monastery—a wooden house with a rickety porch held up by gnarled posts, backing on to the marshes. Mitch slowed the car several times as he spotted likely houses, pulling up just short of them in case Anja was outside.

Then he saw her. Katya. Riding the green bicycle up and down the front path. No one could mistake the blonde braid hanging down her back. It was definitely her. And where she was, Anja wouldn't be far away. He reversed the car along the road, turned on to a dirt track, and parked in the shelter of a large tree. As he hurried back to the main road, a curious mixture of fear and excitement coursed through his body. His daughter was probably no more than a few feet away. He stopped close to the ragged hedge that ran along the side of the garden and watched. Katya was now riding the bicycle slowly around the circumference of a flower bed planted with pale pink flowers. Around and around she went for what seemed an age, then she dropped the bicycle onto the grass and ran up the steps to the porch. He heard mumbled voices and craned his neck. Katya was sitting on an elderly man's lap—a man Mitch took to be her Dedushka. There was no sign of Anja. As he watched, the door to the house opened, and a woman dressed in a dark brown overall with long sleeves came out. She carried a tray on which sat a tall glass and some cups. A knot formed in his stomach. *Where is she? Where's Anja? Maybe she's in the house. What if she's ill? Don't panic,* he told himself. *Check the garden on the other side of the house first.* He stepped out from the side of the hedge and was halfway past the house when a voice shrieked out, "It's Anja's papa!"

He stopped and turned toward the porch where Katya was jumping up and down excitedly. "Is Annushka with you? Did you bring her back?" Her grandmother caught her by the hand as she tried to run toward Mitch.

"Why are you here?" the old man called as he approached.

"Anja. My daughter. She's supposed to be here."

"She isn't here. Not anymore."

Mitch caught his breath. "What do you mean? Where is she?"

"Her mother. She came yesterday and took her away."

The grandmother and Katya had now joined them. "It's no fun without her," Katya whined and stared down at her shoes.

"Why don't you have some tea with us, and you can tell us what's going on in the city?" the woman suggested. "We're hearing conflicting reports here."

"I must get back."

"Surely you can stay a little while. It's a long drive ..."

"Thank you, but I must go," Mitch blurted. "Did my ex-wife ... Natasha. Did she say where she was taking her?"

"*Nyet,*" the man answered. The woman shook her head.

"Annushka didn't want to go," Katya piped up. "She wanted to go to Aleksandra's birthday party."

"Katinka's cousin," the grandmother explained.

"Was anyone else with Natasha?" Mitch ventured.

"No. Just her. She seemed in a hurry. Wouldn't even let Anja finish her lunch."

Mitch began to back away from them, saying, "I must be going. But thank you ... thank you for taking care of Anja."

"We were sorry to see her go," the old man said as he accompanied Mitch to the roadside.

"How was she?" Mitch asked.

"She was fine."

"She didn't seem disturbed about anything?"

The old man looked puzzled. "*Nyet.* She was happy. Like our Katya."

Mitch breathed more easily.

"Is something wrong?"

"No, nothing. I just wanted to see her."

The man gripped Mitch's shoulder for a moment and then turned and walked back to the house.

On the road to Leningrad, Mitch drove like a maniac, hardly slowing as he swept through villages. His mind whirred. *I can't leave her with Natasha ... not with that evil bastard still around. They've been gone nearly a day. They could be anywhere by now,* he thought agitatedly as he pulled out to overtake a car. A moment later, a truck lumbered out of a side road and headed toward him. He put his foot hard on the accelerator and aimed for an ever-decreasing gap. A horn blasted as the driver of the car he was passing braked hard to let him in. Mitch fought with the steering wheel and narrowly avoided going off the road. In the rearview mirror, he saw the driver of the car behind gesticulating wildly.

Take it easy, he cautioned himself. *What will happen to Anja if you end up mangled in a car wreck?* He slowed his speed, turned on the radio, and eventually found a station that was broadcasting. Outside the White House, thousands of people from all walks of Russian life—students, priests, pensioners, defecting soldiers—were surrounding the army tanks. The announcer said that Boris Yeltsin was on top of one, delivering a fiery speech denouncing the coup as unconstitutional and calling for a general strike. "Soldiers, officers, generals," came over the airwaves, "the clouds of terror and dictatorship are gathering over the whole country. They must not be allowed to bring eternal night." *Sounds like an old Bolshevik!* Mitch cursed. *So much for moving away from communism!*

On the outskirts of the city, traffic slowed. Ahead, Mitch saw the blue and white booths of a checkpoint. He was tempted to turn the car around but thought better of it. He couldn't risk losing any more time. It seemed an age until the car in front was waved through. He held his breath. One of the officers walked toward him and indicated that he should pull over.

"Papers." The officer put a hand through the open window.

Mitch fumbled in his jacket pocket.

"Where are you coming from?" He began to leaf through the internal passport Mitch handed him.

"Novgorod."

"But you live in Leningrad."

"My daughter. She's staying in Novgorod with a friend," Mitch said. "I went to see her."

"What work do you do?"

"It's in there," Mitch gestured toward the passport.

"I'm asking you." The officer's words were slow, deliberate.

"Ya ... Ya yurist."

He fixed Mitch with a level gaze. By an effort of will, Mitch forced himself to look back at him. He was sure the man could see into his soul, knew what he was planning.

He held the passport closer to his face. "Mitch ... ell. That's an odd name."

"It's a family name. My mother ..."

"Boris. Over here." He beckoned to one of his colleagues.

The other officer approached, his right hand on the gun in his holster. *Someone must have talked.* Mitch was motionless, his eyes transfixed on the gun as the scene processed slowly through his panic-stricken brain.

"Hey, Boris. How about naming your new son Mitchell?"

The words jolted Mitch out of his trance.

The other officer screwed up his nose. "What sort of a name's that?" he laughed and kicked one of the front tires of Mitch's car.

Relief flooded through Mitch's body. "Not much of a name!" He laughed with them.

After a few minutes of their banter, Mitch tucked the passport back in his pocket and pulled away. He was sweating but closed the window, blocking out the rest of the world. He needed to focus on what he must do.

His progress was slow as he drove through the city. The roads were clogged with traffic and pedestrians, gathering in what food they could in case there was trouble on the streets. Mitch thumped the steering wheel with his fists, venting his frustration as he waited for a traffic light to change. The cars in front began to move and he leaned forward, willing them to go faster, turning over in his mind what he would do when he got to the apartment. "If I ever fucking get there!" he cursed loudly, grinding to a halt again. *Don't get into an argument with Natasha,* he cautioned. *Tell Anja you're taking her back to Novgorod to Katya's cousin's birthday party. That way she won't be scared. We'll spend the night at the dacha in Lyuban, and tomorrow morning I'll explain we're going away. Make it sound like an adventure. One in which we'll have pretend names, like children sometimes have in storybooks.* On the way out of the city today, he would have to take a different route; he couldn't risk being stopped by the same *militsiya* officers again. Would they believe he had two daughters? He didn't want them to question Anja.

He wound the window down to get some air as he pulled away again. *What if she's not at the apartment? They could be with Natasha's parents.* At that moment an old man stepped in front of the car. "What the hell?" Mitch yelled. He banged his foot hard on the brake pedal and yanked the steering wheel to the left. Farther on, he turned into a narrow alleyway and wove between bins and cardboard boxes; it was a cut-through he used when traffic on the main roads was slow. Today he drove faster than he should and clipped the side of a bin. It clattered on to its side, spilling the contents onto the ground.

A few minutes later, he pulled into the street leading to the apartment building. Cars were parked along both sides, and as he went to turn under the archway into the central courtyard of the building, he jammed on the brakes. A garbage truck was parked the other side of the archway. He couldn't get past. Cursing, he slammed the car into reverse and drew in alongside another car, leaving scarcely enough room for traffic to pass. He jumped out of the car. A man on the other side of the street stepped quickly into the shadows. Mitch skirted around the garbage truck and ran into the courtyard. Vyacheslav, the caretaker, came toward him—a toothless grin lit up his face. "Where've you been? We missed you." The old man grasped Mitch's arms. "And that little girl of yours," he shook his head. "My Rodnina was only saying when she saw her yesterday ..."

"Sorry, Slava. I'm in a hurry," Mitch interjected. "My car's blocking the road. The garbage truck ..."

"They won't be long."

Mitch looked around. Natasha's car was in its usual place, so she must be up there. He paced back and forth, lit a cigarette, took a few puffs, ground it out with his shoe. *Calm down,* he told himself. *If I can't get the car in, she can't get out.* After a few minutes, he ran over to help Slava drag aluminium garbage bins across the courtyard to the truck. Anything to quicken the process.

"How much longer will this take?" His voice held the frustration he was trying hard to keep at bay.

"Give me your keys." Slava held out his hands to Mitch. "I'll move the car in here when the truck's gone."

Mitch pressed his car keys into the other man's hand. He took a few steps toward the entrance door and then turned and called, "Leave the keys in the car." He would need to get away with Anja fast. Slava waved a hand in acknowledgement.

The two old women were sitting in their usual place at the side of the elevator as Mitch burst into the hallway. They rested their knitting in their laps, mouths open as if to speak.

He took the stairs two at a time. Outside the apartment, he paused to regain his breath and then knocked on the door. It opened almost immediately.

He scarcely recognized the woman in front of him. Natasha's hair hung in lank strands over her shoulders; her eyes were ringed with red. "You! What are you doing here?" There was no mistaking the sharpness in her voice. She started to close the door. Mitch was too quick for her. The door handle hit the wall inside as he barged in. "I said you weren't to come here," she yelled.

He slammed the door closed and brushed past her. "Anja? Anja?" he called as he strode along the hallway checking each room. "Papa's here."

Natasha ran behind him. "You can't ..."

He threw open his daughter's bedroom door and looked in. "Where is she? Where's Anja?" he shouted.

"She's not here."

"Where?" he barked and spun around to face her. "Where is she?"

"Somewhere you won't find her!"

"I'm not leaving until you tell me where she is." Mitch walked purposefully toward her, his fists clenched.

She edged away from him and then stopped. "He knows. Misha knows it was you."

Mitch gulped, and it was some moments before he was able to force words out of his mouth. "Knows what was me?"

"The newspaper."

"What newspaper?" His steady tone masked the turmoil inside.

"The newspaper in London. Don't try to deny it. Someone told him."

"I've no idea what you're talking about."

"He can tell you himself." She paused and looked over her shoulder toward the front door. "Misha ... he'll be here any minute."

Mitch hoped she was bluffing. "Tell me where Anja is. She's my daughter, for fuck's sake."

"She doesn't want to see you!" She came toward him. "When will you get that into your thick head?"

"You're lying."

She stood in front of him, a supercilious grin on her face.

He had at first felt a pang of sympathy for her, but now the loathing came roaring back. "You whore!" he spat. "You deny me the right to see my own daughter, but you let that ... that vermin near her. If he's done anything to hurt her ..."

"You're the one who's hurting her," she cut in. "Why don't you leave us alone? We were happy before you messed it all up again." Her voice was shrill.

"Happy?" Mitch sneered.

"If you know what's good for you, you'll leave before he gets here."

"I thought he only picked on defenceless girls!"

"And you still deny it was you?" she laughed loudly.

"Deny what was me?"

"The newspaper ..."

"I don't know what you're talking about."

"It was you."

"You're no better than him! Using his dirty money for fancy clothes, fast cars, while young girls hardly older than Anja live in misery."

"Why shouldn't I have nice things? No sense in us all living miserable lives."

"You disgust me!" Mitch turned away, unable to look at her anymore. He walked into the sitting room and with trembling hands poured himself a drink.

She followed him. "Please go," she begged, looking agitatedly at her watch. "I don't want to see anything happen to you."

"But you'd let our daughter live under the same roof as him?"

"She doesn't."

A surge of relief ran through Mitch's body. "Where is she? If you'll just tell me where she is, I'll go." He swigged the drink and picked up the bottle to pour another.

Suddenly, the world exploded. The bottle slipped from his grasp as the building shook beneath his feet. He held on to the table. His eardrums felt as if they were going to burst. For a few moments he couldn't hear anything. Then he looked around, dazed. Natasha was clinging to the door jamb.

His muscles felt rigid, as though set in stone. Then something snapped in his head. "What the? What's happening?" He pushed Natasha to one side and lurched along the hallway. Broken glass crunched under the soles of his shoes. In the doorway to Anja's bedroom, he stopped. The curtains hung in tatters. There was shattered glass everywhere. He picked his way across the floor and grabbed the cover from her bed. Debris spilled onto the floor as he wrapped the cover around his right arm and pushed jagged shards of glass out of the window frame. He looked down onto the street. A column of flame and black smoke rose where his car had been. The car alongside it was also on fire. Then he understood. *The other car! The fuel tank!* He drew back from the window.

"What happened? What's going on?" Natasha stood in the doorway, her mouth open, her hair covered in white dust.

"Get back! The fuel tank!" he yelled. As he tried to get to the doorway, it felt as if he was walking in slow motion. He was almost there when the blast from another explosion hurled shards of metal through the window. His ears boomed with the noise as he groped his way into the hallway. Then he fell to the floor. A deathly silence descended. He couldn't hear the beating of his heart. Moments later, Natasha's cries came to him. He sat up and coughed, trying to clear the dust from his throat.

She was kneeling on the floor, rocking back and forth, wailing.

He pulled his knees into his body and buried his face in the bedcover, which was still wrapped around his arm. *What if Anja had been in her bed?* He began to shake uncontrollably. *The explosion. It must have been a bomb … in the car. My car. The bastard! It was meant for me.* A vision of Slava's toothless grin flashed into his mind. Great rasping sobs came from his throat. "Don't let it be him. Don't let it be Slava," he begged.

"She could have been in there!" Natasha shrieked. "Get out! Get out!" Her fingers were like tallons as she clawed at him. "My baby … she could have been killed!"

He shoved her away and got to his feet, grasping the bedcover in one hand. In the corridor, he leaned against the wall. "It was him! Yagudin!" he yelled back at her. "Your fucking boyfriend. He was trying to kill me! He could have killed my Anja!" He turned and stumbled along the corridor. "You still think he cares for you?" he spat. The sound of her crying followed him.

In the stairwell, voices called, "What happened? Does anyone know what happened?" The words echoed in his head as he gripped the handrail. *Don't let it be him … Don't let it be Slava …* ran through his brain as his feet sought each downward step.

In the courtyard, people were screaming, running everywhere. Sirens wailed in the distance. Mitch crouched against a wall, scanning the crowd for a sight of the old man. He tasted blood in his mouth; his jaw was clenched so tight, he was biting the inside of his mouth. Then he heard a demented cry. "My husband, Slava. Have you seen him?" Rodnina Arkadyevna was grabbing at people. Mitch dropped to his knees and retched. "Does anyone know where he is?" she pleaded. "Slava! Slava!" her voice went on and on. Mitch heaved until he could heave no more. When he looked again, the courtyard was empty. He stumbled out onto the street. Twisted metal littered the sidewalk, and columns of black smoke belched upward. A line of people formed a barrier across the road a few yards in front of where the explosions occurred. The old man wasn't among them. Rodnina was running from one person to the next, screaming, "Slava! My husband! Have you seen him? Have you seen him?" A woman put an arm around her and guided her to the side of the road. Mitch turned and began to walk unsteadily in the opposite direction. He stepped around a group of people huddled together on the sidewalk and sought the seclusion of a shop doorway.

"They're saying it's Vyacheslav Ilyavich, Rodnina Arkadyevna's husband."

Mitch slunk back further into the doorway.

"Someone saw him getting into the car just before the explosion."

"Who would do that to a poor old man?"

"Chechens?"

"Mafiyosa?"

"It could be something to do with the coup."

"Not here! Why would they do it here?"

"Why him? He couldn't have had anything to do with the coup."

Mitch's lower jaw trembled uncontrollably.

"There's a couple of bodies. On the side of the road by the cars." The small crowd gaped at the woman who spoke. "They must have been walking past when the first explosion happened."

The loud noise of sirens obliterated their conversation. Mitch ventured a look at the street. Firemen were now unfurling hoses from the side of two fire engines. *"Derzhi nazad! Derzhi nazad!"* they ordered.

"There was a man." A grey-haired man informed the knot of people. "The car was awkwardly parked. I thought it had broken down." The people leaned further in. "He was doing something underneath the car a few minutes before the explosion." He held up a bag. "I was on my way to the bakery." A small girl struggled to pull her hand away from the grip of a woman in the group. The child stared at Mitch. He averted his eyes.

"You're hurt." Mitch was suddenly aware of a man standing in the open doorway of the shop. "There's blood running down your face. Come in. Let me look."

"*Nyet.* It's nothing." Mitch shook his head and put his hand up to his right temple; it was sticky. "I'll be all right."

"I think you should let me look. It could get infected if there's glass or anything in there." The man stepped toward him.

Mitch drew back. "No. It was just ..."

"You live in the apartment building, don't you?" Mitch didn't reply. "I've seen you in my store. With a little girl."

"My daughter," Mitch said in a shaky voice. "I was in her bedroom when the second blast ..." He gulped and pulled her bedcover close to his chest. "Thank God she wasn't there." His body gave an involuntary shudder.

"We'll get you cleaned up." The man took Mitch's arm and led him into the shop. "Olga, get a bowl of hot water and a cloth," he said to the woman behind the counter. He eased Mitch onto a chair, looked at the wound on his temple, and then took a bottle of antiseptic off a shelf. Olga slopped an enamel bowl of water on to the counter.

He trembled as they cleaned his wound. "It's the shock. We'll get you a drink when we've finished," Olga comforted. He flinched as she dabbed on antiseptic and applied a protective dressing. Then the man produced a small bottle from under the counter and poured some into a medicine glass. As Mitch drank, the brandy numbed his throat. It did nothing to ease the emptiness inside.

Ten minutes or so later, he left the pharmacy, the bedcover under his arm. The group outside had dispersed, and he walked hesitantly back toward the burnt-out wreckage of his car, steeling himself for what he might see. He couldn't get close; a fire engine blocked the street. Foam coated the roadway, like dirty snow. Steam rose from skeletons of twisted metal. The stench of hot metal and fumes, and a smell he couldn't identify, was all around him.

"There's nothing left of him, so they're saying," a voice at his shoulder murmured. "A few bits of charred flesh."

Mitch covered his nose and mouth with Anja's bedcover. *God! What have I done?*

"They've taken his wife away. She was hysterical, poor woman."

Mitch lowered his head and stared at the ground. Tears splashed onto his shoes. He thought of Slava's eager face, his kind words, the warmth of his hands as he took the car keys. *It should have been me. Not him.* He turned, barged past the people behind, and wove a haphazard path along the street, grasping walls, door handles, anything to stop plunging into the dark hole that opened beneath his feet with every step he took.

He heard the screech of brakes. Blasts of horns. He looked around. Nothing moved. The world was frozen in time. Then a voice yelled, "Get out of the way, *Zhopa!*" Mitch felt the heat of a car's engine next to his left leg. The voice came again: "Move!" He walked slowly out of the car's path. Later, in an alleyway, he sank down onto a stone step and cradled the bedcover in his arms as exhaustion overtook him.

He awoke to darkness, lit only by dim street lamps. Unable to make sense of where he was, he fumbled for his cigarettes and lighter and watched as his fingers went through the motions of lighting a cigarette. His thoughts were jumbled. Slava mixed up with Anja ... Anja mixed up with Slava. A chill ran through him. *She's dead? Anja's dead?* Then he remembered. The explosions. The fire. It wasn't Anja who was dead. It was Slava. Relief surged through his body, instantly replaced by guilt. Numbing guilt. He smelled again the stench of burnt flesh and held the end of the cigarette close to his nose, drawing smoke into his nostrils to obliterate the smell.

Tortured thoughts went around and around in his head. *They mustn't find her. They mustn't find Anja. And Papa. You have to stop them before anyone else is killed.* He stared down at the paving slabs. In the flickering light, a face began to form. Dim at first. He leaned forward. It came into focus. Slava. He was laughing. Mitch shrank back, averting his eyes, arms wrapped around his upper body. When he looked again, Slava's face had gone. In its place, the outline of his father's head. An empty space inside the lines. He knew it was him. Then a different image appeared, slowly at first. "Anja?" he breathed. His right arm went forward, fingers touching her face. A jagged crack began to trickle down from the top of her head to her chin. It moved apart. Wider now, until her face was completely in two. He pulled his arm back and scrambled to his feet. "*Nyet! Nyet!* Not her! Not her!" he yelled, moving away from the paving slab. The cigarette burned his fingers. He let it fall to the ground. When he dared to creep forward, she had gone.

Voices drifted toward him along the alleyway. He stumbled on, trailing Anja's bedcover. The voices followed and he quickened his pace, shambling from side to side until the voices were no more. He leaned against a wall and clutched his chest, trying to regain his breath. He looked around. Anja's bedcover had gone.

CHAPTER FORTY-FOUR
LENINGRAD

TUESDAY, AUGUST 20, 1991

He shuffled around the edge of Svetlanovskaya Square, barely able to lift his feet. If only he could think clearly, remember where the house was. The professor took him there that Sunday, the Sunday that was now in another life. The life when he made plans for his daughter's future, a future in which he had hoped to share. Now he didn't even know where she was, his Annushka. *And Slava.* Mitch grabbed at a drain pipe on the front of a building, steadying himself, the acrid stench of burned flesh, hair, still strong in his nostrils. The old man was gone. There was no body for people to file past, to kneel before and pray. Rodnina would spend the rest of her life staring at a photograph or holding a sweater to her face, searching for a trace of her husband.

The ridges in the drainpipe dug into his hands. If only he had stayed at the *dacha* or driven somewhere far away. Slava would still be alive, sitting in his chair exchanging neighbourhood gossip with his wife. Moisture welled in Mitch's eyes, but no tears came. Was this to be his punishment? Denied the luxury of tears, unable to wash guilt away?

He took a step into the road. A truck careened toward him and he stepped back onto the path. He fixed his gaze on the other side of the street and tried to garner the courage to try again. He gave up and stumbled along the path. People passed by, their conversations a jumble of sounds. A few minutes later, by the side of a railway track, he sank down onto a patch of sparse grass and fumbled in his pockets for his cigarettes and lighter. He lit one with unsteady hands, his eyes following the dull metal of the rails as they snaked into the distance. His mind played a constantly changing kaleidoscope of horror. The rails began to twist into distorted shapes, rising high in the air. Beneath them, a doll-sized figure: Slava's wife, reaching upwards, calling her husband's name over and over. He put his hands over his ears and stared at the blades of grass between his feet. Minutes passed. He took his hands away. The only sound was the distant hum of traffic. The rails were back in place.

He inhaled deeply, trying to clear his head. He needed to think. He had to make sure Anja was safe. But what could he do without putting her in more danger? If he tried to find her, they might follow him. And his father. Had they got to him already? He dared not let his thoughts go down that track. *It's all my fault. Slava. That poor old man. He didn't stand a chance. If I get my hands on that fucking Yagudin, I'll … I'll …* He threw down the cigarette, picked up a discarded beer can, and hurled it. It missed the rails.

He stumbled on. Something jabbed into his left foot. He looked down; his shoe was missing. After a while, the tall fence on his left ended, revealing a dirt track with tumble-down houses on either side. A memory stirred. *"Down here toward the railway track."* The professor's voice. He saw now the boarded-up windows, the gnarled tree, the tangled garden. A feeling of peace washed over him as he felt the warm wood of the gate. He opened it, walked slowly up the path, and banged on the door. There were scuffling noises inside, but no one came. He banged again, waited a few moments, and then began to fight his way through the brambles at the side of the house. They snagged his clothes and clawed his flesh. He felt nothing. Disentangling a branch from his hair, he broke free and peered through a gap in the curtains pulled across a window. The red and white bedcover, the woman's face. She looked at him and then began to wave a hand agitatedly back and forth. A man was there now—the man who was here before. The woman pointed at Mitch. For a moment, the man's eyes were wide with fear. Then a look of relief washed over his face. A door alongside the window opened. "Come in quickly, before anyone sees you." He reached out, grabbed Mitch by an arm, and pulled him into the room. "Did anyone follow you?"

The urgency in his voice snapped Mitch out of his trance. *"Nyet."* In truth, he didn't know. He had long since stopped checking behind him. Death had a certain allure.

"You scared us. We thought it was them … the *vory!*"

A wave of exhaustion engulfed Mitch. "My head it's …" The words hung in the air as he hit the floor.

When he opened his eyes, he blinked, trying to focus on the blurred shapes looking down at him. "What happened?" His lips cracked as he spoke. "Where … where am I?"

"You're with us here. You're safe now," Marta Nikolayevna began. "I always said those cigarettes would do you no good." Even in Mitch's confused state, he could tell the words held none of her caustic humour. She knelt down, lifted his head from the floor, and held a cup to his lips. He gulped. Water dribbled out of one side of his mouth as he drifted back into sleep.

When he awoke, he was slumped in an armchair, the room lit by a small lamp on the table at his side. His fingers touched the coarse cloth of a blanket tucked around him. A noise came from the other side of the room. The woman in the bed. She called again. Unintelligible sounds. Tears trickled down Mitch's cheeks as he peered at her through the dim light—tears for Anja, for Slava, and for this woman's dead daughter. He lowered his gaze and cowered in the chair, weighed down again by the burden of what he had done.

Some time later, he struggled upright and padded over to the woman's bed in the soft *tapochki* that were now on his feet. He searched for words. None came. She reached out and took his hand in hers. Her hand was cold, the icy cold he had first felt when he touched Babushka's cheek as she lay in her coffin. He pulled his hand away quickly.

In the corridor, he heard familiar voices. Marta Nikolayevna, the professor, and the other man, the man whose house it was. Maxim ... Maxim Yadov, that was his name. It was coming back now. No one noticed Mitch in the kitchen doorway.

"There are crowds in the street in Moscow. Sixty thousand someone said, standing in the rain defending the White House," Marta declared.

"So much for the curfew!" the professor laughed.

"They're raising the old Russian flag ... the white, blue, and red."

"They said on the radio that Rostropovich flew in from Paris and is playing music within the Parliament building. Can you believe that?"

"*Sumashedshiy!*" Marta shook her head as she spoke. "The whole country's gone crazy!"

"The neighbour," Maxim said as he waved a hand in the direction of the house next door, "he said he heard that two ... or was it three? ... protesters were killed, crushed by a tank outside the Parliament."

"They're saying the Party's lost control of *Izvestia*. The reporters and printers refused to print the paper unless it included Yeltsin's appeal for people to stand firm against the coup."

"Slava! I killed him!" Mitch blurted.

Three startled faces turned toward him.

"It was me! I killed him!" Mitch clasped the fingers of both hands together, as if in prayer.

The professor slid his chair back from the table and hurried over to Mitch. "You haven't killed anyone. You've just had a bad dream," he placated. "Come and sit down. Have something to eat." With one arm around Mitch's shoulders, he guided him to the table.

"You don't understand. *Mertvyy.* Because of me, he's dead!" His voice was loud to his own ears. His fingers seemed locked together. The professor pushed him down onto a chair.

"It's all been too much for you. All this work, family problems." Marta gave him a sympathetic look. "You need to take more care of yourself."

"You'll feel better when you've had a few days rest. You must stay here with us," Maxim suggested.

"Why won't you listen to me?" Mitch pleaded, looking from one to the other.

"I'm sure you've not done anyone any harm."

"Harm ..." Mitch's voice lost its strength. His body sagged.

Maxim Vladimirovich poured a cup of tea, slid it toward Mitch, and said softly, "You were trying to help girls like my Dasha."

"And all I ended up doing was getting an innocent old man killed."

"What old man?" the professor asked.

"Slava! They blew up my car. Don't you realize? The bastards blew up my car!" He unravelled his hands and ran them through his hair. "They killed him! They killed Slava!"

"Who is this Slava?" Marta asked. "I've not heard you speak of him before."

"An old man ... a caretaker. There were only bits of him ..." Mitch's voice broke up.

The four of them sat in silence for some moments, mourning a person most of them had never met.

Then Marta Nikolayevna got to her feet, cut a hunk of bread, and smeared it with margarine and red jam. "You'll feel better if you eat something," she said, nudging the plate toward Mitch.

He lifted the bread to his mouth. "The bomb. It was meant for me." He took a bite. "There were others too. Dead. Lying there ..." The lump of bread seemed to swell in his mouth and he took a swig of tea and gulped it down.

"I think we need something stronger than tea. I'll get the brandy." Maxim Vladimirovich got to his feet. "I bought it in Cyprus when ... when I was there for my Dasha."

WEDNESDAY, AUGUST 21, 1991

Mitch awoke to the sound of birdsong. The curtains fluttered in the breeze coming through the open window. With the breeze came remembrance. As he lay there, he wished the earth would stop spinning and he would be suspended in time, his life reduced to this one instant. He concentrated, tried to will time to halt, if only for a few hours. The birds continued to sing.

He noticed now the faded blue shirt he was wearing, the frayed cuffs of which were some inches above his wrists. He didn't think it was his. Perhaps he was no longer Mitch Galichin. Or maybe he was losing his mind. *What day is it?* he asked himself. He couldn't answer. Nor could he remember how he came to be in this room. His last recollection was of warm liquid slipping down his throat, lodging against the cold stone in his gut.

His gaze strayed to a poster on the wall. Unruly black hair, bushy eyebrows ... the pop singer ... *Philipp Kirkirov.* He could remember that. *It must be her room—the girl, Dariya.* He swallowed hard, imagining the excitement she must have felt on the last night she spent in this room as she anticipated her new job in Cyprus, her mind conjuring up visions of days spent at the beach with friends, evenings in outdoor restaurants; he had heard of these dreams from distraught relatives. How different reality turned out to be. A chill ran through his body, and he pulled the bedclothes up to his chin, trying not to think how she must have longed to be back here in her home, surrounded by the love of her parents.

He breathed softly, not to disturb any lingering trace of her. Jammed into the side of the mirror above the chest of drawers, he saw a photograph. A riot of dark curls framed her face. Her dancing eyes held his gaze, and he felt as though he had been projected forward in time to see the young woman his daughter would become, the one he would probably never know. Maybe this was all he would ever have. It was some moments before Dariya's eyes released their hold.

Voices drifted up to him from below, and he slid his legs over the edge of the bed, walked to the door, and opened it a crack. Someone was trying to tune a radio; the sound came in crackly bursts and then settled into a rhythmic hum. Turning from the door, he searched for his cigarettes and his clothes. The tall cupboard and drawers held a scattering of women's garments. Mitch fingered the coarse cloth of a skirt, as if trying to make a connection with the dead girl. Then he closed the cupboard door and picked up a pair of pants that were draped over the back of a chair. They would have to do.

In the kitchen, Marta was pounding dough on the kitchen table. The professor had one hand on a low shelf and was listening to the radio. Mitch stood for a moment breathing in the normality of the scene, wondering how they could carry on with their lives as if nothing had happened. "How long was I ... ?" he began.

The professor held up a hand, silencing him. Marta scoffed: "He thinks this is going to change everything."

"Two of the coup leaders are heading to the Crimea to talk to Gorbachev."

"At least he's still alive," Mitch murmured.

"Yeltsin ... he said the rest of them are trying to flee the country." The professor pulled out a chair and flopped down onto it.

Marta dusted the dough with flour and put it into a bowl, which she covered with a cloth. "You must be hungry," she said to Mitch.

He was, and ten minutes or so later he had devoured the remains of a loaf of bread, washed down with coffee. "My cigarettes. I can't find them."

Marta turned her back on him and clattered dishes in the sink. He repeated what he had said. When she didn't answer, the professor opened a drawer and pulled out the cigarettes and lighter. Marta turned and fixed him with a steely look. "Now is not the time," the professor hissed at her.

Mitch lit up and inhaled. "Where's Maxim Vladimirovich?"

"He's reading to her, his wife," the professor explained. "It calms her." He picked the coffee pot off the stove and refilled his own cup.

"Did you hear anything about what's going on in the streets ... with that bastard Yagudin?" Mitch asked.

The professor snapped the radio off. "You know they came looking for you at the building? That's why we left."

"They didn't hurt anyone?"

"They don't scare me," Marta declared. "I've lived through worse than that."

"Mariya and Alina?" Mitch spoke the names tentatively.

"Don't you be worrying about them. Mariya can take care of herself. She's ..."

"Your father," the professor interrupted Marta. "Does he know you were coming here?"

Mitch shook his head. "I couldn't call him. It's too risky. I don't even know ..."

"I could get a message to him." Maxim Vladimirovich volunteered as he came into the room. "I'm the only one here they won't recognize. I could make out I was delivering something. Borrow a truck."

"Nyet!" Mitch said emphatically. "It's too dangerous—for you and my father."

"We're wasting time arguing," Maxim said. "Let me do it. At least put your father's mind at ease. Let him know he still has a son. I know what it's like not knowing."

Two hours later, Maxim set off. He carried a delivery note and a parcel, inside which were several books. Tucked into one was a letter from Mitch arranging to meet Sergei at noon the following day, "in the church you first took me to as a six-year-old." He had to take this chance—it might be his last opportunity to see his father for some time. Maxim would go first to Vera's address. If he wasn't there, he would try Sergei's own apartment.

Time passed slowly for those left in the house. The woman in the bed became more agitated, constantly weeping, as if she knew about Slava. Mitch sat by her bed and read to her—to his mind, they were disconnected words without meaning. He checked his watch repeatedly, anxious for Maxim's return. He couldn't take any more, couldn't bear the burden of another person's death. The book slipped from his grasp and he slumped forward and held his head in his hands. "If there is a God, keep Maxim Vladimirovich safe," he begged. The woman's voice quietened, her limbs still. She slept.

THURSDAY, AUGUST 22, 1991

Mitch pulled his cloth cap down and tucked strands of hair inside. He had several days' growth on his chin, signs of exhaustion under his eyes, and, in Maxim Vladimirovich's clothes (his own having been ripped beyond even Marta's view of worth repairing) looked like an old man. "No one will know it's you. Courage, Mitchell Sergeivich," Marta had said as he left the house. In his past life, Mitch would have berated her for the use of his patronymic. But today he was silent, comforted to bear the name derived from that of his father, a sign he belonged to someone and wasn't completely alone in this world. Marta couldn't disguise her smile.

Maxim Vladimirovich pulled the truck in to the side of the road. With one hand on the door handle, Mitch turned to him and said, "I can never thank you enough for what you've done for me. Taking me in ..."

"The debt is ours, all ours," the old man interrupted, grasping Mitch's arm. "Go safely." As Mitch got out of the truck, Maxim added, "I'll be back in an hour."

A few minutes later, Mitch picked his way through the crowds assembled outside Chernyshevskaya station. He felt safer here with the warmth of bodies jostling him. He tucked himself in the middle of a group who were unfurling a banner. They raised it high and chanted loudly: "Yeltsin ... Yeltsin ..." Their words were taken up by the crowd. Voices beat the air like an incessant drum, proclaiming their new hero. Rumour had it that the visibly shaken Gorbachev had returned to Moscow by plane and that all the members of the coup had been arrested, apart from Boris Pugo, the Minister of Internal Affairs, who was alleged to have shot himself in the head.

"They've toppled the statue of Iron Felix!" a man circulating through the crowd yelled. "My cousin in Moscow told me," he added and moved on to impart his news to more of the assembled crowd. *The statue of Felix Dzerzhinsky. The founder of the secret police. Have they really brought it down? Is the iron grip weakening at last?* Mitch's breath was shallow, hardly daring to hope that the long-suffering people of this country—the country that, with all its corruption and violence, had come to be his—would finally be released from tyranny. A faint hope stirred within him that at last someone in authority might clamp down on the trafficking rings and enact legislation imposing stiff penalties. Then he heard Marta Nikolayevna's voice in his head: *"It will change nothing."*

Mitch was swept along with the crowd. The smell of beer-tainted breath, perspiration, unwashed bodies, and tobacco smoke mingled with the stench of burned flesh that had been with him for days. The voices took up a new chant: "Dissolve the Party. Axe the KGB." He scanned the crowd, wondering if any of these ordinary-looking people were agents of the State, or maybe Yagudin's henchmen; he didn't know which he feared more. He stood stock still. The man with his back to him ... the one with long blond hair? *Yuri?* Mitch worked his way unobtrusively to a place where he had a better view. He breathed a sigh of relief; a birthmark splattered from forehead to jaw on one side of the stranger's face. Although Yuri had sworn on his son's life that he wouldn't inform on him, Mitch wasn't taking any chances.

"My father ..." a woman thrust a sepia-tinted picture in front of Mitch's face. Deeply wrinkled skin and troubled eyes looked back at him, the all-too-familiar face of a Russian peasant whose expression held the sorrows of life. "My dear father. He died ... in the camps," she explained. "What had he done? I ask myself." She crossed herself.

Mitch checked his watch and began to fight his way to the far side of the heaving throng. He wished he had their blind faith that things would be different, that the country would emerge from its bloody past. He elbowed people out of the way, and when at last air washed around him, he lit a cigarette and said a silent *"Spasiba"* to Maxim Vladimirovich, who had slid a new packet into his hands when they were in the truck.

Gold crosses above the onion domes of the cathedral beckoned him as he hurried along Kirochnaya ulitsa. He wondered again if he had been foolish to suggest meeting in such a busy place. Reassuring himself that there was safety in crowds, he limped on to ulitsa Mayakovskogo. Maxim's best pair of shoes cramped his toes. A few minutes later, satisfied he hadn't been followed, he extinguished his cigarette and tugged at the door of the cathedral. It opened. Inside, he looked around quickly, removed his cap, and headed for the portico, pausing only to drop coins into a box in payment for the leaflet he now held. Leaning against a pillar in the shadows, the open publication in one hand, he peered through the incense-laden gloom, searching for his father. A few people walked quietly around, pausing to look up at the icons and military memorabilia. The cathedral had been erected in gratitude for the backing the Transfiguration Regiment had shown Peter the Great's daughter, Elizabeth, in her coup against Princess Anja and her appointed successor, the two-month old Ivan. *Not much has changed since then,* Mitch snorted to himself as he scanned the church again.

He had expected more people to be here—the cathedral was high on the list of tourist destinations—but maybe visitors had been warned to stay off the streets in case of trouble with the demonstrators. Mitch took deep breaths, relishing the hushed atmosphere. His mind drifted back to the long-ago day when his father had brought him here. Unlike most religious buildings, because of its age and historical significance, the cathedral had never been closed by the communist regime. But before entering the church, Sergei had impressed on the young Mitch the importance of not telling anyone they had been here. "Religion isn't allowed. People watch the churches and report to the Party. It is our secret," he whispered. The thought that spies may be watching him had thrilled Mitch. Now he tried to still his trembling hands.

He looked up to the blue-painted dome; angels hovered at the side, and in the centre, the divergent rays of a star spread outward. He remembered his father's words all those years ago: *"If you pray hard, your prayers will rise with the incense all the way to the very top of the dome and then to heaven."* Mitch had asked God to let him have the bright blue miniature racing car he coveted. "You will have to get it from Montréal. They don't have them here," he had explained and gone on to give precise instructions as to where the store was. Today, Mitch's prayers were simpler.

A door creaked. The muscles in his shoulders tensed. A priest floated into view, moved slowly toward the altar steps, and dropped to his knees before the iconastasis. Mitch envied him his faith, the strong belief that enabled him to lead a life of devotion to an intangible being. He had never felt secure enough to surrender the direction of his life to another, not even his mother. During the past few months, he had had difficulty recalling her features, the sound of her voice. How could that be, when he loved her so much? By not remembering, had he betrayed her? But now, although she had not shared the religion of this church, he felt her presence somewhere in the shadows.

A figure brushed past. Mitch froze. Then his pulse quickened as he breathed in the scent of his father's cologne and saw the back of the familiar jacket. Sergei lit a taper, held it toward the wick of first one candle, then another, then another, and bowed his head. Then he crossed himself, stepped back, extinguished the taper, and replaced it in the container. He moved toward his son and, staring straight ahead, whispered, "The area where they sell religious memorabilia. Beyond that is a door. Stairs lead to the undercroft." Sergei turned, walked to the right kliros, and began to study the image of Edessa on the lectern.

Mitch moved silently toward the small huddle of people clustered around religious icons, postcards, and books with pictures of the cathedral in various hues on their covers. He approached the door; the priest he had seen earlier nodded almost imperceptibly and opened it. At the bottom of the stairs, Mitch waited. Blood throbbed loudly in his temples. It seemed an age before he heard footsteps descending slowly. The smile on Sergei's face froze as he took in his son's appearance. For a fleeting moment, he glimpsed the old man Mitch would one day be. "Come," he said. With an arm around Mitch's shoulder, he guided him along the corridor and into a small room lit by a bare lightbulb. The door closed. The two men clung to each other. A sob rose in Mitch's throat as he felt familiar arms around him. "Papa ..."

"It's such a relief to know you're safe. I imagined all sorts of things." Sergei's voice was little more than a whisper.

"I was so afraid they'd done something to you, Papa, when they couldn't find me."

"You don't need to be afraid here, Mitch. It's quite safe. The priest, he's a good friend of Vera Alexandrovna."

"How do you know you can trust him? That he won't guide Yagudin's men down here?"

"I said he's a good friend."

"Yuri was a good friend too," Mitch bit back.

"I'd stake my life on him ... the priest." Mitch didn't look convinced, and Sergei went on: "Vera. She helps some of the people he takes in."

"What people? The people in the *dacha*?"

Sergei nodded. "Dissidents, Jews. Innocent people who need to get out of the country quickly. People like you."

"I can't leave, Papa. Not until I know Anja's safe and that maniac is behind bars. You know about Slava?"

Sergei nodded. "Which is why I say you must leave. It isn't safe for you here."

"I'm not going. Not without her ... and you."

"You have to, Mitch. For her sake. If you go anywhere near her, you'll put her in more danger. Don't you see that?"

"I can't abandon her. I have to find her."

"She isn't here. Not in the city."

"Where the hell is she?"

"I spoke to Lyosha. Natasha told them she was taking her away."

"Where? Did she say where?"

"*Nyet.* She wouldn't say. You know what she's like."

"With him? Are they with him?" Mitch blurted loudly.

Sergei put a cautionary finger to his own lips and then whispered: "Lyosha doesn't think they're with him. The piece in the British newspaper ... it stirred up trouble between rival gangs. According to Natasha, Yagudin's in hiding somewhere. She promised Lyosha she wouldn't go anywhere near him."

"Let's hope she's telling the truth." Mitch's voice was low.

"For the time being, for both your sakes, you'll be better out of the way, somewhere safe."

He grabbed his father's arm. "I can't go."

Mitch opened his mouth to say more, but Sergei held up a hand. "At least hear me out," he urged. "We ... Vera Aleksandrovna ... can get you out of the country; it's all arranged."

"I can't. Not until I know where Anja is and that she's okay."

"And what good are you going to be to her on a mortuary slab?"

The words sent a chill through Mitch.

"These people. They're serious. Deadly serious. They've already had one go at you." Mitch said nothing. "Mitch ... listen to me! You have to be sensible. For her sake. Go somewhere else. Build a life for her. I'll do everything I can to find her, and when I do, she can join you."

"Natasha will never let her go."

"Lyosha said he thinks Natasha is afraid for Anja, after she saw what might have happened with the bomb. That's why she's taken her away. Lyosha and Lena more or less admitted Anja would be better off with you when all this is over." Mitch didn't look convinced. "What good are you going to do here? Get away, out of danger. It's your only chance. And hers." Without waiting for Mitch's reaction, Sergei continued quickly, "I've given Vera a photograph of you. The one I always carry in my wallet. They'll use it in a passport—with a false name, of course."

"What if they come after you? Anja?" He barely breathed.

"Please, son. Go for a while ... until it's safe to come back or when I can bring Anja to you."

Mitch paced back and forth in the small space. After a minute or two, he lit a cigarette. "I don't like it, but if it's only temporary and I get Anja back at the end of it ..."

Sergei let out a loud breath and hurriedly explained what Mitch was to do. "It's all written here," he concluded. He opened a desk drawer, took out a small canvas bag, and pulled a black prayer book from it. "Hidden here in the spine, there's a paper with the instructions. Memorize them and destroy the paper before you leave tomorrow."

"Tomorrow? Surely I could stay on here for a day or two. We may get some news of where Anja is."

"You have to leave here tomorrow. If you don't, it'll be weeks before we get another chance," Sergei interjected. "There's a Dutch cargo ship leaving from Vyborg for Rotterdam on Saturday. You're signed on as an orderly in the officers' mess. You'll be working for the captain, so you'll be able to keep mostly to yourself. He's a good man, trustworthy, and speaks Russian and English."

"How is it you know so much about all this?"

"Vera. I ... I help her now and again."

"You help her? In what way?"

"For now, it's better you don't know."

"Those people, the ones who came to the apartment?"

Sergei gave the briefest nod of his head.

"I had no idea you were mixed up in anything like this. You're such a strong Party man."

"I loathe the system as much as you do, Mitch, but we couldn't let you suspect. Maman and I ..."

"She knew?"

"I couldn't have done it without her support. Can't do anything without her ..." His voice trailed off, and it took him a moment or two to regain his composure. "She made things normal when they were anything but."

"All the things I said about you, not caring about anyone." Mitch put a comforting hand on his father's shoulder. "The way you told me that was how it had to be."

"You were angry, Mitch. Angry that Vanya died."

"I was angry about everything, everyone."

"Babushka nearly blurted it out that time."

Mitch remembered now how his father had shouted at Babushka, warning her not to say any more. "I'm sorry, Papa. If only you'd told me."

"It was for the best, Mitch. You know where a careless word can lead. People's lives were at stake."

"Years ago, there was someone else. I remember you were talking in the hallway. Babushka, she made me come away from the door. Told me to mind my own business."

"We had to keep it from you, Mitch."

"I take it Vera really is involved in this, it's not just you?"

"She started it and I drifted in by accident. I used the children's charity as a front, a way to get permission to travel abroad. After it became known that I was involved with your mother, a foreigner," Sergei winced at the term, "all that finished. But I had already set up a network of contacts who could help get people out of the country, provide jobs, homes elsewhere."

"And you couldn't help Maman when she wanted to visit her own mother?"

"It was too risky. They were watching her. I had to stop helping Vera for a while. Then I began to worry that if the situation worsened for people like your mother ... Jews ... I'd need to get the two of you away from here. If I wasn't prepared to help others, then why should I expect help when I needed it? It was as simple as that."

"Doesn't sound simple to me. You're taking a big risk, both of you. And I thought I was foolhardy."

"Maybe we're cut from the same mould, the two of us." A flicker of a smile washed across Sergei's face.

"I hope so, Papa. I hope so."

Neither man spoke for a moment or two, each lost in his own thoughts, his own sense of impending loss. Then Sergei continued quickly. "You'll go with the ship from Rotterdam to Canada."

"Canada? I can't go there. It's too far away."

"You were born there. It's your best chance. When the ship docks in Halifax, there'll be a job waiting for you. Temporary employment until something else can be set up and you can move on. Vera's contact will get a message to you."

"My birth certificate, my old Canadian passport—they were in the car. Maman's papers, too."

"That can be sorted out later. For now, the greater the distance between you and Yagudin the better I'll feel."

Mitch ground the cigarette out on the sole of his shoe and dropped the butt into a waste bin.

"I wish it could be different, son." Sergei swallowed hard. "But you have to go."

Mitch stared at the floor.

"For your mother's sake, if not for anyone else." Sergei gripped Mitch's arms. "It was what she wanted."

Mitch jerked his head up. "She wouldn't want me to leave Anja or you. I know she wouldn't!"

"She always knew that one day you would leave. 'He'll have to go,' she said. 'The system, it's stifling him. What mother would want that for her son?' Those were her words." Sergei put his hand in the inside pocket of his jacket and pulled out an envelope. "You'll need this ... roubles, dollars."

Mitch stared at the envelope in his father's hand.

"Take it, please."

Mitch didn't move. Sergei picked up the canvas bag and dropped the envelope and prayer book into it. "There's something else in there." Sergei's face contorted. "Something your mother wanted you to have."

Mitch took the bag from his father's outstretched hand.

"Look at it later." Sergei opened his mouth to say more, but the words stuck in his throat. He pulled Mitch into his arms.

"I tried ..." Mitch sobbed. "Slava. There was nothing left of him. Those other people."

"They did that, son. Not you." Sergei cradled Mitch's head against his shoulder as he had when he was a small boy. "You did more than anyone has ever done for those girls, those poor innocent souls." After a moment or two, he held Mitch at arm's length and stared at him, as if imprinting his son's image forever in his mind.

"You will come, Papa? When all this is over and Anja and I ..."

Sergei nodded, dropped his hands to his side, and began to walk toward the door.

"Papa! No! Don't go!" Mitch darted in front of his father and barred his exit. "Not yet ..."

"Please, Mitch. Don't make this any harder." Tears rolled down Sergei's cheeks and he brushed them away quickly.

"You can't go like this. We need more time."

"We'll have plenty of time later, when all this is over and we're together again ... you, Anja, and me."

Mitch looked into his father's eyes. Hidden within them he recognized a sense of pleading. As if by mutual agreement, they both took a step to the left. "*Ya lyublyu tebya,* Papa."

Sergei gripped the door latch, put a hand on Mitch's shoulder, and squeezed. "I love you too, son." Their eyes met for a fleeting second. "Go safely."

In the corridor, Mitch watched in silence as his father climbed the stairs. The footsteps faded. His shoulders sagged as he went back into the room and sank down onto a chair. He stared ahead. All he saw was a black void. He had never felt so alone, cast off from everyone he loved, the future cloaked in darkness and misery.

How long he sat there, he didn't know. Suddenly, there was a rustle of robes. "It is time to go." The priest picked up the canvas bag from where it lay on the floor, took Mitch by an elbow, and walked with him to the far end of the corridor. At the top of a flight of stairs, he handed Mitch the bag and turned a key in a lock. "Christ be with you," he intoned and opened the door. Mitch stepped into daylight. It blinded him for several seconds. The door clicked shut, and the key ground in the lock.

Some time later, he found himself at the place where Maxim dropped him. Clutching the bag to his chest, he looked up and down the street and then checked his watch. He was late … nearly an hour late. A feeling of panic washed through him. *He's gone. Maxim's gone.* The chant of the crowd was loud now, close. A truck roared around the corner. Mitch looked up expectantly and then averted his gaze. *Militsiya!* Another truck followed and then another. A glimpse of the officers within was enough. Mitch walked quickly in the opposite direction.

He stumbled on, not knowing where he was. It was quieter now—no chanting crowds, no roar of trucks. He had to get back to the professor and the others. But the more he walked, the more lost and confused he became. By the side of a canal he sank down onto a bench and looked around, searching for a familiar sight. It was as though he was on another planet, in another world. His thoughts drifted back to the time long ago when he had sat on just such a bench by a canal. It was there, haunted by the thought of how his friend, Vanya, suffered at the hands of the *militsiya,* that the reality of what the Soviet Union really was sunk in. Now, despite all the grandiose plans for democratic and economic reform, the country was still mired in corruption. Did he really want his Anja to grow up in a place where the only way she could have a decent life was to do what everyone else did: lie, cheat, inform? *Nyet!* His Anja deserved better than that. *Papa's right. What good can I do here? I'm a danger to her.* He must take this chance to get out of the country and build a better life for her.

He opened the bag and checked that the prayer book was still inside; he would look at the instructions later in the privacy of his—Dariya's—bedroom. He took out a small, brown-paper wrapped parcel, undid the string, pulled the paper back, and let out a cry. His mother's *samizdat* copy of the poems of Anna Akhmatova. He cradled it gently in his hands then unfolded it.

On the top of the first page, in his mother's handwriting:

> *Black and enduring separation*
> *I share equally with you.*
> *Why weep? Give me your hand.*
> *Promise me you will come again.*[5]

5 *From 'In Dream,' by Anna Akhmatova (1889-1966).*

GLOSSARY OF RUSSIAN WORDS AND PHRASES

(NB Russian words often have numerous spellings depending on the tense and/or gender)

Belyye Nochi	White Nights
Blini	Crepes
Brakosochetaniye	Marriage
Burzhuika	Potbelly stove
Byt' ostorozhen	Be careful
Cheryomukha	Bird cherry
Chort!	Damn!
Chto s vami?	What's wrong with you?
Chto-to ne tak?	Is there something wrong?
Da	Yes
Dacha	Country house / cottage
Davayte vyp' em	Let's drink
Den'gi	Money
Derzhi nazad!	Keep back!
Deshovyy	Cheap
Dezhurnaya / Dezhurnyye	Woman on duty / Women on duty
Dorogaya dyevushka	Dear girl
Dvadtsat' litrov	Twenty litres
Glasnost	Transparency in the way a company / organization conducts its business

Govno!	Shit!
Homo Sovieticus	Person uncritically supporting Soviet values / having a Soviet mentality (usually used sarcastically)
Imbetsil	Imbecile
Izvinite	Sorry
Kafe-konditerskaya	Café and pastry shop
Kak dolgo vy budete zdes'?	How long will you stay here?
Kasha	Porridge
Kefir	Fermented milk drink
Khachapuri	Georgian cheese bread
Khorosho	Okay / Good
Khuynya	Bullshit
Khvatit	Enough
Kommunalka	Communal apartment
Kontraktniki	Contract workers
Krasivya	Beautiful
Krasnyy ugol	A corner for Christian iconography in the house (akin to a house altar or a praying spot)
Kresty'yanskiy zavtrak	Peasant breakfast
Krysy	Rats
Kto tam?	Who is it?
Kvass	Fermented beverage made from rye bread
Lyubov'	Love
Lyubov' maya	My love
Mertvyy	Dead
Militsiya	Militia / Police

Moi galubchik	My darling
Monakhi	Monks
Morozhenae	Ice cream
Moy syn	My son
My zdes'	We are here
Nichego	Nothing
Nomenklatura	Bureaucrats in key political positions in Eastern Bloc countries
Nyet	No
Oktyabryata	Political youth organization
Oni yest'	They are
Oni zdes'	They are here
On ushel	He left
Otkuda vy?	Where are you from?
Otstan'!	Leave me alone!
Paka	Bye
Pakhan	Mafia boss / godfather
Pamagite!	Help!
Paslushayte!	Listen!
Pazhalusta	Please
Pelmeni	Dumplings
Perestroika	Restructuring of economic and political system in former Soviet Union
Pirozhok	Small pie / the structure on top of the *Vosstaniya* metro station is often likened to the shape of a pie or inkpot
Ponimaete?	Understand?
Poshol ty!	Fuck off!

Poslyezavtra	Day after tomorrow
Posmotrite	Take a look
Prastite	Pardon / Sorry
Prekrati eto!	Stop it!
Prestupniki	Criminals
Privet	Hi
Propusti menya	Let me through
Rebënok	Child
Religiya	Religion
Ryumochnaya	Vodka house / bar
Samizdat	Dissident underground publication
Sbiten'	Hot sweet honey drink
Shapka	Hat
Sledi za bazarom!	Watch your tongue!
Sleduyushchiy	Next
Solyanka	Thick spicy and sour soup
Sovetnik	Advisor
Sovetskiye Detki	Soviet Kids (privileged kids)
Spasiba	Thank you
Sumashedshiy	Crazy
Syrniki	Fried quark pancakes
Tapochki	Slippers
Tëshcha	Mother-in-law (wife's mother)
Tvoyu mat'	I don't believe it! / What the fuck?
Ty govorish' po russki?	You speak Russian?
Ublyudok!	Bastard!
Vatrushka	Cream cheese buns
Vkusno	Yummy

Vnuchka	Granddaughter
Vory v zakone	Thieves in law / mobsters
Voskresen'ye	Sunday
Ya lyublyu tebya	I love you
Ya p'yan	I'm drunk
Ya yurist	I am a lawyer
Ya znayu	I know
Zakonchenyy	Finished
Zasypai, moya prelest'	Go to sleep, my pretty
Zatknis'!	Shut up!
Za vechnuyu druzhbu	To eternal friendship / toast
Za vstrechu	To this meeting / toast between friends
Zdravstvuyte	Hello
Zhopa!	Ass! / Shit!

Printed in Canada